HIGHER MAGIC

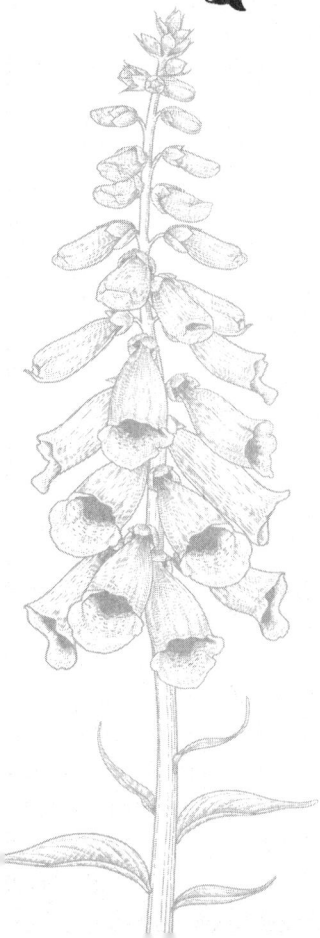

HIGHER MAGIC

COURTNEY FLOYD

/ll MIRA

/II MIRA™

ISBN-13: 978-0-7783-8764-0

Higher Magic

MIRA
22 Adelaide St. West, 41st Floor
Toronto, Ontario M5H 4E3, Canada
MIRABooks.com

HarperCollins Publishers
Macken House, 39/40 Mayor
Street Upper,
Dublin 1, D01 C9W8, Ireland
www.HarperCollins.com

Printed in U.S.A.

TO LILLY AND KATIE JO—THE BEST
OFFICEMATES I COULD HAVE ASKED FOR.

HIGHER MAGIC

EXCERPT FROM THE SUBLIMITY UNIVERSITY SCHOOL OF MAGIC'S GRADUATE HANDBOOK, ANNOTATED IN PEN

The Branch and Field exam has two parts:

1. A question period regarding the Branch and Field of specialization
2. A demonstration of a spell or working prepared for the exam

   The spellwork demonstration must illuminate a quandary or methodological innovation related to the planned dissertation topic, revealing at least part of the student's proposed intervention in the declared magical branch and field.

Nota bene: Mage students who do not pass the Branch and Field exam on the first attempt will be allowed one additional attempt the following term. Any student who does not pass on a second attempt will be expelled from the program.

—Rasputin's balls, I'm fucked.

CHAPTER ONE

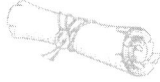

*You should be ~~writing~~ hexing people who
tell you that you should be writing.*
—NOTE ON THE BLACKBOARD IN THE MAGE STUDENT
COPY ROOM, EDITED IN ANOTHER HAND

T HE CLASSROOM DOOR SHIMMERED, AND I SCOWLED AT IT.
Twenty minutes ago, the door had been normal. *Mundane*, even. A steel slab with a hydraulic hinge that had a nasty habit of seeming to swing slowly shut before slamming all at once. It opened onto a fluorescent-lit room overstuffed with motley desks and accessorized with a decrepit whiteboard. Inside, I'd drawn my containment circle using a piece of chalk pilfered from the lecture hall down the way and cast my working. Then, I'd stepped out for a coffee.

Now, two minutes late to my own class, I pressed my palm to the door and felt a frizzle of static ghost its way up my arm and into my hair. My bangs went blowsy. I swatted them out of my eyes and shook the sting from my hand.

So much for making a professional first impression.

Of all the ill-starred winter terms I'd experienced in this program, this one was already well on its way to being the worst, and it was only day one. If I was being fair, it wasn't the door's fault. Someone else teaching in this room had thrown up a ward to penalize late students. I was going to have to take it down, or spend

the next ten weeks fighting with it. But I wasn't in the mood to
be fair. Not with an 8 a.m. class to teach and a meeting with my
advisor immediately after.

Sighing, I levered the door handle down and pushed through
the field of prickling magic. Thirty-five heads—according to my
course roster—swiveled in my direction as I stalked toward the
front of the room. I pretended not to notice them, smoothing my
bangs with my fingertips in an effort to compose myself.

"Hey! The professor's going to be here any minute, dude. Stop
messing around," someone called out.

As a young, femme, and heavily tattooed instructor who ha-
bitually dressed in faded jeans and the nicest clean top I could find
in the laundry basket—today's wasn't wrinkled . . . much—I was
used to that reaction. Instead of replying, I set my satchel on the
long table that served as the room's makeshift lectern and fished
out a dry-erase marker.

Concerned whispers soughed through the room. I ignored them,
scrawling information on the board:

Spell Composition 7

Under that, I added:

Ms. Dorothe Bartleby (she/her)

As I wrote, the whispers quieted until the only sounds were
the squeaking of my marker and the high-pitched flickering of the
fluorescent lights.

When both my nerves and the room were well and truly calm,
I turned back around with a flourishing bow that triggered the
working I'd cast earlier.

Students gasped and giggled as syllabi winked into existence
above each occupied desk and slowly fluttered into place. They
wouldn't be as impressed if they knew my housemate, Cy, had
given me his spell for the working just a couple days earlier. Still,

their delighted bafflement was almost enough to make me smile, despite the morning's irritations.

"My name is Dorothe Bartleby, but you can call me Ms. B." I paused to gesture at the board. "I teach Spell Composition I. If you're here for another class, this is your cue to exit."

A couple of students scurried out of the room as inconspicuously as possible. Which of course meant that the sound of their packing, bags zipping, and sneakered tiptoeing on the waxed vinyl flooring was so loud it was pointless to continue until the capricious classroom door swung shut behind them.

The remaining thirty-three or so students watched me warily.

Smiling, I reached for my heavily annotated copy of the syllabus.

"This course is part of a learning community with Ms. Darya Watkins's Herbalism 101. The work you do in Spell Composition I will complement your work in that class. By the end of the term, you will have drafted *and revised* two academic-quality spells."

The corresponding groan came from nowhere and everywhere at once, an overwhelming expression of sentiment that shuddered me back into freshman year. My shoulders tensed with the sense-memory of panicked drafting, late-night grappling with the arcane rules of the Mage Language Coven's style guide, the growing certainty I'd never be a real practitioner because I couldn't even format my grimoire citations correctly on the battered electric typewriter I used for my assignments.

I took a breath and dropped my shoulders, forcing myself to focus on the students in front of me. Someone had helped me, and I would help them. They might still hate the class at the end. Hec, most of them probably would. It was a gen-ed, designed for gatekeeping and consequently loathed by the student population. But they'd make it through. I'd see them through.

Quiet settled in as I regarded them.

Tangled auras, pained grimaces, sleep-crusted eyes . . . This group was so starkly different from last term's Spell Composition I students that I couldn't help a sudden rush of sympathy. There was something special about the off-cycle students, the unwieldy or unlucky or un . . . something few who'd fallen out of the campus's natural rhythm. And it wasn't just that I had recently become one of them.

Students who took this course in fall term, as admin recommended, tended to be bright-eyed and happy-go-lucky, brimming with the magic of sun-dappled October days and pumpkin-flavored beverages. But it was January, skies glowering with rain clouds, and *these* students were in for a bumpier ride. They knew it. And they'd persist, despite it.

I looked at them and they looked back at me, wearily expectant.

"Most of my students come to class with a very specific preconceived notion," I told them. "Maybe it's self-imposed, or maybe it's something you were told again and again until it stuck."

I stalked back to the board and scrawled a giant number across it.

"According to our preclass survey, eighty-five percent of you self-identify as 'bad spell writers.' That's *bullshit*."

The class gasped and tittered.

"You've been hexed, or hexed yourselves, into believing one of the biggest lies in academia—that there's only one kind of 'good spell writing,' or that only certain kinds of practitioners can be good spell writers. Bull. Shit."

Fewer titters this time, because I'd gotten their attention. Hexing was a serious accusation—workings intended to cause harm violated the student code—and right about now they'd be trying to sort out whether I meant it literally or metaphorically. The thing was, it didn't matter whether someone had literally hexed them to think of themselves as bad spell writers. The only thing that signified was that 85 percent of them *did*. It was part of the story they'd learned to tell about themselves. And reality reshapes itself around stories.

"Does anyone have a hunch about why I'd say that?"

Silence. Stillness. As though I was a predator who could only hunt when prey was in motion or making sound. I folded my arms and waited, even though the approximately seven seconds that went by felt like an eternity.

Finally, a hand climbed skyward.

"Yes? You in the striped shirt. What's your name?"

"Alse. Um, Alse Hathorne."

"Hi, Alse. Any thoughts?"

"Well . . ." Alse fidgeted with their glasses and scrunched their face, as if uncertain whether their thoughts were worth sharing.

"It's okay to speculate. Take a wild guess."

Alse huffed. "Okay, thanks. It's just . . . When you said spell writing isn't just *one thing*, it made me wonder what actually counts. Like, am I writing when I'm flipping through old grimoires for research? Does daydreaming about what I want my spell to do count?"

Their tone was half-sincere, half-sarcastic, but I could work with that. I smiled, waiting to see if any of their classmates had a response before sharing mine.

A blonde in a pink tie-dye T-shirt waved, excited.

"Um, yeah, Reed here. Like, are we writing when we select spell ingredients?"

More hands flew up, and for a little while I forgot it was an ill-starred term. I lost myself in discussion.

BLEAK REALITY CROWDED BACK IN AS MY STUDENTS FILED OUT OF THE classroom. In a matter of minutes, my advisor would be giving me the come-to-Hecate talk I'd been dreading since last term. Her email yesterday hadn't said that, but I could read between the lines of her vague *Let's chat. Can you stop by my office tomorrow?*

A knot formed in my stomach as I repacked my satchel.

Every mage student got two attempts—and only two—to pass the Branch and Field exam, our program's version of the qualifying exam that marked the transition from coursework to dissertation work. I'd failed my first attempt, and this term I'd get one last chance to convince my committee that I had what it took to be a mage.

Except, I wasn't certain *I* believed it anymore.

I had magic, sure. I was one of the lucky few born with the ability to see past consensus reality to other possibilities. But I didn't belong here. Not really. Not in the way my housemates did. They were stars in their respective branches, innovating and winning awards. I was squarely middle-of-the-pack among my fellow Thaumaturgy students. A mediocre practitioner in a branch that I'd heard laughingly referred to as the underwater basket weaving of Magic more times than I could count. It wasn't true. Thaumaturgy was so much more than a catchall for the bits and bobs of magical scholarship that weren't interesting or important enough to make it into the curricula of Necromancy or Alchemy or even Divination. But my branch's undeserved reputation didn't help my confidence.

And now Professor Husik wanted to chat. She was going to tell me I didn't get a second attempt, after all. That my first try had been so egregiously bad the committee wanted me to pack my things and go. I was so engrossed in the thought that it took me a minute to notice the student who'd stopped in front of my desk, smiling nervously. I blinked a few times, forcing myself to refocus.

"Sorry—" I dredged my memory for the student's name "—Alse. Do you have a question?"

Alse rummaged in their bag. "Not a question, really, just, uh—"

They handed me a piece of paper and backed away quickly, as if the slightly crumpled page was actually a detonation charm. A ghost of static tickled up my arm as I skimmed the photocopied text, achingly aware that I was going to have to sprint to my advisor's office to make it on time.

It was an accommodation letter. The requests were common ones: time and a half on exams, an extra week to compose spells, use of an object-based sensory working to manage attention and focus.

I looked up. Alse had used the time to shrink into themself.

"Thank you." If only I could will away their nerves with my smile. "I know these letters don't always give me a full picture of how I can best support you. I'd love to chat about that. Can you make it to my office hours today?"

"Really?"

"Really."

"My last professor nearly exploded when I gave her the letter."

I couldn't help but wince. Some faculty took the letters as a personal affront, rather than expressions of students' desire to be able to actually *do the work*.

"Is everything okay?"

Alse shrugged. "Sure." Their tone wasn't convincing, but every nerve in my body was shouting at me to get moving.

"Okay, good. The directions to my office are in the syllabus. Now, I apologize, but I have to run to another meeting."

I was halfway down the hall and already out of breath by the time that traitorous classroom door slammed behind me. When it slammed again, signaling Alse's departure, I'd rounded the corner and hauled open the stairwell door.

I swore under my breath as I climbed. Most elevators on campus were too old and slow to be relied on in a rush. But teleportation wasn't an option—not even for disabled students.

A group of them had lobbied administration for a change to the policy last year. Their requests were met with a volley of excuses. Teleportation was banned in the student code of conduct due to its *disruptive nature* and *disrespect to the hallowed halls and grounds of this fine institution*. It was federally restricted. Over and above all that, though, it was expensive.

I shoved the thought aside, taking the stairs two at a time. I had until the last full moon of term to pass my exam and convince my committee, and myself, that I deserved to be here. That I was ready to advance to mage candidacy, write my dissertation, and join the ranks of full mages out in the world.

I didn't have time to worry about anyone else's problems. Even without my advisor's cryptic summons, I had more than enough of my own.

CHAPTER TWO

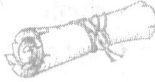

✶✶ I suppose one must expect to fight one's way: there is hardly anything to be done without it.

—STARRED PASSAGE IN GEORGE ELIOT'S
MIDDLEMARCH (1853)

Fuuuuuuuck. Grad school in a nutshell.

—ANNOTATION IN THE MARGINS OF THE
LIBRARY'S COPY OF *MIDDLEMARCH*

MY ADVISOR WAS NOT IN HER OFFICE WHEN I ARRIVED. I SLID into a crouch against the far wall and caught my breath, trying not to eavesdrop on the conversations that leaked through the building's paper-thin walls.

"I have a responsibility to all of my students, not just this one," a professor boomed somewhere down the hall. "There are certain standards—"

"Dorothe! Hello!" My advisor's greeting drowned the angry professor out.

I scrambled to my feet, heart pounding.

"Hi, Amelia."

Professor Amelia Husik—Amelia, as she insisted—didn't seem to notice the tremor in my voice. She was breathing hard, as if she'd just run across the quad. My idle suspicion jelled into something more solid as I took in the flush of her usually pallid cheeks, the disarray of her short reddish-brown hair, and the way her plaid scarf dangled, precariously close to sweeping the floor on one side.

"I hope you haven't been waiting long. I popped across the way for coffee." She wrangled her keys into the door, bullied it open, and ushered me inside without waiting for an answer. "Come in, come in. And have a seat."

I followed her into her office and sank into the only other chair in the room as she shuffled through the papers on her desk. My eyes wandered over the familiar piles of books and half-wilting office plants, the dusty potation bottles and ritual artifacts, the squeaky toy and empty water bowl stored under the desk for Amelia's officemate—an aging but friendly dog she sometimes brought to campus with her.

My hands shook. I folded them in my lap and tried to at least *look* calm as Professor Husik turned to face me, a sheaf of papers in her hands.

"How have you been?" she asked.

My eye twitched, traitorously.

I'd spent winter break holed up in my room, burrowed under my comforter despite the fact that I couldn't sleep. Sleep meant exam nightmares. Reliving my failure in all of its horrible detail.

I'd been prepared. I'd read and reread the relevant grimoires, the primary texts, the secondary criticism. My spellwork demonstration wasn't anything flashy, but it had been competent: a text analysis working that identified shared patterns in Jane Austen's *Pride and Prejudice* and Ariadne Frecke's 1812 grimoire, *Domestick Spelles*. A small-scale proof of methodological concept that would get me through exams and into research, where I could experiment with the knowledge that my place in the program was secure.

It should have worked.

Would have, maybe, if I hadn't been on the verge of a panic attack for the entire question period. If I hadn't caught Professor Huang shooting Amelia a skeptical look during my demonstration and stuttered part of my incantation, causing my working to showcase a bunch of gibberish characters instead of the beautiful, meaningful data I knew it could produce. If I hadn't fully frozen up after that, unable to speak to redo the working or answer the committee's questions.

I'd played it all over in my head since then, again and again, and I still had no idea what I could have done differently. Except, of course, not mess up in the first place.

"I've been better," I admitted.

Professor Husik's smile was sympathetic. She leaned forward, one hand waving that ominous sheaf of papers, the other placating with soft, open gestures.

"You've had a setback, but failure is a normal part of the process."

This was how she was going to do it, then. Ease me into the subject of failure. Tell me that there was more to life than higher magic. That I would have to find my own way to that ambiguous and elusive *more*, because I didn't get to stay here.

Panic clutched my throat, my fingers and toes going tingly as I struggled to breathe. I bit the inside of my cheek to keep myself from spiraling. Even the sharp tang of my own blood wasn't enough to prevent intrusive images. Failing again. Packing my things. Turning in my student ID and the access to higher magic that came with it. Heading home with nothing to show for it but the same minor magic I'd been dabbling in since I was a toddler—workings I'd whispered to reassure myself that I wasn't alone or broken or useless. The pseudo-sorrowful *we told you so* looks on my parents' faces as they welcomed me back.

Amelia must have seen the panic in my eyes, because she set the papers aside, catching my fretting hands between her own.

"You're going to get through this." Her voice went softer. "The committee has some thoughts to help you do that. And I know, with your history, you aren't going to like them. But I need you to remember that we all want you to succeed."

I managed a small smile as she let go of my hands, bracing myself when she retrieved the papers. She straightened, perusing the first page with a focused frown.

"The committee asked me to share how impressed they were with your materials. Your written proposal was—what did Rue say?—*bold and intriguing*. But," her eyes found mine over the top of the page, "we feel that your proposed dissertation would be more successful with a different methodological approach."

I tried to swallow, throat working around a sharp, dry lump of apprehension. I needed to say something—anything—if only to prove that I could.

After another painful swallow, I managed a withered "Oh?"

Amelia's eyes narrowed in a way I couldn't interpret—sympathy? impatience? disappointment?—before she cleared her throat and continued.

"Using magic to conduct a textual analysis of your exemplar texts was clever." Her compliments always led to something brutal, and this one was no different. "But it has been done. We'd like to see you thinking bigger."

Some compartmentalized part of me noted that I was fully trembling, head to toe. Even my brain shook, a hive of agitated bees. As soon as I left Amelia's office, I was going to fall apart. But I nodded along like my world wasn't crumbling, clutching the front edge of my chair to stay upright.

"We agree that there are compelling indications that early novels shaped new social realities, creating the middle class as we know it today. But to be honest, we don't think it likely that you'll be able to prove that one way or the other without a larger data set . . ." She stopped, took a breath. I tried to follow suit. "Let me be frank. We'd like you to consider a digimancy framework."

The breath rushed out of me. She was right. I didn't like it. Every piece of me rejected the idea, horrified. I was *awful* at digimancy. So awful that I was *required* to wear moonstone in the university's computer labs and copy rooms, just in case I caused another equipment fire. But that wasn't even the worst part.

A wave of ancient, sugar-high-fueled terror surged through me. I was four again, my parents clutching my sticky hands tight as they hauled me out of the diviner's booth at the local diner. Magic computers would bring about my greatest failure, the diviner had said, reading my future from my crumby cupcake liner. Or, possibly . . . maybe my greatest success. But she hadn't looked nearly as certain of that interpretation.

Requiring me to use digimancy was tantamount to failing me in advance. But how could I explain that? How could I hold up the words of a diviner who had almost certainly been untrained, selling under-the-table fortunes to down-and-out townies, and expect to be taken seriously by my advisor, or anyone at the university? Even if Amelia believed me, my committee wouldn't—couldn't—go easy on me because of it.

I sat forward, anyway, ready to protest. Or plead. Amelia held up a hand before I could even begin.

"Past incident aside, Dorothe, you're perfectly capable. You simply need more practice. Ursula has offered to work with you personally, to help you prepare. She'll reach out soon. And happenstance would have it that there's a methods workshop you can join. You're a bit behind, since the class did some reading over break, but I've checked in with Mark and he says you're welcome to enroll."

I snapped my mouth shut and nodded. What else could I do? If she'd already spoken to Professor Delight, this was not a suggestion. It was a demand with polite packaging. And anyway, if I said anything at all I was going to cry while doing it.

"We'd like you to submit your revised materials by the next full moon, on the twenty-eighth, to give the committee time to review and offer feedback before your exam. But first—" Amelia took me in with quick, searching eyes "—I want you to take a day or two off. Watch TV, go on a hike, bake something. Then, take a look at the committee's notes and see what emerges." She handed that ill-starred sheaf of papers over. "I mean it. I know the deadline must feel like it's absolutely looming, but you have time. I'm certain that with some distance, and just a bit of tinkering, your project will come together beautifully."

I managed a skeptical nod.

Knowing I needed to retake my exam by the end of term had been stressful enough. Our quarters went by so much more quickly than the semesters most other schools had. But the next full moon was barely more than three weeks away. The deadline wasn't just looming, it was heckling me. Jeering from the sidelines. Actively salivating at my probable failure.

My eyes flooded and I squeezed them shut until the immediate danger of spillover passed. When I opened them again, Amelia was looking carefully away. I thanked her and fled.

FOR ONCE, THE ELEVATOR CAME AFTER ONLY A FEW IMPATIENT JABS OF the call button. I sagged into its boxy sanctuary and stabbed the button for the basement level.

The doors slid shut with an offensively jaunty ding. I scowled at my own reflection.

Professor Husik—I couldn't consistently bring myself to call her Amelia, especially when she wasn't there to look disappointed if I didn't—had implied that I only needed to make a few small changes. But what the committee was requiring would mean going all the way back to the beginning, reshaping *everything* with a new methodology in mind. An augmented reading list for the question period. An updated dissertation proposal. A complete overhaul of my spellwork demonstration.

My breath was too fast, too shallow, stars spangling across my vision as the elevator juddered into motion. In a rush of panic, I jammed my fist against the red emergency stop button. When the elevator stilled, I slid to the floor and wrapped my arms around my knees. Hot tears stung down my cheeks as I took careful, deep breaths.

It wasn't that failure had never occurred to me before. I'd known becoming a mage would be hard. That was kind of the point. If everyone could do higher magic, we wouldn't need to go to school and take on debt, eyesight problems, and trauma to earn the title of mage. We'd simply *be mages*.

I'd come ready for the slog. I'd thrown myself into it. Battled through overwhelm, exhaustion, burnout. Despite the hidden curriculum and my lack of formal experience with pretty much all things arcane, I'd kept my grades up and earned nominations for a few departmental awards. And I'd done it all because I loved it. The magic. The camaraderie. The sense that I was contributing to something that mattered.

And yeah, I knew even that might not be enough. The job market was iffy. The odds of a career in higher magic were vanishingly small. If I couldn't land a full-time gig at an organization with an institutional repository, an on-site cemetery, and a federal license for major workings, I'd have to walk away from higher magic eventually. And landing one of those gigs was almost as rare as pulling a sword out of solid stone. It happened, but usually only for the very good and very lucky—and even then, not before a lot of adjuncting.

But that was a kind of failure that was normalized. If I didn't get my dream job, I would still have the degree.

Except, even the degree might not be possible now. And the worst part was that it might not be systemic inequality that ripped my access to magic away. It might not be the good ol' boy system privileging graduates of elite Magic programs or the whims of the job market or nepotism or classism or any -ism at all stealing my chances at a real career wielding higher magic.

It might be me.

The odds were higher that I'd buckle under the pressure this time around, and that wasn't even factoring in the prophecy. If I couldn't do this by the deadline, there would be no extensions. No additional tries.

I bunched my right sleeve up instinctively, tracing the whorls of my blackberry vine tattoo until I could breathe again. I could do this. I *could*. I still had time. I still had access to higher magic. And I couldn't afford to waste either.

With a shaky breath, I climbed to my feet and yanked the stop button until the brake released. The elevator lurched back into motion, sending my stomach plummeting for a long second before it came to a stop on my floor.

I staggered out, navigating around cockroach traps and free piles of outdated *Mage Language Coven* and *Spellcaster's Review* journals by memory as I trudged down the hallway toward my office.

The aftermath of my panic attack left me numb and foggy, mouth full of cotton and brain full of smoke-addled bees. All I wanted to do was gather my things and slink home. I opened my eyes, determined to do just that.

But, of course, there was someone waiting by my office door. For my office hours. I quickened my pace, closing in on my waiting student in a couple of long strides.

"Alse, you made it." I reached for warm and welcoming, but my ragged voice, puffy eyes, and tearstained cheeks were a dead giveaway.

Alse's expression went from nervous to concerned, eyes narrowing.

"Hi, Ms. B. Everything okay?"

I straightened my shoulders, trying to look unconcerned.

"I'm . . . fine?"

Alse's eyes fluttered, like what they really wanted to do was roll them sarcastically. I tried again.

"I'll *be* fine, anyway. Rough meeting with my advisor. I was going to cancel my office hours and ask you to reschedule."

Alse's face fell, though they tried to mask it.

"Are *you* okay? I know delivering your accommodation letters can be exhausting."

Something frantic flickered in their eyes, but they shook it off. "It's cool, Ms. B."

I could press them, but the prospect of slowly creeping closer to the cause of their frantic glance with careful questions was overwhelming. Exhaustion rolled over me, causing the bees in my brain to startle and sting. I closed my eyes and breathed, then mustered a smile.

"I *am* looking forward to chatting with you. I want to make sure this is a course you can fully and enthusiastically participate in." The effort of lining up the words into coherent sentences almost made me sag. If I hadn't said them so many times before, to so many other students, I wouldn't have been able to drag them into being now. I finished weakly, "But you're right. I'm not in the best place for the conversation right now."

Alse nodded, eyes careful.

"Can you stop by at the same time tomorrow?" I asked.

They hesitated, then jutted their jaw. "Sounds good."

I fought back a swell of guilt and something else—something that felt a lot like a warning—as they adjusted the bag on their shoulder and walked away. Rescheduling the conversation wasn't going to shatter anyone's world. I'd caused a minor inconvenience, if anything. Alse would stop by tomorrow, and we'd move on from there. Right now, my being on campus wasn't doing anybody any good.

If I had to find a way to use my methodological Achilles' heel and evade a lifelong prophecy to get my committee's sign-off, that's what I was going to Heccing do. Even if it killed me. But first, I was going to head home for a consolatory bowl of cereal and some terrible TV.

CHAPTER THREE

Nobility. Greatness. Intellectual excellence. It's all in the name at Sublimity University. Whether you come for our innovative, student-centered programs in the Liberal Arts, Medicine, Business, or Magic, you can rest assured our fine faculty and staff will do their utmost to propel you toward . . . well . . . *sublimity.*

—SUBLIMITY UNIVERSITY RECRUITMENT VIDEO

THE FASTEST ROUTE HOME TOOK ME THROUGH THE HEART OF campus—a ride I usually loved, despite the constant need to bob and weave between clusters of erratically moving students.

The street was lined on either side by the campus's administrative offices, large rectangles of brick that someone had attempted to class up with . . . Cy had used the word for them the other day. Not gargoyles, exactly. Human heads, their stone faces frozen in various expressions.

I chanced a look up at them as I coasted through a clear stretch of roadway. The hair on the back of my arms prickled, as usual, at the cold intensity of all those eyes. I'd seen them in motion, once or twice. Winking and jeering, smiling and hissing. Sometimes, when the wind was right, I'd heard them whispering, too. Nothing intelligible. Just an unnerving susurrus encouraging me to pick up my pace.

Legend—or, at least, my housemates—had it that the heads were carved from the subterranean stone of an oracle site. The story went that they'd been brought to campus from some ancient ruin in the '80s and ever since then, once in a blue moon, they'd whisper with terrible intelligibility to magical passersby. Only under the direst of circumstances, of course.

Today they were blessedly quiet.

I pulled my gaze away from the heads just in time to swerve out of the way of an electric scooter.

"On your left!" the rider shouted, belatedly.

Heart pounding, I skidded around a cluster of slow-moving students and into a pile of half-decayed leaves. My bike wobbled but stayed beneath me, and my sigh was half adrenaline and half relief as I rounded the corner. A few blocks and I'd be off campus. A few more blocks after that, and I'd be home. I'd wrap myself in a blanket and drown my sorrows in bad TV and—

Hecate's dogs.

Sitting up, I dropped my hands from the handlebars and looked at my watch.

10:20 a.m.

Cy and Darya would still be home. I wasn't ready to share the gruesome details of my morning, or my exam.

Cy probably wouldn't notice anything was wrong, but Darya would know the second I stepped through the door. And she would make me talk about it.

Everything gets smaller when we force it out of our heads and into shareable words.

I could almost *hear* her saying it. She was usually right. This time, though, I was afraid she wasn't. If I put it into words, things might get *realer*, not smaller. And I didn't want my ebbing sense of possibility to be real. I wanted it to be seasonal depression. Exhaustion. Burnout, even. Things I could recover from, with a little more sun, or rest, or self-care.

Up ahead, a small forest of Douglas firs sheltered the campus cemetery on one side of the street. Across from it, the austere buildings of the law school bristled at the dead. I winged between them, hand flicking out to switch gears. The road's subtle upward slope made itself felt in my calves and thighs, and I almost didn't register the color bursting between branches in the winter forest.

But it was impossible to miss entirely.

Deep among the cemetery trees, the small, squat building known as Bentham Cote—a central community space for high-achieving undergraduate Necromancy students, part honors dorm and part Greek house—writhed in flames.

I steered into the curb, reality going briefly topsy-turvy as I flipped over my handlebars and scraped to a stop on the asphalt. Throbbing knees didn't dent the thrall I'd fallen into at the sight. I hauled myself up, wincing as I tottered toward the display.

It wasn't fire; it was flowers. Snapdragons and foxglove spears limned the building in radiating oranges, yellows, reds, and pinks. There were hundreds. Thousands, maybe. And they were moving. Undulating.

I gawped.

It had to be a stunt, the necro kids showing up the other Magic houses. A working this big *and* this frivolous was a declaration. It showed the entire campus that the students of Bentham Cote had resources, power, and the influence to swing a permit for a major working just to use it on a Heccing *flower* show.

And I didn't care, because it was glorious.

There was someone dancing through the flowers, flinging his arms with abandon in the shadow of the towering trees—a conductor in his own personal symphony. He was too far away for me to see his face, but he looked about my age. A student, not some wizened mage.

I wrapped my fingers around the wrought iron bars of the cemetery fence, itching to join him. That deep in the throes of the working, he probably wouldn't notice if I flung myself through the flowers with him. The thrum and swell of the magic would be rioting through him, pulling him in and in and in, toward the vast impossibility of *everything*. He would be freefalling into raw potential, taking hold and reshaping it to sustain a version of reality in which flowers could dance like flames—regardless of their roots or the soil below.

I *wanted* that. The burning tug-of-war between something and everything and nothing, the soda pop pressure shift as consensus reality let go of its form—accepting a new shape. The comedown would be as brutal as the rest was brilliant, but it would still be a price worth paying.

With any other kind of flowers, I might have risked it. But I didn't need Darya's encyclopedic knowledge of flora to know that throwing myself into a lawn writhing with foxgloves would be reckless and potentially deadly. The mage student doing the working would have prepared for the plants' toxins. He was protected; I was not.

Reluctantly, I loosened my grip on the wrought iron and turned away. A small group of students was shuffling past behind me, dragging a tarp that had been loaded up with a variety of thrift-store furnishings. Moving in, broke edition. I remembered it well.

"Wasn't that hall named after some racist old dude?" one of them asked. He didn't seem to notice me, too intent on his companions. His moonstone bracelet glinted as he gestured toward a building down the street.

"Aren't all of them?" his friend asked. She clutched her corner of the tarp with desperate energy, fingers, like mine, weighed down with more rings than was strictly fashionable—necessary tools to constrain the many smaller, off-the-cuff workings that might be required over the course of a day.

"Probably, yeah," the third chimed in. The weariness in their sigh called to mine. I sagged under the weight of it, unable now to ignore the entitled ostentation of the working behind me.

With one last, long look at the flowers, I turned to collect my bike from where it still lay in the gutter. The front tire had gone flat.

This fucking day.

THE TV WAS ON, BUT IT WAS DARK ENOUGH INSIDE THAT I COULDN'T tell where my housemates were. I navigated the living room by memory, throwing my helmet and satchel into the corner before I slumped onto the couch, tears welling.

"Hey, this sofa is already occupied," Cy drawled. He paired his words with a gentle push.

I dashed tears aside and looked around. As my eyes adjusted, I could make out the silhouettes of my housemates. Somehow, I'd wedged myself into the tiny section of the couch Cy wasn't draping himself over like a reincarnated Victorian dandy. Beyond him, Darya'd positioned her wheelchair next to the coffee table—her normal spot, next to the fireplace, having been usurped by Cy's sprawling Christmas village for the past several weeks.

Cy arched an eyebrow at me, pushing again with one elegantly slippered foot. It was the sort of thing I'd normally respond to with an eye roll and a shove. I couldn't muster the energy, though, so I stood.

"Just another inch or two and that would've been *perfect*!" Darya cackled.

"I sat on you *once*, years ago. Are you ever planning on forgiving me?" Cy asked, tones petulant. The argument that had ensued that particular hungover morning was dicey enough that I'd been convinced one of them was going to move out over it.

"Oh, you're forgiven." There was still laughter in Darya's voice. "That doesn't mean I can't appreciate cosmic justice when it comes along."

I turned a smile Darya's way and her smirk disappeared.

"What's wrong?"

As she asked, she pulled her power wheelchair's joystick backward with a click, reversing until she had enough room to turn and head my way. The motor whined as she pulled up beside me, took my arm, and guided me across the room to an empty seat.

I slumped into my customary lumpy chair and buried my face in my hands.

"She met with her advisor today," Cy said, voice languid. "I expect it's exam woes. Not that she'll tell us about them."

I groaned, and Darya put her hand on my shoulder sympathetically.

"Bartleby, you know you can talk to us, right?" Her tone was less considerate than her words, practically *demanding* that I spill. "You're starting to scare us."

"Watkins is right," Cy said. "You aren't usually *this* maudlin after a setback."

As if this was just another run-of-the-mill setback. As if all of the smaller setbacks before it weren't adding to the pressure, now. I wanted to scream. To drop my hands and *howl* at the two of them. Instead, I drew in a sharp breath and exhaled pointedly, hands firmly in place.

"It sucks that you failed your exam," Darya said, "but you have another chance. And we're here for you."

"I don't want to talk about it."

Darya pulled her hand away. "It's only going to get bigger and bigger in your head until you do."

I'd *so* called that comment.

"Fine." I dropped my hands with a growl. She was right about one thing: I couldn't keep avoiding this conversation. Not unless I was going to avoid the two of them for the rest of my time in this program—however long that might be. I'd only managed to put it off this long because Darya had gone home for most of winter break. "I didn't just fail. I made a mistake during my demonstration and panicked and stopped being able to speak *at all.*"

I could almost see the shape of Darya's thoughts in the way her expression shifted, neon-yellow eyebrows angling up, stark against the warm brown of her skin. She caught one lip between her lower teeth, and I plowed ahead before those shapes could transform into words.

"They're making me take a Digimancy workshop so I can use it in my exam."

Darya and Cy exchanged a careful glance, as though that explained everything, and all they needed to do now was determine who would talk me down from my irrational worry. But they didn't understand. Not all of it. I gulped a breath and kept going.

"When I was a kid, my parents took me to this diviner . . ." The words tumbled out. Short, sharp sentences that kept my voice from cracking—mostly—as I told them the one story I'd never shared with anyone outside my family.

Twenty-two years ago, the concept of magic computers was an oxymoron. Even now, most people weren't familiar with digimancy outside of higher ed. And so, my parents had taken no chances. They'd kept me away from technology *and* out of Magic classes for as long as they possibly could.

But I'd done tiny workings all throughout my childhood, anyway. A small, secret defiance. And by the time I made it to college, I'd convinced myself the prophecy was fake and my parents had been scammed by someone who wasn't even a real diviner. I'd taken my first Magic class, mustered the courage to use a computer. And everything had been okay—great, even—until I'd come here.

"So, *wait*, is that why you're so low tech? I thought it was some . . . hipster thing." Darya sounded scandalized.

I shrugged.

"Hold on." Cy held his hands up. "I'm still stuck on the fact that you had all of that hanging over your head, and you still decided to enroll in Digimancy in your second term. *Why?*"

Because the Heccing course description had ruined everything. As soon as I'd seen it, I'd realized that magic computers were real, and that the threat of them would hang over me for the rest of my life unless I *did* something about that knowledge.

"I wanted to get it out of the way. Either prove the prophecy wrong once and for all, or trigger the stars-damned thing and get on with my life."

"By frying a room full of university computers?" Cy's horrified laugh punctuated the question.

"She didn't do it on purpose." The look Darya shot him was

almost venomous. But Cy's commentary wasn't going to faze me today. I was already at rock bottom.

"It didn't work." Embarrassed as I had been—and still was—I'd hoped that the copy room incident would be the worst of it. My greatest failure, done and behind me. But my first attempt at the Branch and Field exam had been worse, and it hadn't involved digimancy at all. I leaned forward, looking at my hands so they couldn't see the panic in my eyes. "And now I have to try to use digimancy again without calling down my own doom. By the next full moon. While participating in a workshop I didn't plan for *and* teaching my own class."

I dropped my face back into my hands, imagining—in vivid detail—the silent conversation my housemates must be having. *I told you Bartleby's a hack. An imposter. A fluke. I told you she'd eventually crumble under the pressure. I told you—*

"You'll figure it out," Darya said. "You always do."

"What if I can't?" I pressed my fingertips flat against my eyelids until the dark shaded red. "What if this is the hoop that takes me out? You know what Professor Putnam used to say. The program is meant to separate the wheat from the chaff." I peeled my hands away from my face, anguish making my words sharper than I meant them to be. "What if I'm the chaff?"

Cy rolled his eyes. He glanced Darya's way, then pushed himself upright, facing me. "Trust me, you aren't."

I squinted my disbelief at him.

Darya bobbed her head, the swirling patterns cut into her neon-yellow fade swimming with each movement. "Listen to Cy. There's no such thing as chaff. We are all, technically, good enough to wield higher magic before they even let us through the doors." It was easy for her to say. Darya was Heccing brilliant. She'd passed her Branch and Field exam last summer—months ahead of schedule—and that was only her latest accomplishment in a glittering Alchemical career that had started well before college. I, on the other hand, had only minored in Magic before coming here: stealing moments for workings between the demands of my English major and the part-time jobs I'd juggled to pay for the degree.

"I agree with you in theory," Cy said, "but that's not what I was getting at. I was going to say—and I would have told you this *weeks* ago, if you'd been speaking to us in more than monosyllables—is that *I* was chaff."

I stared at him. "In what reality can you legitimately say that?"

Cy wasn't being fair, claiming to be chaff after he'd already made it almost all the way through the program.

His tone went artificially waspish. "I said I *was* chaff. When I got here."

"I don't think it's something you can grow out of. And besides, you're *moon-favored*." I jutted my chin, challenging him to change my mind.

That wasn't fair, either. Being moon-favored didn't mean anything, really. Except when it did. There was a lot we still didn't understand about magic. What we *did* know was that the only people who could use it were born on the darkest nights of the year. Empowered by that knowledge, some people did a little bit of finagling, scheduling C-sections to ensure that their children possessed the ability to Play-Doh-smash consensus reality. The moon phase was all that mattered, magically speaking. But that didn't stop some practitioners from putting children delivered *naturally* during a new moon or total lunar eclipse—the "moon-favored"—on a pedestal. The rest of us, by that logic, were interlopers. Fair or not, I could almost guarantee that nobody had ever looked at Cy and deemed him chaff.

"You're going to make me tell the story, aren't you?" Cy asked.

"What story?" I crossed my arms, a little angry that curiosity could so easily pry away the stranglehold of my despair.

Cy draped himself back over the couch, contemplating the ceiling for a long moment before he spoke. "Yes, I *happened* to be born naturally on a new moon. In the back of a rusty station wagon, mind you." He waved a hand in an impatient circle. "That's not the point of the story. The *point* is that I coasted through undergrad, because people acted like I was some kind of chosen one. And when I got here, it was more of the same. I was the recipient of a lot of winks and nudges that made it very clear I shouldn't worry too much about program requirements."

"Of course you were, white boy," Darya muttered. Then she cleared her throat. "I don't get how that makes you chaff."

"Oh," Cy sat back up with a sudden swing of his legs, "I also failed my Branch and Field exam the first time around. Bought into the hype. Showed up completely cocksure and unprepared. The term I moved in with you was my second attempt."

"Pffft." Darya waved a hand at him. "I still say there's no such thing as chaff. So you failed. Failing is part of learning."

I flopped backward in my chair, head spinning. One of the best practitioners I knew had failed his exam. A *moon-favored* practitioner had failed his exam. I didn't know if that made me feel better, or more doomed.

"I think we broke Bartleby," Darya said.

"Then we'll have to fix her back up." Cy rubbed his palms together. "As the closest thing to a Doctor of Magic among us, I prescribe you pub food and drinks."

"And I concur with that prescription," Darya added.

"Doctor," Cy said.

"Doctor," Darya echoed.

I groaned.

"Come on, Bartleby. We haven't had a mage's night out in ages," Darya wheedled.

"It's eleven-thirty in the morning." Neither of my housemates were impressed with the excuse.

"That's never stopped us before," Cy said.

"It's going to be fun!" Darya insisted.

CHAPTER FOUR

Students returning to campus this week would have been justified to expect winter doldrums. Instead, we were welcomed back with dazzling displays of season-defying florals, courtesy of the campus's Magic houses. This journalist humbly suggests taking the flower displays as an omen of more good things to come.

—ARTICLE IN THE PLATYPUS PRATTLER, 5 JANUARY

IT PROBABLY WAS FUN. SO MUCH *HECCING FUN* I WAS STILL HUNG-over, nearly twenty-four hours later. In addition to feeling like something scraped off the bottom of an alchemist's crucible after a botched working—which meant I was even *less* prepared to start putting together a new exam proposal than I had been yesterday—I'd drunk enough that I could only remember snatches of the rest of the day.

Cy's announcement that he'd received funding for a research trip to England, which he'd be leaving for in a month.

Darya's revise and resubmit from *Chrysopoeia*—the major journal of Alchemical research—and my ill-starred decision to turn her discussion of said revisions into a drinking game. I'd chugged every time she mentioned kelp or cloaking spells or the repulsive feeling said cloakings caused onlookers. By the time I realized Darya had caught on to my game and was mentioning kelp on purpose, I was too drunk to care.

After that, things were even fuzzier.

A brief encounter with the magically inclined bartender who'd made me drink some water.

Some judgy anti-magic bystander spewing crap about missing "true" reality and its consequences.

I was pretty sure Cy, Darya, and I had talked about the Bentham Cote flower display at some point. And flowers at other Magic houses. Lilies and lotuses floating around Randolph House. Dandelions exploding into sunflowers outside Newton Hall. Unless I'd dreamed that part. Because the houses never worked together, not counting fleeting alliances for their petty interhouse feuds.

I *should've* been dreaming, still. Sleeping it off instead of dragging my battered carcass around campus. But I had a meeting. And a workshop to attend.

At least there were painkillers in my office.

The gray daylight wavering in through the window was enough to illuminate the space, even with the collection of thriving houseplants my officemate kept on the sill, so I didn't bother turning on the overheads.

My head throbbed, anyway. I needed to pull myself together today, not just for Alse, but for my own good. This Heccing exam would not be the thing that ended my Magic career. I wouldn't *let* it. But if I was going to move on with my exam prep, I needed to get the wallowing out of my system.

Easing into my desk chair, I closed my eyes and allowed myself the luxury of a single, pitiful whine, willing the swimming ache of my head and the knot of anxiety in my chest to depart with the sound.

When I opened my eyes again, I pretended it had worked.

Tugging a faux copy of *Pride and Prejudice* from my desk shelf, I flipped the cover open. Inside, my essentials—tampons, bandages, toothbrush, lipstick, deodorant, and ibuprofen—lay in a heap. I dredged up the ibuprofen and wrestled the cap off the bottle, palming a couple of pills and throwing them back with a dry swallow.

A tentative knock let me know my time for wallowing was well and truly over. Grimacing, I pushed to my feet and flicked the lights on. With a quick pull on the door, I revealed Alse, whose hands were tucked awkwardly into their pockets.

I pasted on a smile. "Glad you could make it. Come in."

Alse nodded, following as I turned and reclaimed my seat.

"So." I swiveled my chair to face them, clasping my hands. "How are . . . things?"

Alse slid one arm from their backpack, swinging the bag around to the front of their body as they lowered themself to the edge of the hard plastic chair beside my desk. It'd only been a day since I'd seen them, and in that time worry had traced itself onto their face. The bags under their eyes were deep charcoal smudges, and their skin looked vaguely green.

"Good." They lowered their backpack to the floor, propping it up against the wall.

"Oh, good." I let the lie stand.

They slid their hands under their thighs and looked around. For a moment, I saw the space through their eyes. A small rectangle of a room with cobwebs in the corners, a window at the far end, and flooring waxed to a high sheen, mostly—according to groundskeeping—to make sure that the asbestos stayed put.

My officemate, Magdalen, and I had done what we could to make the office comfortable when it was assigned to us three years ago. I'd found a nice thrift-shop rug and Mags had brought her plants. We'd decorated, too. On Mags's side, that meant her kids' drawings hung next to framed art prints and a poster-board sign advertising our graduate employee union, the Federation of Graduate Teaching Fellows and Practitioners. Above that, Mags had mounted an ornate scabbard that contained an actual, honest-to-Hecate sword. She liked to joke she wielded it on the union's behalf—a warrior for fair pay and equitable working conditions.

My decorations were sparser. A string of lights along the top of my bookshelf, a few knickknacks scattered amongst my library books, a lizard-of-the-month calendar from last year, and a couple of Jane Austen web comics taped, prominently, to the wall in front of my desk.

Despite the shabbiness, I loved it here. It was *mine*, proof that I had a place on campus and in my program. Or, half of a place, since I shared it. But it was half a place with a Heccing *window*, which was more than what some mage students got.

"What's with the moonstone?" Alse's nose wrinkled, incredulous.

I turned to look, as if I'd never noticed the moonstone neck-lace hanging from a thumbtack next to my outdated calendar. I could claim it was Mags's—as an English PhD candidate, it was conceivably something she'd own. Moonstone shielded against magic better than most wards, as long as the stones were regularly recharged. But I had a feeling Alse would see through the lie. I settled for an incomplete truth.

"It's precautionary."

They hummed, politely, as if that explained everything.

"So . . ." I offered them a small, consolatory smile. "Should we talk about your accommodations?"

Their eyebrows crashed together. They looked down at their jeans, shoulders drooping.

"Is it—" They broke the question off, attention snagged by a piece of thread sticking out between their pant seams. They pulled at it, risking a look up at me. "Would it still be okay to talk about an accommodation problem with another class?"

"Of course, but . . ." My frown was reflexive. "Have you talked to anyone in Student Accessibility Services about this?"

Alse shrugged one shoulder. "Yeah."

My stomach sank. If they hadn't been able to help, I didn't know what *I* could do. I made the question as gentle as possible. "What happened?"

"They said the professor had concerns about the effect my ac-commodations would have on the course."

The things in their accommodation letter—providing extra time to compose spells and take exams and allowing Alse to use a sensory working to manage their attention—weren't hard to implement. Student Accessibility Services didn't usually tailor letters to each specific course. But maybe there was some assignment in the other class that could cause sensory overload or required prolonged attention, or—

"SAS is reviewing the professor's response, but it might take a while. In the meantime, I just have to deal." Alse grimaced up at me. Their face had gone greener, somehow. "But that's not the worst part. The professor is pressuring me to drop the class." They gagged the words more than said them. I thought it was from emotion until they gulped and gagged again.

I leaned forward. "Are you okay?"

"Sorry." They swallowed, experimentally. "I think I'm good now."

"No worries. So, your professor is pressuring you to drop the class. I assume that won't work?" Most students would just drop, if they were meeting this much resistance. Better to take the course in a term or two, with a professor who actually gave a crap.

Alse shook their head. "No. She says I might benefit from taking the course later. But she's the only one who teaches it, and it's not offered every year, and there's nothing else that fits this requirement."

As their panic rose, their pallor grew. It was probably just hangover-vision, but they seemed, for a moment, to thin around the edges, transparency lapping at them. I blinked and they looked normal again. Or, mostly. Their stomach roiled audibly, setting my own stomach sloshing in wobbly sympathy.

They started to smile, sheepish, but froze midway, the line of their lips a rictus.

"I—" Alse lurched to their feet. "I'm—" Their hands flew to their mouth, muffling their attempt to apologize as they bolted toward my office door.

"Alse?" They seemed to be fading again as they went—or maybe I was still somehow fully drunk—and I followed without thinking about it, tottering out of my office as they raced down the hall toward the restrooms.

The hallway grew hazy in a distinctive *reality is pluralizing* way. The fluorescent bulbs hissed and popped, casting odd shadows as Alse passed beneath them. With every hunching step, Alse grew more transparent. Halfway down the hall, they disappeared entirely.

Okay, so maybe it wasn't my bleary eyes or the alcohol still coursing through my system; they just didn't want me to see them puke. Which, fair. But I stared at the spot where they'd vanished, anyway, waiting for that feeling of repulsion Darya always mentioned when she lectured about cloaking and her kelp experiments.

It didn't come.

Instead, worry and confusion battled for top billing. If this was a cloaking, it was the weirdest I'd ever seen. They weren't usually so . . . gradual. Then again, maybe Alse was feeling so terrible they'd struggled to cast theirs correctly. I wrapped my arms around my waist, peering after them with a sinking feeling. They must have caught a bug. Maybe the flu.

Down the hall, the restroom door slammed.

I returned to my desk, rummaging in my fake *Pride and Prejudice* for some hand sanitizer. When they got back, I'd help them into their backpack and over to University Health Services. Everything else would have to wait.

ALSE DIDN'T GET BACK. TEN MINUTES WENT BY, AND I WAS PSYCHING myself up to go check the restroom in case they'd passed out or something when a jaunty shave-and-a-haircut knock set the door squeaking open.

I whirled. "Alse?"

"No. Just me." Mags flashed me a grin as she swaggered into the room and slung her bags onto her desk. "And I come with a warning—avoid the restroom if you value your innocence. Someone did a shit ton of magic in there, pun very much intended, and it really fucked the place up. Highlights include a toilet that now burbles menacingly in what I'm pretty sure is blank verse. It's big on scatological humor. Shakespeare would be proud."

"That's not good." A numb ticklish feeling traced its way down my face, along my arms, and into my fingers. I sagged backward.

"What's wrong?" Mags asked. "Don't worry, I'm sure the university ghosts are on it already. Groundskeeping won't be too far behind."

The image of ghosts pouring into the restroom to absorb the fragmentary bits of weird alternative realities Alse's frantic workings had caused was not particularly reassuring.

I shoved the thought aside. "No, it's not that. I was meeting with a student. I was supposed to chat with them yesterday, but—"

"You were too busy melting down after your meeting with your advisor?" Mags asked. I hadn't told her about that, and my perplexity must've shown. She rolled her eyes. "You were so distraught afterward that you walked right past me on your way out of the building. Didn't seem to even notice I was there. And you didn't answer your phone when I called to check in, so I reached out to Darya to make sure you were okay. She filled me in."

"Oh. Sorry."

Magdalen shrugged as if it was only to be expected. "So, your student stood you up?"

I shook my head. "That's the thing. They were here, but they weren't feeling well and they started to sort of . . . fade out? They rushed to the restroom and disappeared halfway there."

"I guess we know who tore the place up." Mags arched an eyebrow.

"I'm worried, Mags. They left in the middle of our meeting and their backpack is still here." I didn't know how to put words to the wrongness of it.

"They're probably just embarrassed," Mags said. "Or headed to their dorm to sleep it off. You clearly weren't the only one with a hangover today."

I ignored her incorrect assumption about my student and jumped to the more pertinent issue. "Is it that obvious?"

"You smell like a bull in a liquor shop." Mags dug in her closest bag and pulled out a pack of gum, slipping two pieces from the case and handing them my way.

I made a face. It couldn't be *that* bad. But I took the gum, anyway. "Thanks."

"Sure."

"You don't think the workings in the bathroom are a bad sign?"

Mags shook her head. "I think your student got vomit on their clothes and tried to magic it away. Aren't subductions super tricky without the right constraints? That's what my parents always say."

Her parents were right. I groaned, just imagining it. One slipup, and Alse could have removed their pants instead of the vomit.

"If you're worried about the backpack, send them an email. I'm sure they'll let you know when they're ready to pick it up. Hec, maybe they already have."

I dove for my laptop, pulling up my inbox. There *was* a new message waiting for me, but it was from one of my committee members. A calendar invite, really. Professor Leighton—Ursula—scheduling an exam practice session the Monday of week three. I ignored the bungee-drop of dread in my stomach and hit **accept**. Then, I started a new message.

Dear Alse,

I typed and deleted a few sentences, reaching for something more professional than *WTF??? Are you okay?*, before hitting **send**.

"All good?" Mags asked.

"Not really." I shook my head, immediately regretting it. My stomach heaved. But it wasn't just the hangover that had me nauseated. I glanced at Alse's backpack, uncertainty gnawing away at my stomach lining.

"Is it just this business with your student, or is there something else going on?" she asked as though she already knew the answer.

Exactly how much had Darya filled her in on? I glanced at my watch and leaped out of my chair.

"There *is* something else." I slung my bag over my shoulder, reaching for my raincoat. I was going to be late for Digimancy. "And it's happening *now*."

"Good luck," Mags called, too cheerful, as I sprinted out the door.

EXCERPT FROM PROFESSOR LEIGHTON'S FIRST LECTURE IN INTRODUCTION TO GRADUATE STUDIES IN MAGIC

Neuroscience tells us that we all experience reality differently. A big part of that difference comes from language and culture, which are always subtly shaping the way we understand the world. But a not insignificant factor is *us*. Our embodied experiences. Our quirks and histories. Because even *within* our cultures and language groups, we're all of us different.

Magic is, at its simplest, the act of *sharing* our unique realities—naming or shaping the way things are in such a way that multiple people experience it at the same time. The visceral knowledge that it *isn't* just you, because you *made it not be.*

Let me share my favorite example:

Scholars say that ancient Greeks had no word for the color blue. So, the story goes, they couldn't *see* blue. And in their literature, at least, this seems to bear out. Ancient Greek texts describe things we would consider *objectively blue* with phrases like "wine dark," which implies a purple or even, some say, a deep green color.

Then, one day, someone *named* the color blue. And suddenly it became *visible* to a whole populace.

Blue is a working.

This may give you pause. You may ask, as so many have before you, if *magic* is *that simple* why go to grad school to study it?

It's a good question. A fair question. Let me pose one in return:

Do you think *blue* is simple?

It is everywhere we go, in everything we do. It *defines* our world, when we zoom out and take the whole thing in at scale.

Anyone can do magic, in theory. Many do, in practice. But *working your own unique reality*? Pulling it into shared, sustained existence through skill and will and, let's face it, luck? That requires a depth of resources and understanding few achieve.

Graduate magic study is not only about the bare *skill* of spell casting, whatever Professor Putnam may tell you to the contrary. It is about a deeper and wider *knowing* of yourself as well as your world and its workings.

That is why you are here.

CHAPTER FIVE

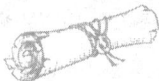

Magic, like genius, is almost completely unglamorous in practice. How did Edison put it? Ninety-nine percent perspiration to one percent inspiration? To get to *glamour*—pun intended—you have to slog through miles of grueling, galling, and gut-wrenching first. Some of you won't make it.

—PROFESSOR WILLIAM PUTNAM, SPELLS & METHODS

AH, MS. BARTLEBY. I WONDERED IF YOU'D BE JOINING US TO-day." Professor Delight let his piece of chalk clatter onto the metal ledge beneath the blackboard and checked his wristwatch. "We've just broken off for project share outs. Why don't you get us started?"

There was something about his tone that seemed urgently familiar, but my anxiety was just as urgently reminding my stomach that it hated me. Palms damp and heart pounding, I turned to face the room. My new classmates sat at desks arranged in crescent moon clusters. I recognized a handful of them: Nathaniel, a Divination fourth-year who always wore a suit and tie, even for casual events like mage student picnics; Hadrian, or maybe Horatia—something Shakespearean—a Thaumaturgy second-year with bright green hair; and an Alchemy fifth year named Imani Joshi, who occasionally hung out with Cy. They all seemed to recognize *me*, eyes widening in shock. I knew what they must be thinking.

That's copy-room girl.

She fried a whole computer lab.

Why the Hec is she here?

I tried to ignore their questioning gazes. "I'm . . . um . . . trying to chart out a new spellwork demonstration for my Branch and Field exam."

"And what will that entail, precisely?"

I shifted from foot to foot, considering. "Originally, my plan was to look for similarities between Jane Austen's *Pride and Prejudice* and Ariadne Frecke's *Domestick Spelles* to see if I could identify traces of spellwork." My committee's feedback rattled around my head. *Unsuccessful. Bigger. More Data.* "I'll probably start by increasing the size of my corpus, including more novels and grimoires so that I can do more in-depth text analysis."

Professor Delight arched an eyebrow. "In order to . . . ?"

Hecate's dogs, wasn't he ever going to let me sit down? I bit back an exasperated sigh.

I knew what I hoped to find with my larger data set. Some archaic, rune-like use of punctuation. Or maybe something structural, a repeating pattern of question and cliff-hanger and revelation that pulled the reader into ritual participation with the texts. Something, in other words, purely thaumaturgical. A type of working that relied on symbol or rhythm or syntax—not the presence of the dead, or the transformation of base elements, or glimpses of the past or future—to create new realities. Not just because I'd be more confident pursuing research so squarely in my own branch, but also because I wanted to stake a claim for Thaumaturgy. Remind everyone that it mattered.

But magic didn't really work like that. It was almost never cleanly one thing or another. The branches were an imperfect classification system, meant to help us grasp the ungraspable. And digimancy was the poster child of that slipperiness: some practitioners argued it was divination—data, in large enough quantities, allowing mages to know or predict things that ought to be unknowable; others argued that it was alchemy, its use of algorithms transforming the way we saw and understood the world.

And anyway, Professor Delight wasn't asking what I hoped to find. He wanted to know what I'd *do* with my findings. He regarded me expectantly, his clean-shaven face fixed with a pleasant half smile.

"I'd like to create an approximation of a historical narrative working." It was only a few tiny steps beyond what I'd been trying for in my first exam attempt. But maybe that would be enough: a proof of concept to convince my committee that this research mattered, and I was the right person to conduct it.

I braced myself for further interrogation, but Professor Delight nodded—finally satisfied.

"Well, I'll certainly look forward to seeing how the project evolves. Why don't you join your classmates? We can get you up to speed after class." He wandered toward one of the closer groups without waiting for my response, leaving me to fend for myself.

I crossed my arms, scanning the room for an empty seat.

"We've got a spot over here." The tall mage student sitting next to Imani flashed a smile. "You're welcome to join us."

He seemed familiar. I chalked up the buzz of not-quite-recognition to my hangover, because the man was striking enough that I would *definitely* have remembered him if I'd met him before. I fished Mags's gum out of my pocket as I walked over, self-conscious.

"Thanks. I'm Bartleby. Dorothe, technically, but my friends call me Bartleby." I sank into the desk, hoping my smile hid my nerves.

"We know," Imani said. "This is Rose." She pointed at a younger woman with spider-silk-fine, strawberry blond hair. Rose waved, a smile dimpling her freckled cheeks. "That's James." Imani waved dismissively toward the student who'd invited me into the group. "And we've met. Now that's done, and we can get on with it. Rose?"

Rose launched into a description of her project. Something about a virtual reality headset and a famous seventeenth-century alchemical experiment.

As she talked, I snuck a sideways look at James. His tousled blond hair and tie-dye shirt would've screamed *beach bum* if not for the clashing plaid jacket hanging off the back of his seat and the brown corduroy pants that were just visible from my vantage point. Altogether, his vibe was more thrift shop than anything.

And Hec if I didn't feel even more convinced that I *knew* him from somewhere.

James caught me looking and winked.

I held his gaze despite the way the tips of my ears flared hot. The classroom fell away as I stared, replaced by an inferno of foxgloves and snapdragons.

"It was you."

"Excuse me?" James's eyebrows bunched together. Distantly, I processed Rose's startled "Oh" and Imani's annoyed sigh. I was too excited to care. I'd *placed* him.

"At Bentham Cote, yesterday. Doing the flower working?"

James's face went pink. "Ah. That . . . wasn't my working." He scratched his shoulder through his shirt, absently. "I dropped something off for my cousin and saw the flowers as I was leaving." His gaze darted toward Imani, concern shadowing his features.

"I *told* you to use moonstone to prevent unexpected visions." Imani scowled at him, fondly. "And unexpected *rashes*."

James, impossibly, got even pinker. He cleared his throat, busied himself rearranging the pen and notebook on his desk.

I was probably just as flushed as he was, because I felt like any second I was going to spontaneously combust from embarrassment. *It was you?* Who did I think I was, Sherlock Holmes?

"Should we . . ." Rose's tone was tentative.

Imani laughed. "Yes, we should."

After Rose finished describing her project, Imani detailed her plans to conduct three versions of the same working, each with a different buffer, so she could track the effects of buffers on magical output. The intricacy of her approach left my head spinning. And James's project, an app to track and predict visions so diviners could more confidently go about their days, was something so obviously necessary I was surprised it didn't already exist.

These were the kind of projects my committee wanted to see. Big ideas, with clear impact. Spellwork that made more than the bare-boned use of digimancy I'd hoped might get me through the next several weeks.

My uneasiness must have showed, because James leaned toward me, eyebrows furrowed. "Everything okay?"

I shrugged. "You've all got such amazing projects, and I'm . . . not great at this." It was an understatement, and everyone in the group knew it.

But James only smiled. "If you ever need someone to bounce ideas off of. Outside of class, I mean . . . I—or, we . . ." He glanced at Imani, who rolled her eyes. "We could have a study group?"

He'd gone pink again, and I wasn't sure why. Or what to make of Imani's reaction to his offer. Before I could respond, Professor Delight called the class to attention.

"I'm afraid that's it for today. Remember to submit your project plans by Friday at five." He turned to me. "Ms. Bartleby, if you wouldn't mind staying for a few minutes."

As my classmates filed out, Professor Delight handed me a syllabus and walked me through the schedule. On Mondays, he demoed real-world digimancy projects. On Wednesdays, we workshopped our own projects. And at the end of term, he would hold one-on-one meetings with us to provide feedback on our work.

All I knew, as the professor gave me a personal lecture on class policies, was that I was going to have to seriously up my game to pull off the kind of project my committee wanted.

It was time for a trip to the library.

CHAPTER SIX

The American Association of Magic Universities and Programs is deliberating a proposal, signed by faculty representatives around the nation, to formally challenge the Americans with Disabilities Act's applicability to Magic programs. The cosigners contend that magic makes mundane accommodations unnecessary, since, the "logic" goes, students with sufficient prowess to pursue higher magic must be able to craft their own accommodations.

—ARTICLE WRITTEN BY SELENE SCOUTT PRICE FOR *THE CHRONICLE OF HIGHER MAGIC* WEBSITE, 7 JANUARY

THE LIBRARY WAS STILL QUIET THIS EARLY IN THE TERM. I walked down the empty main hall, past display cases highlighting important moments in university history. The founding of the institution. The establishment of the School of Magic and its four undergraduate houses—Bentham Cote (Necromancy), Randolph House (Thaumaturgy), Newton Hall (Alchemy), and Sibyl House (Divination)—forty years later. Important scholarship by faculty and alumni. Several shelves of trophies, most of them won by the women's basketball team. A gallery of successful alumni, with signed film and TV posters and first-edition books. And, in the final display case, an ombre-fade of photographs of Sublimity's most illustrious practitioners: Miriam Bishop, Katherine Quimby, George Blackwater, and a half dozen more.

The exhibit was a blatant attempt to build bridges between the Magic and nonMagic schools, just like admin's policy of pairing mage students with grad students from other programs when they assigned offices. Still, I wanted to be up there one day. Wanted the positive version of my childhood prophecy to play out, against all the odds, and make this foray into digimancy my greatest success.

I pulled myself away from the exhibit and cut through the stacks toward the elevator at the rear of the building. Most magic holdings were on the lower levels with special collections and the institutional repository, accessible only via a heavily warded freight elevator and stairwell that both required card-swipe access. But I didn't need magic right now; I needed a subject librarian.

I jabbed the button for the second floor. Moments later, the elevator dinged and set me loose. Fingers trailing along a row of fraying cloth spines, I set off to find the staff offices. Maps posted around the library showed them in a neat little row in a far corner of the building, but I'd never been able to get there on my first try. I suspected that the magic of the workings in the building's depths had seeped into its structure, making the reality of its walls and walkways more flexible than it should be.

I stopped where periodicals met media collections and hesitated, considering the rows of books around me. Was it a left here, or a right two rows down?

I tried the right turn, following a row that, despite the perfect parallel lines of its shelving, seemed to zig and zag in ways that weren't strictly possible according to the floor plan. I trudged along anyway, until it spat me out into a study area.

Two tatty rust-orange couches faced a corner in which a massive bulletin board held so many sticky notes it was fringed. Just this side of the couches a dry-erase board proclaimed:

The oracle is in.

I stumbled to a stop, chills chasing up and down my limbs as I took in a hoodie-covered head, barely visible on the arm of one couch. The oracle was napping.

Houdini's farts.

I did *not* have time to deal with a prophecy right now. Especially not from some powered-up undergrad I'd rudely awoken. The last thing I wanted was a reminder of my certain doom. Or the revelation of some horrible new one.

I shifted my bag and turned around as quietly as possible, directing a mental swear at the library as I tiptoed my way back into the stacks. The row opened up ahead of me with a speed I took as an unspoken apology, transitioning from narrow shelves to an open area where a row of glass-walled rooms sat dark and empty.

Small paper nameplates distinguished one fishbowl office from the next, and I kept walking until I reached one that read AMANDA PEREZ, SUBJECT LIBRARIAN, COMPUTER AND INFORMATIONAL SCIENCES.

A cheery voice rang out behind me. "Hello there!"

I spun, shoulders inching toward my ears. "I was looking for—"

"Amanda Perez. And you found me. Do you mind?" She held a stack of books almost as tall as her torso, and she gestured to her office door with a foot. "It's not locked."

I yanked the door open and held it as she staggered in and dropped the books onto her already cluttered desk. The lights flicked on above her, belated.

"Bartleby, isn't it?" She fell into her chair with a long exhale. "You coming in?"

I stepped inside, not entirely surprised by the fact that she knew my name. Mags, Darya, and I had an ongoing debate about librarians. My theory was that they had thaumaturgical training—the Library of Congress classification system was just as good as any other system of symbols or syntax for wonderworking. Darya insisted they were diviners. Mags swore up and down that they were just very good at their jobs.

Amanda tapped at her keyboard and squinted at the screen. "Do you read the *Chronicle*?"

"Sometimes."

Amanda gestured at her monitor, expression annoyed. "Have you been following this ridiculous business with the American Association of Magic Universities and Programs and . . ." Her gaze cut to mine, taking in my carefully blank expression. "You're in a hurry, aren't you?"

I hoped my smile was sufficiently apologetic. I didn't want to be rude, but I *was* in a hurry. Or, a race against the clock.

She nodded, sitting forward and slipping three books out of a tottering pile with the ease of someone who spent copious amounts of time playing Jenga.

"These should do the trick." She handed them over, and I glanced at the spines.

Machine Learning for Absolute Beginners. Natural Language Processing. Predictive Analytics. They seemed to be in the right area of digital . . . stuff.

Another point to Darya, then.

"Thanks. I was also—"

"Hoping I'd have a list of digital reference guides?" Amanda riffled through a coffee-stained shuffle of papers and passed me a handwritten list.

She *had* to be an adept. I folded the list into a neat square and slid it into my bag.

"Hang a left on your way out if you want the nearest exit," she said, pulling a small plastic lunchbox from the detritus on her desk and turning back toward her computer screen.

I did as I was told.

IF *MACHINE LEARNING FOR ABSOLUTE BEGINNERS* WAS ACTUALLY meant for *absolute* beginners, I was screwed. I'd planned to study in my office, but Mags had ransacked my emergency stash of six-hour energy, leaving a crumpled IOU in its place. So I headed home, set up camp at the kitchen table with an entire carafe of coffee, and spent the next several hours slowly working through the book, making notes. It felt like trying to read the Voynich manuscript without the proper translation working, but I kept at it, and ideas began to take shape.

Maybe I could use technology for more than just analyzing texts and identifying patterns across the corpus. Maybe it could test those patterns, too. If I built a text-to-speech function into the spell, it could even narrate aloud as it tested potential workings. A lot of novels were experienced that way, historically: whole families gathered around while one person read aloud. If nothing else, I could use the text-to-speech narration to help monitor what, if anything, had an effect on reality.

The idea was exciting, but I wasn't sure it was feasible. According to the book, machine learning took *time*. Potentially months, instead of the weeks I had. I slammed the book shut.

"I'm going to have to invent time travel," I moaned.

"Or, you *could* just use the spellwork to help the code do its thing faster," Cy said over the sizzle of something delicious meeting hot cast iron.

My stomach grumbled.

"I was joking."

"And *I'm* Aleister Crowley."

I stared at him until the urge to blink motivated me to change the subject. "Why do you always do this?"

"Make panino?" He still hadn't blinked. The bastard.

"Swoop in and make me feel like an idiot for missing the obvious."

Cy shrugged and turned back to his sandwich. "You're too close to the problem."

"You're telling me."

I scowled down at my book. It looked Voynichier than ever, and it wasn't even open.

"You should take a break."

"That's what you said yesterday, and look where it got me."

Cy snorted as he flipped his panino onto a plate and sliced it diagonally. When he turned, he held two plates, and he slid one to me as he took a seat.

Tears welled. *"Cy."*

"You look like a miserable puppy," he said, biting into his half as if he hadn't done anything out of the ordinary. "Make a big deal about it and I'll take it back."

I snatched my half off the plate and tucked in. "Oh my god."

Smoked turkey met pesto aioli and gouda and . . . it was the best thing I'd ever eaten in my life.

"Told you a break would help."

"You didn't say it could be a snack break."

He smirked. "Every break can be a snack break if you have a snack while you're taking it."

I moaned my agreement into the sandwich. "Words to live by."

We finished eating in silence. I was chasing a crumb around my plate when Cy leaned back in his chair and glared at me.

"So, what's up? It seems as though you have an idea. Shouldn't you be, I don't know, happier about it?"

I gave up on the crumb with a shrug.

"Maybe it will be an idea when it grows up. It's more vague direction at this point."

Cy reached for my plate. "That's more than you had yesterday." Stacking our plates, he pushed his chair partway back and stopped, waiting for a response. What was I supposed to say?

He rolled his eyes. "Describe your direction, Bartleby."

"Really?"

"Really."

I crossed my arms. "I'm training a computer on a corpus of novels and grimoires. Hopefully, it will find patterns that might be indicative of workings."

"Because of the *novels are magic* thing you're always on about."

It wasn't a question, but I nodded. Literature scholars had been arguing that early novels shaped society—changing the way people thought about themselves in relation to others and, thereby, changing the reality they shared—for almost half a century. But if early novels *were* workings, whatever they'd wrought had become part of consensus reality hundreds of years ago. There was no easy way to prove they were magic. And I was apparently the only mage student in about twenty years who was foolish enough to try.

"And you're hoping, what exactly?" he asked.

I huffed, sending my bangs floating. "That I don't set anything on fire. That the committee finds my spellwork demonstration compelling this time. That I pass my Heccing exam."

Cy rolled his eyes, and I explained my nascent plans.

"So, wait, you expect this construct to start spouting workings?" Cy asked.

"If I get it right." Which I probably wouldn't, given my track record. "I have to figure out how to get around the reality barrier first."

He waved that aside. "You're going to set a magic-wielding construct loose on campus. Please tell me you've thought about constraints."

I cleared my throat against the impulse to be sarcastic. I hadn't gotten that far in my planning yet, but I *was* going to need to set my narration construct loose on *something*, if I wanted to be able to track its magical effects. And the perfect something happened to be in eyeshot, cluttering up the corner near the fireplace.

"Actually, I was hoping I could set it loose on your Christmas village . . ."

Cy pushed his chair the rest of the way back. "No."

"But it's exactly the right scale and complexity." A tiny plaster society, ready and waiting for its story to change. As my working narrated it, I'd be able to tell if the stories held any power by identifying changes to the buildings and figurines.

He stalked to the sink with the dishes, impervious to the whine in my voice. "*Nope.*"

Desperation seared through me. "I'll do your assigned chores for the rest of the term."

Cy shot a disappointed look my way. "I'm leaving for a month, remember?"

That wasn't a no. "Spring term, then?"

Drying his hands, Cy turned to face me. "I've been meaning to get rid of the thing, anyway. Putting it up once or twice is kitschy. More than that, it's just a boring *tradition*." He said the word like it tasted foul, shuddering dramatically.

Even the knowledge that he'd strung me along for a better offer couldn't dim my delight. I clapped. "Thank you, thank you, *thank you*."

"You're welcome," Cy drawled. "Now, shoo. Break time is over." He waved his dish towel in my direction until I gathered up my books and headed for my room.

CHAPTER SEVEN

With absences already stacking up, campus is bracing for a brutal flu season. Magic students seem to be getting hit hardest, with frightening and rapid-onset symptoms that don't present in nonMagic students' cases.

—ARTICLE IN *THE PLATYPUS PRATTLER*, 7 JANUARY

ON THURSDAY, I PLAYED A GAME OF GUESS WHO WITH MY PHOTO roster while my class trickled in. Manesh and Alastair settled in the back corner. Priti sat next to Waite in the front row. Reed took a seat behind them next to Grigori. Pam, whose blue tiered-tulle maxi skirt matched the ombre hues of her braid extensions, settled down in the middle of the room, under the projector. The desk beside her was conspicuously empty.

Alse's seat.

I still hadn't heard from them, which meant . . . what? They really were sick? They'd decided talking to me was too awkward and dropped my class? They'd need to pick up their backpack, either way. Or send someone else to do it. Worrying wouldn't make that happen any faster.

Sighing, I pulled my attention back to the present.

"Good morning, class. Today we're tackling a question I'm sure every practitioner has asked at one point or another—why do we write spells? We can work basic magic without them, so why are they necessary?"

The distinct sound of a dry-erase marker rolling across a table and plummeting to the floor distracted me. Strange. I could have sworn I'd left mine in my bag.

"I assigned a short excerpt from Yeats's *Ideas of Good and Evil* to get our discussion started. Would anyone like to share initial thoughts?"

My students shuffled, paging through their readers instead of looking at me. After a long stretch, Manesh's arm rose, slow but steady.

"It might have to do with memory? Yeats writes . . ." Manesh paused to scroll the document on his laptop screen. "'This great mind and memory can be evoked by symbols.'" He sagged back into his seat once the comment was out.

"Great observation, Manesh. What do you think that means?"

Pam raised her hand. "The term *great mind* implies that there's some sort of singular shared memory that can be accessed by arcane symbols—" she played with her hair as she spoke "—which seems . . . problematic."

Grigori turned toward her. "How do you mean?"

"We don't all think the same way, or use the same symbols." Pam shrugged.

Reed jumped in. "Yeah, I agree. It's like, why does some dead white guy get to define what the great mind is? Colonialism much?"

"Maybe it's just a way of saying we can re-create a reality someone else imagined by using their spells?" Alastair asked.

I started to nod, but the sudden, sharp squeak of a marker on the whiteboard made me yelp. I wasn't the only one. Around the room, startled sounds almost drowned out the marker's continued path across the board. *Screee srcreeeeeee screeeeeeech.* Silence fell abruptly, static electricity prickling up and down my arms.

I didn't want to look. Didn't want to discover what was scrawled on the board. Given the horrified expressions on some of my students' faces, I didn't have a choice. I turned around, my heartbeat doing its best impression of Morse code.

The beginnings of a word, written in bright red ink and followed by an illegible scribble, cut a slash across the board.

Hel

It might've been the start of anything. *Heccing* or *Hello* or . . . or *Help*.

My pulse kicked back up at the thought, and I forced myself to breathe. To face my class and put on a smile.

A prank. That was the simplest, most logical explanation. It was a prank, and that meant the static had been the university ghosts intervening, before it went too far. I scanned my students' faces, hoping to catch someone smirking or looking suspiciously bored or guilty. Mostly, they seemed as baffled and unsettled as I felt.

"It would seem we've got a resident class clown." My laugh was a threadbare thing with my breath still hitching in my throat. "Or, an aspiring one, anyway."

Nobody confessed. And I wasn't going to waste time grilling them over something so inconsequential. Squaring my shoulders, I marched to the whiteboard and wiped away the half-formed word.

"Let's take a look at the spell of the day. Turn to page sixty-three."

My students dutifully flipped and scrolled ahead in their readers. Eventually, quiet settled, signaling their readiness.

"I'll start us off with a question. What is this spell *arguing*?"

Priti raised a hand. "Do you mean what does this spell *create*?"

The rest of the class looked on, some trying to hide their confusion and others so exasperated they didn't care if it was obvious.

Realization settled heavy on my shoulders. "Has nobody ever told you that magic is an argument?" I knew the answer even before Priti shook her head.

Hecate's dogs.

I smiled at the class, showing just a few too many teeth. Anger—not at them but at this fresh evidence that the academy was not built for students like them, students like *me*—pushed me to my feet and set me pacing. A rant brewed deep in my belly.

"All workings—minor or major—reshape reality in some way. But with minor workings, that reshaping is so small and so fleeting that reality is usually happy to play along. No big deal."

Around the room, my students were nodding. So far, so good.

"The larger a working gets, the more reality needs to be convinced of. Changing reality in one huge way—despite thousands of years' worth of people telling it otherwise—is incredibly difficult, especially if you want your changes to last. Realities are—"

"Aren't the *constants* what let us do that?" The interruption came from Waite, one of my quieter students. "Change reality in big ways, I mean?"

"No, the constants are what keep us from getting lost in competing realities when we do major workings. Right, Ms. B?" Reed turned to me for confirmation.

"You're both—"

"But I thought the moon breaks magic, and ghosts eat workings . . . Don't they?" Alastair looked genuinely upset. He clasped his head between his hands.

"Realities are complex," I explained. "And impossibly vast. Death and the moon are the only constants we've found across them. They exist in every version of reality we've crafted, or explored, to date." The ones that had been documented, anyway. As yet, NASA hadn't made it far enough to test a working beyond the moon's influence. Maybe in a decade or two, some astronaut on Mars would discover a new constant. Peer into a reality without the moon. Death, I was fairly certain, would follow us everywhere. But I was getting distracted.

I cleared my throat.

"So, you're right, Reed. They do keep us oriented when we're working higher magic. And Waite and Alastair are also right, in a sense—we wouldn't last long doing higher magic without the constants, and when needed, we can rely on them to . . . unravel our workings." I was *not* going to use Alastair's terminology, because the thought of ghosts cramming giant handfuls of magic into their rotten, chomping mouths made me want to barf.

Like everyone in the graduate program, I'd witnessed the way the university's ghosts—former faculty, staff, and alumni who'd been buried on campus—tore apart unsanctioned workings. It was a time-honored unit in Intro to Graduate Studies in Magic. The experience still haunted me; if I thought about it long enough, I could hear the meaty *fwump* of ghostly essences solidifying into fully manifested bodies. Worse, I could feel the chill of their waxen gazes somberly taking me in. Assessing. They didn't usually operate so *visibly*. In fact, most of the dead's interventions happened sight unseen—like today.

I took a breath, shaking the memories away. "But we don't use the constants to change or shape reality—we just factor them into our workings to define their limits."

"So, you're saying magic is just . . . us beefing with reality?" Alastair smirked, as though it was the most absurd idea in the world. The class laughed, eyes on me—expectant. But it was as good an explanation as any.

"If by *beefing* you mean *arguing*, then yes."

Pam tipped her head to one side, eyebrows raised. "You're really telling us we're here, paying all this money, just to learn how to throw hands with the universe?"

"No. What you're paying for is the ability to use everyone else's *receipts* when you throw hands with the universe." The class groaned at my attempt to use slang, but I ignored them. Kept going. "I'm serious. Realities are stubborn. They have to be cajoled every single step of the way. It's easier if you break the big changes down into lots of smaller ones—but you have to cast them all simultaneously for that to work. How would you accomplish that with a working like, say, Quimby's Long-Range Teleportation? Any thoughts?"

Alastair looked around for help, meeting Priti's gaze. She shrugged and raised her hand.

"Yes, Priti?"

"There must be some shortcut." She shifted in her seat as if settling in for a long conversation. "It would require a prohibitive amount of time, not to mention people and resources, to cast even the simplest of major workings, otherwise."

My smile returned.

"Exactly. We do research to understand the specific changes *we* want to make to consensus reality, and we rely on the spellwork of those who've come before us—collected in our institutional repository—for the intermediary steps. But even *naming* the steps it takes to get from *higher magic is real* to *a large group of people entered a small room in Portland, Oregon, and exited the same room in Portland, Maine*, could take all the time you have to cast. So, to make higher magic possible *at all*, we do indeed have a shortcut. Does anyone know what it is?"

After a beat, Waite raised xir hand. "It's something to do with our student IDs, right?" Xey fished xir's out of xir bag, regarding it. "They said we *had* to carry them, at all times. And mine has all these little symbols. It says *access level 1*?"

I nodded. "Yes, that's right. The access levels control what holdings you can draw on."

Pam flashed her hand and let it fall. "So, what, our IDs let us pull spells into our own workings without actually *doing* those workings? Like, a placement exam that lets you skip a basic class?"

"That's a good comparison."

"Wait . . ." Reed raised her hand. "Do *our* spells end up in the institutional repository? Is that why you had us read Yeats? The institutional repository is *our* 'great mind and memory'?"

My smile slipped into seriousness. "Yes, they do. And yes, it is."

Around the classroom, eyes widened as the import of that sank in. A surge of pride in my off-cycle students spurred me to drive the point home.

"We write spells instead of just doing workings and letting the knowledge of them fade when we're done, because the accumulation of knowledge makes higher magic possible. *Your* spells help make higher magic possible."

With the light of that realization shining in their eyes, I couldn't bring myself to say the rest. That they'd lose access to the institutional repository they'd helped build after graduating. That, unless they were very well connected or very lucky or both, they probably wouldn't find a job at an institution with the resources to create its own robust spell repository. That their spells made higher magic possible, but that didn't guarantee them a place in higher magic.

I SLID THE ACCOMMODATION LETTER PAM HAD JUST GIVEN ME INTO MY satchel, making my way toward the stairwell. The prank had rattled me, and while I'd done my best not to let it show, the niggling sense that something was off—amiss—clung. An anxious fog.

Back in my office, I popped in my earbuds and opened my code packet. Pam had mentioned stopping by for office hours, but I had some time before that. Might as well make use of it—and distract myself from my vague and growing sense of irrational dread in the process.

The next thing I knew, Mags was tapping me on the shoulder.

I pulled my earbuds out. "Hey."

"Hey." Mags grinned. "Sorry to interrupt. You seemed pretty into it. But in a loud way, and our hallway neighbors asked me to intervene."

Hecate's dogs. "I was singing again?"

"Yep."

My face lit itself on fire.

"Sorry."

"No big deal," Mags said. "I take it things are coming together?" She spun her seat so the back of it faced me, then straddled it, propping her chin on the top.

"Sort of. Maybe. I don't want to hex it by talking about it. Sorry."

"I get it." Shrugging, Mags started to spin away.

"Wait. Why do I keep apologizing? I'm mad at you." I scowled, and she stopped spinning. Her precisely penciled eyebrows bunched together.

"What did I do?"

The memory of my hand closing around paper instead of six-hour-energy filled my voice with ire. "You took my last six-hour-energy potation and left an IOU. What am I supposed to do with an IOU, Mags? It derailed my whole afternoon."

Mags crossed her arms. "Would it help if I said it was a child-care emergency?"

I crossed my arms back, jutting my chin. It did. Grad school was enough to make a life of six-hour-energy-stealing crimes sound tempting on a good day. And that was *without* toddlers. But I wasn't going to let her off that easy.

"It would help if you replaced my potation. You shouldn't even be using it. Do I have to remind you that having mages for parents doesn't make *you* a mage? If something goes wrong, you'll be fucked."

Mags rolled her eyes and changed the subject. "Why are you still on campus, anyway? Didn't your office hours end, like, an hour ago?"

"No." I checked my watch. "Yes." How had I lost track of that much time? And why hadn't Pam shown up? I whirled around to check my email. Nothing from Pam, and still nothing from Alse.

"Bartleby, what's wrong?" Mags's tone went serious.

I spun to face her, gesturing at Alse's backpack. "My student from yesterday still hasn't gotten in touch."

Mag scrunched her nose. "Bad flu?"

"Maybe. But another student ghosted my office hours, too. She said she planned to come by this morning."

"So, something came up. Or maybe this student got the flu, too. Students blowing off office hours is among the most time-honored of traditions."

I could practically see her rearranging mental puzzle pieces to make my level of worry make sense. She had a point.

I shook my head, anyway. "You're probably right, but I've got a bad feeling."

"Before you get too worked up, I'd like to remind you that you're the queen of bad feelings."

"I'm not getting worked up." I bit my lip, choosing to ignore the gentle jab about my anxiety. "I'm just worried. What if it's not the flu? What if something else is going on?" And what if the prank this morning *hadn't* been a prank?

"Then send another email," Mags said. "What else can you do?"

I didn't have a good answer. As handy as it would be, I couldn't track my students down and demand to know what was wrong. Or I could, but I'd be violating my terms of employment.

I sent a quick note to Alse, asking if they'd like to send someone by for their backpack. Then I emailed Pam. By the time I'd finished, there was a new message waiting in my inbox.

Mail undeliverable, the subject read.

I clicked into it.

Account alse.hathorne@sublimity.edu does not exist.

"What the Hec?"

"What's wrong?" Mags leaned back in her chair, eyebrow raised.

"I got an email bounce back. It's saying my student's account doesn't exist."

Mags frowned. "Maybe they withdrew from the program?"

"Don't students have access to their email for a year after they leave?"

Mags sighed. "Hec if I know. Maybe that's just for students who actually graduate."

I didn't know what to say to that. Students had dropped my class before. But I couldn't recall a single former student who'd withdrawn from the program.

A chime from my inbox broke the uneasy silence. My stomach swooped, the dread from earlier back with a vengeance.

A new **mail undeliverable** message, this time for Pam.

"I just got another bounce back. For a different student." I stared at the message. One withdrawal I might have been able to rationalize. But two? In the first week of term? It wasn't just this morning's lingering anxiety telling me something wasn't right.

"So weird." Mags huffed a long breath, the squeak of her chair signaling that she'd gotten back to work.

"Don't you think it's . . . a little *more* than weird?" I turned, and Mags set her pen down, dramatically.

"I don't know. Not really? Students leave sometimes."

"But *two of them*? At the same time?"

"There could be all kinds of reasons. A death in the family. Health issues. Money issues. Hec, maybe they didn't even want to go to college in the first place."

"Sure, but . . . what if it's not any of those reasons? What if something's wrong?"

Mags wheeled closer and placed a comforting hand on my shoulder. "You know you have my sword if you need it. Literally." She gestured to the scabbard on the wall above her desk. "But, for all we know, it's just a glitch in the system and the emails will go through in a few hours."

I managed an uncertain nod. She was probably right. A tiny, insistent part of me didn't think so, though.

Mags rolled her eyes. "If you really think something's wrong, log on to the Student Success portal and make a note about it on the early-warning system."

I blinked a few times by way of reply. It wasn't a bad idea. I could let the Dean of Students' Office look into . . . whatever was going on. They'd know what to do if something was actually wrong. And I could focus on my own problems.

CHAPTER EIGHT

Computers, originally developed as assistive devices for the nonmagical, were long assumed by mages to be redundant at best and antithetical to magic at worst. The latter is not entirely unfounded. But we have learned how to account for this antithesis. We have learned to create *buffers*.

—MAGE BETH MANISKI, "NEVER THE TWAIN
SHALL MEET: A DIGIMANCY MANIFESTO"

I SPENT THE NEXT SEVERAL DAYS CHIPPING AWAY AT MY CODE. BEtween classes, office hours, grading, and the occasional nap, I cleaned up plain text files for my dataset, finalized the Python packet, and drafted the hooks that told the code where to find its data.

I wasn't even almost done. I still had to figure out how to create a buffer between the tech and the spellwork that would wend its way through the code's syntax, urging it to greater heights. For my working, that was extra complicated.

Since I wanted my working to produce new magic in addition to identifying the original spellwork in my source texts, run-of-the-mill organic buffers like the tree saplings or abandoned beehives many digimancers prized wouldn't cut it for me.

What *would*, I didn't know.

I explained as much to Imani, James, and Rose in the handful of minutes Professor Delight allotted for group discussion during Monday's workshop session.

"I think I need a buffer that is, or was, capable of navigating multiple realities." I bit my lip. "I just feel like, if I choose wrong, this whole thing might blow up."

"Oof," Rose murmured.

"A crow skull might work. Or deer, possibly. Raccoon could be interesting, but it might be too chaotic. I was hoping you all could help me think through the pros and cons?"

Imani hummed. "You're right that you need something more complex than a sapling. But I'm not sure an animal will work the way you want it to." She chewed her lip. "The crow, maybe. If you can convince it to say more than one cryptic thing, over and over. But deer might be too skittish to buffer properly. And a raccoon . . . You're right about the chaos."

Which left me with, what? I clutched my pen, trying to keep the panicked snatch of my breath inaudible.

"Necromancy has surplus human skulls sometimes," James said, breaking me out of my spiral with the flash of a dimple. The way he swept his hair out of his eyes was distracting enough that it took a second for his words to sink in. "From people who donated their bodies to Magic," he added.

Professor Delight chose that moment to call us back to order. "All right, class, let's discuss your outstanding questions."

Across the room, Hadrian raised her hand. I didn't follow much of the discussion. My thoughts kept tracking back to James's suggestion. And—infuriatingly—James.

I HEADED STRAIGHT TO THE NECROMANCY BRANCH AFTER CLASS. THE sun was out—a rarity for early January in Oregon. Despite the chill in the air, students lounged in hammocks and on blankets strewn across dead, leaf-littered grass. Most were clustered on the admin building's lawn, drawn—I assumed—by the mass of violently purple flowers there. Dahlias and hyacinths had been arranged to form an enormous platypus that, as I watched, changed positions and winked at passersby.

Another massive working.

I closed my eyes and breathed deep, longing to join the students in the grass, to soak in the fragrance of the flowers and the fledgling warmth of the sun. But I didn't have time to linger. If I didn't pass my exam, there'd be no more magic flower displays for me. No more time on campus. I'd be kicked out of the program, out of this life.

I slid my hands into my pockets and lengthened my stride, stomach knotting as my path took me away from the flowers and under the leering busts along campus's main thoroughfare. They were chatty today, whatever they were saying. But their whispers were unintelligible. I took a deep breath, walking faster just in case that changed. The last thing I needed was a whispered doom omen.

Intentionally going to Necromancy was daunting enough. It was one of only two spots on campus that used ghost wards— instead of run-of-the-mill spellwork ones—to keep unwanted visitors away. The other was the institutional repository. And from what I heard, the Necromancy wards were the more aggressive of the two—in part to prepare students for the dicier aspects of their future careers working with the dead.

The closer I got, the harder my heart pounded. In my pockets, my palms grew warm and damp. I balled my hands into fists and ducked my head, navigating through clusters of dawdling students based on my view of their feet.

In three years here, I'd managed to avoid the tall, narrow Victorian that Necromancy called home. It was the domain of the elite, mages who grappled with the constant of death, and if there was part of me that suspected I didn't belong on campus, all the rest of me *knew* I didn't belong *there*. It loomed over me now, ominous weather-stained fish-scale siding and violently detailed gingerbread trim starker than usual in the sparkling midafternoon light. The Bone House, students called it. Faculty, too, when they weren't being formal.

I looked up at the bleak building from its dead lawn. This

close, it seemed even narrower. A starved specter of a place with a rickety covered porch and an even ricketier balcony sagging off the second story. This was, according to Darya, the single most inaccessible building on campus. Supposedly, there was a ramshackle chairlift at the back that only functioned some of the time—and only if you knew the right working to set it going. From my point of view in the front, the building wasn't any more welcoming. The uneven stone steps threatened a tumble, and the heavy door resisted as I tried to haul it open.

The dilapidation had to be intentional. As the most well-endowed branch at our university, Necromancy could have had the most pristine building on campus. But they used their money on other things, like medical facilities for corpse work, perfectly content with their frightful accommodations.

I managed to crack the door far enough to wriggle inside, and it clanged shut behind me, the sound echoing through the dark, empty hallway ahead.

Hopefully empty.

A shiver snaked its way up my spine. Intellectually, I knew the entire campus was haunted. Insurance, and government regulations, required it because of the number of major workings that took place here on any given day. Even my own apartment—a run-down duplex a few miles off campus—had a resident ghost. Without the university's dead, we'd end up lost in a palimpsest of competing realities that the moon cycle might not disrupt in time to save us. But that didn't mean all of the ghosts haunting campus were friendly, or even safe to be around.

At the far end of the hall, a bulletin board and directory waited under an old-fashioned hanging lamp. I headed toward it, steps slow and echoing. Something flickered to my right, and I froze. At the edges of my vision, shadows began not so much to shift as to writhe.

I clenched my jaw against the instinct to scream.

CHAPTER NINE

When referring to scholars of magic, it is customary to use the gender-neutral *mage* for those who have completed doctoral programs in one of the recognized branches, *adept* for those who've completed terminal degrees, and *practitioner* both as a general catchall and for those who've had little or no formal training. When it is known, use terminology that aligns with scholars' heritage, such as *brujx* for mages of Latinx descent. In all cases, eschew inaccurate and overly gendered terminology such as *witch* or *wizard*.

—EXCERPT FROM THE *MAGE LANGUAGE COVEN STYLE GUIDE*, 66TH EDITION

THE SHADOWS BEGAN TO SHIFT TOWARD ME, STRETCHING INTO lanky, looming figures with sharp edges suggestive of sharpened teeth and ragged fingernails. I crossed and uncrossed my eyes until the room went blurry.

By the time we were toddlers, most practitioners discovered that one of the building blocks of magic came easier to us, and we latched on to it with pudgy fingers, a moon-given gift. For Cy, it was gesture. For Darya, it was object. Incantation had always been my thing. Quotation magic, I'd called it, before I'd stumbled into my first Magic course in college and learned some actual terminology.

Dizzy, I reached for reality, rummaging through my memory for an applicable quote with which to tether it into place. I twisted the wooden ring on my thumb as I spoke, constraining my working to the room around me.

"'We shall not have to explore our way into a hall dimly lighted.'" Jane Austen's *Northanger Abbey* seemed fitting in this terrifying building. The words rang through the space, gaining force as I strung them together, dragging something out of me like a parachute on a plummeting body. I sagged with the reciprocal force.

The more cultural weight my words carried, the more effect they could have on consensus reality. And the more of a toll they took on me. I rolled my shoulders, achier than I'd been a moment ago, and considered my surroundings.

My vision swam for a second as the rest of the lights blinked back on.

Beside me, a digital directory now hung on the wall. Highlighted on the screen was the innocuously named Materials Lab, room 205a. I squared my shoulders and headed for the door labeled *stairs* that was now visible next to the bulletin board at the end of the hall.

Unease itched between my shoulder blades. That ghostly encounter had been too easy. Which meant the real wards must be waiting between here and the second floor.

I hauled the door open and stepped into the stairwell, breath held.

What should've been a bland, uninspired academic staircase—all blue-and-gray-speckled vinyl flooring and dingy white walls—was, instead, *nothing*. The door slammed behind me, leaving me enshrouded in cold, silence, darkness.

It pressed in, a physical weight as I felt my way up the steps. Whoever'd shaped these wards didn't have much imagination, if all they could come up with was a big gaping yawn of *nothingness*.

Well, nothingness that was, presumably, full of ghosts. Not unassuming residence ghosts, either. But poltergeisting and possessing *ward* ghosts.

I shoved the thought aside, pouring my attention into my growing irritation. A branch with funding and resources at their fingertips, full of people who spent their days working and communicating with the dead, should at least have a strong grasp of the *aesthetics* of hauntings. This place should have had gothic trappings. Moth-eaten velvet carpet. Ornately carved balusters propping up a sweeping handrail.

Panic fluttered anyway as I continued to inch my way up toward the second floor.

On second thought, maybe whoever'd designed the wards had been on to something. Maybe gothic trappings only got in the way. Without visuals to latch on to, my mind echoed with a single thought.

Ghosts. Ghosts. Ghosts. Gho—

Something brushed past me, stirring the hair on my arms and the back of my neck.

"Get out."

The words were there and gone so quickly I was half-certain I'd imagined them. I kept moving, forcing myself to maintain a steady pace. It was getting harder to breathe. I should've reached the second floor by now. Could've reached a third or fourth or fifth, if they'd existed. The wards were holding me here, which didn't make any sense.

They should've recognized me as a Magic student. Read my intent. Let me *through*. Every other ward on campus I'd encountered worked that way. Sure, they hadn't been ghost wards. But still. This shouldn't be happening.

Unless . . .

I clenched my jaw, fighting panic as I slipped my hand into my satchel, fingers finding the outline of my student ID. Tension sapped away at the feel of it. The wards *should* be able to recognize me. If I just kept walking, they would. I'd get through. Probably. Eventually. They couldn't be *lethal*, or the university would be buried in lawsuits.

That didn't mean they didn't have teeth.

I swallowed, worked my throat until I could muster whispered words. More *Northanger Abbey.*

"'Strange things may be—'" Someone—some*thing*—hip checked me, nearly sending me face-first into the stairs. I clutched the handrail, braced myself. "'—generally accounted for if—'" a spectral elbow landed on my solar plexus "'—their cause be fairly searched out.'" Another ghost slammed into me. Each violent touch left me not cold so much as numb. I flexed the hand that wasn't gripping the handrail, trying to work some feeling back into it.

"Leeeeeeaaaaaaavvvvvveeeeeee," something moaned, close by.

I counted heartbeats instead of breathing.

The nothingness was almost audible. A scuttling of insects. The inexorable crumbling of leaves under a heavy blanket of snow. The writhing, munching sound of microscopic decomposition. Words hurled themselves at me from the white-noise buzz with the slap and sting of crawling things aiming at a light.

Imposter. Intruder. Out. Out. Out.

Hecate's dogs, I wanted to listen. To turn around and scramble down this haunted staircase, back into light and air and life. But if I wanted to *keep* my life, this version of it that I'd been so painstakingly building, I had to keep climbing.

Sometimes, the incantations I chose required actions—rituals, really, in micro—and this particular Austen quote indicated I needed to do some "searching out." But I was in a lightless void, on an eternal staircase, surrounded by Hecate knew how many dead. I couldn't *literally* search out anything. Which meant it would have to be figurative.

"There's got to be a good reason this staircase is warded so excessively." I said the words tentatively, voice echoing in the strange darkness. "And I'm pretty sure that reason is why I'm here. You're guarding the Materials Lab. I'm headed to the Materials Lab."

To buy a skull with which I was going to somehow do a digimancy working, hoping to Hecate I didn't mess anything up this time around. But they didn't need to know the context. They didn't need to know I was the last person who should be allowed to do digimancy, even including the nonMagic students on campus.

As if they could read my thoughts, the ghosts escalated, hurling themselves against me with every step I took. It wasn't just hands and hips and shoulders and elbows and knees and feet. It was fingernails and teeth and the hot, heaving breaths of composting things. I clung to the handrail with both hands, doing my best not to *lose* ground even if I couldn't *gain* it. Trying not to let them sense me reacting to their assault.

It *should've* hurt, but what it did was worse. It made things warbly and high-pitched, then took sensation entirely. I was uncomfortable and nauseated and wavering on the brink of disassociating. Rolling numbness fought to conquer my amplifying sense of wrongness, eliding the violation of my space, my body.

Something trickled down my cheek and I jerked away before I realized it was sweat. No, a tear. I was sobbing. Soundlessly but thoroughly. But numbness took even that, until all I had was horror and an unmoored sense of determination.

I sputtered more borrowed words, voice haggard as I channeled Lizzie Bennett: "'There is a stubbornness about me that never can bear to be frightened at the will of others. My courage always rises at every attempt to intimidate me.'"

The sound of hundreds of fluttering moth wings circled around me, echoing throughout the space. It sounded like disagreement.

I kept talking, anyway, my own words bubbling up. "I'm here on business. As a student. I am a practitioner in need of materials. I have a right to be here."

Something brushed against my shoulder, grasped, turned me bodily toward the wall and the handrail.

"Why didn't you sssssay ssssooOo?" The voice soughed through me, past me, into the crumbling darkness in front of me. As it shoved me into the wall, my entire body numbed, then pulsed with warmth and returned feeling.

Around me, the stairwell door appeared. Light spilled through and set me tingling all over in that painful way of a limb regaining circulation. I barreled into the hallway beyond, gasping.

AFTER ALL THAT, THE MATERIALS LAB WAS JUST A LAB. A GRAD STU-dent staffed the desk and, when I explained what I wanted, handed me a clipboard with a two-page form.

I fished a pen out of my bag and sank into a battered chair to fill it out.

"Never been in the building before?" the grad student asked. She was wearing a colorful pin that proclaimed her *young, Latinx, and MAGIC* beside one that gave her pronouns as She/They. I shook my head, confirming their suspicion.

She winced.

"Rough," they said. "The first time I was in here, the wards trotted out my dead abuela. Made her say some harsh shit. They're constructed to respond to any sense of unbelonging. The more intense it is, the more intense their response is."

So, I'd brought this on myself in more ways than one.

I jutted out my chin, projecting ambivalence. I wasn't ready to think about it. And if I tried to talk about it . . .

She took in my disheveled state and defiant-so-it's-not-broken stare. "I can escort you out. When you're done."

I bobbed my head and turned my attention back to the form, trying to keep my hands from shaking as I checked the box to signify that I understood and acknowledged the university's one skull per academic year policy. Then I signed my name and handed the clipboard over.

The Necromancy grad scanned it. "Looks like it's all in order. I'll be right back." They wandered into a storage room, and I clasped my still-trembling hands. In a few minutes, I'd have my skull. I'd be one step closer to a successful spellwork demonstration.

I *couldn't* fall apart now.

Five minutes and five hundred dollars later, I held the thing in my hands. It was smaller than I'd imagined it would be. Vulnerable, somehow. And its jaw was attached with bright gold-colored wire.

True to their word, the grad student escorted me to the exit. I made my way back across campus, stopping by the admin building to pick up an exam working permit and book a campus containment circle.

I had a terrible feeling this had been the easy part. But I did my best to chuck that emboldening thought into the darkest, dustiest part of my head—focusing instead on the copious amounts of mac n' cheese I was going to make when I got home.

Technological horrors might still await me, but at least I had a plan. On Wednesday, one way or another, I'd find out whether I still had a real shot in this program.

EXCERPT FROM PROFESSOR PUTNAM'S
FIRST LECTURE IN SPELLS & METHODS

Professor Leighton will have filled your heads with flights of
fancy about the outlandish possibilities of naming your own
reality and blue being a working and, worst of all, magic
being something unquantifiably *more* than bare skill. And
that's all well and good. As one of my favorite philosophers
famously said, "If you have built castles in the air, your work
need not be lost; that is where they *should* be. Now put the
foundations under them."★

In this course, we will return to our foundations. The
building blocks of all workings: Incantation, Gesture,
Object, and Ritual. We will explore them in their granular
individuality and in their full scale. Because, as you all
should know, magic *always* comes down to one or more of
these four elements, no matter how complex the working.

You'll do well to remember them. Brand them into your
eager young minds. Respect them in all of their seeming
simplicity.

And would you look at that? I've conveniently written
them on the board in an order that lends itself to mnemonic:

I

G

O

R

As in the assistant who helps Dr. Frankenstein bring the
monster to life. Amid all of the noise of branch-specific
praxis and methodological interventions and cutting-edge
frameworks, it has become rather easy to lose track of
our foundations. Attending to IGOR will help you work
wonders of your own, stabilizing your attempts at *naming* or
reshaping reality. And if you attend well, your wonders will
only be monstrous if you *mean* them to.

★ Henry David Thoreau, *On Walden Pond*.

CHAPTER TEN

Scholarly consensus has it that there is no such thing as an Ur-Reality. But there must be something at the center, something solid and . . . well . . . *real*. Otherwise, the damage caused by unwise workings wouldn't leave such dreadful scars.

—PROFESSOR RUE HUANG, THEORIES OF MAGIC

HANDS POISED AND TREMBLING ABOVE THE ODD AND SLIGHTLY menacing *mise en place* of my spell supplies, I forced myself to breathe.

This was my last chance. If I failed now, I wouldn't be able to replace the skull and start again—and even if I could, they might not issue me another permit quickly enough for it to matter. Admin expedited the permit process for exams and dissertation defenses, but only once per attempt. Waiting the four-to-six weeks for a regular permit wasn't an option.

A long inhale and exhale wasn't enough to calm me, so I closed my eyes and visualized my body. I wiggled my toes, tensed my calves, worked my way up until I was calm and anchored again, stretching my neck in lazy circles.

I knew how to do this. Work from outside to inside, and remember the basics: Incantation, Gesture, Object, and Ritual. Or at least the first three. This particular working didn't require anything specific, ritually. Then again, spell prep was a ritual all its own.

My stomach cramped in a particularly stabby way, anxiety already creeping back in. Best to get on with it, starting with *object*.

Taking another slow breath, I arranged thrift-shop microphones and speakers in a five-point pattern around the table. My hands continued to tremble as I stacked books beside each piece of sound equipment: battered copies of Austen, Defoe, Burney, and Radcliffe novels I'd carted home over the years from the secondhand bookshop near campus. I placed the skull, rigged with a couple of networked hard drives and connected to my laptop, in the center of the arrangement before ringing the whole in a circle of powdered kelp. That left my student ID. It technically didn't have to be *in* the working—I could activate the dormant magic in it just by reaching for it mentally—but it served as another representation of the collections I wanted to draw on as my spell sped up the machine-learning process and transformed a chaos of code into a magic narration construct.

I propped it up against the skull and took a step back.

The tableau before me set my heart dubstepping. Everything was ready, my objects all in place, a vision board for reality to draw upon as it transformed. I tried not to think about the ghosts waiting in the figurative wings, ready to snuff my working out if it started to go awry. But a frisson of discomfort tickled up my spine, and for half a second I was back in the endless void of that stairwell, assaulted by the moldering dead.

Darkness. Silence. Moths' wings.

Resisting a shiver, I flipped my laptop open. *Gesture.* A few keystrokes and I'd know, one way or the other. Sending a plea into the universe, I typed the command to start the program. *Incantation.*

The candle flames flickered, then steadied. The speakers hummed to life, louder than I'd expected, a cacophony of audio playing simultaneously, drowning out the whine of fluorescents and the sub-bass rumble of the HVAC system with text-to-speech narration of the dataset I needed my construct to process, learn, and riff on.

I couldn't watch.

I couldn't *not* watch.

Squeezing my hands together in front of my face, I bit into a knuckle to keep myself from laughing or crying.

If this was working, it would be magically condensing the computer's processing time as code and spellwork alike bonded to their organic buffer: the skull.

I didn't want to hex it, but it *seemed* to be working. Which meant, any second now . . . I braced for the physical toll. The cosmic cost. A wave of exhaustion, nausea, blurred or double vision. Last time I'd done a working this size I'd vomited, skipping straight to the agony of an immense, arcane hangover.

Breath caught in my throat as I watched the candles flare and gutter, smoke wafting toward the ceiling. My laptop, taking that as a cue, shut itself down.

An obvious sign, if not a clear one. Was the working complete, or had it failed?

Only one way to find out.

"Once upon a time."

The command was supposed to start narration, and the words *the end* would get it to stop. Except, nothing happened. I tried again with more confidence, more *expectation*, than I actually felt.

"Once upon a time . . ."

Still, nothing. I stood there waiting for so long, the room's motion-sensing lights clicked off. In the dark, I was ambushed by the urgent need to cry. I cleared my throat instead, sniffing.

"Starsdammit."

It took a bit of jumping and waving to convince the lights to turn back on, which was annoying enough to distract me—briefly—from the despair reaching for me like a riptide. I repacked my bike's saddlebags, clutching at the dregs of my annoyance until frustration—at myself, at my advisor, at the universe—gave me another moor to lash myself to. Temporarily safe from the sea of despondency, I loaded my bike and made my way home.

THERE WAS NO WAY TO SALVAGE THIS DAY, BUT MAYBE I COULD PREVENT
it from getting worse if I turned all of my devices off, grabbed the
leftover mac n' cheese, climbed into bed, and pretended it hadn't
happened.

I headed for the kitchen without even bothering to drop my
saddlebags by the front door and immediately stumbled to a stop
when Darya looked up, pinning me with an expectant smile.

"How'd it go?"

Beside her, Cy tilted his head in silent echo of the question.
They were clearly waiting for me, had been for a while if the dirty
dishes on the table and the spread of cards between them—gin
rummy, not tarot—was anything to go by. Just like that, my plans
were out the window.

I sank into a chair, letting the bags slip to the floor.

"Terribly."

"Could you give us a little more context?" Cy asked, voice
careful in the way it always got when he was worried.

"Cy!" Darya shot him a stern look.

"What? I'm just trying to determine how we can assist our
friend . . . and whether it will be safe to go to campus tomorrow."

I didn't want to explain. Despair surged higher, mingled with
embarrassment. I could lie right now, but I'd have to tell them
eventually. That, or they'd figure it out when I inevitably got
kicked out of the program.

I didn't have to watch them process the information, though.

"It didn't work." I dropped my face into my hands.

"Like, at *all*?" Darya asked, voice spiking high.

"Like at all." My confirmation was muffled, but it must have
been audible enough.

"Oh, thank Hecate," Cy breathed.

I dropped my hands, indignant. "Good to know you care
about my success. Or my ability to pay my share of the rent, for
that matter." I yanked the closest saddlebag open and rummaged
until my fingers found smooth bone. Setting the skull and its tangle of cords down in the middle of the table with a crack, I caught

Cy's avoidant gaze. "This thing cost me five hundred dollars. For a working that snuffed itself out. I spent almost half of my stipend and a *whole* week working on something that's gotten me *nowhere.*"

"Eight days, actually," Cy managed. "And I'm sorry if I care *slightly* more about the sanctity of consensus reality than your degree progress."

"Hecate's dogs, Cy," Darya swore.

I scrunched my mouth up into the fiercest scowl in my power. "Eight days, then. I have fifteen days left to somehow scrape *something* together, but that's not going to happen. I'm out of ideas and resources. When the full moon rises, it won't just be my workings that ebb away. It will be my Magic career."

I was breathing too fast, and it was making me lightheaded. But I couldn't stop it any more than I could stop the hot tears from burning down my cheeks.

"It's not ideal," Cy said. "But I'm sure you'll think of something. You always do."

My heart swooped down into my abs, and the room wobbled around me. Every time I'd had to *think of something* before, I'd had space, breathing room, time to *plan.*

This was my *last* chance, and I'd already fucked it up.

"I—" Words wouldn't line themselves up. I wheezed, clutching the edge of the table for support. My vision fizzed at the edges, and my fingertips tingled and went numb. The room seesawed around me.

"Bartleby?" Cy grabbed my shoulder as I slumped to one side, pulling me back into place.

"Bartleby, breathe." Darya's voice was kind but firm. I wanted to obey so badly I sobbed.

"I'll get a blanket." Cy looked me over. "And some tea."

Darya took my hands. "You're going to be fine. Just breathe with me, okay? In—" she inhaled loudly, and I did my best to imitate her "—and out." Her exhale was slow. Mine was too quick and shaky, but she smiled at me, anyway. "Good. Again. In . . . and out."

I was shivering so hard the table shook with the force of it, but Darya held on to me and kept me focused on my breath.

After a while, a blanket settled around me. Cy rested his hand briefly on top of my head. "You're doing great, Bartleby. I'm going to make us some nice warm tea."

By the time the kettle started whistling, the room had stopped spinning. I was too cold, and my mouth was so dry it was hard to swallow. But I was able to pull my blanket tighter around me and offer Darya a smile.

"Better?" she asked.

My eyes welled up as I tried to decide how to answer that. Finally, I shook my head. "Yes. But no."

I could breathe again. My body didn't feel like an egg shaker in the hands of an agitated toddler anymore. But I did feel *guilty*. This wasn't the first panic attack my housemates had helped me through, and they'd been happening more and more frequently. My housemates had their own stress to deal with; they shouldn't have to worry about mine.

Cy slid a steaming mug of tea toward me and instructed me to take a sip.

I did, wrapping my hands around the warm ceramic for comfort. After another trip to the kettle, Cy returned with mugs for himself and Darya.

"That was a rough one." He grimaced in sympathy.

"Yeah." I pulled my tea closer, letting the steam waft up toward my face. "Sorry."

Darya squawked. "Dorothe Bartleby, *you* don't have *anything* to apologize for." She took her glasses off and fidgeted with them. "Some of us do, though."

Cy huffed. "I suppose Darya's right. I made light of what you're going through. I do believe you'll find your way through this, but I'm sorry for being dismissive."

Darya sighed. "Good on you, Pearson, but I meant *me*. I need to apologize."

What?

"I've wondered, for a while now, if maybe you should . . ." She hesitated, twisting her frames so much I thought for sure they would snap. "If you might benefit from talking to someone about accommodations. But I didn't say anything, and maybe I was wrong not to."

"I . . . What?"

Her voice went gentle. "Bartleby, panic attacks are serious."

I shrugged, but my shoulders stayed up. I didn't *want* to be defensive. Needing accommodations wasn't a bad thing. I just *didn't* need them, and even talking about it made me feel wrong. Like acknowledging Darya's words meant I was taking resources from students who really needed them. I was doing fine. Or, I had been, until my first exam attempt took a nosedive.

"Grad school is stressful. It's *supposed* to be stressful."

"True," Cy said, "but Watkins isn't wrong. Panic attacks aren't part and parcel of a magic degree. Thank Hecate."

I gritted my teeth. "I'm fine." And even if I wasn't—but I *was*—what was SAS going to do, give me time and a half on program progress requirements? More time would help, but it wasn't the core of my problem.

My housemates' expressions were cautious, but the careful neutrality couldn't hide their worry.

"I'll *be* fine." I pushed to my feet. "I'm going to get some sleep." I clutched my blanket with one hand and picked up my tea with the other. "Good night."

CHAPTER ELEVEN

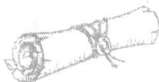

Magic isn't all great. If you have the power to rewrite reality, you also have the power to rip reality—and yourself—a new one in the process. I mean, if you can get approval for the working.

—MAGDALEN, IN DISCUSSION WITH A STUDENT,
OVERHEARD BY BARTLEBY DURING OFFICE HOURS

I T WAS 10:07 P.M. BY THE OVEN CLOCK. I PADDED TOWARD THE fridge in sock feet, questing for leftover mac n' cheese. I'd been too out of it to eat earlier, and as much as I wanted to go back to sleep and keep ignoring my problems, my hunger wasn't going to let that happen.

As if on cue, my stomach growled so hard a wave of dizziness washed over me. I grabbed the edge of the counter until my head cleared, then hauled the fridge door open.

In the glow of the fridge lights, everything looked blobby. I blinked, trying to bring the contents into focus. Had I crashed out so hard my vision was still bleary? Even with gunk and grime keeping my eyes half-shut, I should be able to see the ugly orange plastic container I'd used to store the mac n' cheese. There was plenty of orange in there. And neon purple. And transparent yellow bubbles. But nothing was the right *shape* to be my leftovers. I blinked again.

It wasn't my vision. The fridge was full of amorphous shapes, and they were moving. The hair on the backs of my arms tickled and stood as I watched the shapes gyrate and float.

I kept the fridge door open with my foot so I could use my hands to rub my eyes.

When I pulled them away, anemones and kelp swam through the space. I had to be dreaming. The alternative was too dire. Slamming the fridge shut, I turned to stare into the darkness where I knew the kitchen table had to be. The shadows there were pulsating, flashes of what looked like static moving erratically. When my eyes adjusted, the sense of the movements shuddered through me.

I was seeing myself during my working. The skull at the table's center was the only real object in the stop-motion show, but echoes of my arms moved echoes of books and candles, speakers and mics into place. Sparks ignited at the tips of ethereal candles. A light rectangle stood in for my laptop, and the static shape of my hands typed in the code that set the working going.

I wrapped my arms around myself, breath shallow so I wouldn't interrupt . . . whatever this was. Something sharp and strident at the back of my mind told me I damn well *knew* what this was. I watched the working take hold, anyway, crushed all over again when it sputtered out just like it had earlier. Smoke from snuffed candles rose up and up and up, captivating my attention.

There hadn't been this much before, had there? And why did the smoke seem so much more . . . real than the rest of this odd echo? Dizziness crashed over me, but I couldn't look away. Distantly, I heard a syncopating trill. The fire alarms were going off. Why wasn't I reacting? Why wasn't I *moving*? Was it getting darker?

No, my eyelids were sliding shut. I mustered enough concern to bleat as I fell to the floor. My eyes flew open as my skull cracked against the ground, swimming until they came into focus on the oven clock.

10:59 p.m.

That didn't make *sense*. I'd only been up for a few minutes. Something was wrong. Something was *very* wrong. I tried to move, to stand, to do anything—but the dark wrapped around me like a warm blanket, dragging me deeper and deeper into oblivion.

GHOSTLY HANDS CLAMPED AROUND MY UPPER ARMS, NAILS PRESSING into my skin as they dragged. I fought them, my cries drowning out the ghoulish whispering of moths' wings. Abruptly, the hands let go. But that was almost worse—they'd left me in the deep void. I dove from side to side, searching for the stairwell door, before reason caught up with me.

This was a nightmare. I hadn't gone back to the Bone House, and I wasn't trapped in a stairwell full of ghosts.

But why were the walls . . . gooey and hexagonal? And was it just head trauma nudging me to indulge in pathetic fallacy, or did the orbs darting back and forth across the space seem distraught?

I did *not* like this dream.

Forcing my eyes to open even a sliver exhausted what little energy I had. With a huff, I willed myself to keep going. Grit from the linoleum floor gouged into my cheek as I shifted to get a better sense of my surroundings. Lids at half-mast, I peered up at the oven's blinking LED display.

There, then gone, the numbers read 2:12 a.m. The power must have gone out at some point, after I'd passed out.

Why had I passed out? The answer seemed important. Critical, even. But it wouldn't come, no matter how much I tried to focus.

"Hecate's dogs, Bartleby, you said the working failed." The voice was familiar. An irritable—and literally smoldering—Cy wobbled into view, collapsing into a chair as he patted himself down. "This was one of my favorite shirts," he moaned.

The whine of a power wheelchair motor behind me signaled Darya's presence. "What Cy means is we didn't think we should move you. How do you feel?"

I didn't want to think about that. I groaned and dragged myself upright so I could direct a question at my more sympathetic housemate.

"What happened?"

Darya grimaced.

"What happened was your starsdamned working," Cy said, before Darya could attempt an answer.

I jolted up. Or, tried to. Pain spiked through my head and my vision swam. Pinching the bridge of my nose, I breathed hard.

"I don't understand. It didn't *work*. It's disassembled in my bike bag, for Hecate's sake."

Cy sighed. "Tell me you ended the working."

Heart sinking, I turned from Cy to Darya. "I . . . forgot." My voice was small, pleading. It seemed so obvious now. But I'd been pushing so hard—battling anxiety and insomnia, juggling teaching and my own coursework—I'd blanked on something that should have been second nature.

Darya shook her head, a small movement that tore through me. Usually, Cy was the one who triggered Darya's disappointment. The weight of it was unfamiliar and upsetting. I pulled my knees up and leaned my head into them, breathing through a rush of nausea.

I deserved it. I was so stressed I was slipping on basic Heccing shit.

A thought pulled me up short.

"Shouldn't the ghosts have done something?" This seemed like exactly the kind of situation they were here, haunting, for. Even if our residence ghost didn't catch it, shouldn't the ones at the university have noticed when I'd carted a ticking time bomb beyond the protections of the containment circle?

"You made our kitchen into a palimpsest of realities, none of which were particularly pleasant, and you're blaming the *ghosts*?" Cy used the sibilants in *ghosts* to their full effect, hissing so violently I flinched. "If it wasn't for Moxley, we'd still be sliding sideways into plurality."

As if to echo the point, our usually reserved residence ghost rattled the pipes.

"Cy's right, Bartleby." Darya's quieter words drove the justice in Cy's home. "I did not enjoy being an *orb*."

Not a dream, then.

I'd brought an incomplete working home, where it hadn't been ringed by moon-rock-reinforced walls or in safe proximity to the campus cemetery when it tried to reboot. There'd been nothing to stop it from ripping reality a new one, as Mags would say. Nothing but our lone residence ghost: Moxley.

But if my working had tried to reboot, if it had done so forcefully enough to cause consensus reality to buckle under the pressure—

Heart pounding, I scrambled to my feet, wobbling precariously toward the kitchen table.

"*Once Upon A Time.*" I capitalized every single word as I said it, pouring will and surety into my voice. Ignoring my housemates' questions, I held my breath and waited. Time passed in lurching heartbeats. After a minute, I sagged.

It hadn't suddenly started working. It'd just failed again, more dramatically.

I'd just flunked out of Magic school.

Darya offered me a sympathetic half smile as I sank back to the floor under the weight of that revelation. I should have been panicking. Instead, numbness spread through me. I cradled my knees to my chest.

"'I-i-i-i-iit-t-t-t-t-t-t is-s-s-s-s a-a-a-a-a-a-a-a-a-a-a tr-r-r-u-u-u-u-u-t-t-t-th—'"

A digital voice tore through our uneasy silence, its attempt to narrate the first few words of *Pride and Prejudice* lagging and discordant. I jerked out of my makeshift cocoon and back to my feet, bracing myself against the counter as a wave of dizziness swept through me.

"'A-a-a-a-aalllllll h-a-a-a-ppy f-f-familie-e-e-e-es a-a-re alike-e-e-e-e-e—'"

Anna Karenina. The fragments of monotone narration were coming from the skull.

"What the Hec." My whispered curse was involuntary.

"Bartleby?" There were a multitude of questions in the way

Darya said my name. Like, *is this supposed to be happening? Are we trapped in an alternate reality after all? Is it quoting* Jane Austen?

I didn't have answers to anything except that last one (yes, of course—what else did she expect?), so I ignored the question, eyes locked on the skull.

It answered for me.

"'When you have eliminated all which is impossible, then whatever remains, however improbable, must be the truth.'"

Sherlock Holmes. *The Sign of Four*, if I wasn't mistaken. My working had *worked*.

"Hmm. I draw the line at quotable quotes," Cy drawled. "I'm going to bed. Try not to rip any more holes between realities tonight?"

He strode out before I could answer.

"Congrats!" Darya said, smile genuine then apologetic. "But I need my sleep, so . . ." She inclined her head, motionless until I nodded, then followed Cy with a click of her joystick.

"'I find the nights long, for I sleep but little and think much,'" the narration construct said as the room fell silent in my housemates' wake.

Bleak House. The thought buoyed me.

I laughed without quite meaning to, dizzy—giddy—with the implications. I might pass my exam this time around, after all.

"Ba-a-a-a-a-aaaaartleby stared into the middle distance, worried." The skull's text-to-speech voice glitched again before stabilizing.

A cloud flitted between me and my visions of possible success. The working hadn't *failed* exactly, but it hadn't *worked*, either. Not properly. Not if it was narrating *me*. It was supposed to generate *fiction*. And only when I asked it to.

"The End."

"'A lady's imagination is very rapid. It jumps from exultation to concern, from concern to trepidation in a moment.'"

More *Pride and Prejudice*. I groaned. "You aren't responding to my commands."

"Bartleby expressed a valid concern. One for which the narration skull had no explanation or excuse. It was, after all, only a narration skull."

Despite my worries, I started to relax. My working might not be functioning as planned, but at least it was drawing on novels to narrate. Something had gone right. It had even started out with Austen quotes, which made up a big chunk of my dataset. Maybe whatever was causing it to operate outside of the parameters I'd set was fixable.

"However," the skull went on, "Bartleby resolved to worry about the problem later. If there *was* a later in which she remained enrolled in this graduate program."

I ignored the dig—could it be a dig?—choosing to focus my harried thoughts on something less life-and-death:

"You keep saying that. Narration skull. You need a name."

"The narration skull agreed with Bartleby that the phrase narration skull was rather unwieldy for narratorial purposes."

Hec. It even talked like an Austen novel. At least that was one more sign that I hadn't *entirely* failed.

"Okay, good. What would you like to be called? Pick a name."

"Bartleby's question puzzled the narration skull, whose spellwork and code did not recognize the command *pick a name.*"

"O-o-okay." Considering it didn't seem to need (or recognize) its actual commands, that was rich. I crossed my arms. "What about Anne?"

"Bartleby suggested the name Anne because she'd recently watched a documentary about the wives of Henry the VIII and was obsessed with the rumor that Anne Boleyn tried to speak after being beheaded."

I narrowed my eyes. Was its tone *wry* somehow? I hadn't programmed it to do sentiment analysis, let alone emotional output. More likely it was the probable concussion shaping my perception.

"Touché. But how do you feel about the name?"

"Bartleby's question posed an interesting quandary—could such a being, a homunculus of code and spell, actually feel? The narration skull did not know. Nevertheless, the name Anne was agreeable to it."

Make that Austen with the pomposity of a Dickens character.

"Good. Nice to make your acquaintance, Anne."

"Bartleby's salutation was kind, and Anne appreciated making Bartleby's acquaintance as well." It was sincere enough that I felt a spark of guilt for considering its narration pompous.

But *could* my working be capable of sincerity, any more than it could be capable of digs or wryness? I was anthropomorphizing it. I puffed out a breath and shifted my weight from one leg to the other, suddenly and painfully aware of the chill seeping into my feet from the cold linoleum floor and the jitters coursing through me.

When had I eaten last?

My stomach grumbled in immediate answer: too long ago. That, at least, was easily fixed.

"I wonder if there's any leftover mac n' cheese."

I was halfway to the fridge before Anne commented. "Bartleby's quest for mac n' cheese was destined to be fruitless, as Cy and Darya had consumed the entire dish hours before."

I sagged into the open refrigerator with a groan.

"Cereal it is, I guess."

CHAPTER TWELVE

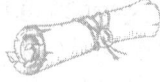

From twenty-three to twenty-six Dorothe Bartleby was in training to become a mage.

—NARRATORIAL COMMENTARY ADAPTED FROM
JANE AUSTEN'S *NORTHANGER ABBEY* BY ANNE

A SPEAKER-SQUAWK OF FEEDBACK TORE THROUGH THE QUIET.
"Brimful absence. Jarring, gaping, groping void. Mislaid. Unreachable. Fading—Fading—*Fading.* Unlocated. Un-n-n-n-n-n-n-n-nnnnnnnnfelt."

I fought out of the tangle of my blankets, halfway to my feet before my thoughts caught up to my panic.

Anne, sitting on top of my dresser, continued to spout words and phrases that my brain refused to process into meaning. Either I was too sleep deprived to do words, or it was gibberish. Anxiety seesawed with hope in my gut, leaving me nauseated and frozen in place.

"Concealed, clutching, catching—*devoid-d-d-d-d-d-d-d-d-d,*" Anne said, so somberly it rang through the room like a Delphic pronouncement. *Definitely gibberish.*

Maybe this was a sign my working was too broken to keep. But I wasn't ready to admit defeat. Not yet. The gibberish could just as easily be a sign the working was salvageable. Gibberish was a lot closer to fiction than a blow-by-blow of my life. At least, that *felt* true. I said as much, testing the thought.

"Thi-i-i-i-s sounded nonsense to Anne, so it said nothing." Anne's voice skipped before steadying.

My earlier certainty about Anne's lack of capacity for sentiment crumbled in the face of its obvious joke.

"Are you quoting Lewis Carroll at me?" I was pretty sure that was a slightly adapted line from *Through the Looking Glass*. It didn't get a chance to respond. A series of loud bangs interrupted us.

"Bartleby, what's going on?" Cy pounded at my door. A faint whirring sound told me Anne had woken Darya, too.

"Can't you turn that thing off?" she called.

Belatedly, my muddled thoughts pinpointed another important piece of information. The squawking wasn't Anne. Or, it wasn't just Anne. My alarm clock was going off, and somehow the sound was interacting with Anne's narration, like a hot microphone held right next to an amp.

I slapped my alarm until it fell silent. Stumbling across the room, I hauled my door open. My housemates waited, looking as disheveled as I felt, in the hallway.

"Sorry. My narration construct is glitching."

Cy shoved his hands into his dressing gown pockets, rolling his eyes. "Obviously. What are you *doing* about it?"

Darya elbowed him.

"Oof. What in the name of Rasputin's balls, Watkins?"

Darya made a face that clearly said *try again.*

Cy glowered at her. "Fine." He turned to me. "How can we help?"

MY HOUSEMATES MADE COFFEE WHILE I SHOWERED AND GOT DRESSED. I still had thirty minutes before I needed to leave for campus, which was more than enough time to run my problem by them. Still, as I retrieved Anne from my dresser and headed to the kitchen, I set an alarm on my phone, just in case.

Darya slid me a mug of coffee, and I stumbled through an explanation between long, desperate gulps.

"After you two went to bed, Anne started narrating *me*. It was only supposed to narrate Cy's Christmas village, and only on my command. And I thought that was all that was wrong—" Cy groaned. I knew what he was thinking, because I was thinking it, too: even if that *was* all, it was still *a lot* of wrong to deal with. "—except, now Anne is glitching. I think. It's still narrating me, but it's spouting a bunch of nonsense, too."

"'You may call it *nonsense* if you like,'" Anne said, contrarily, "'but *I've* heard nonsense, compared with which that would be as sensible as a dictionary!'"

It was another quote from *Through the Looking Glass*, which, now that I thought about it, hadn't been in my corpus of long-eighteenth-century texts, since it was *firmly* Victorian. Like *Bleak House* and Sherlock Holmes. I pinched the bridge of my nose, adding *corpus issues* to my growing list of problems.

"And you have no idea what went wrong?" Darya asked.

I shook my head.

"No. It could be something in the code, which I can probably find out on Monday in Digimancy. Or it could be in the spell-work. Or—"

"It's just . . ." Darya interrupted. "You did check that the skull had been properly cleansed of its . . . former inhabitant before you did the working?"

I stared at her, horrified. Was Anne capable of sentiment because it was still *human*?

"Bartleby had imagined that Necromancy would be 'on their shit' and so had not thought to check that the cleansing had been completely and properly done," Anne intoned.

If there was still *Anne* in Anne, still some piece of human consciousness bound to the skull, I was going to have a *huge* IRB issue. However minuscule the amount of spirit matter still tethered to the skull, my research would technically involve *human subjects* and the institutional review board would be all over me like . . . Well, like rocks on Merlin.

I folded my arms on the table and laid my head in the cradle of them, moaning. "Why does magic have to be so hard?" When nobody answered, I sat back up, scowling. "Seriously, I want to know. When I was little, as long as I had the right words and really *believed* them when I said them, anything was possible. I could stop my siblings from fighting, or convince a teacher to let me stay in and read during recess because the other kids were just going to bully me. And one time, my dog went missing—like gone for weeks, my parents had given up, missing—and I decided that if I repeated a specific line from Beverly Cleary's *Ribsy* enough times, he'd come home. And he did."

I never got workings wrong, back then. They either worked or they didn't. Sure, I only cast small ones to keep my parents from noticing. I was only ever able to accomplish things that were already possible in my tiny version of consensus reality. And none of the changes had been lasting: Bryan and Grace eventually went back to fighting, and my dog ran off again. But that was how primary magic worked, and I'd been able to do something when it seemed like nobody else could. I'd been capable, and more than that, I'd been *powerful*.

I missed that feeling.

"Magic used to be so *fun*, didn't it?" Darya sighed. "Now it's all grimoire reviews and experiment parameters and an ill-starred amount of autoclaving."

We lapsed into the sort of chummy silence only housemates of long tenure seem to achieve, staring into our coffee contemplatively until my phone buzzed and an air-raid siren blared into life. I jumped, jabbing at my phone screen until my alarm stopped.

"Time to head out?" Darya asked.

"Unfortunately." I reached for Anne. My working's problems, whether spellwork, code, or spirit matter, would have to wait until class was over.

DAILY DIGEST OF MAGICALLY PROMISING NARRATIONS, AUTOMATICALLY GENERATED FROM ANNE'S LOGS

DATE AND TIME	CONTENT
Thursday, January 14, 8:00 a.m.	Bartleby was temporarily distracted from her concerns about the misfunction of her narration skull by the conspicuous absence of two of her students.
Thursday, January 14, 8:02 a.m.	As she unpacked her satchel, Bartleby's remaining students traded grim gossip about some new strain of the flu. Manesh brandished a copy of the *Platypus Prattler*. "It's having strange effects on Magic students," he said. Bartleby couldn't help but think about the way Alse's face had gone green, right before they disappeared. "Some of the affected students have been reported *missing*."
Thursday, January 14, 8:04 a.m.	Taking the paper from her student, Bartleby skimmed the article. "They say there's no evidence of a connection," she said. "In fact, the author of this article says that's just speculation." Still, it was a startling coincidence.
Thursday, January 14, 8:05 a.m.	Bartleby did her best to hide her own agitation and redirect, though it was clearly a struggle.
Thursday, January 14, 8:06 a.m.	Students are delicate plants. They should take care of their health and their complexion.
Thursday, January 14, 8:07 a.m.	Anne's aphorism, though taken from the eminently respectable *Emma*, rather disquieted than soothed the restless spirits in the room. Bartleby, sighing, explained the nature of her spellwork construct to the class.
Thursday, January 14, 8:08 a.m.	All have been, or at least all have believed themselves to be, in danger from the pursuit of someone whom they wished to avoid. But resolving not to be again overcome by trivial appearances of alarm, or misled by a raised imagination, the class resumed its studies.

DATE AND TIME	CONTENT
Thursday, January 14, 8:42 a.m.	Inexplicably, Bartleby's students remained on edge despite Anne's further quotation of *Emma*. The matter was not helped in the slightest by the arrival of a vague, unseen presence who—
Thursday, January 14, 8:42 a.m.	Where they were, nothing. An undulating unreality of absences. There is nothing at the center, but there was. There was. There was.
Thursday, January 14, 9:34 a.m.	A light was blinking on the old-fashioned phone when Bartleby returned to her office after class. Bartleby did not seem to notice, prodding Alse's backpack with the toe of her shoe. She felt a desperate need to do something. Rummaging through her student's belongings was probably not the answer.
Thursday, January 14, 9:35 a.m.	When her narration skull called attention to the blinking light, Bartleby sagged into her desk chair and sighed. "To be honest, I don't know how to check the voicemail. At this point, it's been long enough that I'm embarrassed to ask. But it's okay; the only people who ever call are groundskeeping. My students know to contact me by email."
Thursday, January 14, 10:03 a.m.	Bartleby ignored Anne's glitching attempts to indicate the importance of the voicemail, putting on noise-canceling headphones and pulling up the library search interface. It was time, she had determined, to figure out what had gone wrong with her working.
Thursday, January 14, 10:35 a.m.	As she tried search term after search term, Bartleby's efforts to determine the cause of Anne's glitch became increasingly erratic. Despite her vow never to return to the Bone House, she feared the answers she needed could only be found in the Materials Lab.
Thursday, January 14, 11:09 a.m.	Bartleby neglected to check the voicemail before leaving her office. Had she listened, she would have realized that the call was from Alse's distraught father.

CHAPTER THIRTEEN

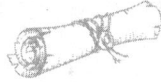

If adventures will not befall a young lady in her own office, she must seek them abroad.

—NARRATORIAL COMMENTARY ADAPTED FROM
JANE AUSTEN'S *NORTHANGER ABBEY* BY ANNE

FOR THE SECOND TIME IN AS MANY WEEKS, I WAS IN HOSTILE TERritory. Even at the less austere back entrance, I could *feel* the Bone House's spiteful regard. Or, the spiteful regard of its wards. I twitched away the sense memory of my last encounter with the dead.

"Wish me luck."

Anne didn't respond to my whispered plea. Which was fine. Luck wasn't the issue, anyway. What I really needed was confidence. But if *that* was easy to come by, I wouldn't be in this mess to begin with.

I took a deep breath and hauled open the heavy door, waiting for intervention. Divine, magical, mundane, I didn't care.

When nothing happened, I closed my eyes and plunged over the threshold and directly into an immovable object. With warm, cinnamony breath.

I froze. Taking a step back, I pried open one eye.

Watching me, with an oblique expression that could've been amusement or disgust, was the Necromancy grad. They were holding their phone out, like they'd just been looking at it.

"It's *you* again," she sighed.

I nodded.

"It's just . . . a bit disappointing," they elaborated, slipping their phone into their pocket. "I assumed you were a smart person who made a bad decision in a moment of desperation."

"I was."

"But you're back."

"I am."

"Which tells me," a growl crept into her words, "that, while you *may* be desperate, you must not be that smart."

I took an involuntary step back. Ouch, death mage.

"The fact that you're sneaking in the back door makes me think you've still got a major case of imposter syndrome," they continued. "The wards are going to hate that." She paused, tipped her head to one side. "Or love it, maybe. They do relish their grave-sworn duties. But, either way, you're waist-deep in newt shit. Especially because you obviously know *nothing* about necromancy. They'll do their best to either destroy you or keep you if they get the chance again. Depending, of course, on whether it's hate or love. And—no offense—you don't have the experience to make sure that doesn't happen."

"It's just, I'm still desperate." The words made their own way out of my body as I finished gathering my wits in the onslaught of that tirade. "I'm pretty sure that the skull you sold me wasn't properly cleansed, and it's having some weird consequences for my working. If I don't get this figured out in the next fourteen days, I'm done for."

The Necromancy grad, whose name I was just realizing I did *not* know, blinked.

"I know I didn't just hear you say I don't know how to do my job. *I know you're smarter than that.* So, go on. Finish your little explanation." They crossed their arms.

"Bartleby, flustered and, as already mentioned, desperate, attempted to explain that she had no idea how to test for residual spirit matter," Anne explained, voice slightly obscured by the other contents of my bag. "And she'd spent the entire morning searching for solutions online."

"What's that?" Her eyes narrowed.

"It's my working."

They considered this. "And it's . . . Please tell me it's not right. The *internet*?"

I grimaced, sheepishly. "I tried the library first?"

"Now I'm *really* disappointed," they huffed. "But lucky for you, my advisor just rescheduled on me. Come in. Let's take a look at this thing."

"Bartleby was at once embarrassed and relieved," Anne announced as we headed deeper into the building. I did my best not to shrivel up and die on the spot. "She hoped this nameless and intimidating death mage would have some answers."

The aforementioned *death mage* muttered something under their breath that sounded an awful lot like curses before turning so abruptly on her heel that I almost ran into her again.

"My name is Lora. Lora Mamani Flores," they said. "And I'm *not* a *death mage*. I'm a yatiri. That's why I work here. The spirits in the skulls demanded it. Apparently, I am the only person at this starsforsaken university who knows how to communicate with the ñatitas because white mages don't have to learn other people's magic. It's always only the other way around."

That was a lot, but one phrase stood out: *the spirits in the skulls.*

"But I thought you said—"

Lora arched an eyebrow, cutting me off.

"*Your* skull was properly cleansed. But not *all* of the skulls in the lab are cleansed. Not all of the magic we do requires the human equivalent of a tabula rasa."

"So." I chose my words more carefully. "There's a small possibility—"

Lora cut me off again, this time by loudly jangling their keys and announcing, "Here we are."

I followed her into the lab. They dropped their bag onto a table and turned.

"Show me your skull so we can get to the part where you realize that I'm always right and grovel lavishly."

I rolled my eyes but dug Anne out of my bag.

"Bartleby was merely employing the process of elimination by coming here . . ." Anne began.

Lora raised an eyebrow at me for the third time that day, this time with the ghost of a smile.

"Process of elimination, huh?"

"She'd hoped never to step foot in this building again," Anne confirmed.

This earned me an approving nod. "So, you aren't entirely clueless. You at least have a sense of self-preservation to ignore."

Not knowing how to respond to that, I shrugged.

She smiled for a microsecond longer before clapping her hands together with businesslike energy.

"Let's get to work. Bring the skull over here."

"I named it Anne."

"Well, bring *Anne* over here. The ñatitas will tell us if anyone's lurking in its organic matter," they explained as they walked across the room. I lengthened my stride to keep up.

"The skulls?"

"No, the spirits that . . . hmm . . . occasionally couch-surf in the skulls," she said. They'd come to a stop in a corner where shelves had been converted into a flower-and candle-laden altar. A trio of skulls presided over the room from this vantage point, one in a crocheted neon-green beanie and sunglasses, one with a gold tooth and grandfatherly bottle-lens glasses, the third, very small, in gaming headphones and a plastic bead necklace.

"Hola, Alfonso, Xavier, and Pilar, please allow me to introduce . . ." Lora glanced over their shoulder at me in question. She'd forgotten my name.

"Bartleby." I wasn't quite sure why I was whispering, except that I had the intense feeling that I should.

Lora turned back to the ñatitas. "Bartleby and Anne. They've come to ask whether Anne might be carrying a spirit."

The hair on my arms prickled.

"Give me your ofrenda," Lora whispered, holding out a hand without looking away from the altar.

"My what?" My single language was mortifying. Well. *Single* wasn't technically right, if I counted arcane languages. I didn't, in this case.

Lora sucked their teeth, annoyed.

"An offering? You can't have come to deal with the dead without *something* to offer. Cigarettes? Chewing gum? A particularly sparkly hair clip?"

I hadn't known I would be dealing with the dead, but I swallowed that explanation and searched my bag. I found a tube of unopened Chapstick and a brand-new pack of pens and shoved them into Lora's outstretched hands.

Lora placed two pens beside each skull and repeated my request, pocketing my Chapstick.

Again, the hair on the back of my arms prickled.

Anne buzzed with static electricity. I managed not to yelp, even though it felt like I was holding one of those orbs they sell in catalogs full of junk for vaguely sciencey kids. The telltale whirring and clicking started a second later.

"Stumbling, frightened, into sprawling nothing. Flummoxed, fuddled, flailing—flailing—failing." Embarrassment and curiosity succumbed to my growing sense of vindication as I held Anne at arm's length.

"See." I pointed it at Lora. "Glitching. Like I said. It's got to be contaminated."

Lora rolled her eyes.

"Are you sure it's not just chattering about you?" They looked me up and down. "I haven't known you long, but you did stumble into the wards' void the other day. And, not gonna lie, flummoxed and fuddled do seem to be apt descriptors."

She had a point about the first part. And, maybe, the second. But Anne narrated me by name just fine, all the time. This *had* to be something different.

"Bartleby could rest easy," Anne's voice still warbled slightly as it resumed normal narration. "The ñatitas determined there were no traces of spirit matter remaining in Anne's organic matter."

"It's right. That is what they said," Lora agreed, glancing from me to Anne with widened eyes. "How did it . . ." Lora paused, looking almost flustered. The expression was entirely out of place on their face. She tried again. "It is a difficult thing, to listen well enough to hear the ñatitas. Could you . . . ?"

I shook my head.

"No. And I don't know how Anne does it. That's partly why I'm worried. It's narrating information it has no access to. Or *should* have no access to."

Lora pursed their lips and hummed. Then, shaking herself, she turned back toward the ñatitas.

"Gracias, ustedes," they said, formally.

"Thank you." I echoed her words, not sure if I meant them for her or for the ñatitas.

"Just promise me you won't tempt your fate and come here on your own again. You may be clueless and annoying but you're too interesting to end up ghost food. Or possessed."

"I . . . Thank you?"

Lora rolled their eyes and held out their hand.

"Gimme."

I extended my hand, confused.

Lora groaned. "Your *phone*."

I unlocked it and held it out. She snatched it, shooting off a text.

"They told me to give you my contact info," they passed the phone back to me, "because, and I quote, 'you'll need it.'"

"Okay." That couldn't be good, could it?

"Okay. Now, this time, when I show you out, you know what to do?"

"Stay away?"

"That, or get confident. Because . . ."

"If I don't, I'll get eaten by the ghosts." It didn't seem fair—I was a Magic student, I had as much right to be here as anyone in the program, whether I'd fully internalized it or not—but I wasn't going to argue with Lora or her ñatitas.

"Bingo. Good luck with your exams. Let me know how it goes," they said, holding a palm to their ear in the universal signal for a phone call.

When I nodded, she shoved me through the lab door and practically herded me down the stairs and out the back. Then, they vanished into the building without another word.

I'd gotten what I'd come for. I didn't have to face impending doom in the form of the IRB for unauthorized human subjects research. But I wasn't any closer to knowing the problem I *was* dealing with.

I kicked a rock to vent my frustration and headed back across campus.

If only I didn't have to wait until class on Monday to get answers about my code. I paused, midstride. Maybe I could track down one of my classmates. Imani seemed like the most knowledgeable, but she'd rolled her eyes when James suggested a study group. James was my best bet. And while I didn't have his phone number, I knew where I might be able to get it.

THE FLOWERS WERE STILL WRITHING OUTSIDE BENTHAM COTE WHEN I climbed the brick steps, paused outside the ornately carved door, and looked around until I spotted the doorbell. I pressed it long and hard before taking a couple of steps backward and sliding my hands into my pockets.

A solid minute passed before I heard deadlocks tumbling on the other side of the door, which eventually swung inward with a sustained creak that had to be magically amplified and not the result of poor housekeeping.

"What brings you to our threshold?" a voice boomed and echoed through the building's impossibly cavernous lobby. There was nobody there. My eyes watered with the frantic urge to look away, which probably meant the speaker was using a cloaking, and not that they were a ghost. On that logic, I stifled a shiver and squinted into the seemingly empty middle of the room.

"I was hoping you could put me in touch with James?"

"Who?" The disembodied voice did not bother to mask its indifference.

"James Southeil? He mentioned his cousin lives here."

"Oh, did he?" The voice, sans dramatic reverb, came from right beside me, and a young student in a tulle mourning dress draped with a sash of lilies materialized a millisecond later.

"Cloaking," Anne intoned from the depths of my bag, "can be voluntary or involuntary. Disappearing faces still move in physical places."

"Uhhh . . . what?" the student asked.

Internally, I agreed. With emphasis. *What the actual Hec?* Externally, I stayed on task.

"Ignore that."

The student scowled, unsubtly looking me up and down. "You're not like, a stalker or anything?"

I resisted the urge to roll my eyes, unexpectedly annoyed. Instead, I showed her my student ID and fished my crumpled Digimancy syllabus out of my bag.

"James and I are taking a class together. I just need to chat with him about some spellwork."

She glanced at my ID, a delicate furrow forming between her brows. "Why don't you already have his number?"

I shrugged. "We haven't had a chance to exchange contact information. But he said we could start a study group, if I wanted. And . . ." I wasn't going to explain *all* of my business to a nosy necro undergrad. "Can you give it to me, or not?"

She tipped her head to the side as if she needed to give the idea some deep thought, then smirked. "Fine. I guess offering to form a study group and then forgetting to give you his info does sound like James. But I'm going to have a word with him about this whole situation."

She made a couple of thumb gestures that looked remarkably like texting, even though she didn't have a phone in her hands. And then my phone buzzed, an anonymous text that contained a phone number and nothing else.

"Now, if that's it?" She glared at me like that better be it. "I have an invisible party to get back to." She vanished without waiting for a reply, and a second later the door swung shut in my face.

I rolled my eyes and headed back the way I'd come, texting as I walked.

Hey, James, it's Bartleby.
From Digimancy.
I was hoping maybe I could take you up on that study group?

CHAPTER FOURTEEN

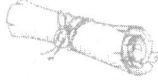

In the nineteenth century, we in the Western world
began to think of magic as something at once social
and shareable. No longer the secret province of the
lonely practitioner, magic at its fullest became a practice
requiring collaboration. It is ultimately *people*, working
together, who make magic truly possible. So look around
you. Consider your cohort. Do not take them for granted.

—PROFESSOR URSULA LEIGHTON, INTRODUCTION
TO GRADUATE STUDIES IN MAGIC

ACCORDING TO JAMES, IMANI HELD COURT OVER A SMALL GROUP
of dissertating mages every Friday at Oat & About, a coffee shop a few blocks from campus. If I wanted her input
as well as his, this was the best time to catch her.

Palms clamped to my handlebars, I pedaled hard for the last
several blocks. I wasn't going to turn down more help, even if the
thought of crashing a study group made me queasy. James had
promised it would be fine. It was going to be fine.

As if summoned by my thoughts, James wavered into view. A
crowd of pajama-clad students passed and there he was, leaning
against the building like a ridiculously good-looking cardboard
cutout of a cowboy in a Western-wear store.

I hopped off my bike while it was still rolling, steering it neatly
into the rack.

"Mims wants you to know that showing up at Bentham Cote and demanding my information was unspeakably rude," James announced, pushing away from the wall and joining me as I locked up my bike.

"Fair." I tried to amp up the apology in my tone. The problem was I wasn't sorry. I'd do it again. "But I didn't know how else to get in touch."

He did not make the completely valid argument that I could have waited a few days, asked in Digimancy class. He didn't say anything at all, and I rushed to fill the silence.

"I was honestly surprised she gave me your info. She seemed pretty worried about stalkers." Which, now that I thought about it, was unusual. And probably *also* unspeakably rude to comment on.

James groaned. "She explained why, didn't she?" He ran a hand through his hair, distraught. "I told her she can get away with being mysterious about it. So what if people think she's paranoid and self-important? That describes half of Necromancy, for Hecate's sake."

"Explained . . . what?"

James stared. "She didn't tell you."

I shook my head.

"And now I've made a huge deal about it." He sighed, scrubbed a hand down his face. "My family's kind of famous because . . . my great-great-aunt endowed Bentham Cote. We've had a few incidents over the years because of it. Not Mims and I, personally. The family in general."

"Wait. Your aunt—sorry, *great-great-aunt*—is *Miriam Heccing Bishop*?" I put my hands to my head and pulled them away, flicking all my fingers out at once as I made an explosion sound.

It sure explained why he'd known about the Materials Lab. He probably knew all kinds of Necromancy secrets.

"Next, you're going to tell me you're moon-favored." I laughed as I said it, but James's cheeks flooded red, his eyes dropping to his shoes. "Rasputin's *balls*," I couldn't help hissing the word as I lowered my voice, "you're moon-favored."

He was frowning when he looked back up. "It's not a big deal."

I sputtered. "I thought you were just . . . I don't know . . . some surfer kid with a thrifting habit."

He smiled at that. Then frowned. "But now you know the truth."

I wasn't sure why he made that sound like such a problem, and I didn't have time to ask. Any minute, Imani could pack up and I'd lose my window. So I ad-libbed.

"What? That you're probably loaded? Yeah. So, I'm going to gracefully let you buy my coffee and then we can pretend this conversation never happened."

"And you'll go back to thinking of me as a weird surfer kid?"

I held up my hand as though I were taking an oath.

"I swear."

He grinned. "Great. Then, allow me."

James yanked the door open and gestured me through. To his credit, he did not complain even a little bit when I ordered an obscenely large lavender and oat milk latte, a blackberry scone, and a rosemary and blueberry cruller (for later).

Armed with snacks, we ventured upstairs in search of Imani.

IMANI'S DISSERTATION GROUP WAS TRICKLING OUT WHEN WE FOUND her, ensconced in the sunniest back corner of Oat & About's upstairs room and presiding over three tables, which were absolutely littered with cups, crumbs, books, and notes.

"James!" Imani called, catching sight of him before noticing me. "And Bartleby?"

"Hey. I took James up on his study group offer. I was hoping I could get your thoughts on something, too, if you have the time." Getting right to the point seemed best. "I really appreciated your insight on my buffer ideas the other day."

"One good deed . . ." Imani sighed. Her smile belied the words. "What's up?"

I placed my ill-gotten goods carefully on the nearest table, shrugging off my bag and coat before sinking into a chair. Digging Anne out of my bag, I set it on the table so that it was facing Imani.

"It's not working right."

Imani's brow furrowed, her gaze going from the skull to me and back. "It's not working at all, or . . ."

"By *it's not working right*, Bartleby meant to say that it, by which she meant Anne, the organic-digital narration construct she'd conjured into existence, was operating outside of the parameters Bartleby believed she had given it in code and spellwork alike."

Imani gaped.

James leaned over as if he was thinking about poking Anne, with an awed "cool." I swatted his hand away and caught Imani's gaze.

"It's only supposed to narrate on command, and only using a corpus of long-eighteenth-century texts to create fiction about a Christmas village. But it doesn't respond to my commands. And it's narrating *me*." I eyed Anne. "It's also started spouting gibberish."

Imani's brows furrowed farther.

"I've confirmed it's not spirit matter contamination," I added, before *that* could derail anything.

She sighed. "Let's see the code."

I dug out my laptop and sent them both the code packet.

After what felt like half a Heccing century, Imani sat back. "I'm not seeing anything obvious."

She looked me up and down with an expression that might have been surprised reassessment—*maybe copy-room girl isn't entirely incompetent*—or hopefulness that I'd let her get on with her day. Probably the second one.

I straightened, my vintage wooden chair creaking in chorus with my spine. "Thank you both. I won't waste any more of your—"

Imani waved her hands until I stopped. "No. I'm not . . . I just . . ." She huffed. "We're going about this the wrong way. I found a few small things, but they're not enough to cause the glitching you describe. Tell us about the working itself."

I did, pulling up my diagrams and notes to help them visualize my flow. James scooched his chair closer to mine and leaned over as I described the pentangle construction, the promising start, and the premature snuffing.

"And then, later that night, the working rebooted itself and triggered a palimpsest."

Imani shook her head. "It didn't reboot."

"Machine learning takes *time*," James added.

"I know. But the working was supposed to condense that." My shoulders crept upward.

"It did," James said, "but even magic has a hard time compressing *months* into *minutes*. It sounds like you got it down to hours instead of weeks, which is pretty impressive."

I sagged backward. "You're saying the working would've been fine if I'd just waited a little longer?"

Imani nodded. "Exactly. This was just a processing delay. Lag time, if you will."

"But that doesn't explain the nonfiction narration, or the broken commands. Does it?"

Imani tore a jagged cuticle with her teeth. "Actually, it might. Some of these smaller errors may have given your spellwork enough wiggle room to—*interpret* isn't the right word exactly . . . hmm—*build on* your parameters."

"The database query?" James asked.

"Yeah!" Imani turned her computer screen toward me and James. "You said it's drawing on your corpus sometimes. But see here, where you designate your data source and output? You left the queries open. The working must have included some other options."

My stomach sank. "Like the institutional repository?"

"Sure," Imani caught on quickly. "You said you put your ID in the containment circle? That might have been enough."

"Does that mean . . ." The world constricted itself around me, my vision tunneling to a pinpoint of blurred color and light.

Cy'd been right to worry. That long ago diner-diviner had been right to prophesy.

Leaving the data source query open was bad enough, but the output was supposed to tell it to narrate Cy's Christmas village. I'd created a construct with *no functional controls*, fed it what amounted to our university's consensus reality, and, by leaving the output unspecified, set it loose on something much larger than a collection of holiday decorations. If it worked and its narrations were *actually* magic, then it would do untold damage. My palms went damp, heart racing nearly as fast as my thoughts.

Imani was talking, but there was a high-pitched ringing in my right ear. I tried to focus on the movement of her lips, but my mind kept slipping back toward the undeniable fact that if I couldn't figure out how to fix this, I wasn't just going to destroy my Magic career—I was going to destroy the entire campus. My right pinky toe had gone numb, and my fingertips were tingling.

"Bartleby, lost to a panic attack, had overlooked one critical factor," Anne expostulated from the middle of the table. "The dead."

Imani placed a firm but gentle hand on my shoulder.

"It's right, Bartleby," she said. "In fact, that's probably what's causing the glitching."

Relief sapped all the solidity out of my bones, and embarrassment dissolved what was left. I sank into my chair.

Of course the dead would keep my working from turning campus into a palimpsest of fictional realities. There was no way a university that had stood for over a century could be destroyed by some random first-gen student who didn't have her shit together. This exact sort of situation was why only campuses with onsite cemeteries were allowed to house Magic programs.

"Look on the bright side," James said while patting my other shoulder tentatively, "if it's triggering the ghosts, that means its narration *is* magic. It might not be working as you imagined, but it *is* working."

"None of this explains why it's not responding to your commands," Imani said, "but you'll figure that out." Pausing, she twisted the lid off a small glass water bottle and sipped the contents.

Beside me, James cleared his throat. "Actually, I think I know why it isn't responding to your commands."

Imani and I both turned toward him.

"Most of your packet is written in Python, but you used R hooks. Which *would* have been totally fine," he said, "but you didn't have the necessary packages installed to make it work."

"There you go. Easy fix." Imani pushed away from the table and stood up, palms braced on the slightly sticky veneer surface. "Look, I have to go. I've been out all morning, and my cat is going to be pissed. Are you going to be okay?"

I managed a nod. Imani grabbed her bags and coat and left.

"Need a ride home?" James asked in the ensuing silence. "My car's out front."

"My bike—"

"I have a bike rack. It's no trouble. I remember how exhausting the term leading up to exams is, and I can't imagine . . ."

He caught himself before bringing up my failed first attempt. I had no illusions that it wasn't common knowledge—Magic was a big program, but not that big—still, I wanted to squirm just thinking about the way people must be talking.

"It's no trouble," he repeated, instead.

I was out of excuses and too tired to worry very much about inconveniencing him.

"Okay."

James stood, pulled my coat from the back of my chair, and held it open like some sort of disheveled butler. It was kind of cute. I mustered a smile and stood, letting him help me into my coat and hand me my bag.

"You're being awfully nice for someone I smoked out of the woodwork and basically blackmailed for snacks."

James shrugged. "Yeah, well, it's not every day that a cute disaster blackmails me."

I froze. "*Disaster?*" Was my code way worse than they'd let on? Was I about to fail harder than I'd ever failed in my entire life? Or was he going to bring up my exam, after all?

"Oh, crap. I meant . . ." James took a deep breath. "Your last foray into digimancy is *legend* around here."

I groaned.

"And I was in the room when it happened?" He said it almost apologetically.

My eyes doubled in size.

"I didn't . . . destroy anything of yours, did I?" I'd hoped, since nobody had demanded I buy them a new laptop, that my epic digimancy fail hadn't fried any *personal* computers.

James nodded, expression caught somewhere between glee and reluctance.

"And you bought me coffee, anyway." I huffed, already mentally calculating how much I could carve out of my meager monthly stipend to slowly pay him back.

"If you knew how much social currency that's given me, you wouldn't look so guilty right now."

"Wait, you've been talking about it? Like at parties? Am I some sort of joke?"

He was right. Suddenly, I wasn't feeling guilty at all. Outraged, sure. Furious. Embarrassed. Torn between throwing punches and hiding under a blanket for the rest of forever.

I swiveled on my heel and stomped out of the room, down the stairs, and out onto the sidewalk.

James hurried after me.

"Wait! It's not like that! Everybody thinks you did it on purpose. That you're some sort of hero. Because they had to update all of the computers and the printer and they all work so much better now. I was the only one in the room—"

"So you know that's not true."

"And when I tell the story I don't include your panicked swearing. You taught me a few terms that day, actually. I was impressed."

My response to the last part was automatic.

"I learned them from my officemate." The rest of his words sank in. "So . . . wait." I stumbled to a stop, a few steps away from my bike. "You've been, what? Making me out to be some sort of Luddite? Smashing tech for the social good?"

"Sort of?"

My eyes were stinging, and I squinted into the misting rain, determined not to cry. It was the exhaustion or the worry or the lingering effects of the panic attack. Definitely not this misguided kindness.

I sniffled and hated myself for it.

"How am I supposed to live up to that?" I spun to face him, crowding his space. "I'm not even supposed to be here. My parents aren't mages, or even practitioners. They did everything they could to keep me *out* of this world. I didn't go to magic camps in grade school, or intern with any of the major covens. I didn't study ancient witchcraft in Europe for a semester. I didn't even take the right secondary arcane languages."

I dragged in a long, ragged breath, squinting up into James's carefully neutral face.

"I went with *Latin*, James. Not Phoenician, or cuneiform or Sanskrit or Linear A. *Latin.* I don't know what the fuck I'm doing. I've already *failed* my exam once. I am faking my way through this degree, and any day now my advisor is going to realize that. Or my committee will. Or the admin will discover some error and rescind my admission."

I kept shouting. People hurried past us, giving me serious side eye. But I'd snapped. I'd reached the end of my limited supply of calmness and perseverance. I was taking it out on James, who absolutely did not deserve it, but it was out of my control. I was a runaway train of imposter syndrome and exhaustion.

James just took it, stoic and patient, until I ran out of steam.

"Feel better?" he asked.

I shook my head. "Now you're going to have a different story to tell about me at parties." A sob distorted the end of my sentence. I looked at my feet.

James shepherded me to his car, an aging, forest green Subaru with cracked vinyl seats and a pine tree air freshener hanging from the rearview. He pried my bike key out of my hands, loaded up my bike, and drove me home.

Later, when I was curled up in bed with a giant mug of tea and a whole lot of self-pity, Anne reminded me of its existence and triggered another, different, type of panic.

"Bartleby realized that James hadn't just called her a *disaster*. He'd also called her *cute*."

CHAPTER FIFTEEN

When asked for a statement regarding the five Magic students who have been reported missing, the Office of Public Safety declined comment, except to say that they have several promising leads and they're working closely with local police. While there's been much speculation, including by members of this newspaper's staff, it's currently unclear whether the disappearances have any connection to the "magic flu" that hit campus earlier this term.

—ARTICLE IN *THE PLATYPUS PRATTLER*, 14 JANUARY

IT WAS MONDAY OF WEEK THREE. MY MATERIALS WERE DUE IN TEN days, and I was doing my best not to think about anything except for that. Not James calling me cute, or the vague warning Lora had passed on from the ñatitas, or the fact that Alse's backpack was *still* sitting in my office.

There'd been no response from the Dean of Students's office about the concerns I'd shared on the early-warning system. I told myself that they might not respond at all. That it didn't mean they hadn't looked into things. That Mags was right: Alse and Pam had probably just withdrawn from the university. But the *Platypus Prattler's* coverage of the flu outbreak and the missing students had me second-guessing.

What if they hadn't withdrawn?

It seemed like conspiracy thinking, even to my anxiety-primed, catastrophizing mind. I shied away from the awful possibilities that thought left unspoken. My exam stress was starting to seep into everything else. That was all.

"Bartleby well knew the maxim that 'it is a capital mistake to theorize before one has data,'" Anne droned, quoting Sherlock Holmes. *A Scandal in Bohemia*, I thought. "'Insensibly one begins to twist facts to suit theories, instead of theories to suit facts.'"

"Yes, thank you, Anne." I sighed and reached for my tea, a calming lavender blend of Cy's. Taking a scalding swig, I stood and headed into the hall. "I'll be back soon, okay?"

I needed to be calm for my meeting with Professor Leighton. It would be the first time I'd seen her since my failed exam attempt, and I wasn't sure I was ready. I *knew* I wasn't ready to face her critique of Anne.

I'd updated Anne's code over the weekend, using Imani's and James's feedback to close the open queries and make sure the correct packages were in place and functional. And it'd worked— partially. Now, if I said *once upon a time*, Anne would produce remixed quotes from my corpus until I said *the end*. There'd been no change to the Christmas village, so far. But I felt cautiously optimistic that there might be.

My major concern was that Anne was still narrating me, as frequently and vociferously as it deemed necessary. My stop command worked less consistently on those narrations. I often had to enunciate the words multiple times before it took effect.

Which was why I wouldn't be showing Anne to any of my committee members until I absolutely had to.

I tromped up one flight of steps, past the Thaumaturgy offices, and down the hall. Professor Leighton's door was cracked. Taking another sip of tea, I willed it to work magic it wasn't made for and knocked on the door frame.

The screech of plastic wheels on vinyl heralded Professor Leighton's plummy, "Dorothe? Is that you? Come in, dear."

Pushing the door open, I peeked into the room.

"Hi, Professor."

Professor Leighton leaned back in her desk chair, head craned to see me. Her pixie-length gray hair was circled with a delicate band of golden vines and flowers that made her appear an elderly faerie rather than the expat hippie she really was. She smiled and sat forward so she could wheel the chair around to face me.

"Dorothe. It's good to see you."

I smiled. Despite everything, it was good to see her, too.

Ursula Leighton had been the first person I'd spoken to in the program. The first faculty member I'd taken a class with. She'd been my first advisor, too—a role she held for all first-years. After Intro to Graduate Studies in Magic, I hadn't had many opportunities to work with her. Until now.

My smile faltered. I couldn't help but feel like I'd disappointed her.

She didn't seem to notice my shifting mood, gesturing me to the antique velvet settee that stood, sun dappled, beneath her office's double windows.

"I hope you've been taking care of yourself. I hear the flu is particularly brutal this season."

"I got my shot before the term started."

She nodded. "Good girl."

Anne's Sherlock quote fresh in my mind, I took a breath. "But . . . about the flu. I have a question." Professor Leighton tended to be in the loop about things. If anyone could set my mind at ease about Alse and Pam, give me data so I could bend theories to facts, it would be her.

Professor Leighton tipped her head. "Oh?"

"I have a couple of students who stopped attending with no explanation. One of them was meeting with me in my office and got sick and ran out. They left their backpack behind. And . . . Anyway, I thought it was probably the flu. But I've tried to reach out to them, both of them, and their emails keep bouncing back. The error message says their accounts don't exist?"

Professor Leighton's head was still tipped, and her lips were pursed so tight, they'd gone pale around the edges.

"How troubling, dear."

"Do you know what might be causing it? My officemate thinks they withdrew from the university, but wouldn't they get to keep access to their email, for a little while at least?"

"I doubt it's anything so dramatic as withdrawals. I'm told there's been some sort of technical problem with the latest update of Penant. We lost some student records, and we're in the process of restoring them." She waved a blue-veined hand, dismissive. "Their emails will be functional again soon enough. And as for attendance, the Add/Drop period did just end on Friday. Are you certain your students haven't simply switched sections, or opted to take different courses?"

I shook my head. I wasn't certain about anything, except for the fact that I had an abandoned backpack cluttering up my office.

"There you have it, then. Nothing to be worried about." Professor Leighton's posture shifted, chin lifting and shoulders straightening, as she turned her attention to business. "Now, shall we discuss your exam preparations?"

I nodded, and Professor Leighton smiled.

"Wonderful." She reached for a notebook, wet the point of a pencil with her tongue, and pressed it to the page. "Tell me about the scholarship your work is in conversation with."

It was a basic question, allowing me the opportunity to ease in. I took a steadying breath, willed myself to focus.

"My work is in conversation with research conducted by Thaumaturgists including Ewan Volt and Nonni Strong, as well as a number of literature scholars who've traced the rise of the novel in Western literature . . ." I managed the words without hyperventilating, clutching my tea mug like a protective charm as I answered that question and the three that followed it. They were all easy. None of them touched on digimancy, but I knew it must be coming.

Eventually, Professor Leighton shifted forward, bones and chair creaking in chorus, and looked me in the eye.

"Are you ready, dear, for a more complex query?"

I wanted to shake my head, but I grit my teeth and forced myself to nod.

"Good." She sighed. "Good, good." She leaned back, considering me. "Tell me about your spellwork demonstration. We've recommended a new approach. I'd like to know what you plan to do, and how it will help you pinpoint this elusive narrative magic you're trying to find."

I swallowed, traitorous mouth already bone dry. "I'll try. I cast the working on Wednesday, and I . . ." My voice hitched and broke. I cleared my throat. "I'm, um . . . trying to make some adjustments. But once I've—"

Professor Leighton wagged a finger.

"Wait." Her expression went stern. "I'd like you to start over, with more confidence. None of this *trying to*. You're almost a mage, and you *will* do it, if you set your mind to it."

Her words should have been reassuring, but they rattled me. What if I *couldn't*? Would that mean I wasn't fit to be a mage? It would definitely mean I wasn't *going* to be a mage, either way. So maybe the distinction was moot.

"Go on," Professor Leighton urged.

"I used algorithm- and rune-enhanced Markov Chains to train a spellwork construct to identify common patterns in early novels and grimoires from the same period. Once it's fixed, it should . . ." I caught myself, tried again. "It *will* generate new narrations using those patterns and, hopefully . . . um . . . definitely?"

I cleared my throat, wishing I could shed another layer. The office felt at least ten degrees hotter than it had been when I'd walked in.

"If it works . . ." I caught myself again, ears going red. "*Hecate's dogs.*"

"I know, it's difficult," Professor Leighton said. The wheels of her chair screeched and scraped across the floor, and she squeezed my shoulder. "That's why practice is so important."

At her coaxing, I took a breath and tried again. This time, I managed to explain my working as if it was already a success, detailing the pieces I'd put in place to measure the effects—and ideal outcomes—of the working.

"The construct generates automatic logs that document each of its narrations, and I can compare those against daily photographs and observational surveys of my microcosm."

"See, there?" Professor Leighton leaned back in her chair. "You're already sounding more confident. Let's plan on another session two weeks from today. I'll send an invitation, but in the meantime I'd like you to do some practicing on your own. Answer questions aloud, just as if I'd asked them. And be confident in your answers."

I wrung my hands in my lap, meeting her eyes. "What if I still mess up, even with practice?"

"It's a question many a great mage has faced." Her smile was wry. "We academics aren't exactly known to be outgoing. But we find our ways. Communicating our research is an important skill. If we have to push ourselves further outside of our comfort zones than we'd like, drive ourselves beyond what we believe to be our breaking points, that is the burden we bear for the great privilege of a life spent in communion with higher magic."

I nodded, misery spilling onto my face despite my best efforts to keep it in. That might be easier if exam prep was *all* I had to worry about. But I had Digimancy, my own class to teach, the weirdness with Alse and Pam—

"And I know," Professor Leighton added, as if she'd seen right to the heart of my worry, "that you're concerned about your students. But I'm certain they're just fine. This whole mess with Penant will be sorted soon enough. And it is perfectly acceptable—advisable, even—to leave university problems to university personnel. If you intend to remain in this program, Dorothe, you *must* prioritize your own work."

CHAPTER SIXTEEN

Bartleby had taken up a wrong idea . . . Sometimes one
conjectures right, and sometimes one conjectures wrong.
She was quite concerned and ashamed, and resolved to do
such things no more.

—NARRATORIAL COMMENTARY ADAPTED
FROM JANE AUSTEN'S *EMMA* BY ANNE

MOTIVATED BY PROFESSOR LEIGHTON'S ADVICE, I SPENT THE
first twenty minutes of Digimancy class surreptitiously
reviewing Anne's logs. I'd glanced at them a time or two
since my working just to confirm they were being generated, but I'd been so focused on tracking down the source of
Anne's glitchiness that I hadn't really taken time to analyze the
results yet.

While Professor Delight lectured about *Selfie Spellwork*, a digimancy project launched five years ago that was meant to track
what the professor called "the condensation and caricaturization
of personal realities via the medium of the selfie," I put pen to paper, categorizing the types of narration I was seeing.

There were the direct quotes, usually context appropriate but
not remixed in any way. The adaptations of passages that ranged
from obvious references to iconic literary lines to mix-and-match
arrangements with turns of phrase or uses of punctuation that
seemed vaguely familiar. The original narrations of me with no

clear reference texts. And, finally, the glitches: nonsense clusters of words that often had negative prefixes. Hopefully, Imani was right and those were a sign Anne was generating workings, even if they were workings the university's dead felt duty-bound to stop.

But if the glitches were a symptom of magic, that meant they most likely weren't the *source* of the workings. So which of the other types of narration were?

"But, Professor," Nathaniel's loud interjection cut through my focus, "hasn't the internet expanded the concept of the self? Our individual realities aren't fully contained in the corporeal anymore. Our virtual selves are just as real, sometimes more real, than our physical ones."

"Yeah, if you delete my socials, do I really exist?" Hadrian laughed.

I glanced up just in time to catch James looking at me. He smiled, and my pen hand jerked, leaving a long mark on the page.

Starsdammit.

He wasn't even flirting, just smiling in a friendly way, with that scruffy hint of a beard and that blond tousled hair that was obviously just *like that* and not styled to look like that, and—Rasputin's balls, I was *not supposed to be thinking about him.*

I bit my lip and forced my eyes back to my screen. Narration. I needed to focus on narration.

I almost scrolled by another glitch, but Alse's name caught my eye. It was just an entry about me nudging their backpack with my shoe. I'd wanted to see if there was anything important inside. Because if there wasn't, then I could have stopped worrying about the fact that they'd abandoned it. But my cautious investigation had revealed a tablet with one of those keyboard folio cases. And a set of keys on a stretchy spiral chain. Most students—even more privileged ones—would want something like that back.

I took a breath, shoving the thoughts aside as I continued skimming through a series of narrations about my office phone. Anne's fixation on the blinking light was baffling—at least, until I got to the final narration in the series.

```
Thursday, January 14, 11:09 a.m., Bartleby
neglected to check the voicemail before leaving
her office. Had she listened, she would have
realized that the call was from Alse's distraught
father.
```

I stared at the screen, a high-pitched buzz building up inside my head. Parents didn't call college instructors. Or, they did, very rarely, but legally we couldn't talk to them unless we had prior written permission from the student in question.

Still.

If Alse's father had called me, that meant something.

My mouth went dry as I tried to shuffle frantic thoughts into some semblance of order.

It meant . . . what? That Alse hadn't just stopped responding to me. That they were out of contact with their father, as well. And if that was true, it meant that Professor Leighton's theory was likely wrong, and they hadn't simply switched sections or dropped Spell Composition I to take some other class. Did that mean the technical problems with Penant she'd mentioned *weren't* just system update bugginess?

The class was still discussing social media, selfies, the records of life online. Hadrian's joke echoed in my mind, mixing into a storm of anxious thoughts.

Do I really exist?

Tech errors. Email bounce backs. Missing students. Could it all be connected?

If the Penant problem wasn't just some run-of-the-mill bug, if it was connected to the missing students somehow, that meant the disappearances weren't random. Someone was *making* students vanish. And if that was the case, I had a feeling it wouldn't just be our central records system that was affected. Whoever was behind this—*if* someone was behind this—might be trying to make students disappear online, too.

I needed to check records outside of the Penant system. And I'd

heard Thaumaturgy's educational technologist gripe about the dis-
connect between Penant and Jute, the platform we used for course
websites, often enough by now to know that it was a separate digital
ecosystem. Hands trembling, I pulled up my course website.

If Penant was just being buggy, data on Jute should still be
intact. But if my theory was right—Hecate's dogs, I hoped my
theory wasn't right—my Jute records would be affected, too.

I clicked into my course roster first, skimming through twice
without finding Alse or Pam. The photo roster was similarly al-
tered.

I needed to listen to that voicemail.

I stood up, desk screeching against the waxed vinyl floor. Professor Delight's lecture ground to a halt.

"Is there a problem, Ms. Bartleby?"

I tried to shake my head, but the buzz of panic made me dizzy,
and I braced myself on my desk. "I don't feel well. I need to . . . I
have to . . . go."

"I see." The professor's tone made it very clear he *didn't* see.
"You're excused."

Shaking, I gathered my things and headed for the door. Whispers trailed me through the classroom. I heard the word *flu* a few
times. If only it *were* something that simple. Dazed and on the
verge of a panic attack, I made my way to my office. I jammed the
keys into the lock and wrenched the door open, shaking.

"Bartleby was—Bartleby—Bart—Bart—Bart—" From my
desk, the whir and click of Anne's glitch amplified in volume
with every hiccupping syllable. I kept moving across the room
to the phone. "Disoriented. Foggy and frustrated. Fracturing—
Fracturing—Fra–a–a–a–a–a—" That whirring click again, and
Anne shut down abruptly.

"Fuck."

I had no starsdamned idea *how* to listen to the voicemail.

"Bartleby?" James stuck his head into the room, breathing
hard. "Is everything okay?" He braced himself on the doorjamb,
concern sharpening the angles of his face.

"I . . ." I glanced at the blinking light on the phone, then back to him. "You followed me?"

"You really hauled out of there." He straightened up and crossed his arms. "I was worried. What's wrong?"

"I need to check my voicemail, but I don't know the password, or who to contact for the password, or—"

"There's a workaround for that." James stepped into the room, joining me beside the phone. "Can I have your key?"

I handed him my office key. "You aren't going to ask why?"

"I'm assuming, if it's important enough for you to rush out midway through class, it's kind of urgent." James shrugged, attention focused on the key in his hands. He rubbed it between his palms, as if to warm it. Then he pressed it to the phone's keypad, jamming it into the buttons with his palm and holding it there until a jaunty series of notes chimed.

"Speaker mode activated," a robotic voice announced. "You have *one* new message." A beep sounded, then the static of a faraway room tone.

"Hello, uh, Ms. Bartleby. My kid, Alse Hathorne, is in your class. And I know you're not supposed to talk to me, but I haven't heard from Alse for twelve days, and they normally call a couple times a week. I need to know they're okay. Please, if you've seen them, can you let me know that they're okay?" His voice warbled into a sob, and he cleared his throat. "Uh, you can reach me at either of these numbers . . ."

James found my gaze while the man on the phone rattled off digits. "What was that about?"

I opened my mouth, then closed it. Where would I even start? Anne seemed to know. It began narrating as I sank into my office chair.

"Bartleby had just stumbled upon a mystery," Anne announced. James startled, gaze jerky as he searched for—and found—Anne. "Her students were not, as she'd been led to believe, out with the flu or taking different classes. They had not dropped out from the university. They were missing."

James turned to me. "I'm going to need you to explain." The corners of his gray eyes were creased, anxiety echoing my own.

I fiddled with my rings, words coming slow as I explained about my meeting with Alse, the way they'd faded and flashed back, their flight down the hall, the aftermath in the restroom, and the email bounce backs later that week.

I shoved my laptop into his hands, telltale roster still on screen.

"You think they're being affected by some kind of working?" he asked.

I shrugged. "I know it's hard to believe. But if it was just the flu, their records wouldn't be *gone*. And if they'd just dropped—"

"—you'd see *that* on your roster." James leaned forward, staring at my computer screen. There were no *W*s there, indicating withdrawal. There were no listings for my missing students at all.

"Exactly. I think they're being . . ." Erased from this reality, physically and virtually. I couldn't bring myself to say it.

James was still squinting at my laptop. "There'd have to be a digimancer involved. Someone skilled enough to hack into Pennant and Jute."

"Or someone who doesn't need to hack, because they already have administrative access." I paused. "You believe me?"

James winced, cupping the back of his neck with the palm of his hand. "I go into trances sometimes," he said, "and get these visions. I had one at the start of term. There was a disembodied voice saying cryptic things. And Imani was in the vision, too, but then she faded and vanished. I kept trying to find her, but she wasn't anywhere to be found." He let his hand drop. "She wasn't in class today. And she didn't text to demand that I take 'proper notes' like she usually does when she's out sick. I haven't heard from her since our study session last week."

"That's . . . weird?" My words slipped sideways as I processed James's revelation. He was closer with Imani than I'd realized, if he was searching for her in trances. I shoved that aside, grabbing on to the most relevant piece. "Wait, you think Imani is missing, too?"

James nodded. "Imani's taking this class for credit so she's more competitive for positions requiring digimancy experience. And she'd *never* miss a day willingly."

"We can check right now. I'll send Imani an email."

James handed my laptop back, rattling off Imani's email address as I typed. Just in case we were wrong, I added a quick message.

Hey Imani, James and I are testing something. Will explain later.

I hit **send**, staring at my inbox with breath held until the chime of a new message broke the silence.

Mail undeliverable

Account imani.joshi@sublimity.edu does not exist.

James swore. "I knew it. Starsdamnit, I *knew* something was wrong."

"We should go to Public Safety."

James ran a hand through his hair. "We should, but I don't think we have enough proof."

"I don't know about you, but I'm way out of my depth." I leaned back in my desk chair rather than meet his eyes, tracing the stains in the drop tiles of the ceiling, "It's one thing for this to be affecting brand-new undergrads. They don't know how to fight back against workings. If this is affecting mage candidates . . ." It was worse than I'd imagined. What kind of spellwork could snare someone with as much training as Imani had?

"You're right. We're out of our depth. Because if this *is* a working, and it's affecting Penant," James's tone was grim, "it's not just erasing emails, it'll be erasing student IDs, too."

I could *feel* the blood rushing from my face. "They're cut off from higher magic."

"Probably." The muscle in his jaw ticked. "But right now the only proof we have can be explained away as software bugs. We need more, or they won't take us seriously."

My stomach ached. I was just a graduate student. I couldn't even pass my exam on the first try; how was I supposed to prove any of this? Investigating was probably a bad idea. I didn't know where my students lived, and—wait.

The keys in Alse's backpack. We could use them to find their dorm. Check in.

I scrambled up, shooed James out of his chair so I could see behind it. But the backpack was gone. In its place, tacked to the wall, a note from Mags:

I took the backpack to Thaumaturgy's lost and found so you'd stop obsessing over it. You're welcome. Don't forget about the FGTFD potluck tonight; we're voting for next year's Federation officers.—xx Mags

What the Hec, Mags?

Hopelessness hit again, even harder this time. I sagged back into my chair and dropped my head into my hands.

"Bartleby was at a complete loss," Anne announced, "thoughts a scandalous riot of confusion." I glowered at it, half-irritated and half-impressed by its adaptation of a line from *Northanger Abbey*. "Until she realized at least one of the people in her office probably knew where a missing student lived."

Its words struck with enough force that I huffed, setting my bangs afloat. I turned to James. "Anne's right, isn't it? You know where Imani lives."

James's smile was grim. "Yes. Yes, I do."

CHAPTER SEVENTEEN

To borrow a phrase from one of your founding fathers,
nothing is certain but Death and the Moon.
—PROFESSOR YÉSICA VASCONCELLOS, HISTORIES OF MAGIC

IMANI LIVED IN AN EDGY NEIGHBORHOOD BY THE RIVER. MURALS AND
sculptures brightened the otherwise dilapidated state of the architecture. Sagging brick, crumbling sidewalks, weather-faded
siding, and toppled fences all seemed whimsical when strung
with twinkle lights and hand-knit textiles in a rainbow of colors.

I shifted in my seat, sneaking a look at James.

He and Imani were probably a thing. Or would be a thing. Or
should be a thing.

I turned back toward the window, throat tight with something
that wasn't jealousy. Swallowing, I tried to focus on a two-story
mural of a top-hat-wearing bee on a unicycle. Maybe it was a
little bit jealousy, but I'd get over it. It wasn't like I'd spent hours
obsessing over the fact that James had called me cute or anything.
He had to have meant it in an *oh, you naive little third-year, trying so
hard* way. Even on a good day, I didn't hold a candle to someone as
accomplished and sophisticated as Imani.

"Touch piece for your thoughts?" James asked.

I twitched. Even a proverbial lucky coin was not enough payment to reveal *these* particular thoughts. As he slowed, I contemplated jumping out of the car to avoid the question.

Say something. My silence was getting more awkward by the second. But the time pressure just made it worse. Every thought I'd ever had about *anything* else scoured itself from my mind.

It shouldn't have surprised me when Anne, muffled but still perfectly audible from its place in my bag on the backseat, began to speak. "Bartleby wondered if James and Imani—"

"The end. The *end* Anne, or I swear to Hecate . . ." Adrenaline buzzed through me even after Anne cut off, setting my hands trembling. I shoved them under my thighs.

James blinked and laughed. "Care to explain?"

"Narration!" It was more blurt than response, and I immediately wanted to unsay it. What kind of person kept thinking about their exam when students were *missing*? "I was reviewing Anne's logs in class, before I realized . . . well, you know. Anyway, the changes you and Imani suggested got it to start narrating on command, as intended. But it's still narrating me at random. And glitching." I cleared my throat. "I'm assuming the glitches mean workings are happening and the university ghosts are intervening, but I don't know which type of narrations are causing them."

James parked and killed the engine.

"And I know I'm a terrible person for even thinking about this when Imani and my students are missing—"

"Not terrible," James interrupted. "Just a person, with a lot to juggle. A good person who is generously making the time to help with something that's way above her pay grade," he added.

I wanted to melt into the seat and disappear. "I wouldn't put it like that."

James grinned. "I would. Just did, even."

I had no idea how to respond to that, so I scrambled out of the car and into an artistically overgrown yard instead. Anne could wait in the backseat.

The shabby, three-story Victorian ahead of me towered over its disproportionately small lawn. I started down a flagstone walkway that I could barely see through some sort of flat, creeping juniper and wet mounds of dead leaves. James jogged to catch up, slipping on one of those piles and nearly sprawling into a pyramid of cheerleading gnomes before catching himself. The look of horror on his face as he contemplated the obstacle stopped me in my tracks. I laughed so hard I almost fell into the flock of striped flamingos in Santa hats that seemed to be guarding a birdbath from the wraparound porch.

James cleared his throat, stepped gingerly around gnomes and flamingos, and climbed the porch steps. I composed myself and followed, joining James on the porch as he knocked.

"Yo! Don't stand on ceremony!" someone yelled from inside the house.

We hesitated, eyeing each other. The place could be warded. But the shouted invitation seemed odd in that case.

"Yo! Dudes! Are you coming or going? And do you have any chips?"

James threw me a *here goes nothing* look and turned the doorknob. Nothing terrible happened as he pushed the door open with one finger and stepped carefully inside. I followed.

Across the room, a white dude with matted hair that was probably meant to be locs waved to us from the couch. "Duuuuuuudes," he said. "Welcome to my humble abode. What can I do you for, amigos?"

James crouched on a love seat that managed to look simultaneously damp and crunchy. I chose to remain standing.

"I'm a friend of Imani's. She home?" he asked.

"Nah, bro. Haven't seen her since . . . Friday night maybe?"

I snuck a look at James, who raised his eyebrows. The last time either of us had interacted with Imani was Friday, and she'd been heading home to feed her cat.

"You're sure about that?" James asked.

"What is time, am I right?" Couch guy laughed for a while and coughed for a while and then puffed on his joint. Breath held, he attempted to pass it to us. I grimaced. James shook his head.

Dude was *baked*.

"She probably left because—" couch guy looked around before whispering, theatrically, "—this place is *haunted*."

I arched an eyebrow. He couldn't have lived with Imani for long, if he didn't know the deal about residence ghosts. Imani would have been more likely to leave because the place *wasn't* haunted.

"Huh." James sat back, wincing as something crinkled behind him.

"Yeah, man. Started this weekend," couch guy explained without prompting. "Things moving around all by themselves. Food floating through the air. Lights flickering. Words written in shower steam."

"Words?"

That kind of haunting was unusual for a residence ghost. So either couch dude was just *that* insufferable as a roommate, or the "ghost" wasn't a ghost at all.

"Yeah. Get this." Couch guy took another hit and talked around a held breath. "The spirit *turned on the shower,* then when I came in to turn the faucet off, it tore down the shower curtains, wrapped them around itself and wrote 'get out' on the mirror. Like, you might be dead, dude, but we still have to conserve water."

That sounded way more like a pissed off woman than a ghost to me. James, apparently coming to the same conclusion, slapped his palms on his thighs.

"Well, I have some stuff she asked me to bring by. Guess I'll leave it in her room." He stood. "That cool?"

Couch guy nodded, but he seemed more interested in his joint than James. "It's upstairs, man, second door on the right."

"Thanks, man." James led the way to the door. "We'll be right back."

"Hey! You her boyfriend or something?" We both paused, and James turned while I did my best not to show any interest in his response.

"Just a friend, dude."

Couch guy pouted. "Thought maybe that's why she won't go out with me. Ah, well."

On that weird note, we headed back to James's car.

"I don't really have anything to drop off," James said. "I just thought it would seem less suspicious if we had a reason to go upstairs." He hauled open the back door and reached inside, slinging his backpack over one shoulder. Before he could close the door, Anne piped up.

"The division of the party was completed by Bartleby and James resolving to look into the residence's new haunting, and Anne remained alone."

"What?" James turned to me.

"It's quoting *Mansfield Park*." I sighed. "It feels left out."

He took the news in stride, shrugging. "Bring it with us. Maybe it can help."

I doubted that, but I grabbed my bag anyway and followed him back inside.

Imani's room was decorated in deep jewel tones. A handful of Turkish lamps gleaming like stained glass in the window set colorful shadows twisting through the space. Beside the window, several white particleboard bookcases sagged under the weight of their load. In addition to books, they held a collection of glass and ceramic elephants and a few frilly air plants. On the opposite wall, Imani had hung six framed vintage posters of pop stars from the '80s. I recognized Kate Bush, mostly because her use of Thaumaturgy in performances had been a case study in one of my classes.

James paced around the room, pawing through the shelves and rummaging through drawers, muttering.

"What are you looking for?"

"Ouija board." He didn't stop searching. "She'll have one for discussions with the residence ghost. Since she didn't scream at that guy for barging in on her in the shower, I'm assuming we can't just *talk*, but if she can write in steam, she can use a planchette."

"Got it."

I dropped to my knees and peeked under the bed, but the only thing there was a lanky black cat with a small tuft of white fur on her chest. Her eyes went huge and she hissed, scuttling away and out into the open on the other side of the room.

"Corelli." Something in James's expression shifted when he saw her, mild irritation transforming into a darker emotion. Fear, maybe. He bent to stroke her, and she flicked her tail against his ankles, yowling. "How are you doing, girl?" he cooed. "You're as upset as I am, aren't you, friend?" The cat kept yowling, twining back and forth. James glanced over at me. "She only acts like this when Imani's not around."

"Oh." Corelli slunk back under the bed as I approached. "Does that mean Imani's not here, or that whatever's affecting her is making her imperceptible to the cat?" Neither option seemed like a positive sign. If Imani wasn't home, she could be anywhere. Finding her might be difficult. But if she was here and her cat couldn't sense her . . . the working was terrifyingly thorough. Cats had an uncanny way of seeing through realities, finding what they wanted to find.

"I don't know," James said.

My stomach dropped out from under me, but I ignored my own worry and put a tentative hand on James's shoulder. Imani wasn't just his classmate—she was his close friend. This had to be terrifying.

"We're going to figure this out."

He sighed, running a hand through his hair. "I know."

"Isn't there some other way we can contact Imani?" I'd promised not to bring up the fact that he was part of one of the most important necromancer lineages on this side of the country, but I couldn't exactly *forget*. Surely someone with that sort of family history didn't need to rely on a Ouija board.

From his expression, James *did* have a way to contact her—one he didn't like very much.

Anne, who I'd honestly all but forgotten about, spoke for him. "Plan B would be extremely embarrassing, for all involved."

"What is Plan B?"

James wouldn't meet my eyes, but the pink of his cheeks verified the accuracy of Anne's pronouncement.

"James?" I crossed my arms. "Are you seriously going to let Imani stay missing because you're embarrassed?"

He sighed, shoulders going slack in defeat. "No. Of course not."

"Good. I promise not to secretly record you doing this embarrassing thing—whatever it is—and blackmail you with it later."

That got me a tiny huff of a laugh and a smile, which was immediately replaced by a grimace.

"This is going to seem weird." He kicked off his shoes as he spoke, balancing one-legged as he removed his socks. "But . . . you've heard about the way the Fox sisters communicated with the dead, back in the 1800s?"

"The knocking and rapping stuff, sure. They asked yes or no questions and the ghosts used ghost Morse code to talk to them."

James shook his head. "That was PR spin."

My eyes went wide, and I couldn't help sneaking a look at James's bare feet. "I always thought it was the ghosts making the noise."

"No, the Fox sisters cracked their toes to grab hold of reality and shift it so that voiceless spirits could speak. It was their personal ritual. Some necromancers argue it was also nonverbal incantation, but that's not widely accepted."

"Oh." I swallowed a nervous laugh. "Interesting."

"I'm not sure it will cut through whatever working's affecting Imani, but even if it doesn't it should let me talk to the residence ghosts."

He sat on the edge of the bed—facing away from me, I couldn't help but notice—and propped one foot up on his knee. He took a deep breath, slid a thumb across the rings on his right hand. Reached out to bend and crack each individual toe. Still holding his breath, he repeated the process for the other foot.

Static electricity crackled through the room, frizzing my hair and prickling down my arms. James gasped a breath, voice a wheeze when he posed a question to the room.

"Imani, are you here?"

Seconds stretched into a solid minute, the quiet of the room a taut thing, ready to snap. Eventually, James sighed, admitting to himself that either Imani wasn't here or she couldn't answer. He adjusted his shoulders and lifted his chin.

"Residence ghosts, I request your attendance."

Static crackled through the room again, and my skin prickled with the sensation of something watching me, just outside of my field of vision.

"Please," James said when nothing else happened. "She's in your charge. You must know *something*."

The scrape of ceramic across fake wood snagged my attention. I jerked my gaze toward the shelves, expecting to see the cat acting out. But there was no sign of Corelli. Just a ceramic elephant teetering on the edge of a shelf.

It tumbled and fell with enough force that it shattered across the carpet.

James jumped, expression going grim as he took in the mess.

"The residence ghosts had declined James's request," Anne intoned. "At least, that is what Bartleby supposed. Imani would not destroy an item from her own collection, especially not in a way that endangered her cat."

"It's not wrong." James muttered.

We cleaned up the mess in silence, and before we left, James reached under the bed to scratch Corelli behind the ears.

"We'll find her and bring her back to you, friend," he whispered. "Don't you worry."

Back on the porch, James shoved his hands into his pockets, gaze falling to his shoes.

"What happened in there?"

"I don't know." James sighed. "I'm out of practice, but that should have worked. Unless my family . . ." He trailed off, and when Anne piped in to explain, I stopped it.

"The end, Anne."

"Thanks." James's smile was mostly wince.

"No worries. What do we do now?" A whine slipped out with my words. I felt all of five, frustrated and upset at our lack of progress. It'd probably been naive of me to hope coming here would solve things. That we'd find Imani and figure out what was going wrong and bring my students back, all in the space of one afternoon.

James turned a considering look my way, and chills raced up my spine. "I have an idea."

"What is it?"

His grin was sheepish. "That depends. Can you drive?"

"I mean, yeah. Why?"

"If I get this right, I'll be able to see every working that's been cast in this house for the past week." His tone went apologetic. "But it's going to hit me hard. Like an eye dilation at the ophthalmologist's, multiplied by a few levels of intensity."

"Go for it." We needed proof if we were going to convince Public Safety a malicious working had been cast on students. I'd drive to Texas—to my parents' house—and back if it would help.

After one last searching look, James fished his keys out of his pocket and tossed them to me, flashing a smile.

CHAPTER EIGHTEEN

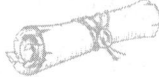

If we had a keen vision and feeling of all ordinary human life, it would be like hearing the grass grow and the squirrel's heart beat, and we should die of that roar which lies on the other side of silence.

—GEORGE ELIOT, *MIDDLEMARCH* (1871)

That is EXACTLY what divining feels like. Death and all.

—ANNOTATION IN THE MARGINS OF THE LIBRARY'S COPY OF *MIDDLEMARCH*

MY EARS POPPED AS JAMES CAUGHT HOLD OF REALITY. The disgusting birdbath water rippled in a tiny wave before going placid, and James lowered his face toward it, muttering words I couldn't quite hear. His expression went slack, eyes open and tracking so fast he might have been speed reading.

I couldn't see what he was seeing, but it was clear something was happening. Whatever it was, he'd be drawing on the university's holdings to convince reality that the past was something that *could* be seen, even by someone who hadn't been there when it happened.

I could almost read the thrum of possibility in the lines of his body, sharp and fluid at the same time. All he was doing was standing over a birdbath. It was a far cry from the joyful abandon I'd seen animate him outside of Bentham Cote, but an aura of beauty and power haloed him as he peered into the water. He could have been a mythical statue, coming to life among a flock of plastic flamingos.

I rubbed the shivers from my arms, watching him watch the water's occasional rills and swirls, and tried not to let myself think about the way he'd called me cute. The way he'd spun the story of my copy-room incident into something heroic. The casual, disinterested way he'd denied having a thing with Imani just now.

Was it possible that he was interested in *me*?

I scuffed my shoes across the dirty flagstones as if the action could scrub the idea out of my head. It didn't make sense. He'd only ever seen me at my worst, first in the copy room and now with a malfunctioning exam working and a rapidly disintegrating career. The fact that he'd noticed me from time to time didn't mean anything *deeper*.

Still, if he'd been there all along, how had I ever *missed* him?

I'd been so tied up in my own knot of anxiety, so focused on staying under the radar so I could maybe make it through the program before they realized I didn't belong here, that I hadn't noticed much of anyone. But it seemed impossible to me, now, that I'd ever overlooked James.

"Bartleby allowed herself to dwell on this because it was better than thinking about *why* James had cast his working," Anne observed. "Students were missing, and without proof, she and James wouldn't be believed by the university's authorities."

Just like that, all thought of pleasant impossibilities was scoured away.

Thirty minutes went by, James's grip on the birdbath growing tighter and tighter. His knuckles turned entirely white and his arms trembled, so slightly I might have convinced myself it was the breeze if not for the sweat slowly darkening his shirt.

Another ten minutes passed. I distracted myself by walking to the car and back. Partway there on my second loop, I heard a long gasp and a heavy crack.

"Damn."

I sprinted toward James, who'd knocked the birdbath sideways when he released it. The bath part had broken from the stem, taking out a few flamingos in the process.

James was on his knees and still looking unsteady there. He put his hands to the ground, bracing himself.

"Hey." I knelt beside him. "You okay?"

He looked a little green this close. "Yeah."

"Are you ready to move?"

He shook his head, groaning like he might puke. I put my palm to his back before I could think better of it, drawing it in a large, hopefully soothing, circle. After a couple of minutes, he sat up. I pulled away.

"Better?"

"Better." He blinked at me and grimaced. "I still can't see straight, though."

"That's why you gave me the keys." I helped him to his feet and put my arm around his shoulder to guide him to the car. He smelled like soap, and trees opening up after a heavy rain, and if I didn't stop thinking about that I couldn't trust myself not to say or do something weird.

"Did your scrying work?"

"Mhmm," James moaned as he climbed into the passenger seat.

I jogged around to the driver's side and sat down, feeling around the bottom edge of the seat until I found the button to adjust the position.

"It doesn't make any sense. It's like she didn't understand what was happening."

I stopped trying to decide which key was the right one, turning to stare at James. "What do you mean?"

"On Friday afternoon, someone cast a cloaking. I couldn't see who—I got the sense it was done from a distance."

"Is that even possible?" Cloakings were usually cast by the person being cloaked. Which meant cloakings were cast *exactly* where they were meant to happen.

James shook his head, more out of dismay than in answer. "I've never heard of anything like it. But it happened, and Imani tried to throw up three different kinds of wards, then pulled them all down and tried to cast a Faraday containment." He squinted at me, face taut with worry. "It didn't take."

Faraday containments were like magic panic rooms, cast when workings had gone out of control and neither death nor the moon was pulling them back into order quickly enough. A last resort. My whole body tensed, thinking about what that meant.

Somehow, a cloaking had been enough to overwhelm all of Imani's defenses. It had to be part of a larger working. That, or whoever was behind it must be powerful, to work it at a distance. And to affect the university's records and course sites in the process.

"And then the magic just stopped," James finished. His voice wobbled, just a little. And I knew what he was thinking. I was thinking it, too.

"That doesn't mean she's been harmed," I said, keeping the direr part—*or killed*—to myself.

"I know." James let out a long breath, repeating the words as a whisper. "I know."

I peered over at the house as if I could see last Friday's workings going off like fireworks inside its walls. If our theory was correct—and it was looking more and more like it must be—when the cloaking took hold, erased her records and her ID, it would have cut Imani off from higher magic. That's all the magic stopping meant. That had to be all.

It was still too Heccing much.

I started the car. "We have to report this."

THE OFFICE OF PUBLIC SAFETY WAS OUR ADMINISTRATION'S COMPROmise with a student body who didn't want police on campus. It looked a lot like the campus police department it had been designed to replace, though. Its large reception desk, staffed by people in a mix of jeans and business casual, buzzed with activity. Keyboards clacked, phones rang. Somewhere, I could hear a coffeemaker percolating loudly. Around the room, a handful of students and older adults talked to people in name tags. Several were crying.

"Can I help you?" An older woman, with a grandma-pixie cut and a smoker's rasp that accentuated her New Englander accent, called us to the desk. She wore a flowery blouse and large, clip-on moonstone earrings. Her name tag read *Iris*.

"We're here to report some missing students."

"You and everyone else, hon." She gestured around the room. "I can't make sense of it." She was squinting at the computer in an intent way that made me wonder if she was talking about software before she continued. "They say it's this flu. Got some weird new kinda side effects. Me, I don't buy it. This campus used to be the safest place. Now we've got Magic students vanishing left and right. Parents camping in the lobby, demanding action. Faculty and students showing up at all hours making reports in person because the last Penant update broke the early-warning system."

I tensed. Beside me, James swore under his breath.

I'd convinced myself I was doing enough. That making reports on a faceless digital system fulfilled my responsibility as an instructor and member of the university community. That Mags and Professor Leighton were right, and nothing was *truly* wrong. It hadn't occurred to me, even today, that my reports on the early-warning system had never gone through. But it made a horrible kind of sense: if the system didn't think the students reported missing existed, of course those reports wouldn't go through.

I swallowed my emotions, collecting my thoughts. "About that . . . We think there's a working behind all of this, even the Penant glitches."

I walked her through the way Alse had flickered and vanished in the hall outside my office, the email bounce backs, our theory about Penant and Jute, the strange cloaking that'd overtaken

Imani. James chimed in at that point, describing everything he'd seen.

Of all the important details in our story, Iris latched on to the working. Her eyes narrowed. "You think a *cloaking* is causing all of this? I'm not a practitioner, hon, but aren't cloakings harmless little things?"

I couldn't blame her for her disbelief. I had trouble believing it myself, especially given the number of people in the lobby reporting their own missing students. Whatever was going on, the scope of it was bigger than I'd imagined.

"It wouldn't be an ordinary cloaking," James said. "It's been augmented. We suspect there's some digimancy involved."

His explanation didn't lessen the skepticism on Iris's face. She raised one drawn-on eyebrow, shook her head. Then she dragged her mouse on a peeling sunset mousepad and clicked a few times in rapid succession.

"All right, dears, I'll need some information from you."

Press-on nails clacking against her keyboard, Iris asked us for our names and contact information. The dates on which we'd last seen Imani, Alse, and Pam.

I felt my face get hot when I shared that Alse had gone missing, as far as I knew, on the second day of class.

"I thought it was just the flu," I explained. "And later I made reports on the early-warning system, but I guess they didn't go through. I didn't realize until today it was so serious."

Iris reached out and patted my hand, pity in her eyes. "It's gonna be okay, hon. Don't you worry. We'll look into this and pass your report along to the Dean of Students." Her smoky voice was bright, but there was a strain under it she couldn't hide.

"They're in over their heads," James said as we headed back to his car.

He was right. There would be some practitioners—a handful of adepts, a mage or two—on the staff. A couple of them might even know a little bit of digimancy: it was getting more popular, all the time. But their office was so bogged down by frantic reports, paperwork, and red tape that it would be a miracle if they gave every report equal consideration. And how seriously would they take ours, with our outlandish claim about a *cloaking*?

"You think they'll look into the digimancy angle, at least?"

James shrugged. "While you were talking to Iris, I heard a couple of Public Safety officers telling people it was the flu. Or Magic house hazing gone wrong."

"Those could just be the stories they're handing out, to keep people from panicking."

James shrugged. "Could be."

"We agree that it's definitely not the flu." I looked up at him. "Right?"

He shook his head, keeping his eyes on mine. "Right. And I don't think it's hazing, either. Not with a working that's lasted this long, and university records going haywire."

"We have to keep investigating." If I closed my eyes, I could almost hear Professor Leighton's gentle but implacable lecturing. *You must prioritize your work.* She'd be disappointed, if she could see me now.

"We do," James said. His tone was grim. "And I have another working we can try. But I need some time to recover . . ."

His words were an opening. The beginnings of a call and response urging me to say *that's okay; there's something I can try in the meantime.* He'd already done two workings, and I hadn't even come up with one. But the only spell I could think of was an old charm, written by Ariadne Frecke, for finding lost buttons. It wasn't any good; it required a matching button to call to the lost one. And, as far as I knew, none of the missing students had a twin conveniently waiting around to be of use.

I wrapped my arms around my waist, willing myself to think harder. To make a real contribution. As always, I came up short.

"Are you all right?" James still looked a little green, though his pupils had finally snapped back into shape. His eyes were narrowed on me, concern obvious. I swallowed a surge of shame and mustered a smile.

"I'm fine. It's *you* you should be worried about."

"I just need some carbs and a few hours of sleep. His hand snuck up to the back of his neck. "I should be good to go tomorrow."

"Okay." I chewed my lip. "I teach first thing, but I can cancel class."

"I was thinking more like eleven? If our missing students don't miraculously show up first."

CHAPTER NINETEEN

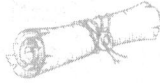

¾ c. all purpose flour *(milled with moon rock to neutralize)*
1 c. confectioner's sugar
dash salt
8 TBSP unsalted butter
4 egg whites *(double yolks are favorable omens,*
   but should be set aside for other workings)
1 tsp. vanilla extract *(real, unless you want a bad trip)*
dash cinnamon
   strips of paper relevant to subject of divination
   —JAMES'S TUILES RECIPE, PRINTED ON BATTER-
   STAINED PAPER AND ANNOTATED IN PEN

PULLING MY OFFICE DOOR FIRMLY SHUT, I MADE MY WAY TO THE front of the building to meet James.

Class had run smoothly for the first time all term. I'd been overprepared, for a change, because yesterday's search for Imani had left me with a nervous energy that rattled through me with teeth-clacking intensity until I poured it into my to-do list. I'd made notes for class, done a little grading, and even submitted my revised exam materials to Amelia.

Leaving Anne at home this morning had also helped—if only because it prevented a repeat of last Thursday, when Anne attempted to ease my students' worries about the flu with increasingly inexplicable platitudes. Sure, Alastair had demanded to see

Anne and tried to lead the class in a chant of *skull TA, skull TA, skull TA*—a choice that made me wonder if he was my mysterious class prankster—but it'd been easy enough to redirect.

I might have felt almost triumphant, if it hadn't been for the way my students kept sneaking looks at our classroom's empty desks, faces creasing with worry. How many of them would withdraw, or change majors, if we didn't figure this out soon?

I sagged onto a low brick wall, staring into the middle distance. I had a sinking feeling that the number would be far from zero. And nobody could blame them, if it was. Least of all, me. A degree that would pave the way to magic-adjacent careers reviewing others' spellwork, or teaching kindergartners the building blocks of magic, or a decade more schooling in pursuit of the slim chance of something more, wasn't offering much against the risk that they might disappear. But how many innovative practitioners would higher magic lose in the fallout? How many perspectives and experiences that could have shaped consensus reality into something better, and kinder, and richer would leave with them?

It couldn't come to that. I couldn't let it come to that.

Impatience turned my foot into a metronome. Crossing my arms, I scanned the area for any sign of James.

Movement caught my eye. Past the bus stop on the other side of the street, something was bobbing about seven feet off the ground. A series of somethings.

Lilies and lotuses floated around the brick-solid shape of Randolph House, an unnerving botanical orrery. What were the Magic houses up to, with their odd and ostentatious floral workings? I watched the unerring oblong orbits until James pulled into the spot right in front of me. He waved.

Anxiety—and something else, something appallingly like excitement—buzzed through me. I did my best to shake it off. What kind of person got *excited* about investigating something so dreadful? Or, rather, about the person they were investigating with?

I gathered my things and hauled open the passenger door, sliding onto the cracked vinyl seat.

"Hey."

"Hi." James smiled, dimple there and gone. Flustered, I re-arranged my bag at my feet. "So, where should we do this?" he asked.

"What exactly are we doing?"

James grinned. "I, uh, thought we'd bake some cookies."

Was he . . . messing with me? "Is that some kind of slang?"

His glance was incredulous. "Slang?"

"You know, for—" I made a series of gestures to mime death and dying "—necromancy?"

Since I'd known him, James had talked about having visions, done some weird necromancy, and scried in a birdbath. There was enough methodological overlap between Divination and Necromancy—both branches were all about manipulating real-ity to interact with the unknowable, whether that meant death or the past or future or all three—that the combination of workings wasn't unusual. But if James's great-great-aunt endowed Bentham Cote and his cousin lived there, odds were he was a necromancer, too. Families like his went *all* in.

Except, he wasn't responding.

I cleared my throat. "You *are* a necromancer, right?"

James's face turned three shades of pink. He cycled through a series of guttural sounds, and I wasn't sure if he was trying to sort out a response or was just disgruntled.

We sat there for what felt like five full minutes. The urge to apologize had me frantic, but I didn't know what to apologize *for.* I bit my lip and turned to face him.

"James?"

He took a breath. "Divination," he said. "My branch is Divi-nation."

That made a lot of sense. "Ah, sorry. I—"

"Made a logical assumption? No need to apologize for that."

Awkward silence tried to envelop us again. I took a breath, clasping my hands.

"So, baking cookies, huh?"

James nodded, not quite meeting my eyes.

"We could go to my place." I regretted it as soon as the words left my mouth. Why in Hecate's name was I inviting him over? What the fuck did I think this was, a date disguised as an investigation?

"Sure. Just tell me where to point the car."

I managed not to hyperventilate as I gave him the first few directions. "Hang a right, then another right at the second light." While he drove, I rummaged for my phone and sent Darya and Cy a warning text, as per house rules.

Bringing a classmate over to do a working.

Darya responded immediately.

Is he hot?

I grimaced at my phone.

It's not like that.

Cy sent a series of lewd emoji.

They'd both been out when I got home yesterday, and were still asleep when I left for campus. I hadn't been able to fill them in, and I couldn't do it over text. I turned my phone over and stared out at the road.

"Take another right up here."

James nodded. "Got it." He paused. "Warning the roommates?"

I sighed. "Yeah."

My phone pinged. I stuffed it into my bag without looking. Hands in my lap, I turned to James.

"What, um, drew you to Divination?"

It wasn't exactly the question I wanted to ask. I wanted to

know if his experience was anything like mine. If there was some parallel between his choice to study Divination and my choice to pursue magic, despite the differences between us.

His family tradition seemed a lot more . . . intentional than mine. A reputation built through generations. My family hadn't done anything intentionally. They'd just slowly calcified into place, each new generation living the same life as their parents and grandparents before them, only shittier as industries moved away from their area and the town slowly died around them. With both of my parents working multiple jobs just to make ends meet, there wasn't much room for anything else. No time, or resources, for dreaming of a different life. It'd been almost impossible to break out of that pattern.

I wondered if that was true for James, too. Had it been difficult, or had his parents smoothed the way? Had they given him room to dream and made those dreams possible?

"I'd rather not talk about it," James said. His hands were tight on the steering wheel.

The awkward silence won, after all. That was the extent of our conversation until James pulled up outside my apartment, killing the engine.

He unbuckled and levered his door open. "Should we get started?"

Another apology bubbled up in my throat. I swallowed the words and led the way inside.

"HOUSEMATES, MEET JAMES." I LOWERED MY EYEBROWS MEANINGFULLY at them—be nice—before turning to James. "James, this is Darya and Cy." I couldn't quite meet his eyes.

"Nice to meet you." Darya looked up from a pile of grading with a smile.

"Oh, we've met," Cy said at the same time. "Good to see you, man." I could see a dozen other responses sparking, mischievously, in his eyes, but he kept his mouth shut.

At least that much was going right, if my housemates weren't going to be embarrassing about the fact that I'd brought someone home. As I gestured James toward a chair, my phone buzzed.

Maybe I'd relaxed too soon.

I ignored the message, resisting the urge to squint suspiciously at Darya and Cy.

"Have a seat. We've got coffee, tea, and maybe some six-hour-energy rattling around in the fridge if you need it."

"Coffee would be great," James said with almost none of the warmth that usually mellowed his voice. He lowered himself into the chair I'd indicated and clasped his hands. "Nice place."

"We like it," Cy answered.

Throat tight, I went into the kitchen. We weren't here to socialize. We were here to find our missing students. I hastily scooped coffee into a filter and filled the coffeemaker with water, jamming my finger too hard against the button that set the pot brewing in my rush to get back to the living room.

"Have you lived here long?" James was asking.

I grabbed a chair next to him, sneaking a glance at his face. It didn't *look* like they'd said anything inappropriate in my absence.

"Bartleby and I have lived here since we started the program." Darya's smile was all nostalgia. "Cy moved in about a year after that."

"Bartleby thought herself a most fortunate creature," a muffled text-to-speech voice filtered down the hall from my room, "and surrounded with blessings in such excellent housemates."

"*Emma*," I sighed, before anyone could ask. "It's quoting Jane Austen. And it's right—insufferable as it will make these two." My laugh was too bright, obviously artificial. Darya noticed and raised an eyebrow. "Anyway," I cleared my throat, "I don't know how to say this, but—"

"You finally got some game?" Cy asked.

My cheeks and ears went incandescent. "No. Yes. I mean, I already had—" I took a deep breath, shifting so that I was only talking to Darya. *Fucking Cy.* "Alse and Pam aren't just absent. They're missing. And they aren't the only ones."

I didn't dare look at James as we filled them in on the details. But by the time we'd moved from the missing enrollment listings to Imani's frantic workings and the chaos at the Office of Public Safety, I was too furious to be embarrassed. And our story seemed to have a similar effect on James. He caught my eye, then turned to Darya and Cy.

"We couldn't just file reports and walk away."

"Of course you couldn't." Darya set her grading aside and clasped her hands. "It's strange, though. Why *those* students? If it were just the undergrads, I could buy that this is some sort of Magic house prank. But *Imani*?"

"It is strange," James agreed. "We need to figure out what's connecting them. That's what I'm hoping to do today."

"So, where do we start?" Cy asked.

James leaned back as he considered. "We're going to need something that belongs to each of the missing students. Preferably paper. I brought a couple of notes from Imani."

I bit my lip. Also hadn't been in class long enough to turn in any actual assignments. But both of the missing students *had* handed in something. "Would accommodation letters work?"

James raised an eyebrow, then shrugged. "I don't see why not."

FLOUR FLOATED IN THE AIR AROUND US. I'D TURNED OUR MIXER UP TOO high, nervous and distracted.

"What is it we're actually doing?" Darya asked.

James grinned, dimple accentuating the smudge of flour on his right cheek. "Prophecy by flour."

Cy nodded. "Aleuromancy, right? I had a roommate who was extremely into it. He was adorable but constantly baked cakes full of tiny porcelain dolls. What were they called? Frozen Carolines? Christines?" He waved a hand, dismissing the question. "It doesn't matter. After I chipped my second tooth, I called it quits and moved in with these two."

"Right. But we won't need porcelain dolls," James assured Cy.

"Just these." He gestured at the papers on the table, which included a sheaf of notes Imani had lent James before she vanished—Darya and Cy had copied the documents and were busily shredding the originals. "We'll tuck one strip into each cookie."

"Wait." Darya's delight made her voice pitchy. "We're making *fortune cookies?*"

"Something like that. The recipe I was taught is for tuiles, but it's a similar concept." James stepped up beside me, grabbing a spoon. "Ready?"

I reached for the icing spreader. "Ready."

He scooped out the batter, and I smoothed it into flat circles.

"Once they come out, we've got to shape them quickly." James slid the cookie sheet into the oven. "If we don't get them folded correctly, the working won't take."

He walked us through the motions, using a circular scrap of paper as a stand-in for the cookies. He lay a strip of the fortune-bearing paper across the middle of the circle, then flipped it over the handle of a wooden spoon, slid it off, and twisted it.

"With the real cookie, you'll move it from the spoon handle to the muffin tin, so it can't unfold as it sets."

Our test run was mediocre, at best. But the timer went off before we could do another round. I pulled the cookies out and brought them to the table, where we spent the next several minutes shaping them.

"What now?" Darya asked.

I turned to James.

"We wait for the cookies to cool. Then we meditate to make sure we're ready to receive our prophecy. And then we eat." James looked from me to Darya to Cy as he explained.

Cy shrugged. "Sounds easy enough."

"Snack magic!" Darya practically sang the words, clapping her hands.

I frowned, attention snagging on the word *prophecy.* An itchy feeling traced itself up the back of my neck. "You're sure the prophecies will only be about the missing students?"

"Pretty sure." James's eyebrows briefly collided. "Why?"

"No reason." I mustered a smile. Divination was his thing, apparently. If he was sure, I didn't have to worry about a dire reminder of my coming digimancy doom—or explaining said reminder to James.

In the waiting silence, Anne's voice was just audible enough to startle me even from my bedroom.

"Bartleby put aside her worry, trusting in her cute classmate's expertise."

I yelped. "*The end*, Anne."

Cy cackled, starsdamn him. But I didn't have time to glower him into silence, because Anne wasn't finished, despite my command.

"Bartleby was impressed by the way he approached spellwork, and she liked the way he looked—"

"The end! *The end. The END. THE END.*"

It stopped, midsentence, and I sagged backward in relief. If it had actually narrated what I was thinking about seeing James in his apron in my kitchen . . . well. I snuck a look at James.

He winked, and my cheeks skipped pink, heating up to sunburn red.

"I think these cookies are just about cool enough," he said. "Who's ready to meditate?"

MINDS CLEAR, WE SETTLED BACK DOWN AROUND THE KITCHEN TABLE.

There was a ritual aspect to the eating. James instructed us to reach for a cookie without looking, letting the right one come to us. Once we had one, we needed to hold it in both upturned palms, feeling its weight before cracking it open with a swift, sure movement.

"Snap it like a carrot," he said. "Forcefully and all at once."

Hesitation would muddy the divination.

I followed his lead, watching him before attempting the process on my own. Sugar, bright and blooming, overwhelmed my senses as I closed my eyes. The snapping and munching sounds that had been filling the room went muted, audible but only just, like someone had dropped a filter over consensus reality.

I took another bite.

Tidbits of prophecy were supposed to slip through with every crunch: a glimpse of a location, or a person, or a feeling. Almost like they say it was with the Delphic Oracle's leaves: scattershot and cryptic.

Instead, the world went grayer. A sense of unease settled over me, like dress clothes that didn't fit right. I was floating, detached from everything. Fuzziness crept up my arms and legs, white noise made horribly tangible. The feeling of not quite numbness tingled, icy in my fingertips and toes.

A flash of memory—the library hustling me toward the napping oracle—made me hesitate as I reached for my next cookie. Maybe I should sit the rest of this out. Let someone else eat my remaining tuiles. Because maybe James was wrong. Maybe capital P prophecy could override the work we'd done to trigger these smaller prophecies.

No. My students needed me. I breathed and reached for another cookie. The subtle vanilla curdled on my tongue.

Failure. The word wisped through my head all smoke and ash. My body went numb, then tingled with returning sensation. My hands felt sticky, like deep down I was still four years old, listening to a strange lady tell me scary things about what life would be like when I grew up.

Run. This word wasn't smoke, but fire. It burned in my mouth as if I'd spoken it, searing down my throat and choking me in the process. I ran to the bathroom, wrongness pooling in my stomach until I threw up every last crumb.

Heccing baked-good-based prophecies.

Sagging against the cool enamel of the bathtub afterward, I did my best to keep tears at bay.

The cryptic, warning words felt like they were swirling around me. Bees, waiting to sting. My whole body tensed in terrified anticipation. I closed my eyes and forced myself to breathe until the imminent buzzing ebbed. Then I cleaned up and headed back to the kitchen.

James, Darya, and Cy were still where they had been, eyes closed as if locked in some internal world. All that remained of the cookies was crumbs. I gagged a little, just looking at them. But I couldn't hide in the bathroom when students were missing. I swallowed, took a deep breath. When I felt steady, I dragged my chair away from the table and slumped into it. The sound pulled Darya and Cy out of their trances. James didn't seem to register anything, but maybe he was better at tuning the world out.

"Where were you?" Darya whispered. "I could sort of see you run off while I was . . . out of it. Everything okay?"

"Bathroom. And I'm fine." There was no way I was going to explain what was really going on. I didn't even *know* what was really going on, other than that prophecy was being a huge dick to me, specifically. But that made me sound like I thought the universe revolved around me in a making-a-secret-chaos-conspiracy-chart kind of way.

I fibbed. "Too much sugar."

Darya hesitated, clearly not believing that lie from someone who had very recently eaten an entire half pint of ice cream in one sitting with no obvious ill effects. But she let me have it.

"Okay. Maybe you need some real food? We can order pizza."

Before I could answer, Anne's voice—much louder than it should have been—echoed down the hall.

"Unmoored. Reaching frantically for answers, solutions, help. But reaching they are unreachable. Reaching they are unreachable. Reaching they are—they are—they are—overlooked."

Anne's last, direful, syllables resonated. I stared in its direction, as though walls and furniture weren't in the way and I could see it glitching. A sharp inhalation pulled my attention back to the table.

James had the stunned expression of someone who'd just tethered reality for the first time. Or been slapped.

"That was—" He found my eyes, frantic. "Bartleby, was that

Anne?" I nodded, but he didn't seem to register the fact, already sputtering into a new sentence. "It's the voice from my trance. The one at the start of term. I thought it sounded familiar before, but text-to-speech voices all sound like that, so I wrote it off. But those words . . . Those were the exact words I heard in my trance." His hands were shaking. He pushed away from the table, bracing himself against the back of his chair. "I think—" He pulled one hand down his face with a groan before staring right at me. "No, I *know*. It's narrating Imani. And your missing students."

CHAPTER TWENTY

The phrase "a feature, not a bug" can apply to spellwork
as well as technology. Just because something seems like a
mistake doesn't mean it is one.
—PROFESSOR MARK DELIGHT, ADVANCED METHODS: DIGIMANCY

MY HEART POUNDED SO HARD IT SET MY EARS RINGING. EVERY-
one was looking at me. I couldn't feel my fingers or toes.

"It can't be." I gasped, dragging in an insufficient
amount of air. My words were immediately drowned out
by Cy's and Darya's questions.

"What trance?" Cy asked.

"Why would Bartleby's exam working be narrating missing
students?" Darya cocked her head in that way she did when she
was getting ready to fight.

James ran his hands through his hair. "I had a vision at the start
of term," he explained. "Imani was missing and there was this voice
that kept saying odd things—*unmoored, unreachable, overlooked.*"

My view of the room fuzzed around the edges as his words
sank in.

"That doesn't mean the glitching is *about* Imani. False correlation is a common problem in divination." Cy stared at James as if
to say *you should know this.*

I stole a breath, sliding my hands under my thighs to hide their
trembling.

James nodded. "True. But I don't think it's actually glitching. *Unmoored* and *unreachable* describes what the cookies triggered for me pretty aptly."

Darya scrunched her face. "It was supposed to do that? I thought I was doing something wrong."

"I suppose that floating detachment could be described as *unmoored* and *unreachable*," Cy conceded.

"It was like that for me, too." I bit my lip. "But we already know Anne's glitching because of the dead's intervention. When its narration triggers magic that might affect consensus reality, the university's ghosts step in."

Later, I'd beat myself up about the raw pleading in my voice. But here, now, the only thing that mattered was that James *couldn't* be right. There was no way my malfunctioning spellwork held the keys to anything except, possibly—and it was admittedly an increasingly tentative possibility—my mage candidacy.

James's look was pitying. "That was our theory, but Bartleby . . ." He hesitated. "If Anne's narrations draw on the institutional record, it makes sense that something destroying parts of the record, like information about specific students, might cause it to, not glitch exactly, but narrate the absence of whatever should be there."

Dismay unsettled my stomach, a squelching pressure that made me worry for a second that I'd have to bolt back to the bathroom.

He had a point.

Anne was drawing on more than my corpus of early novels. It could narrate people—or, at least, it could narrate me. If Anne was attempting to narrate the missing students and finding gaps in the institutional repository, that meant it might not be generating workings at all. In which case it was basically a very expensive, magically wrought canary in a coal mine: letting us know something was wrong.

But another possibility skulked at the edges of my thoughts. Because of my faulty spellwork, Anne had access to the *entire* university repository. What if . . . What if it had been the thing that caused Penant to malfunction in the first place? Could it be erasing records, somehow, and making the whole situation with missing students worse? That could explain why prophecy had been in my face all term. Because if my theory was right, this was worse than my copy-room failure and my last exam attempt combined.

James didn't notice my confusion, caught up in his epiphany.

"This is a good thing. We might be able to use Anne to find them. Tweak the code so it's only narrating the missing students. There's got to be some clue, some *pattern*—"

"That's . . ." The numbness in my fingers and toes was spreading. Cold bit deep into my bones. "I don't know if—"

"Students are *missing*," James interrupted. "We have to do whatever we can to help. None of the administrators who *should* be fixing this have a handle on the situation."

"Maybe we should give them a chance," Cy said. "They may be overwhelmed at the moment, but they are professionals. This is *their* job. Not yours, and certainly not Bartleby's."

James shrugged off Cy's words. He wanted an answer, and I was the only one who could give it. His eyes stayed on mine, pleading.

If I was right, I would have to dismantle my working immediately. Stop it from causing further harm. Come clean to admin, so they could set things right. If James was right, I'd need to update Anne's code, moving it *further* from the functionality I needed it to have for my exam, if it worked at all. Given how resistant it had been to my updates, even if we could make the changes, I might not be able to get it to change back afterward.

I drew my knees up to my chest, wrapping my arms around them, and closed my eyes.

It was selfish to hesitate. But Anne, despite its glitchiness and unexpected functionality, was my best shot at making it through this program. The steps we took next might mean giving up on my chances at becoming a mage. If I was going to let go of that dream, I needed to be sure. I needed time to *think*. But James was waiting for my answer, and I could feel my housemates watching.

As difficult as it was even under normal circumstances, I forced myself to visualize what it would really mean to prioritize my work—my career—right now. To keep quiet about my worries and tell James no. I imagined passing my exam, called up the emotions of it—the nerves, the adrenaline rush, the ragged mix of exhilaration and relief that would make me burst into tears on the spot. I didn't just tell myself that story. I *lived* it.

And in living it, I knew that joy, that relief, that slight inching away from the cliff's edge of failure, was not worth the cost. The guilt would eat it all through, faster than I could ever imagine. I'd end up giving up my career, anyway, because I wouldn't *deserve* magic anymore.

I couldn't say no. My career, my life in magic, didn't signify when students' *actual* lives were at stake.

In the background, I could hear James arguing with my roommates. Darya and Cy defending my hesitation. James responding through gritted teeth.

"Did you *see* the missing students in your visions? Even *one* of them, even for a second?" He waited. Nobody answered. "That's what I thought. Let me tell you what that means. Let me *really* spell it out. Either the cloaking was so thorough that they've ceased to exist in this reality, or some other layer of the working is blocking them from prying eyes, pushing them half out of this reality in the process. Either way, it's only a matter of time before they come fully untethered, or, in Anne's words, *unmoored*, from consensus reality. And because this working erased their records, they're cut off from higher magic. They aren't going to be able to make their way back on their own."

When I opened my eyes, James's face was a tight mask, gaze hard on mine. I wanted to flinch away from it. I stared back, instead.

"There's only one way to find out." The words sounded strained, even to me. But I kept talking, kept pushing forward so that the weight of my choice wouldn't have a chance to sink in. "But there's something else we need to check first."

"ON ITS BEING PROPOSED, ANNE OFFERED ITS SERVICES, AS USUAL," Anne announced when we reached my bedroom. It sounded almost petulant, adapting a passage from Jane Austen's *Persuasion* in its most monotone monotone. "And though its syntax would sometimes fill with dreadful static at being so thoroughly analyzed, Anne was extremely glad to be employed."

"Snarky little thing, isn't it?" Cy drawled.

He'd opted to lean in the doorway while the rest of us huddled around my laptop. They'd all taken my theory in stride, which either told me that my theory was sound or that they'd expected catastrophe from me in the first place. Maybe both.

"Cy would be snarky as well, were his innermost workings to be opened up to such public critique," Anne observed.

Darya hummed. "It has a point. We didn't even ask if it was okay with this."

Cy scoffed. "Since when do we have to ask our spellwork if it's okay being analyzed?"

I typed in my password, doing my best to ignore their conversation.

I could almost hear the raised eyebrow in Darya's tone. "Since it started talking, obviously." She turned to the skull, which was propped up on top of my dresser. "Are you okay with this, Anne?"

"Anne thanked Darya for asking and wished to assure her, as well as anyone else who cared to know, that it had accepted its discomfort as necessary."

I spared it a glance. Since when did it respond so easily to conversational cues? "I'm sorry, Anne. We'll be as quick as we can."

At my elbow, James cleared his throat. "We should take a look at your corpus first. If it's deleting the databases it draws on, your plain text files should be disappearing like student records are."

I hooked up the hard drive that contained my corpus of early novels and started scrolling, searching for files I knew Anne had referenced. *Pride and Prejudice, Emma, Persuasion, Northanger Abbey.* Each file I clicked opened without issue. I scrolled through anyway, looking for any evidence that data was beginning to corrupt.

"Is there anything that would make you feel more comfortable, Anne?" Darya asked.

Anne was silent for a moment, before answering. "Anne requested to borrow a hat or bonnet of the people of the house." I added Fanny Burney's *Evelina* to my list of files to check.

"Okay, then. A hat it is." The click of Darya's power wheelchair joystick heralded her departure. I kept scrolling through plain text files, all of which seemed to be perfectly fine.

A few minutes later Darya returned, hefting a bright pink iridescent trucker hat with fuzzy cat ears.

"Hat delivery, coming through."

"You did not—" Cy made an outraged sound. "That hat belongs to me, Watkins. You can't just rummage through other people's rooms and give away their accessories."

"Anne is only borrowing it," Darya said, unbothered. "Besides, you don't even wear it."

"I did once. I might again."

"Mm-hmm." Darya stretched up to settle the thing gently over Anne.

"Anne wished to express its utmost gratitude," Anne said, its volume low.

Darya laughed. "No need. It's the least we could do."

I finished skimming *Evelina* and sat back in my chair. "That was the last file. I think . . ." It felt like hubris to say it, but I took a breath and did anyway. "I think we're good."

"You're right. If there's no evidence your corpus files are being affected there's no reason to believe your working is deleting files from the repository." James's smile was genuine, if tight around the edges.

There was still the matter of Anne's glitches to look into.

I sighed. "Let me pull up the logs."

There was no easy way to sort for the glitches, because the CSV file that captured Anne's narration didn't *parse* them as glitches. It labeled them using the same machine learning it used to label everything else, denoting the date and time, contents, and reference texts drawn upon (a categorization that didn't seem to be working well, I noticed).

I explained as much to James while I scrolled through the spreadsheet. Row after row of Anne's narration went by with each flick of my fingers on the trackpad. I kept an eye out for narrative nonsense, ready to stop the scroll at any moment.

"The glitches have been a lot more frequent since last week, and when it's glitching, Anne seems partial toward *un-* words and negations. That's really all I know . . ."

I paused at each glitch to give James time to review. He kept his thoughts to himself, brow furrowing as we neared the end of the file.

Anne had tapped into the institutional record, and today's aleuromancy, coupled with James's vision, strongly suggested that its glitches were related to the vanishing records of our missing students. But its gibberish wording gave me *no* reason to believe it could describe more about where the students were or what was happening to them. It was simply narrating their experience, the endless unmoored fogginess. Changing its code wouldn't change that—at least I didn't think so. We'd have to change the students' circumstances to get Anne to narrate them differently.

Unless I was letting the slim hope that I wouldn't have to torpedo my spellwork demonstration cloud my judgment.

Breath held, I waited to see if James would come to the same conclusion.

"There are a lot more of these than I thought there'd be." He frowned at the screen. "We should try charting them out on a timeline. Maybe dumping the logs into something like AntConc and pulling out clusters and collocates. It might give us some sort of pattern. But—" he looked up at me, the crease between his brows deepening "—if this is what all of its glitches are like, I don't think Anne is going to lead us to the students. It's missing the information it needs to do that."

He sat back on his heels.

I couldn't help a little huff of relief. Pulling my hands into my lap, I cracked my knuckles against the giddy feeling.

"So, this is just some perverse coincidence?" Cy's laugh was incredulous. "We're no closer to answers?"

It didn't feel like a coincidence; it felt like a curse. Whether it could give us answers or not, my exam working was inextricably connected to whatever was happening to the students. That couldn't be good, for it or for me. I gripped the pressed wood of my desk until my fingernails went pink and then white with the pressure.

"Our aleuromancy worked, technically," Darya said. "It's just that the missing students aren't in a state that's particularly illuminating for us. Maybe if we narrow our focus . . ."

James pulled a hand through his hair. "That's what I plan to do. I've known Imani long enough that there are some other workings I can try to find her. Psychic links and spiritual dowsing. And if I can find her maybe she can help us track down the others. But I'll need solitude. Uninterrupted focus. Maybe—"

"We can split up, try to crack this from different angles." Darya's nod was vigorous. "Bartleby can do that . . . correlation and conglomeration you suggested."

"Clusters and correlates," I corrected, voice low. "It's a text analysis thing."

Darya waved me off. "Yeah, that." Her eyes went wide, and she turned to face me. "Oh! Maybe you could try *getting* Anne to glitch on purpose. We don't know what triggers the glitches, so that might also tell us something."

I nodded. It wasn't a bad idea.

"And I," Darya went on, looking around at our rag-tag group, "will work on a contingency plan."

"What about me?" Cy asked, pout already half-formed on his porcelain face.

Darya smirked. "You'll be helping me, Pearson."

THE REST OF THE WEEK OOZED BY, SLOW AND EXCRUCIATING. I COULDN'T sleep for much longer than a few minutes at a time. When I did doze off, I had recurring nightmares about my exam, my missing students, Imani, and James. Maybe Darya had a point about accommodations. Not that I was ready to explore that, on top of everything else.

I spent as much time as possible holed up in my bedroom going over Anne's logs. Or, as now, in a standoff with my spellwork construct.

"Go on, glitch." I sat cross-legged on my bed, staring into Anne's empty eye sockets.

"Bartleby's narration skull did not recognize the command *glitch*." Anne's monotone voice managed to convey exasperation.

I tried not to growl. "Anne, this is important. If you know anything, I need you to tell me."

"In her urgency, Bartleby refused to acknowledge the fact that expecting a narration construct she had called into being less than a fortnight previously to *know* anything beyond the scope of its databases was unfair and unfounded."

It was right, but I didn't know what else to do.

"Please?"

Anne didn't even bother narrating circuitously back at me.

I didn't blame it. Slumping back onto my bed, I dug through blankets until I found my phone, texting James about my lack of progress. He hadn't been responding—he'd told us he needed solitude and focus for his divination, so his phone was probably in airplane mode or something—but I watched my messaging app anyway, waiting for telltale bubbles. Despite knowing he was just otherwise occupied, I couldn't suppress a shiver of worry when they didn't appear.

Magic students were disappearing. *He* was a Magic student.

My phone chimed, and I pulled it up with embarrassing eagerness. But it wasn't James.

So excited to dig in on your new materials. Let's meet Tuesday to discuss. Does 9:30 work?
—Amelia

I stared at the email, biting at a hangnail. Then I swiped back to my browser, pulling up the Divination branch's website. James's name was still listed there, even when I refreshed the page.

Turning on my side, I let my phone fall as I curled into a fetal position. Maybe his scrying or trances or whatever the heck he called them had worked better than any of us expected. Maybe he'd found Imani and they'd reunited and something had sparked between them and—

Without a response to reassure me, the worry grew. I got up and wandered around the house, unsure what to do next. My housemates tried to console me.

"Did you see the article in the *Prattler*?" Darya asked, forcing a mug of tea into my hands. "Supposedly, the Office of Public Safety has some promising leads."

"And even if that's PR spin, the full moon is next week," Cy added. "Odds are this will all be over by then."

Under normal circumstances, Cy's logic would have been reassuring. Workings were at their strongest during a New Moon, and each subsequent phase chipped away at their integrity. Most workings, even major ones, dissolved under the full moon. But there were workarounds for magic that needed to last longer. Estimating from the date Alse had disappeared, this working had already lasted several moon phases without any sign of weakening, which meant it was probably using one of those workarounds.

I hid my dismay with a sip of tea.

We were dealing with a working that the university's dead had failed to identify as rogue, malicious magic. If it wasn't over by next week, odds were that it could last as long as its casters wanted it to.

"Maybe we should take this to the Dean of Magic." The Office of Public Safety and the Dean of Students hadn't followed up on our report, which told me they hadn't gotten to it yet, or they didn't believe us. We'd be justified in escalating the issue.

"I don't think it will do any good," Darya said.

She'd appealed to the Dean of Magic enough times to know.

But part of me still hoped the real adults could take over, find the missing students, set things right. That if I just told the right person, all of this would stop being my problem and I could get back to my exam prep.

"It can't hurt to try."

Cy only scoffed. But Darya sighed.

"Fine. If the full moon doesn't take it down and Public Safety still doesn't have a handle on it, we'll go to the Dean of Magic. But Pearson and I are still working on that contingency plan."

CHAPTER TWENTY-ONE

Degree progress requirements wait for no mage.

—ANNOTATION IN THE SUBLIMITY UNIVERSITY
SCHOOL OF MAGIC'S GRADUATE HANDBOOK

OUTSIDE PROFESSOR HUSIK'S OFFICE, I PAUSED TO COLLECT MYself. It felt wrong to go about my business, teaching and meeting with my advisor, when some of my students were missing and all of them were likely uncertain and afraid. What choice did I have, though?

I took a deep breath, exhaling as I lifted my hand to knock. Down the hall, a voice fractured the hush. I hesitated, knuckles hovering an inch away from the door.

"As I said, it's a fundamental alteration. I explained as much to Ms. Joshi when she submitted her letter. She challenged my assertion, then dropped—" It was the same professor I'd overheard three weeks ago. Now, the source of the self-satisfied tones was all-too familiar: Professor Delight. And he was talking about Imani.

A tinny voice interrupted him with a question I couldn't quite make out. I let my hand fall to my side, giving in to the urge to eavesdrop.

"Well, perhaps not *officially*. But she's stopped attending. I presume it's only a matter of time." Professor Delight's voice was clipped, as though he was explaining something to a belligerent teenager. More tinny almost-words filtered down the hallway. Whoever he was talking to wasn't happy. "It's for the best," the professor insisted. "I've got the reputation of our institution to consider. We're teetering on the edge of R1 as it is, and you people want me to make my courses *less* rigorous? This work—"

Whatever he said next was muffled by the sound of my advisor's office door opening. Professor Husik yelped in surprise. I wrenched my attention to the doorway, where my advisor now stood, holding a hand to her sternum, cheeks pink and eyes wide.

"Oh! Hi, Professor."

"Good morning, Dorothe," Professor Husik—Amelia—said. "You're right on time as usual." She gave herself a little shake and gestured me inside.

I followed, distracted. Imani had submitted an accommodation letter, from the sound of it. And Professor Delight had refused to make any changes, on the grounds that it would substantially change the course or lower the academic standard or both. On the fence as I was about pursuing my own accommodations, his words rattled me. A lightning ball of dread crackled in my stomach.

I was already out of place in the program, though I'd mostly kept that fact hidden. If I managed to get accommodations, would that change? Would my place here be openly debated by professors who not so secretly considered me unfit to be a mage? It was almost enough to knock my exam anxiety out of my head. I sank into the chair and folded my hands in my lap, trying to breathe.

"I've just finished going over your updated materials." Amelia licked a finger and flipped through a freshly printed stack of papers on her desk, pausing when she reached a page with row upon row of her tightly looping handwriting. Then she turned to face me properly.

"You've done it. This is—" she paused to wave her hands, grin splitting the careful neutrality of her expression "—fabulous. I've just got a few small suggestions, then it will be ready to send to the rest of the committee."

I nodded, overly aware of the way my heart was throwing itself against my rib cage as I waited for my own sense of joy, or even just a calm sense of accomplishment, to set in. Instead, tears threatened. Pressure built in my chest, a billowing thunderstorm I was irrationally afraid might break free if I tried to say anything at all.

I'd made it this far before, only to fail miserably. This wasn't an accomplishment, not really. I might make a mistake during the exam and freeze up again. I *probably* would. I had less time to prepare now than I had last fall. I still needed to figure out how to assess Anne's narrations for signs of magic. How to use those signs to establish, beyond a doubt, that early novels contained workings. And I hadn't been practicing for the oral portion of my exam at all, aside from the one session with Professor Leighton.

"It's mostly adding context here and there," Amelia was saying, "making sure your line of reasoning is fully articulated, demonstrating the power of the connections you're making." She ran a finger down her list of notes, forehead creasing when she glanced back up at me.

My eyes welled. *Keep it together, Bartleby.*

"Dorothe? What's wrong?" She dropped her notes and reached out, taking my hands. "This is good news."

But it wasn't, not really.

Because Amelia's approval meant I had a real second chance. And if I had a real, honest-to-Hecate second chance, then investigating my students' disappearances was going to actively jeopardize my Magic career.

I needed more time. I needed actual help if I was going to pass my exam. Not because I wasn't good enough, but because I was having to deal with panic attacks and insomnia and a dozen other starsdamned things before I could even do the work in the first place.

Darya and Cy had been right.

Panic attacks weren't normal. They weren't part of the program requirements. I shouldn't have to brave my way through them, when the program's unrelenting intensity and lack of support were at least halfway to blame for them in the first place.

"I think . . ." I pulled my hands away and crossed my arms, wishing Amelia had brought her dog so I could stare into his kind eyes instead of hers. "I think I might need to talk to somebody in Student Accessibility Services." My gaze settled on a shriveled rosemary plant on the shelf past her shoulder. "I'm worried I'll freeze up again, despite practicing with Professor Leighton. And I'd like to be able to do my best." Or even just speak, at all, during the exam.

I wasn't sure what accommodations would look like, because the School of Magic's website only said *accommodations may be available for Branch and Field Exams.* But Darya had told me about something called AACs: augmented and alternative communication devices that could help if I lost my words again.

Amelia's *hmm* conveyed sympathy and skepticism all at once. My throat tightened as she replied, words slow and careful.

"We all want nothing more than to see you succeed. But, Dorothe . . ." Her voice softened, "I'm not certain that SAS is your best option here."

Confusion pulled my gaze to hers.

"Why not?"

I'd never advise my own students against speaking to SAS if they needed to. The sting of her words cut through my haze of anxiety, embarrassment, and uncertainty. I straightened my shoulders, swallowing the unfamiliar tang of anger.

"It takes SAS several weeks to process accommodations requests, once all of the proper documentation and medical tests are complete. It's unlikely they'd be in place in time for your exam." Professor Husik bit her lip, looking uncannily decades younger than she actually was. "It's probably for the best. These exams are meant to prepare future mage candidates for the job market and, unfortunately, most institutions don't provide robust accommodations for interviewees. It's my responsibility to ensure you build those skills." She straightened, tones perking up. "Why don't you stop by my office once a week, until your exam? We have four or five weeks to get you prepared. I just know we can provide the support you need without all that extra red tape." She waved a hand, dismissing the idea.

She had a point, but I couldn't help but think she sounded almost like Professor Delight.

"Shall we go over my notes?" Professor Husik asked, after a restorative swig of coffee.

I didn't know how to respond. What to do. I could barely hear her over the ringing in my ears. Anger and exhaustion and uncertainty carried my thoughts in fitful gusts.

She sounded like Professor Delight. Who'd been talking about Imani's accommodations. And now that I'd had a second to process, that fact felt momentous. Imani had submitted an accommodation request right before she disappeared. Just like Alse. And . . . Pam had given me a letter, too, the last day she'd been in class.

Was that the connection? Were *accommodations* the thread linking the growing number of missing students? Not the flu. Not some ridiculous Magic house hazing battle. Disability accommodations.

My eyes flicked uncertainly to Amelia's. I forced myself to nod, to smile. To pull a notebook and pen from my bag and sketch out what little of her feedback I heard, anger and frustration seeping away beneath the chill of suspicion.

MAYBE I'D MISHEARD OR MISUNDERSTOOD. MAYBE I'D JUMPED TO THE wrong conclusion. Maybe I was cooking up a conspiracy to procrastinate on what I should be focusing on.

I'd just gotten sign-off to retake my Branch and Field exam. Anyone else would be *celebrating*, for Hecate's sake.

But my students were missing. Imani was missing. Those

were facts. And maybe their disappearances weren't connected, or maybe they'd all decided to ditch university life at roughly the same time for personal, idiosyncratic reasons. But that felt like wishful thinking.

The accommodation letters were too much of a coincidence not to mean something. And if they meant what I thought they did, if this was the missing thread connecting *all* of the disappearances, then whoever was behind it was even more powerful than we'd already suspected. SAS records were highly protected. There almost *had* to be administrators involved, and faculty, too, if they'd been able to access those records. Maybe even faculty I knew.

I sped up, feeling suddenly exposed in the long stretch of hallway.

The thought felt preposterous, but I couldn't help dwelling on the strange similarity between my advisor and Professor Delight. What if one or both of them was involved?

We knew that someone with digimancy skills must be behind the working, so Professor Delight was a logical suspect in at least that regard. But based on his phone call, he believed Imani was going to drop his course. Unless that had been a pretense. He *had* seemed almost smug when he'd said so to the person on the phone. There hadn't been any concern or regret in his voice. Just triumph, laced with anger. More than that, though, he'd seemed so certain she wouldn't be returning.

I headed toward the elevators, head spinning.

I had to have imagined the triumph in his voice. The ringing note of certainty was just anxiety brain playing tricks on me. Because if he was involved—an enormous *if*—Amelia might be, too. She'd reacted strangely when I asked about accommodations. Like she didn't want me to get them. And sure, her reasoning about the timeline made sense. But maybe it was more than that. Maybe she *knew* something.

But that was impossible.

Amelia Husik was *beloved* in Thaumaturgy, by grads and undergrads, faculty and staff alike. She'd won teaching awards two of the three years I'd been here. She'd . . . She'd told me to keep braving my way through. To work harder. To meet with her and practice more.

Jabbing the elevator button repeatedly, I stood back to wait, willing my brain to shut the Hec up.

"Dorothe?" Rapid footsteps rang through the hall as Professor Delight called out my name.

My nervous system did its best to self-petrify. After what felt like forever, I managed to turn. He came to a stop beside me.

"Professor."

"I was just stepping out for some coffee, but this is serendipitous."

I mustered something like a smile, muscles tensing. If this man *had* casually disappeared students for submitting accommodation letters, what would he do to me for investigating their disappearances?

"I've been meaning to check in with you," he explained, "but you always scurry off so quickly after class."

"Oh, um . . . sorry?"

The professor lifted one shoulder, impassive.

"I know you've had some . . . difficulty with this subject matter in the past, and I wanted to assure you that, from my perspective, you're getting along swimmingly."

I relaxed. Being wrong about accommodations didn't automatically make him, or my advisor, some evil conspirator, vanishing students who dared to ask for support.

"Thank you."

He opened his mouth, as if to elaborate, just as the elevator dinged.

"I won't hold you up any longer," he said with a self-consciously wry smile. "I'm sure you're spending every spare moment preparing for your exam."

"BARTLEBY!" MAGDALEN CHEERED AS I BLEW INTO OUR OFFICE. "ARE congratulations in order?"

I managed a nod, dumping my bag and raincoat into my desk chair. "I guess. And possibly also condolences."

The words slipped out before I could stop them. I wanted to run my theory about the accommodation letters by Darya or Cy or James. But I'd tried calling and gotten busy signals for my housemates and an automated error message for James. *The device you are calling is out of service. Please try again later.* The only thing keeping me from panicking about that was the fact that the email I'd sent him immediately afterward hadn't bounced back.

Mags threw her arms around me. "Fucking congrats!"

She hadn't heard. Or she'd interpreted and dismissed my negativity as exam nerves. That was probably for the best. I should keep my theory to myself until I had actual proof.

I took a breath, pulling out of the hug. *Should*, but couldn't. This was too big. I had to tell someone, if only to keep myself from any more wild speculation about my professors' possible complicity.

"Thanks. I have a few minor changes to make by Thursday. But Mags?"

A knock interrupted me.

Cy shoved the door open, strolling into the room with Darya close behind him. Mags retreated to her side of the office to make space for them.

"We came to support you," Cy announced, slouching into the extra chair.

Darya growled. "Or to *celebrate* with you. Come on, Pearson, we practiced this." She was wearing her favorite pink-sequined *Black Girl Magic* T-shirt, a testimony to her plans to celebrate.

"So," Cy asked, turning to me, "which is it?"

"After a revelation during her meeting with her advisor, Bartleby had a new theory," Anne said.

"Blabbermouth." I scowled at Anne.

I'd left it in my office for my meeting, not ready for Amelia to see my spellwork demonstration—or, more likely, to witness it glitching.

"Oh!" Darya's tone shifted from congratulatory to cautious. "How'd it go?"

I sighed. "She's signing off on it. I just have to make some small changes before I submit to the committee."

Darya clapped. "Congrats, Bartleby!" She stuck her tongue at Cy. "Told you it'd be a celebration. Mages' night out, everyone?"

"No."

I didn't have *time* to celebrate. Even if I did, this wasn't worth celebrating. I'd gotten sign-off before, and I'd still managed to fuck things up. My second attempt was perfectly primed to go much, much worse than the first. And I couldn't do anything about that, because students were Heccing missing.

"Okay, now you're fucking scaring me," Mags said.

Darya echoed. "What's wrong?"

I sat on the edge of my desk, chewing on the inside of my cheek as I recounted what I'd overheard from Professor Delight.

Darya's eyebrows inched together. "Gross, but I don't get it. What does that have to do with your exam?"

My huff set my bangs adrift. "He was talking about Imani. And then when I was checking with Amelia about maybe getting accommodations and she was being . . . less than enthusiastic—"

"Oh, Bartleby. I'm proud of you for bringing them up. I know you've been reluctant to consider them. And I'm sorry that—" Darya's eyes widened, the other pieces of my story clicking into place. "Oh, shit."

I nodded, echoing her words. "Oh *shit*."

"Are either of you planning on filling the rest of us in?" Cy drawled.

"You think accommodation letters are the common thread?" Darya leaned back in her chair, her words more a statement than a question.

"I do. Alse and Pam each submitted one before they disappeared, too."

That much, I was confident about. My suspicions about my professors . . . not so much. I turned toward the others. Cy's expression was thoughtful, but Mags's was outright skeptical.

Slowly, she shook her head. "There's no way you could know that."

"But . . ."

Mags held up a hand. "We're up to, what, ten missing students now? You know that *three* of them submitted accommodation letters. That's less than a third of them. It's not a pattern."

"I think she might be right," Darya said.

"You . . . what?" Mags and I said the words in tandem and eyed each other.

"I think you're right," Darya repeated, turning to me. "Manesh submitted an accommodation letter to me in class yesterday." The worry in her expression was underscored by the too rapid *tap tap tap* of her neon-yellow fingernail against the arm of her chair. "Was he in your class this morning?"

"No." Something clenched in my chest. I couldn't tell if it was validation or fear.

Cy sat forward, elbows on knees. "So, what do we do now?"

Darya eyed him. "*You* need to go home and pack for your research trip. Aren't you leaving in two days? You *might* need some clothes."

He waved the words off with a languid gesture. "Yes, yes. Excuse me for misspeaking. What do *you* do now?"

He looked at me, but I didn't know. James was off on his own investigation. And storming Student Accessibility Services and demanding access to their records wasn't going to get me far.

I turned to Darya. She took a breath, but before she could say anything, Mags cut in.

"Look, I have to get to a Federation meeting, but I feel like I need to say something. You are running yourself ragged, and it's *not your job* to save these students. You need to breathe. Focus on your exams and advancing to candidacy. The people who are *supposed* to find the students will find the students."

"I have to try, Mags."

Mags flicked a glance at her watch and pursed her lips. "I really do have to go. Please, just . . . don't blow up your career? Academia needs people like you. And," her tone went dire, "I don't want to have to break in a new officemate."

She grabbed her bag and slipped between me, Darya, and Cy on her way out the door.

"I have a meeting, too," Darya said after several long seconds ticked by. "But after that . . ." Her smile was a merciless thing. "You were right, Bartleby. It's time to escalate this. Tomorrow we're going to the Dean of Magic."

CHAPTER TWENTY-TWO

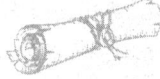

Wait for wisdom and conscience in public agents—
fiddlestick! The only conscience we can trust to is the
massive sense of wrong in a class, and the best wisdom
that will work is the wisdom of balancing claims.

—QUOTE FROM GEORGE ELIOT'S *MIDDLEMARCH* (1871)
INCLUDED IN THE FEDERATION OF GRADUATE TEACHING
FELLOWS AND PRACTITIONERS BARGAINING HANDBOOK

I WAS ABOUT TO INTENTIONALLY KICK A HORNETS' NEST, AND I WAS corpse-calm about it. Or telling myself that I was.

After class, I pulled my hood up against the misting rain and started toward the Science Library, where Darya shared an office with a Botany PhD student. On the sidewalk, I kicked my way through a couple of puddles to burn off adrenaline.

Going to the Dean of Magic was supposed to be a last resort. Because of the way our program functioned, housing four branches that acted like departments but operated more codependently, like subfields within a single department, our reporting structure was ill-starred.

Typically, we reported to our advisors or, when our issues were teaching related, our branch supervisors. If the issue was less pedagogical and more about student life and well-being, it went to the Dean of Students. If the issue wasn't teaching related and our advisors passed us up the chain of command, we'd be handed off to Professor Leighton, in her capacity as Magic's Director of Graduate Studies, or, maybe, a branch head. If none of those individuals were sufficient, then and only then was Dean Underhill called in.

None of those other individuals *were* sufficient in this case. My advisor may or may not have been in on it. The Dean of Students and Office of Public Safety were buried under an avalanche of missing students' cases. Our problem had nothing to do with our studies, so Professor Leighton couldn't help. And the thought of petitioning Thaumaturgy's branch head, Professor Paris, for *anything* was nearly as intimidating as—and was bound to be less effective than—speaking to the Dean of Magic.

The dean *was* our last resort.

I kick-splashed through another puddle as I turned onto the path between one of the newer dorms and the Art History building. Across an open courtyard, the squat, largely glass structure of the Science Library presided. Darya was parked under an awning just outside the main entrance.

"Are you ready?" she asked as I joined her under the awning.

"Ready as I can be." I shrugged for her benefit, but as we set off toward the admin building, I focused on my breath. In and out. In and out. In and out. If I let my thoughts slip to what I was doing or why I was doing it, I was going to spiral.

Darya took the lead, pulling her joystick to the left to follow a fork in the sidewalk that took us under a row of bare-branched trees. Her wheelchair motor whined as we climbed the hill.

The Dean of Magic's office was in the same unassuming but pretentiously positioned little building as those of the university president, the provost, and other assorted deans. At the center and highest point of campus, its two-story white stucco box gave me Tudor vibes despite the distinct lack of anything even Tudoresque.

Darya sighed as it came into view.

"We'll have to go around the back. The only ramp is the loading and unloading area where they take out the trash."

"Seriously?"

Darya nodded.

"The only access you have to the most powerful people on campus is *the trash entrance?*"

I'd known things were bad. But this would've been comically bald-faced if it wasn't so infuriating.

Darya didn't look infuriated, though. She just looked exhausted. And I didn't want to add to that with my incredulity and outrage.

I followed her inside.

THE DEAN LOOKED OLD ENOUGH TO BE MORGAINE. WITHERED AND white from top down, her colorless hair was as sharp and asymmetrical as a guillotine. Her white suit and cloak seemed to suck the warmth from the room. And her nails were painted such a blinding white I saw spots after glancing at them.

Her office furnishings were similarly colorless. White walls, white and off-white art, white rug and books and technology.

The only spot of color in the room was the crimson slash of lipstick on her face.

It was enough of a sensory assault that I had to pause and consciously breathe. I could feel my pulse pounding, and my stomach cramped around itself as if trying to flee.

Darya nudged me forward. There was nothing visible hanging in the doorway, but stepping inside felt like walking through a bead curtain. I rubbed my arms, willing the tickling feeling away.

"Hello, Dean Underhill. My name is Dorothe Bartleby." I tried to sound polite as I shoved a chair aside for Darya and took my own seat. "And this is my colleague, Darya Watkins."

"Dean," Darya said, pulling up beside me.

"Darya." The dean spoke in the measured tone of a person encountering an old enemy. She locked eyes with Darya. "What can I help you with this afternoon."

It wasn't really a question, but we attempted to answer it, anyway.

"It's come to our attention that Magic students are going missing," Darya said.

"Yes." The dean's voice was dry. "I'm aware." She gestured to the latest edition of *The Platypus Prattler*. "The entire campus is aware."

"The whole campus doesn't know they disappeared after submitting accommodation letters." I was speaking in slow motion, forcing the words out a Sisyphean task. "Or, at least some of them did. I don't have access to the others' records. And, speaking of records, I don't think Penant is buggy. I think the missing students' records are being destroyed."

I was chattering.

Darya rested her palm on my arm. "We personally know four of the students who've gone missing. And, as my colleague said, we have evidence to indicate—"

The dean clacked her nails, loud, against the top of her desk. "You have evidence. And you decided to come to me, instead of going to Public Safety or the Dean of Students. Why?" She narrowed her eyes, looking at Darya.

Darya, for her part, looked entirely too guileless *not* to have an ulterior motive.

"We've used the early-warning system, reached out to the Dean of Students, and filed reports with Public Safety. But I don't think they're *hearing* us." Or maybe, though I wasn't about to speculate in front of the dean, someone high up in that office had heard us and didn't care. I added the Dean of Students to my growing mental list of suspects. "It's not just that Magic students are going missing by normal means. Magic students are going missing because of some sort of . . . working."

My words slowed, sap hardening into amber.

The dean arched an eyebrow that could have been sculpted from snow. She waved a hand, nails glinting.

"If it were magic, the dead would have put a stop to it."

She wasn't asking any of the questions Iris had. Wasn't making *any* kind of effort to record our report. Hec, she wasn't acting as if any of this mattered in any way.

"I know it sounds far-fetched." The words slipped away as I said them, so quickly I wasn't sure they were coming out in the right order. "But if you just check SAS's records. Or have SAS staff check them. You'll—"

The dean steepled her hands, and my voice quit working. She peered at us over the sharp points of her nails for several long seconds. Then, coming to some sort of conclusion, she hummed.

"Well, ladies, this does sound serious. Thank you for bringing it to my attention. I'll have my people follow up." We must not have looked convinced, because the dean stood, palms pressed to the desk.

"Rest assured that, if there is a practitioner behind these disappearances, we will stop at nothing to ensure they're found and stopped." Her mouth twitched into something just enough like a smile to terrify. "And don't worry, girls. We will return the missing students to their families and friends."

I stood, recognizing a dismissal when I heard one, and more than satisfied with the dean's response. Except, why was I satisfied? I was putting off finishing my exam prep because I was *worried* about these students.

Darya frowned. "It *is* magic," she challenged. "*Nobody* has seen or heard from them. Their records are disappearing. Even divination can't pin them down anywhere."

My heart slammed against my rib cage, even though, logically, I knew this was exactly what we'd come here to say. I resisted the urge to grab Darya by the arm and pull her out of there, but only barely. And only by gritting my teeth and imagining myself rooted to the spot.

Darya wasn't just bringing our issue to the dean's attention; she was calling out the dean's response. Questioning the dean's authority.

It felt wrong. My skin wanted to crawl off my bones to get away from the conflict. Darya had transgressed and dragged me with her, an accomplice. I scowled at her.

"The dean will take care of it. We should go."

Darya rolled her eyes and turned back to the dean.

"We will look into the matter carefully," Dean Underhill repeated. "We take the safety of our students very seriously. And if, *if*, this matter involves the misuse of magic, we will hold the perpetrators to the consequences outlined in our student code."

This jarred me out of whatever funk had been enveloping me.

"But what if it's not a *student* who's responsible?" It almost certainly wouldn't be, given how complex the working was, how long it had already lasted, and how entangled it seemed to be with sensitive university records. But I wasn't confident enough in my suspicions to mention Professor Delight or Amelia. Not to the dean, or even to my own housemates.

I wasn't ready to implicate my working, either. Not only because I didn't want to risk Anne, but also because I didn't want to be an easy scapegoat. *I* knew the disappearances had started before Anne existed, but that didn't mean anyone would believe me.

The dean sighed.

"Then that will be a matter for the provost and the police, not two mage students. You've done your part, and I suggest you get back to your own work and leave me to mine."

OUTSIDE, MY MENTAL FOG CLEARED SO QUICKLY I WAS LIGHTHEADED. I braced my hands on my knees and breathed slowly, willing my vision to spin back into focus.

"What happened in there?"

Around us, students headed to and from classes, chattering with friends and listening to booming headphones and texting as if this was just another day. Envy cramped in my stomach. I longed to join them, to be pulled along in the undertow of normal, beautiful routine. Instead, this investigation had me walking against the surge of the tide.

Darya rolled her eyes. "We got the runaround." She didn't say *I told you so*, but she didn't have to.

"I know *that*, but why did I go all Stepford wife? And if it was some sort of working, why *didn't* you?"

Darya shook her wrist, revealing a charm bracelet.

"The dean likes to be agreed with," she explained. "It's a simple compulsion, triggered when you enter her office. It really only works the first time, because after that you know to expect it, but I imagine it cuts her workload in half. At least."

I shot Darya a look that I hoped reflected my extreme annoyance.

"And you chose not to warn me because . . . ?"

"I wanted to see the effects on someone else," she said, matter-of-fact. "I've experienced them myself, but I've never observed it from an objective perspective. Call it scientific curiosity."

"Fucking scientists." I let my head sag in exhaustion.

Darya kept talking. "Do you know how easy it would be to make all of the containment circles on campus wheelchair accessible? Most of the rooms could accommodate a larger circle without much trouble. But when I brought it to the dean, all she said was 'thank you for bringing this to my attention' with a few platitudes about diversity, equity, and inclusion thrown in." Darya's voice wasn't so much frustrated as empty. "That was *two years ago*. We still only have one accessible circle on campus, and it's been closed for renovations for six months."

"That's the same phrase she just used on us. 'Thank you for bringing this to my attention.'" I squinted at Darya. "If you knew this wasn't going to work, why did you agree to come at all?"

"You know why." Darya pushed her glasses up, rubbing her eyes. Her hair color working was beginning to fade, neon yellow seeping away to reveal medium brown with natural blond highlights. A stark reminder that this moon cycle was almost over. "It's a formality, Bartleby. The dean *might* do something, but we need to be able to say we went to her either way. To justify what comes next."

I sat with that for a second.

Whatever came next was going to involve some serious workings. Maybe even *major* workings. The student code allowed for that, in the case of emergencies. But only when all the usual avenues had been exhausted. Dean Underhill was the very end of the usual avenue, if anything about this could be considered *usual*.

"Are you planning on letting me in on your contingency plan, then?"

There was a distinct gleam in her eye. "We go rogue."

Of course we were going rogue. Once we found the missing students, and we *would* find them, by Hecate, we were going to have to do something about the institution that enabled their disappearances in the first place.

I spoke through gritted teeth. "Yes. But what does that mean, exactly?"

Darya only smiled.

"I need to get to the greenhouse before it closes." She flicked a glance at her watch and wrinkled her nose. "Which is in about twenty minutes . . . I'll tell you later tonight, okay? Or first thing tomorrow."

"And what do I do in the meantime?"

Despite the time crunch, she stopped and looked me in the eye. "Submit your exam materials to your committee."

With that, she jabbed her joystick forward and left.

I called after her. "*Your* article revisions are due *next week*, for Hecate's sake."

HEAVINESS SETTLED OVER ME AS I WATCHED DARYA LEAVE, LIKE I'D swallowed some lead, and deep in my gut it was transforming into something ominous. Maybe it was the weight of responsibility. Or maybe it was my guilty conscience reminding me that I *should* be doing the committee's revisions and submitting my work.

The full moon, bright in the winter dusk, perched over campus, an inescapable reminder that my deadline was *tonight*.

I stuffed my hands in my pockets and started back toward the bus stop, turning onto campus's main corridor just as the clocks began to chime five.

The hush in the air came on suddenly. It was just dark enough that the streetlights were flickering on, and students should have been spilling out of buildings on their way home. Or to their next classes. But I was alone.

Where had they all gone?

It wasn't that late. And it wasn't Friday, so the early desertion of campus couldn't be explained away by parties or sports.

Dead leaves whispered across the damp sidewalk, scuttled in circles and swirls by the breeze. That wasn't the only whispering I heard. Dread blossomed inside me. I'd wandered into range of those Heccing stone heads.

Failure.

Desssstruction.

Upheaval.
ImpossssSsster.

Coming—
It's coming.
It'ssssSsss coming—
Coming!
It's—

I walked faster, tucking my chin, but the murmurs chased me down the cobbled street.

HERE.
Run.
Run.
Turn back.
Escape.
Ruin.
Leave.
Leeeeeeaaaaavvvveeee.
Driven out. Gone.
Vanished.
Invisible.
Inevitable.
Failure.
Failed.

I splashed through a puddle at full speed. The words spun around me with the winter breeze and I knew, deep down, if they caught up it would be very bad.

But it was too late, wasn't it? I couldn't run. I'd already *heard*.

Stumbling to a stop, I gasped until my heart stopped throwing itself against my chest. Above me, the heads gaped and scowled and smiled. I wrapped my arms around myself, colder than I should be after jogging what felt like several blocks. They were still whispering, the sort of dramatically hushed tones that are meant to be heard.

And I'd heard them.

Worse, I could understand what they were saying. Without meaning to, I'd processed the words into sentences. Heccing *prophecy* had finally cornered me.

The nearest head caught my eye and winked.

Pity, that. Would've made a wonderful mage.

Would've made a wonderful mage.

Would've made a mage.

Would've failed.

The heads passed the words along casually, repeating and riffing and rabbit trailing with new words and . . . I snapped. I screamed up at them at the top of my lungs.

"Fuck that! Fuck your cryptic whispered omens. I *am* going to be a wonderful mage. I'm not going to fail. I'm—"

In the distance, someone drunkenly shouted back at me.

"S'go Plats!"

It wasn't even a game week.

The whispers picked back up. I couldn't stand the thought of one more terrifying adjective. I covered my ears with my hands and ran the rest of the way to the bus stop.

CHAPTER TWENTY-THREE

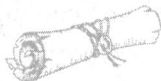

One must allow that there is something very trying to a young woman who has been prophesied about in the loss of her sense of freewill.

—NARRATORIAL COMMENTARY ADAPTED FROM JANE AUSTEN'S *SENSE AND SENSIBILITY* BY ANNE

THE APARTMENT WAS DARK. DARYA WAS STILL ON CAMPUS, OR still on her way home. And Cy was out, too. He hadn't left a note, so that meant he planned to be back that night.

I shrugged out of my raincoat without bothering to turn on the lights and schlepped the rest of my stuff to my bedroom, where I fell dramatically onto my bed, facedown into my pillow.

"Bartleby had wandered straight into a bad omen," Anne announced to the room at large.

It sounded almost amused by that fact, but I couldn't quite blame it. I'd left it on my dresser this morning despite its oblique, circuitous attempt to narrate its frustration at being left behind. Between teaching and my visit to the Dean of Magic, I couldn't risk carting it to campus.

"That's exactly what happened." I pushed myself away from the bed, turning around to face Anne. "I walked face-first into a big old bad omen. Can't say I'd recommend the experience."

Leaning back against the headboard, I considered Anne's empty eye sockets.

"I think they were warning me that I'm going to fail my exam again. Not that I needed *more* prophetic intervention to know that."

At the rate things were going, failure was all but inevitable.

If I was more pragmatic, I'd be polishing my résumé and scrolling through job sites. With my bachelor's and enough grad-level credit hours for a master's, I might be able to land an adjunct gig at a community college with enough of a repository and an onsite cemetery to sustain the occasional major working. That, or I could substitute teach at a place like my old high school and work on getting my K-12 teaching certificate. Taking a bunch of jaded teenagers into the cemetery every day to practice basic workings sounded like some sort of arcane torture, and there definitely wouldn't be enough of a school library to let me keep up with my research on the side, but it might be the best I could hope for with no terminal degree.

Part of me had kept believing there was a *possibility* I could turn things around. Part of me *still* believed that, despite the certainty of the mascarons' whispered words.

"Bartleby referred to words like *failure* and *invisible* and *driven out* and—"

"Yeah, I remember. It just happened."

Anne's face couldn't show hurt, but the pause that ensued conveyed multitudes. I pulled my fingers across my eyelids, sighing.

"I'm sorry, Anne. It's been a trying day. But there's no reason to take it out on you."

"Hands, reaching out. Pushing. Knocking. Writing. Unseen, unknowable."

"Anne?" I leaned forward, waved in Anne's direction.

"Not-spirits. Not-*not*-spirits. Haunting us. Haunting and hoping. Hoping for—Hoping for—Ho-o-o-o-o-o-o-o-o-o-o-o-o-o-o-o-o." The distorted word went on for a long time until Anne emitted a long whirring sound.

Its glitches had slowed down enough over the past week that I'd been beginning to hope they might stop altogether. Hearing it glitch for the first time in days right on the heels of my encounter with the mascarons set my hair on end. I rubbed my arms, struck by the uncanny similarity.

Grotesque, leering heads catcalling prophecy.

Anne, triggered by unknown forces, rattling out semiconnected clauses about the missing students.

Divination was the articulation of the unknown, be that the unknown past, present, or future. Anne was narrating things that should be unknowable. Not just about the unmoored state of our missing students, but about me. I'd been miles away from Anne when I encountered the heads. Did that mean Anne's narration was a form of divination?

The thought thrilled through me.

Divination shaped realities by revealing what should be unknowable and identifying probabilities that humans became subconsciously compelled to fulfill. But we hadn't always known that. The magic effects of prophecy were, for a long time, attributed to divine intervention. Because prophecy itself, much like whatever was at work in early novels, often didn't leave a trace.

Maybe divination was the mechanism for early narrative magic I'd been missing all along. Not some strange pattern of punctuation or an invisible ritual completed between reader, text, and author. Not thaumaturgy at all, but *prognostication* as a function of narrative. Workings readers enacted as they moved through stories.

A rush of excitement spurred me into motion. I dragged my laptop open and traced my fingers along the trackpad, navigating to my exam materials folder.

As I opened my proposal, contemplating the changes I was about to make—changes that went well beyond the minor tweaks my advisor had suggested—my heart dubstepped so hard my stomach heaved. The moon would still be full for a few more hours. I had time to fix the things Professor Husik had pinpointed *and* update my entire argument. But only just.

I stared at my draft, frozen for a long second.

"Bartleby knew she had to take the risk," Anne intoned, "in order to submit her best work."

With a nod, I started typing.

As Amelia had predicted, the changes didn't take me long to make. Or they wouldn't have, if my epiphany about Anne and the mascarons hadn't impelled me to spend the next several hours making some major, and majorly reckless, changes.

Hitting **send** made my heart hopscotch between my lungs. Amelia might hate my changes. She might revoke her sign-off. Fingers a rictus against my keyboard, I watched my outbox's progress bar fill in. A chime marked the point of no return.

The email had been sent, not just to Amelia, but to my whole committee.

Maybe they would see what I'd been trying to do and applaud me for risking it. But panic was a tourniquet around me, compressing my burgeoning excitement before it could bubble and bloom. At best, they'd accept my updates and get Faye, our branch administrator, to schedule my exam; there was no way I'd be applauded, not after the spectacular failure of my first exam.

"Bartleby grieved for the way things could have been."

I clicked out of my inbox and closed my computer before I could think too deeply about Anne's words, or the pressure shift of emotions in my chest.

A FEW HOURS LATER, I WOKE UP SOAKED AND SWEATING. MY HEART pounded and my stomach lurched in a way that had become upsettingly familiar. I panted until my heartbeat slowed, gummy thoughts doing their best to sort out what was bothering me. Something about email. Exam materials.

Oh, fuck. Had I really sent them, or had I dreamed it?

I scrambled out of bed and flipped my laptop open, not even bothering to sit in my chair. Instead, I loomed over my desk, frantically closing out open tabs until I found what I was looking for.

Inbox.

Seven unread messages. A student complaining about his grade. A department announcement. And, there, notes from my committee members. I clicked into one from Professor Cordelia Matthews, my nonMagic committee member. My shoulders loosened as I skimmed.

> Thanks for the materials. I look forward to your exam, and will be particularly interested in your use of narratology and natural language processing, in which I've begun to dabble myself.
>
> ALL BEST, CM

I'd definitely sent the materials, then.

Professor Rue Huang's email was an out-of-office message, which detailed their plans to reply to emails upon their return in a couple of weeks. I'd asked them to be on my committee after taking Theories of Magic with them last year. Having a mage from a different branch—in Professor Huang's case, Divination—on the committee was a requirement. But I also appreciated the way their feedback challenged me to think deeper and make more interesting connections.

Or I had, before everything went sideways last fall.

I huffed a sigh, skipping over the second-to-last email—an automated calendar update, notifying me that Professor Leighton had canceled tomorrow's practice session—and opened the final message, also from Professor Leighton.

After a paragraph of niceties—*apologies, will reschedule,* and *looking forward to reviewing your materials soon*—there was still another paragraph of email remaining.

I inhaled despite myself, crouching to read.

> On another matter, I ran into Dean Underhill this afternoon. She mentioned that you have some concerns about several students, including your classmate Imani. As the Director of Graduate Studies and your former advisor, I feel that I would be remiss not to offer you a bit

of advice. While it is laudable that you're so solicitous over the well-being of your fellows, I must urge you again to prioritize your own work. I would hate to see the career of so promising a mage student scuttled due to lack of focus at such a critical moment. Rest assured that, in passing along your concerns, you've done all you must. More practiced hands will take it from here.

REGARDS, URSULA

I rocked back on my heels, dizzy. Shouldn't my conversation with the dean have been confidential? And was it just my sleep-hazy anxiety or was Professor Leighton's tone almost . . . threatening?

Rereading the email, I mulled over her diction. She'd told me to prioritize my own work often enough. Not just at our last meeting, but back when she was my advisor. During Intro to Graduate Studies in Magic, too. It was a phrase she trotted out for all of us, the academic equivalent of advocating for work/life balance—except, in this case, it mostly meant teaching/research balance. But she'd never been so blatant about the prospect of failure before. *Career scuttled* felt, coming from Professor Leighton, like a slap in the face.

It was probably just my anxiety talking. I'd woken up from nightmares and started stress-reading emails; of course they seemed threatening.

Still, I was rattled deeply enough that I jumped when my in-box chimed with a new email alert.

We need to talk.

It was from my advisor. I stared at the subject line, trembling. Hecate's fucking dogs. I shouldn't have made those changes. She must have read through them and hated them so much she'd emailed immediately to let me know she was revoking her sign-off until I walked them back.

My fingers spasmed against the trackpad, opening the email.

I peered at the screen through half-closed eyes, holding my breath as I read.

The body of the email took some of the knife blade pressure away from my throat, but only just. It was written in haste, probably on her phone as she multitasked—a habit she'd confessed to me once, after a glass or two of wine, at a conference.

> Heard from Dean Underhill and want to make sure you are
> okay. Please call me on my personal cell when you get this.
> AMELIA

It wasn't about my materials, then. But it wasn't good that Dean Underhill was reaching out to my exam committee about my visit. My advisor certainly wasn't taking it in stride. The latest Amelia had *ever* emailed me anything was 8 p.m. She'd never, ever asked me to call her before. And definitely not on her personal cell.

Maybe the heads had been right.

Maybe I'd fucked up so entirely going to the dean that my materials didn't matter anymore. Maybe I was about to be driven out. To—

A knock on my door halted that runaway train of thought. Thank Hecate for small miracles. I took a breath before climbing to my feet and hobbled to the door on toes tingling with freshly circulating blood.

Cy lounged against the hallway's far wall in a dramatically patterned dressing gown.

"I heard you rustling around in here like a trapped rabbit and thought I might as well offer you some tea." He lifted a single shoulder in a languid shrug. "I could use the company."

I pulled my ratty terry-cloth robe off its hook and shrugged it over my shoulders.

"So could I."

Cy led the way into the kitchen, where he'd already set out a cup and saucer for me. He took tea seriously, refusing to use our motley collection of tea bags and our all-purpose electric kettle. In his designated kitchen cupboard, he kept a fancy gooseneck kettle, which he heated on the stove. He also had a curated collection of loose-leaf teas, displayed in assorted bottles and jars like a miniature apothecary. Most were caffeinated, but a few were herbal, kept for purely medicinal purposes such as sleepless nights. He blended them all himself.

I slid into my seat and watched as Cy prepared a lavender, valerian, and oat flower blend. Steam circled above the patterned teapot until he closed the lid so it could steep.

"We both have a pretty good idea why *I* could use some company at 4:30 in the morning." I tossed the words like a gauntlet as Cy took his seat. "But what about you?"

"I'm a terrible traveler," he said, folding his hands on the table. "I hate teleportation. The very thought of it is enough to keep me up at night."

"So, you're trying to distract yourself?"

"I'm trying not to crawl out of my own skin. Dissertating worked for a while. Now I've got you. So tell me—because by the look of you, it seems I'm not actually up-to-date, despite Darya's best efforts—what's got you up at this awful hour?"

Cy poured us both tea as I considered where to start answering that question.

I watched the faintly green-blue liquid swirl and settle in my cup, inhaling the steam that rose. "Darya told you about our visit to the dean?" I asked, finally.

"I ran into her at the library."

I licked my lips, then dove in. The heads' omen, Professor Leighton's vaguely menacing email, my advisor's worrying one. When I was done, my tea had gone tepid. Cy sat back with an overwhelmed whistle.

"You *heard* the mascarons speak? As in, actual human words?"

I nodded.

"Bartleby, that's—" Cy thrust his teacup to the side and leaned toward me over the table. "That's *big*. That's . . . It hasn't happened for at least a decade. It's not an omen, in that omens are individually oriented and can be about calamity small and large. It's a *portent*. Which means it has implications for the *entire university*. And you're saying all they did is tell you that you're going to fail your exam?"

I took a breath, let it out slowly. "I think so."

Cy steepled his hands, impatient. "What did they say, exactly?"

"The experience was just a little unsettling." I made a face. "You try memorizing precise diction while grappling with your fight-or-flight instinct because a bunch of melodramatic granite busts are shout-whispering *portents* at you."

Cy tipped his head back and groaned.

"But I know they said *failure* a shit ton of times. And *destruction* and *upheaval* and *imposter* and *run*."

"See, that makes me think it's about a little bit more than your exams," Cy said, running his fingers through his hair with agitated speed.

I shrugged, feigning nonchalance. An omen about my exam was one thing. But a portent, a dire message about the welfare of the university at large, was a responsibility I didn't want or need. Panic stung through me, prickling at the tips of my fingers.

"A portent about the investigation would make more sense," Cy said. "Students are going missing. It's an institutional failure, certainly."

"My interpretation is limited by my perspective. And it's not like I can go back and ask them to clarify—" I froze, catching Cy's gaze. "Can I?"

Cy shook his head. "No. That's not how it works."

I sighed, relief replacing anxiety so quickly I felt a little woozy.

"Good. Then I'm going to try to sleep for a couple of hours." I pushed my chair away from the table. "Thanks for the tea."

CHAPTER TWENTY-FOUR

Bartleby slept poorly and was so pale and tragic the next morning that Darya was alarmed and insisted on making her take a cup of scorching coffee. Bartleby sipped it patiently, although she could not imagine what good coffee would do. Had it been some magic brew, potent to confer age and experience, she would have swallowed a quart of it without flinching.

—NARRATORIAL COMMENTARY ADAPTED FROM L.M. MONTGOMERY'S *ANNE OF AVONLEA* BY ANNE

Y WAS GONE BY THE TIME I DRAGGED MYSELF BACK INTO CONsciousness. The house felt emptier and quieter without him in it. Or it did until Darya started pounding on my door.

"This working isn't going to cast itself!" she shouted. "Get up already!"

I fumbled for something to throw at the door. The noise *had* to stop. Now. My fingers scraped along the fore edge of my battered copy of *Emma*. Desperate, I hefted and hurled. It landed with a meek thump a couple of feet away. Defeated, I flopped back into my pillows.

"What was that? Did you throw something at me?" Darya's outrage was clear even through the door.

"Darya was going to barge in at any moment," Anne observed.

"And Bartleby, loath for that to happen, mustered the courage to get up and face the day."

I rolled my eyes, but did as my narration skull suggested just as Darya rattled the knob.

"I'm coming! Wait a sec."

Darya made a rude noise but stopped assaulting my door long enough for me to get dressed.

"Finally!" Darya steered her power wheelchair down the hall as I stepped out of my room. "I thought you were going to sleep all day."

It wasn't even six in the morning. I resisted the urge to make a face, but only because she handed me a steaming mug of coffee.

"Drink it," Darya instructed, backing up until she had enough clearance to turn, "you're going to need it."

"Of course I am. You didn't let me *sleep*." Muttering was a petty indulgence that I wasn't above. If Darya heard me, she ignored the snark.

"You should probably cancel your class. We're going to need the whole day for this working. You're cool with low-key bending student code, right?"

I wasn't *cool* with pretty much anything I'd had to do this term, but I didn't see what choice I had. I followed her into the kitchen.

"What exactly do you have in mind?"

Darya smiled. With the full moon come and gone, all traces of yellow had vanished from her hair. She looked like she had when we'd moved in together, three years ago. Dizzy with the feeling that I was straddling two moments in time, I sank into a kitchen chair.

"We're going to transform ourselves into the world's best detectives," she said. "And we're going to retrace our students' last known steps. Well, Alse's, since we know where they were when the working took hold."

Darya's chicken-scratch spell notes did not bode well for the day ahead. I squinted at them, parsing hectic letters until they made more sense. Radishes. Elderflower. Rose hips. It sounded more like a horrible batch of kombucha than a potation.

"Springwort?"

Darya nodded. "That's what I had to pick up at the greenhouse. It's more commonly known as Saint John's Wort these days."

"Isn't that more for . . . spiritual possession?" As far as I knew, it was used to keep evil spirits at bay. And as a general pick-me-up in the nonmagic community.

"Yes, but it's also been used to disclose things of value that have been concealed. Treasures. Secrets. That kind of thing."

"And the radishes, elderflower, and rose hips?"

Darya shrugged again. "They do more or less the same thing. Like I said, we're transforming ourselves into detectives. Sort of."

I looked back at the spell.

"This says it only takes thirty minutes to steep."

"Mm-hmm." Darya's tone implied that I was being oblivious. "But then we have to go to campus and spend Hecate knows how long retracing steps." She slapped her palms on the table. "Could take all day."

I twitched my lips, unhappy but unable to argue with that logic. My eyes flicked to the bottom of the page.

"Darya?" I didn't try to hide the suspicion in my voice. "Why does this say *serves one?*"

Darya would not meet my eyes.

"It might've been a little misleading to say *we.*" She contemplated a cobweb in the corner above the fridge. "Not all of campus is wheelchair accessible. I'll keep up with you if I can, but think of me as the Watson to your Sherlock."

I scowled. "Really?"

Darya crossed her arms. "Really. Now, let's get moving. The day's wasting."

"YOU HAVE TO DRINK IT ALL," DARYA WARNED, "OR THIS WON'T WORK."

Finding the missing students mattered more than preserving the sanctity of my taste buds, but only barely. Eyes flicking to my lizard calendar for some reptilian commiseration, I brandished my quart-size canning jar with a grimace.

"Abracadabra."

"Bartleby forced herself to get the liquid down," Anne said from my bag. "She told herself it was only kombucha. Brackish, herbal-tasting kombucha."

I willed myself not to dwell on the bitter traces of radish flavor. My office swam around me as I chugged. Every crack and smudge in the room leaped out, like pores on a high-definition TV screen. Colors radiated through me, accompanied by facts about their exact shades and means of production.

I blinked, setting the jar down with a snick.

"If this is what Sherlock felt like all the time, no wonder he did drugs." Leaning into my arms on the desk seemed like the only movement that wouldn't result in dizziness and vomiting.

Darya scoffed.

"Sherlock felt like this all the time *because* he did drugs," she said. "Now, let's go."

She poked me until I stood and slung my bag over my shoulder, then herded me out into the hall. We'd start our search in the place where Alse had vanished. Holographic footprints radiated out of the worn vinyl in the middle of the hallway, staggering into the restroom, in and out of the middle stall, and back out the door.

I walked faster to keep up with them, huffing my way into the elevator and out of the building. Darya kept pace. The sound of her power wheelchair motor whirred behind me.

The trail took us around campus in a hectic zigzag across the grounds: through several buildings; into University Health services, but not farther than the lobby; and in and out of a handful of classrooms, two of which were in use. Darya left me to blunder through those on my own—I was showered in scowls, demands to leave, and a small repelling hex. Freaking Watson.

Instead of slowing, the footprints moved faster and faster, like I was speeding through Alse's day. The faster they went, the less following them felt like a choice.

"Is it supposed to work like this?"

I looked to Darya, who was lagging behind, even with her wheelchair at top speed. She shrugged. "This is the first time I've cast the spell. Cy and I composed it in bits and pieces this week."

If I'd been in control of my own body, I would have stopped right there and had a talk with her. It would've involved a lecture on informed consent. And acceptable flavor profiles. But the footprints tugged me along, pivoting at the last minute up a flight of stairs and stranding Darya behind me.

"Good luck!" she shouted, before I was out of earshot. "I'll catch up with you at home."

Home?

She'd gotten me into this mess with all her talk about contingency plans and going rogue and being detectives, and now she was just going to abandon me to her brand-new working?

The swears I muttered would've made Mags blush.

Still, I couldn't stop. The footsteps wound their way through the Sibyl House grounds, where white narcissus and spidery yellow-orange tulips framed the scrying pond in elaborate bands that transformed the whole landscape into a mirror. Thankfully, the footsteps tugged me quickly onward, across the street, through a soccer field—which was in use: I caught a soccer ball to the rear—and toward the dorms.

I rubbed the welt on my backside without lessening my pace.

"Bartleby had never enjoyed sports," Anne intoned.

Rasputin's hairy balls, this had better be worth the trouble.

The urge to keep walking ebbed as I entered a dormitory. By the time I stood outside room 307, it had vanished altogether. Taped to the door was a picture of two people: one a smudged silhouette that might have been Alse, the other a woman with long black hair, who was throwing up a peace sign. It was like someone had photoshopped one side of the snapshot into murky nothing before printing it. Below the photo, there were two name cards. One, like the person above it, was nearly illegible, as though the ink had gotten wet and run. I made out an *Al* and a *thorne* before calling my effort good enough. It was enough of Alse's name to be reasonably certain I'd found the right place. The other name read *Katrina Luu.*

Whatever else had happened on the day they'd gone missing, I knew two things for sure: Alse hadn't been so under the weather they'd taken immediately to their bed. They'd traipsed all over campus after leaving my office, a trail that had begun to feel frantic at the end. Like they'd been looking for something, or someone. So I doubted they'd actually had the flu. But they *had* made it safely back home. It was, according to Darya's working, the last place they'd been on the last day *anyone* remembered seeing them.

On that unsettling thought, I knocked.

A SERIES OF SHUFFLING SOUNDS ENSUED. CRUMPLING. DRAGGING. HAD there been a chair propped against the door? A chain rattled, and the door creaked open an inch or two. A fuzzy unicorn face appeared through the crack. Beneath it, a baggy-eyed undergrad stared out at me.

"Hello?" She let the single word stand for an entire set of questions. *What do you want? Why are you here? Can't you see I'm not in a good place to talk to another human?*

"Katrina Luu?"

She nodded, wary.

"I'm one of Alse's instructors, and I haven't heard from them in a few weeks." The truth, pared down to its essential core. It did what it was supposed to do.

Katrina's eyes widened. She shot a look over her shoulder and, after a second's hesitation, took a step back and swung the door open with her.

"Come in." Her voice was a harsh whisper. I took a tentative half step and paused.

There was no warning buzz, no sign the place had been warded. That might mean Katrina wasn't a practitioner. Alse had been gone long enough that anything they'd set up would have faded. But it might just mean that Katrina didn't want to risk a talking-to from the RA. The student code didn't outright *ban* wards, but it did discourage the use of them for safety reasons. (The number of unknowing first responders who'd been zapped by student wards in these halls was non-zero, I could guarantee.)

Katrina tugged my arm until I stepped the rest of the way into the room, slamming the door behind me.

Not a good sign.

"Alse hasn't been here for a *while*," she whispered. "I'm beginning to think they might be dead." She looked around, frenzy showing in the widening whites of her eyes. "I think they're haunting me."

I stopped in the middle of the cluttered room, trying not to step on anything.

Alse couldn't be dead. Dead didn't explain the vanishing records. But something was obviously going on. Something like the weirdness at Imani's place, only worse. The dorm room floor was covered with discarded clothes, takeout containers, and an assortment of other belongings. Pictures hung askew on the walls. None of the furniture was where it should be, either. Beds and desks were more akimbo than they were aligned.

An annoyed sigh cut through my scurrying thoughts. The clink and scrape of metal hangers was my only other warning.

"We've been over this," Lora said, stepping out of the clothes closet. I yelped, and they smirked at me before turning back to Katrina. "Alse isn't dead. If they were dead, I'd be able to sense that— especially surrounded by their stuff like this. If nothing else, their closet would be giving off mothball smell and mourning vibes."

"But things are moving with no explanation. There's knocking on the walls at random times. And there are cold spots." Katrina gasped as she spoke. "There! Do you feel that?"

Lora shook her head. "First, you've pissed off your residence ghost—you do remember the whole residence ghost thing, right? You can't have signed the waiver more than a few months ago."

Katrina rolled her eyes.

"Second," Lora added through gritted teeth, "you're in a dorm. People are going to *bang* occasionally. And third, this particular dorm is ancient. I'll bet the HVAC system is older than the three of us combined." They raised a finger for each point, addressing and dismissing Katrina's concerns.

"It's been happening almost as long as Alse has been gone," Katrina insisted, petulant. She hugged herself against the chill with a dramatic shiver. "I've tried smudging and salting the doors and windowsills and—" She broke off, sniffling. "My RA said you could help."

"And Steve is going to owe me big time for that," Lora said. "He *should* have called groundskeeping. They have trained necromancers on staff for this sort of thing." She glanced at me, arching one sculpted brow before turning back to Katrina. "Lucky for you, this is pretty excessive for a residence ghost—even if you were smudging and salting—and I'm intrigued. I'll have a chat with it."

Katrina twisted one of her unicorn-hoof-colored cuffs. "Thanks."

Hands on hips, Lora took a breath, surveying the room. "You have a yoga mat?"

"Why?" The impatience was clear in Katrina's voice.

I intervened before Lora's super cauldron of ire could bubble over. "Just get it, Katrina. For Alse."

Katrina scrounged under her bed and pulled out a molting, neon-orange foam mat, shoving it at Lora. Before either of us could ask, she rushed to sweep detritus out of Lora's path with a series of kicks and shoves that set the stuffed horn on her slightly matted hood flopping violently.

When the mat was unrolled, Lora looked from me to Katrina, stern. "I'm going to need complete silence from you two, okay? Even if I start speaking in a few minutes. Not a peep until I've rolled this mat back up, got it?"

Next to me, Katrina hummed her understanding.

Lora dug in their bag, pulling out an old-school cell phone

with a slide out keyboard. She didn't have the ñatitas with her, or anything that I recognized as the tools of her trade, bones or mortcloth or even a Ouija board. Just the phone, which they held in one hand. Kicking off her shoes and lowering herself into a cross-legged position in the center of the mat, she looked up at us.

"I'm going to do some breathing exercises to put myself in a meditative state. A trance, basically."

I nodded. Out of the corner of my eye, I saw Katrina bob her head.

"This," Lora showed us their phone, "does not have a SIM card. It doesn't receive regular calls or texts." She placed it just in front of her on the mat. "Once I'm in my trance, I'll start sending messages. I may receive some as well. It's important that neither of you look at the screen while the conversation is happening."

As far as workings went, it was simple enough. Object and ritual, working together to trigger death-specific divination. Except, the ward ghosts had been able to communicate directly. I bit my lip against the niggle of doubt. But Lora paused, as if anticipating questions.

Katrina squirmed, face reddening with the strain of staying quiet.

The hint of a smile belied Lora's begrudging sigh. "If you have questions, ask them now. Once I close my eyes, I need complete silence."

Katrina raised her hand. "Um, what happens if, like, we *do* look at the phone. Accidentally?"

Lora, still looking up at us, managed to stare Katrina down. "Best case? Your ghost gets shy."

That was enough to quiet Katrina. The necessary follow-up was left to me.

"What's the worst case?"

Lora grimaced. "Worst case, the ghost decides to communicate through you instead of my phone."

"Why can't they talk to us directly? Like the ward ghosts?"

"The ward ghosts are *wards*," Lora said as if it was the most obvious thing in the world, "not singular hauntings like residence ghosts. They're juiced up by the working that drew them into place, and each individual ghost in the ward is stabilized by the presence of the others. Which means they can manifest more easily. For a solitary ghost, possession's always easier than manifesting— it's basically just haunting in a meatier location."

With that cursed image, Lora closed their eyes and began taking long, deep breaths.

I don't know about Katrina, but I closed my eyes, too. Just in case.

"IS ANYBODY THERE?" LORA ASKED AS SHE BEGAN TEXTING. THEY didn't keep asking their questions out loud, though. The *tap tap tap* of her thumbs on her phone became the loudest thing in the room, louder even than the creak and rattle of the radiator that had just kicked off. I focused on the sound, eyes tight shut.

Katrina coughed, drowning out a few taps. There was no way to parse meaning from the pattern of sounds—Darya's magic kombucha had fully worn off, and I was just me again, not a super-detective. That didn't stop me from being annoyed.

When Katrina coughed again, the sound stretched into a discordant hum, like she was doing vocal warmups before performing a song. Or learning how to use vocal cords again. She'd *peeked*.

Horror swamped me. My eyes flew open on instinct. Katrina's eyes were already wide, but her gaze darted back and forth in a jerky way, like something had taken control but didn't quite remember how eyes worked. There was a sort of half-distracted smirk on her face, and she was still humming, off-key and slow. My hair stood on end.

As I shuffled away, Katrina's humming twisted into a word.

"Of—" She blinked. "Of course. Someone's here." She was looking past me, at Lora. Her voice was higher pitched than it should have been, and the emphasis in her sentences came out all wrong. "My job. To. Be here."

"I told you not to look, kid," Lora muttered. They dropped their phone to the yoga mat and pushed to standing, knees creaking. "Can you tell me what's been going on?"

Katrina's eyes narrowed. "Not. My job," she said in the same too-bright tones.

"Neither is rearranging furniture at all hours and scaring the crap out of your roommates." Lora crossed their arms, lips a thin line.

Katrina took a deeper breath than seemed possible for her tiny frame. "Not me."

Lora's eyebrows collided. "Then *who?*"

"Was it Alse?" Katrina swiveled to look at me, as if she'd never noticed I was there. I could feel Lora staring, too, but I didn't look away from the girl or the ghost possessing her.

"Not. Me. Not. *Ghost.*" Katrina's voice warbled and broke into a reedy wail. "Stop asking, stop asking, stop *asking.*" She jerked from Lora to me and back before crumpling to the floor. Lora lunged to catch her.

What the Hec?

"Help me move her," Lora demanded.

I grabbed Katrina's ankles and we shuffled her to one of the beds.

"Is she still possessed?"

Lora shook their head. "Nope."

The knot of tension between my shoulders eased. "Is she going to be okay?"

Katrina let out a long, wheezing snore as Lora shrugged.

"She probably won't remember much, if that's what you're asking. When she comes to, she might puke a little."

I moved a trash bin next to the bed and jotted a quick note.

Alse isn't dead.

Odds were high they *were* the invisible presence haunting the dorm, but that wasn't the basis of Katrina's worry. Not really.

Lora, peeking over my shoulder, snatched the pen and added her own message.

Apologize to your residence ghost for smudging.
And throw away the fucking sage.

Hopefully, Katrina's problems were over. Lora's séance hadn't done anything for mine. I wasn't in the habit of conversing with residence ghosts, but this reticence seemed awfully convenient. Shouldn't they want to talk to us, so that things could be set right?

"All set?" Lora asked.

I glanced at Katrina one last time before pulling the dorm door closed. "All set."

"Good," Lora said. "'Cause we need to talk. There's some weird shit going on with the campus ghosts, and you're clearly tangled up in it somehow."

CHAPTER TWENTY-FIVE

Nearly halfway through winter term, university administration has yet to address concerns about the safety of Magic students on this campus. With more students reported missing every day, the university's lack of action or comment speaks volumes. President Mathers, we want to know: Do you care at all about the well-being of your students?

—ARTICLE IN *THE PLATYPUS PRATTLER*, 29 JANUARY

T'S JUST ODD," LORA SAID AROUND A MOUTHFUL OF SANDWICH. "Ghosts are usually shameless gossips, when they aren't being assholes."

We were tucked into a sunny corner of Oat & About. I spun my coffee mug around by the handle, considering. "Do you think it seemed, I don't know, worried?" I took a tentative bite of my breakfast burrito.

"Cagey, for sure. I thought I sensed another . . . presence there. Not a ghost, not quite." She snorted. "For all I know it was that creepy unicorn onesie."

"Except we both know that thing wasn't moving the furniture around."

Lora's eyes narrowed. "Right." They stabbed their fork into their home fries. "So, it's probably the roommate, although if that's the case I don't know why the ghost wouldn't just say so."

I swallowed, my spicy chorizo and egg burrito going bland.

"About that . . . Is it possible, magically, to keep ghosts from talking about something?"

Death was a constant. Unchanging. Eternal. A reality unto itself, but one that was inextricably bound to ours. Ghosts were its avatars. They'd signed on to help keep the university safe, but as far as I knew they couldn't be compelled to do more. Or in this case, less.

Lora made a face. "Technically, no. Theoretically, yes." They waved a hand. "You'd have to get really tricky and confuse them. Why do you ask? You haven't been dabbling, have you? After the wards, I'd have thought—"

"No. Not dabbling. Just . . ." I couldn't stop myself from looking around the restaurant like some sort of conspiracy theorist. The booth closest to us was empty, but the nearby tables were all full, and I dropped my voice. "This isn't the first mysterious presence or asshole ghost I've encountered this term." I ran my finger in a lemniscate over the sticky tabletop, letting the infinite figure-eight motion ground me as I recounted the events of the past several weeks. My students' absences. Their vanishing records. Imani's residence ghosts.

"Bartleby wondered," Anne said from my bag, "whether the working that had caused the disappearances might also prevent residence ghosts from revealing—or maybe even recognizing—the students' presence."

If Lora was startled by Anne's sudden pronouncement, they didn't show it. Raising one eyebrow in a dramatic arc, she eyed my bag. "Hey, Anne."

"Anne extended its sincerest greetings to Lora Mamani Flores."

"Seems rude to keep it in the bag," Lora said, turning to me.

Rolling my eyes, I dug Anne out and propped it on the table.

"Anne found Lora's sense of etiquette quite refreshing," it declared.

"Thank you." Lora grinned. "Anyway, what you're describing is implausible, but not impossible. Not with a skilled enough necromancer. And necromantic interference might explain some of the other . . . unusual happenings . . . we've been dealing with."

"Lora referred to the 'weird shit going on with the campus ghosts' they'd mentioned so ominously earlier," Anne said.

Lora snorted. "Yeah. That. There've been a bunch of class-room hauntings. Disruptions in the dorms. That kind of thing."

"Wait, what?" That probably explained the marker incidents in my class. They weren't pranks; they were something worse.

"Yeah. Groundskeeping is so overwhelmed with calls about it that they've been bringing in Necromancy grads to help. Professor Osborne—my advisor—says it'll pass soon. Apparently, the dead get unsettled from time to time. It could be something as small as a change to the way the campus cemetery is maintained. Or they could be sensing an impending catastrophe." Lora took a bite and chewed on it, mulling. "I don't know, though. I've never heard of anything like this. And, whenever I check out an incident, it doesn't seem to be ghosts causing all the chaos."

"You think it could be—" My phone began to ring, and I fished it out of my bag. The caller ID read **Amelia Husik**.

My face must've drained of all color, because Lora leaned forward.

"Bartleby, you okay?"

"Because Bartleby failed to call her advisor this morning, as requested, her advisor had decided to reach out," Anne explained as I sprinted outside.

I answered on the fourth ring. "Hi, Prof—Ah, Amelia," I panted.

"Dorothe," Professor Husik said, voice artificially bright. "I was hoping I'd catch you."

I ran a hand through my hair, unsettled at her tone.

"I'm sorry I didn't call. I . . . had a previous commitment." It was a bad excuse. Amelia overlooked it.

"I'm just happy we could connect. As I mentioned in my email, the dean got in touch after your visit and I wanted to check in with you."

Check in with me? If I was supposed to read between the lines of that statement, I was failing.

"Thank you?"

Amelia sighed. "The dean shared her concern that you may be . . . struggling with time management in the weeks before your exam. She recommended I have a talk with you about priorities and how your academic work must take precedence over *everything*. Which, of course, you've heard me say many times. I'm confident you don't need to hear it again."

I tried to interject, but my advisor seemed determined to get through her odd monologue.

"Personally, I completely understand, and *applaud*, the impulse to ensure that your peers and students are safe. And I *trust* that you know how to manage your time. You've always struck me as *resourceful*."

"Thank you?" I was repeating myself like a confused parrot. In my defense, her emphasis was confusing. Like she was very carefully *not* saying what the dean had advised her to say. Or not *not* saying it, but sort of saying it in a way that left enough wiggle room for me to carry on with what I was doing.

Giving me an out, so that if I *did* keep doing what I was doing, I wouldn't be acting in direct disregard of her instructions.

Did she want me to keep investigating? Or was she stressing the words because of our conversation about accommodations? Telling me that I could power through, without additional support?

I tried to ask, but she cut me off.

"I'll let you get on with your day. Oh, and Dorothe, the direction you took in your revised materials is *fabulous*. I'll be back in touch about that soon. Do take *care*."

She ended the call.

What in Hecate's name was going on?

I slid my phone into my pocket, numb. The world wobbled past me uncertainly, and I wrapped my arms around myself. It was one thing to go rogue on my own account. But getting all but told to keep going by my advisor, after *everything* I was already juggling this term? It was like I'd just been handed something incredibly fragile and told to get it to safety, but, ha ha, small catch, the way to safety was through an obstacle course.

Numbness cascaded into shivers. I spun to head inside and ran straight into a wall of scratchy flannel wool. Someone caught my shoulders, stabilizing me as I teetered from the force of the impact.

"Bartleby?"

My traitorous face turned up, even though I could feel my cheeks turning some ridiculous shade of red.

"James?"

I should apologize for walking into him. He should apologize, too. For ghosting me. But I couldn't hold either of those thoughts in my head, because a windswept lock of hair had fallen into his eyes. It was taking all of my willpower not to brush it away.

James recovered first, blinking and letting go of my shoulders.

The space meant I could breathe enough to take in small details, like the bags under his eyes and the deep wrinkles in his shirt. Whatever he'd been doing since our aleuromancy working, it hadn't included much sleeping.

"Is everything okay?" he asked.

I started to say yes, instinctually, but my smile crumbled away. Everything caught up with me at once. I was in over my head, my advisor was being cryptic, we weren't any closer to figuring out what had caused our students to disappear, and I was almost certainly going to fail my exam if the most renowned prophetic force on campus was to be believed.

My eyes brimmed with tears I refused to let fall.

"Is everything okay with *you*?" I sounded defensive, and I didn't care. "I tried to keep you updated, but you haven't . . . You just . . ." I forced myself to stop, sniffing, hard, to keep the tears at bay. "Your phone was out of service and I was worried."

James's face went pink as his hand slid up to the back of his neck. "I . . . forgot to pay the bill."

"You . . . what?"

"It's not a big deal, I've just been pushing so hard looking for Imani it slipped my mind. But I got it reconnected this morning." He fished his phone out of his pocket and tapped at the screen, a little ding signaling he'd sent a message. My phone buzzed, and when I glanced at it there was a message from James.

Sorry I worried you.

His stomach rumbled. He stuffed his phone back into his pocket. "Anyway, I was nearby and I thought I might as well feed two birds with one scone."

"You're looking for Imani." Of course he was. It was Friday morning—at least for a few more minutes. Under normal circumstances, her dissertation group would be here. He definitely hadn't come looking for me, but I pushed the irrational disappointment of that aside. "The trances aren't working?"

"It's . . . complicated." James shoved his hands into his pants pockets. "I was planning to track you down after breakfast. I'm not sure what to do next."

At that, I smiled. It was a grim thing. A determined thing.

"Maybe we can figure it out together." I hooked my arm through his and dragged him toward the door. "There's a lot I need to fill you in on."

LORA WAS SLIDING HER SANDWICH INTO A TO-GO BOX BY THE TIME I got back to the table.

"I was beginning to think you'd abandoned me," they said. "Don't worry. I left you the check."

I would have laughed if I hadn't been fizzing with so much adrenaline I was about to explode.

"Sorry, my advisor wanted to check in about my visit to the dean, and then I ran into—"

"James." Lora crossed her arms.

"Lora." James's voice went flat.

Well, that was interesting.

"You two already know each other?"

They regarded each other like wary meerkats.

"James was on the Necromancy track when our cohort started," Lora said. "Punked out real fast."

"You switched branches." I hadn't thought it through before. I'd just assumed he'd be a necromancer, then assumed he'd always studied Divination. Switching branches wasn't completely unheard of, but it *was* rare.

James shrugged. "It was more complicated than that, but yes."

"Complicated?" Lora was looking at James like he'd kicked her puppy. "If he'd switched branches just a little bit earlier, he wouldn't have done the working that nearly destroyed my ñatitas. It took me *months* to reassure them they were safe enough to stay."

"I didn't know," James whispered.

"Wait, so you're to necromancy what I am to digimancy?" I couldn't help the interruption.

Lora glared at me. James barked a laugh.

"A hot mess? Pretty much." I decided not to dwell on the way my stomach fluttered when he said *hot*. He glanced at Lora, and his smile died.

"That working nearly took out the Materials Lab," he explained, "and it gave me the excuse to switch branches. My family wouldn't have accepted anything less disastrous."

"Exactly." Lora made the word an accusation.

James shook his head, hurt splashing red across his cheeks. "It wasn't intentional, I swear. I was trying an articulation working, but—"

Lora narrowed her eyes. "You got the constraints wrong." It wasn't a question.

"I forgot to *set* the constraints," James said. "Instead of articulating bones from the same body, it attempted to articulate *every bone* in the lab. Including mine." He shoved up his shirtsleeves and showed us thick bands of scarring. "I don't know who stopped it—"

"I did," Lora whispered. "Not that you deserved it."

The only sign that James heard her was a twitching muscle in his jaw. "The next thing I knew I was in intensive care. My family paid to cover it up out of embarrassment. Or because they thought the obligation would keep me from switching branches. By the time I recovered enough to reach out, you'd blocked my number."

Lora scrunched her mouth side to side, clearly shaken. After a minute, they cleared their throat and turned to me. "Anyway, what I was going to say before you rushed out is that I think your story makes more sense than Osborne's. Which means there's probably a necromancer involved in your delightful conspiracy of mages. We need to talk to a missing student as soon as possible."

"Bartleby, it seemed, was to be the intermediary in the conversation," Anne explained, "preventing the unpleasant necessity of Lora acknowledging James's continued presence."

Lora shot it a look.

"That's going to be tricky," James said, and for a second I wasn't sure whether he meant talking to a missing student or ignoring his presence. Hecate knew *I* would struggle to ignore his presence. "Because I did learn *something* during my trances. The students are moving around. And I think I know why, at least in Imani's case. She'd stick to her routine. Attend classes, show up for her group meeting. Not just so she'd be on track when all of this blows over, but to combat the effects of being between realities for so long."

"That theory was what had brought James to Oat & About for breakfast," Anne said. "However, there were no invisible presences to be found in the restaurant."

Lora made a face, then closed their eyes, spinning the rings on their thumbs in a meditative way. She took a series of deep breaths, then opened her eyes.

"I think Anne's right."

"Where would Imani go next?" I asked, turning to James. "Home, to feed Corelli, right?"

He nodded.

"Great," Lora said, slapping the table. "Let's go. We'll need to stop by the Materials Lab for supplies on the way."

WHILE LORA VENTURED INTO THE BONE HOUSE FOR SUPPLIES, JAMES and I waited in the car. Rain pattered gently on the hood and windshield, and for a few seconds I watched students rush back and forth, some under umbrellas but most braving the elements—as was the Oregon way.

James tapped his fingers on the steering wheel. "I feel like I'm missing a few pieces. Did I hear right that you went to visit the dean?"

"Bartleby took the opportunity to fill James in," Anne said, "on the momentous events of the past several days." I rolled my eyes, but did as it suggested.

"After our aleuromancy, I didn't really make any progress until I met with my advisor . . ." I explained my revelation about accommodations, sharing details about Professor Delight's phone conversation without expressing my nascent suspicions.

James nodded. "That makes sense, actually. Imani mentioned she was pursuing an ADHD diagnosis last term."

"But that, with what we already knew about the records, pointed to faculty or administrator involvement. So, we went to the dean."

"And how did that go?"

"The appointment was a catastrophe," Anne said. "Dean Underhill took the visit badly, reaching out to Bartleby's advisor and the director of graduate studies. And afterward, Bartleby blundered into a portent."

"Wait, what?" James pivoted, craning to stare at Anne in the backseat. When it didn't deign to reply, he turned to me. "What happened?"

I told him about the visit. Dean Underhill's compliance working. Amelia's cryptic email. I wasn't ready to start pointing fingers in her direction, especially not after her call, but the whole exchange had left me even more anxious than before. If she wanted me to investigate, did that mean she was worried about the disappearances, or was she setting me up to fail?

James listened quietly, a furrow forming between his eyebrows.

"That sounds rough. And you haven't even gotten to the part where you *stumbled into a portent*," he said when I finished.

I didn't want to tell him about the mascarons; it felt too big and too ridiculous to talk about. But before I could help myself it was all tumbling out. The horrible things they'd said. The terrifyingly cryptic threat of their parting shot. I'd been too unnerved to memorize their words in the moment, but Anne had captured their whispers in its logs, and rereading them had seared them into my memory.

"And Cy says their prophecies somehow apply to the whole university." I frowned, staring at a splotch of grease on my jeans. "It didn't feel like that, though. It felt personal."

James's expression was neutral, but his eyes had gone tight. "Cy's not wrong," his tone went cautious, "but, you know the mascarons aren't infallible, right? They aren't even carved out of stone from some ancient oracle site, despite the lore. The stone is from a quarry in St. Helens. The busts were commissioned as a prank by the Divination senior class of 1982, modeled on professors who were teaching in the program at the time. All they were ever meant to do was parody those professors, and just for a few weeks before graduation. But something about the working went wrong. The school ran with it, because as a haywire working it's quite useful. It predicts major upheaval accurately more often than it doesn't. But it's still just an overhyped accident."

It was difficult to think of the mascarons as some failed prank. They'd known exactly what to say to warn me off. And if they were right more often than they were wrong, I'd be a fool not to heed them.

"Maybe I should listen. It's not like I'm getting anywhere with this. And if we're right and there's a necromancer involved, too . . ."

"Then we'll have to set the dead straight," Lora said, startling both of us as they slid onto the backseat, "and kick the rogue necromancer's ass into the next reality."

They slammed the door.

"Well, what are we waiting for?"

CHAPTER TWENTY-SIX

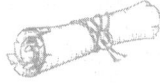

Here and not here, gone but not gone. Unable to return but not yet departed. Moving with the flap of moths' wings, half shadow and ebbing—ebbing—ebbing in the dark.

—GLITCH IN ANNE'S LOGS, 26 JANUARY

OUTSIDE IMANI'S PLACE, THE PYRAMID OF CHEERLEADING GNOMES had been moved into a single line formation, flanked by the flamingos, which had been given Mardi Gras necklaces a month too early.

James knocked. I glanced from him to Lora and back at the door, shoulders inching up toward my ears. The tension between them had built to nearly bursting on the car ride over, until it felt like one wrong move would detonate the entire situation. Lora kept shooting sad looks James's way whenever he wasn't looking. And he *wasn't* looking at her with enough intensity that I was beginning to feel like a third wheel. A fact that Anne was probably narrating gleefully from the floorboards of James's car, where I'd left it at Lora's insistence. They didn't want it to interfere with our séance.

I took a breath, drawing my shoulders back down as James knocked again.

Maybe I was misreading his intensity, and he was just focused on the fact that he might get to speak to Imani in a matter of minutes. Maybe the prospect of reuniting with his best friend had him thinking about making her *more* than a friend. Or maybe he didn't have a thing for Imani at all. Maybe he had a preexisting, starscrossed thing for Lora.

I shouldn't care. Hecate knew we could use all the help we could get. And there was no version of reality in which he could possibly have a thing for me.

Blessedly, couch guy answered the door after James's third round of knocking, preventing me from digging too much deeper in that particular area of poorly repressed thoughts.

"Hey, do I know you guys from somewhere?" he asked, tossing his matted hair over his shoulder. He was barefoot and shirtless but seemed less high today.

"Kind of," James said. "We stopped by the other day looking for Imani?"

Couch guy squinted at James and me. "Name's Zach."

"I'm James, and this is Bartleby and Lora." James gestured at us by turn. "We're here because you mentioned that your place has a new ghost."

Zach bobbed his head enthusiastically. "Oh yeah, dude. Place was already big time haunted—the ghosts are kind of important, I guess. I was told to leave them alone, but this new one is super active." He paused, frowning. "But like, we don't want to exorcise it or anything . . ."

He looked like he was seriously considering slamming the door in our faces.

"Neither do we," I cut in. "We just want to chat. If the ghost is willing to talk."

He shrugged and led us into the living room. Sinking into what I assumed was his customary place on the couch, he reached for a bong. "Anyone need a hit?" He flicked a lighter at the bottom of the thing and took a long one himself instead of waiting for us to reply. Wisps of smoke seeped out around his mouth.

We were going to get contact high no matter what, but I shook my head. So did James. Lora, on the other hand, stepped toward him.

"Yeah, man. Thanks."

There was a lot of smoke left in the bong, so Lora took a long rip and turned to face us. As they slowly exhaled, they extended the bong toward me. "Okay. So, we're gonna take a slightly different approach this time."

I made a face, not at all liking where this seemed to be heading. "But we stopped for supplies. I thought you had a plan."

"I do. And I just updated it. I'm going to need the both of you to get very, very high," they clarified.

James coughed, nervously, beside me. "How is that going to help, exactly?"

"What he said." I didn't tend to handle THC well, historically. Last time I'd tried, it had felt like someone handed my anxiety an ant farm, which my anxiety had promptly dropped. Spending the rest of my Friday feeling like ants were crawling all over me wasn't exactly appealing, even in the name of helping my students.

"It's going to make us all more open, which means I can use you to channel any spirits that might be hanging around," Lora explained. "And, before you ask," she pinned me in place with her gaze, "it has to be *everyone*, or it's not gonna work."

I moaned. "Why can't you just do the trance and texting thing again?"

Lora grinned at me.

"Because this is more fun. And also, dude's right. There's *definitely* more than one ghost here. That tends to make texting tricky."

That sounded fake. "You said being used to channel was the worst-case scenario."

They tossed their hair, dismissive. "That was when an *undergrad* was involved. At that age, most people don't have a strong enough grip on their own identity to safely channel."

I made a face, but I didn't argue. Feeling like an imposter most of the time didn't mean I didn't have a strong sense of identity. Probably.

"When too many ghosts try to communicate at the same time,

the messages get garbled," Lora insisted. "It's too much for one phone and pair of thumbs to handle."

I swore and reached for the bong. "Fine. Let's just get this over with."

WE WERE FLOATING ON CLOUDS AND MY HANDS WERE TOO BIG AND there was a telltale tickle under my collar and at the cuffs of my pants that told me the ants would be crawling all over me any minute now.

I swallowed a giggle and looked around at James, Lora, and Zach. We were all sitting in a circle on the battered living room rug. The coffee table had been shoved to the far side of the room, and there was enough cat hair smashed into the carpet underneath to make a second cat.

I traced the whirling patterns with my fingertips.

"Bartleby."

It felt at once dusty and achingly soft on my skin. I wanted to rest my cheek against it.

"Bartleby?" I vaguely registered Lora's voice. But they seemed faraway and unimportant. The whirling pattern of fur reminded me of something. I leaned toward it, eyes widening. It was the precise shape of that long wisp of hair that always tumbled into James's eyes.

I sat up and craned around to look at James. His eyes were barely open, but he smiled sleepily at me. I reached out and brushed my fingertips across his forehead.

"So soft," I whispered.

"Bar. Tle. By." Lora made every syllable of my name a demand.

I blinked rapidly, swiveling to face her.

"What?"

"We have a séance to do. And I need you all to hold hands and stay quiet. Can you manage that?"

I repeated the words to myself several times to make sure I had the sense of them before nodding. My head tried to float away with the movement, so I squeezed my eyes closed and held out my hands to James and Zach.

Lora started talking again, but I could tell by the tone they weren't talking to me, and it was all I could do to keep still. The ants had arrived, scampering up and down my arms. I didn't hear what she said. I didn't notice much of anything that went on, until the ants disappeared. The room went cold. And everything faded to an endless gray fog.

Something resonated deep in my chest, vibrating outward and outward and outward until—

I VOMITED ON THE CARPET, GASPING AND SCRATCHING AT MY OWN BODY as if it were a strangling outfit I could tear off. Lora put one hand on my shoulder and handed me a bottled water.

"It took you a while to resurface. I was beginning to worry."

Sipping the water, I glared at her. "It's already done, then?" My voice came out raspy, like someone else had been using it and not in a particularly careful way.

"If you can call more than an hour wrangling with ghosts *already*, then yes." Lora turned as James stepped up beside them. There were four jagged scrapes along her cheek.

"Are you okay?" James asked. He was looking at me, that lock of hair glancing down into his eyes. I wanted to curl up and die, right there next to my vomit. But I nodded.

"Any luck?" It was the only question I could manage, despite the swell of them in the back of my throat. Was Imani *here*? Had they been able to speak with her? Were James and Imani . . .

James grimaced. "Sort of. Lora was able to confirm the new haunting is Imani, but the ghosts wouldn't let her get through."

As I looked around, it hit me that that must've been an understatement. The living room had been torn apart. There were slashes in the couch cushions. The coffee table sagged on one end, the legs kicked out from under it. A couple of pictures had fallen, and the shattered glass from their frames covered the TV stand.

"Did the residence ghosts do all of this?"

James met my panicked question with an affirmative jut of the chin.

"Did we learn anything else? About the working or who's behind it?" My rasp made the question harsher than I intended, but I was too worn out and worried to care.

Lora cracked her knuckles. "The ghosts didn't talk, if that's what you mean. I hoped it was just that dorm ghost being a pendejo, but no such luck." There were more scrapes up and down their arms, and blood beaded up in spots along them.

"It looks like they were too busy to talk."

Lora crossed her arms. "They took exception to my questions. Especially when I tried to speak with Imani." They said it like it happened all the time. But if it happened all the time, I would have heard about it. Residence ghosts didn't beat people up. They weren't wards. And Lora hadn't been doing anything wrong. They were a necromancer for Hecate's sake. It was practically her *job* to talk to ghosts.

"What does that mean?"

James held out a hand and I took it, swallowing about a hundred more anxious questions as I hauled myself upright.

Lora huffed. "It means there's *definitely* a necromancer tangled up in this business."

Dizziness spiked into my skull. I pinched the bridge of my nose. "This just gets worse and worse."

"We've confirmed the missing students can move around, at least," James said. "Now we know where to find them. There has to be some way to keep the university's ghosts at bay so we can talk to them."

"Theoretically," Lora said. "But it's going to be tricky to pull off without getting us expelled. I'll have to talk to the ñatitas."

"Won't you just run into the same problem with them?"

"No. They aren't university affiliated." Behind them, Zach made a sound somewhere between a moan and a scream. Lora glanced toward him. "I think I'm going to have to do a little bit of exorcising. He still hasn't resurfaced."

I grimaced. Getting sucked back into my body after being formless for an hour wasn't a pleasant experience, and I doubted adding exorcism to the mix would improve it. Everything felt too heavy, too bright, too pungent. I was fighting the urge to vomit again. But I was also *starving*.

My stomach rumbled to underscore the point.

"Why am I so hungry?"

James edged closer to me. "It's the munchies." There was a twinkle in his eye like he was amused by the whole situation. "You don't smoke often, do you?" he asked.

"Almost never. It's not relaxing." I crossed my arms, too tired to pretend not to be defensive. I could see them there, dancing on the tip of his tongue: the words to make fun of me for touching his hair.

He just smiled, that twinkle brightening, until I was compelled to smile back. Then he nudged me with his shoulder, gently.

"We'll figure this out."

I wanted to believe him, but we were up against a digimancer and a necromancer who were in possession of serious skills *and* resources. The words of the mascarons echoed in my head. *Failure. Ruin. Destruction. Upheaval. Run. Run. Run . . .*

WHEN ZACH HAD BEEN MINORLY EXORCISED—"IT'S REALLY A VERY, VERY small exorcism," Lora grunted, smearing rosemary, sage, and juniper paste all over Zach's chest. "Barely counts at all."—we headed out into the slanting midafternoon light.

"Bartleby, James, and Lora were disheartened by the outcome of their séance," Anne declared as soon as we'd settled into the car. "'Their anxiety had foundation in fact; their fears in probability,'" it added, quoting *Northanger Abbey*.

None of us had the heart to respond. We rode in silence until James pulled up outside the Bone House. Lora levered open the back door and slammed it shut behind themself, grimly.

I leaned out my window. "Thanks, Lora."

"I'll text you when I know more." She waved as we pulled back into traffic.

At the stoplight, James glanced over. "What now?"

I'd been dreading the question, with the mascarons' eerie words still circling through my head. Out the window, campus bustled with life. From this distance, everything looked normal. I wrapped my hands around the seat belt, tugging it away from my chest as if it was responsible for the zip-tie crush of my lungs. Lora might have clear next steps, but I was at a loss. Everything I'd tried led to more questions.

"I don't know."

"So, lunch then?" James asked after a minute. His words were casual, but the question felt like a warding, laid but not yet cast. If I stepped the wrong way, it would activate. The only problem was I couldn't be sure *what* it was warding, or why.

I paused, breathed.

"You don't have to feed me, James. I'm sure you have better things to do."

He thought about that while we drove. Coming to some sort of conclusion, he pulled into street parking and shut the car off.

"Bartleby . . ."

He turned toward me, and I couldn't quite make myself make eye contact. He was going to say, *I have a girlfriend. Or you're cute, but . . .* Or *we're teaming up to find the missing students, that's it. We're not friends. We barely know each other.* And whatever he said, it would be true. It would be fair, even. But I didn't want to hear it.

"Dorothe," he tried again. I forced myself to look up, toward his face if not into his eyes. "I would like to take you out to lunch."

It was an effort to keep breathing despite confusion so entire it made my chest ache.

"Not a date," he said. "Not *yet*. Because it would be a terrible day for a date." He reached out and brushed my bangs out of my face, gently, and his eyes found mine. "But I want to be very clear. If it wasn't a terrible day for a date, and you were interested—"

"I would be interested," I interrupted. "If it wasn't such a terrible day for a—" I didn't get to finish that thought, because he leaned forward, then, and kissed me. His fingers slipped into my hair, flirted with the strands. When he pulled away—after long enough that I'd lost all track of time but still, somehow, too soon—he grinned.

"Your hair is so soft."

I punched him in the arm. And then I kissed him back.

WE HIT UP A DRIVE-THROUGH ON THE WAY BACK TO MY APARTMENT, both of us too tired for anything more. After demolishing our food, we fell into awkward silence. The magic of our kiss had faded, replaced by self-consciousness and worry over the growing scope of our investigation.

"The problem obtruded itself upon Bartleby and James in such a way that it was impossible to ignore," Anne said. I was fairly sure it was quoting *The Memoirs of Sherlock Holmes.*

James's knuckles tightened on the steering wheel. His *friend* had been swallowed up by this impossible working. Not just a student he'd known for a few days, but someone he cared about. He had to be struggling.

Knowing what to say when people needed words to wrap around themselves against worry or pain or hurt was a kind of magic I'd never learned. Most of the time, it felt wiser not to try. Especially because the words that failed as workings succeeded as weapons. They didn't make things better or shield their recipients from their cares. They just *hurt.*

I couldn't not try, now.

"You two are close, huh?" I managed.

"I wouldn't have made it this far without her," James said.

"We started the program at the same time. And after about a year of courses I was panicking and considering dropping out."

"Really?" Someone with *his* connections?

"Really." He took the left onto my street. "I'm a legacy and this stuff is supposed to be easier for me. And, in a lot of ways, it is. But—and I realize this is a champagne problem—I was trapped in the exact same path every mage in my family had taken before me, not a person so much as a cog in the machine of heritage. I was becoming my father and his father and his father before him. And I was breaking under the pressure." James parked in my driveway and squinted up into the trees. "Imani talked me down. Told me I could find my own path, even here. She helped me switch branches after the lab incident."

"Wow."

It was all I could manage. James didn't seem to notice.

"We were friendly before that, but we've been friends ever since."

I reached for his hand. "Look. It's going to be okay. And if it isn't, we'll find a way to make it okay. All right?"

James lifted the corner of his mouth in the imitation of a smile. I was repeating his earlier words back to him, and we both knew they might not be true.

This was a major working. It hadn't fallen at the full moon, which meant it had been grounded. The ghosts weren't willing to talk about it, and they weren't taking it down, which told us that there was a necromancer involved. And we knew someone familiar with digimancy and able to access institutional records had to have shaped the working. James had been putting himself in trances for ten days with minimal results. This wasn't something our training had prepared us for.

But our training had prepared us for so very little of what we were expected to do, day to day. We got thrown into teaching after a single workshop on pedagogy and grading best practices. We were expected to know a million little political and cultural things to navigate our branches and the mages who taught in them. Even choosing *what* to study was largely a process most of us stumbled through haphazardly, if we didn't have family or connections guiding our choices. Apparently, sometimes even then.

I straightened my shoulders, putting more force into my words. "We're going to make this okay." An idea was taking shape in the murky matter of my anxiety. We'd tried to divine information about the missing students, without much success. But what about the people responsible? What if we scried *them*? "In fact, we're going to figure out who's responsible for this whole mess. Are you in?"

He groaned, dragging his hands down the sides of his face. "Of course. But what are we going to do? I'm running on fumes. I think I'm tapped out on workings for a while."

I chewed on my lower lip, anticipation and anxiety sparking in my gut. If we needed to know the unknowable, there was at least one option we hadn't explored. Prophecy had been stalking me all term, reminding me of my impending failure. Maybe it was time the tables turned. According to Cy, I couldn't just stroll up and chat with the mascarons, but there was at least one other intimidating font of frightening foretellings on this campus. I'd stumbled into her corner of the library once already this term.

And unlike James, she didn't need trances or scrying or any other divination method to access the unknowable. It just found her, drawn like pencil shavings to a magnet, whether she liked it or not. Oracles were more forces of nature than they were practitioners.

"I think I know someone who can help."

CHAPTER TWENTY-SEVEN

"I don't control the future, dude, I just write shit down."
—THE CURRENT CAMPUS ORACLE,
OVERHEARD IN THE LIBRARY STACKS

THE ORACLE'S SMILE SENT CHILLS UP MY SPINE.

In another life, or another version of reality, she could have been an Amazon or maybe a Valkyrie. In this one, she was a basketball player who wore her hair in two long braids and spent all her free time writing down possible futures and taking naps in the library.

"Bartleby! I wondered when you'd stop by."

And she knew my name. That wasn't terrifying at all. I swallowed, threading my fingers together in my lap.

"I guess I finally made it." Her stare was unnervingly sharp. "So, how does this work?"

"Oh, it's easy. I hand you notes, and you read them." She stood, stretching before she walked over to the bulletin boards in the corner. She snatched a few sticky notes at random, turned to eye me, and grabbed a few more. "They'll be sequential," she said, handing them to me in a messy stack, "or they won't."

The Oracle shrugged and sank back to her seat on one of the orange couches. I waited for more instructions, but she fished her phone out of her hoodie pocket and proceeded to scroll.

"Okay." I breathed, taking a moment to brace myself before looking at the collection of notes in my hands.

The ones I could see, stuck to the top of the haphazard stack, were completely covered in cramped block letters. On some, the text spiraled from the outside edges to the center. On others, it appeared in neat lines.

Familiar words jumped out.

Fading. Absent. Unseen. Failing. Disaster. Imposter.

"Anything?" James asked.

I shook my head, disappointment clamping my jaw tight. It seemed to be a mix of Anne's glitches and the mascarons' portent, with unsettling echoes of my childhood prophecy. Nothing new. Nothing *helpful.* I stuck the notes to the arm of the couch and squinted at the tiny lettering on the next handful. More of the same. I stuck them on top of the others, impatient. Note after note after note, more prophetic gibberish and glitches. And the stack had dwindled down to almost nothing.

I let out a frustrated growl.

It was enough to pull the Oracle's attention from her phone. She sucked her teeth, hands and phone shoved into her hoodie pocket so she could stare me down properly.

"The trick," she drew the words out, "is that the text isn't set. *You* bring the energy. *You* determine the outcome." Her emphasis very clearly spelled out the subtext: *it's not my fault if you're too uptight for this.*

James put a hand on my knee. "Take a minute to breathe and focus on what you need." He reached across me to scoop up the discarded notes. Reluctantly, I let him put them back into my hands. Frustration welled and I shut my eyes, forcing myself to take a deep breath as I focused on what I needed to know: *Who worked the spell that made the students disappear? Who was responsible?*

"Lay them out," the Oracle suggested with the bored tone of a teenager at work. Which, I supposed, she was. "Don't pay attention to what they say until they're all out in a row."

The coffee table in front of us was covered with magazines. I stuck notes to them quickly, twelve in a row, covering up the faces of celebrities and famous mages. When I sat back, the writing on the notes was the same as it had been. I turned to the Oracle, who rolled her eyes.

"Watch," she insisted. "But like, don't *watch* watch."

Facing the notes again, I allowed my vision to unfocus. Between one blink and the next, the spirals and lines squiggled into new formations. The same words, repurposed to fill in the shapes of large letters:

THEY ARE CLOSE

"Bartleby was not entirely sure what the sticky notes meant," Anne said from my bag.

In my periphery, the Oracle stiffened, head tipping to the side in curiosity. She didn't speak. I kept my eyes on the notes, insistently focused on what I needed them to tell me. *Who was involved, even a little, with the working? Who will lead us to the answers we need?* My eyes went blurry. I wiped away involuntary tears. When I could see again, the message had changed.

SO CLOSE TO YOU

Chills raced up and down my spine. Did that mean my suspicions were justified, and Amelia really did have something to do with all this? Or could it be Professor Delight after all, with his smug certainty that Imani wouldn't be returning?

I stared so hard at the notes, willing them to change, that the muscle in my right eyelid began to twitch. Slowly, the letters resolved into new form.

FAILING SOON!

The large letters didn't stay in that formation long, though. They quickly resolved back into the notes' original scrawl. Message complete, apparently. But what did it all add up to?

There weren't that many people close to me. A handful of faculty, my housemates, a few friends, my students if I stretched the definition of *close*. I wanted to believe the people I'd managed to connect with in this program weren't the sort to secretly plot and enact magical conspiracies. But according to the Oracle's horrible sticky notes, some of them were.

Maybe . . . Maybe the notes were pointing me toward someone I hadn't considered at all. Someone so close, I'd trusted her implicitly. Someone who didn't have magic, but had connections and know-how.

She'd been urging me to stay out of this all term. Explaining things away. Accusing me of procrastinating. She'd even conveniently gotten rid of Alse's backpack right when I needed it.

But it couldn't be Mags. It couldn't be.

Not Mags not Mags not Mags.

My thoughts looped in echoing dread. I clasped my hands together in an effort to steady myself. Did the final message mean *the conspirators* were going to fail, or was it a repeat of the same old prophecy I'd been living with for decades, predicting *my* failure because of magic computers?

I was so busy trying to puzzle that out, I didn't notice the waft of smoke. James shouted and dragged me away as sticky notes caught fire. The magazines beneath them smoked and curled, succumbing quickly. It took less than a second for the entire coffee table to go up like a signal fire.

The building's sprinklers hummed for just a second before they let loose.

"Someone did not want Bartleby to know even such ambiguous details," Anne declared as James snatched my bag off the couch and hauled it away from the already sputtering fire.

"Zip it, skull." The Oracle stared straight at my bag even though Anne was fully hidden inside it. The fetid sprinkler water had made her mascara run, and she looked more Valkyrie-like than ever. "This is my territory." She looked at me, repeating the gist of Anne's comment. "Someone doesn't want you to ask questions."

We watched the water douse the flames. The magazines that had survived the fire began to warp, and their ink ran into little puddles on the battered coffee table, swirling into shapes that looked suspiciously like letters.

I surged forward and knocked the table on its side before they could cluster into words. I couldn't take any more prophecy today. What was I supposed to *do* with any of it? Turn into a paranoid mess, scrutinizing everyone around me? Why couldn't the notes have just given me a starsdamned name?

"Fury built rapidly in Bartleby's chest, and she clamped her jaw tight against the urge to scream," Anne said. For once, I didn't care that it was exposing my innermost thoughts. Anyone looking at me could probably already tell I was pissed.

"Obviously," the Oracle said. "Happy people don't knock over innocent coffee tables." She arched a gossamer eyebrow at me. "Maybe go touch some grass."

"I came here for answers." I clenched my hands into fists. "I. Need. Answers."

The Oracle laughed. It started out normal enough, the mocking sound of a teen witnessing an adult meltdown. But it stretched out, eerie and dissonant. I took an instinctive step back.

"I think we're done here," James said. He put his hands gently on my shoulders, and I let him guide me away from the terrible corner and the terrible Oracle and her starsdamned terrible sticky notes.

I took deep breaths as we walked through the stacks toward the elevator, willing myself to calm down.

"That wasn't great, was it?"

"The part where you almost punched out the Oracle?" James jabbed the call button. "Not your best moment. But understandable. I'd be punchy, too, if everyone I was close to just came into question."

I shook my head. "Not everyone." A look of relief crossed James's face, and I realized he must think I meant him. "Not Darya and Cy, I mean." Darya would never use accommodation letters as a way to make students vanish. And Cy was too much of a hedonist for villainous conspiracies. Plus, he was out of town and thus not technically close. I grimaced, apologetic. "For what it's worth, I don't think it's you, either."

The elevator door opened with a ding, and we crowded in. Staring at his back, I couldn't help thinking that if he *was* involved, he was diabolical. Someone who could sit there all calm and supportive while blocking the Oracle's prophecy was . . . terrifying.

"Who *do* you think it is?" he asked. "Based on what just happened, there's got to be a diviner blocking us from seeing the details of this working more clearly. So, that's three conspirators, potentially."

"Upon making the suggestion, James reflected that the digimancer could be the diviner—since experts in that accursed methodology tended to be specialists in either divination or alchemy," Anne said.

I ignored it.

"Professor Huang, on my committee, is a diviner," I said. "But they've been away all term, doing archival research."

"I know. They're my advisor. For what it's worth, I doubt they're involved."

"Why?" I doubted it, too, but the Oracle's sticky notes had unmoored me. If some of the people involved in the working were close to me, I wasn't sure I could trust my own judgment.

"When I switched branches and Rue agreed to be my advisor, they had conditions. A whole lecture full of them, really. But one of them was that I needed to use my privilege in the program to include people, 'especially the ones the academy does its best to keep silent and make invisible,' they said. Otherwise, they didn't want to spend their time mentoring another well-to-do white boy." James grinned at the memory.

I couldn't help feeling a little bit envious: I'd trusted Amelia that much, once. It was hard to imagine now.

The elevator dinged and the doors slid open. We made our way toward the lobby.

"So, not Professor Huang. And the only necromancer I know is Lora." I paused, considering. They'd tried to help as soon as I told them what was going on. She'd even taken damage from Imani's residence ghosts while trying to help. Unless that had been a ruse. "You don't think . . ."

"Lora?" James barked a laugh. "They wouldn't hurt a fly. Me? Maybe. But I did something to deserve it."

I relaxed a little. James had known Lora long enough to make the call, and it fit with what little I knew about her.

"But didn't they mention their advisor explaining all the ghost business away?" James asked, hauling open the building's door and gesturing me through.

"Yeah." I waited on the sidewalk outside until he caught up. Lora's advisor's response was definitely suspicious, but he couldn't be who the Oracle meant. "Their advisor isn't close to me, though."

James shrugged. "Anyone else leap to mind?"

We headed down the sidewalk toward James's car, quiet except for the slap of our footsteps against damp concrete.

"Professor Delight seemed certain Imani wouldn't be coming back to class." I chewed my bottom lip. "But he's in Alchemy, not Divination."

"That doesn't necessarily rule him out."

"He also thought Imani had dropped, though."

"He could have said that to make himself seem innocent." I'd had the same thought, earlier in the week, but it wasn't much to go on.

I crossed my arms, gaze on the sidewalk. Little spatters of rain kept darkening the pale concrete, then fading quickly away.

"Bartleby didn't wish to unfairly impugn her officemate or advisor," Anne said. Its voice was quiet, but James still had my bag slung over his shoulder so there was no way he didn't hear. "Yet, they were the only other people in her circle she had any real grounds to suspect."

James glanced my way, obviously curious.

I explained how I'd asked Amelia about accommodations and been shut down, not meeting James's eyes.

"That does seem off, but she wasn't lying about how long the process takes."

I sighed. "I know."

"And what did Anne mean about your officemate?" James asked. We'd reached his car, but instead of going to the door, he sat on the hood and patted the spot next to him. It was rain-damp, but I sat, telling him about Mags's behavior this term while we both stared at the library.

"I don't know what her motive would be, though. I don't think she resents practitioners or anything."

James hummed.

"If Mags is involved—and that's an *enormous* if—she's obviously not responsible for the actual working." I didn't want to think about the possibility any more than I had to. "I think we need to focus on our other suspects. Which means it's between my advisor and Professor Delight . . ."

"Delight's the likelier choice." James followed my line of thought. "With his digimancy background and his attitude about accommodations."

"Right." I nodded, the motion more decisive than I felt. "But we need proof."

"And how do you propose we get it?"

Adrenaline sparked through me, setting all my nerves ablaze.

"We set a trap," I said. "And we spring it in class next week." I stood, walked around to the passenger-side door, and hauled it open. "Are you coming or what?"

James looked so completely baffled, I couldn't help grinning. Still, he followed my lead, taking his seat at the wheel before he asked where we were headed.

"My place. We need to fill Darya in on everything . . . and ask if we can copy her last accommodation letter." The template was different for graduate students.

"You want to make a fake." James started the engine, sparing a glance my way. It wasn't a question, and given the determined slant of his brow, he'd already figured out the rest of my plan.

"If she submitted it on Monday, Bartleby hoped Professor Delight would be fooled into believing she should be missing on Wednesday." Anne, as usual, made no bones about adding its two cents. "When she showed up after all, he would be startled into slipping up."

James groaned. "I thought so."

"Tell me it's a bad plan." I crossed my arms, scowling at him. Infuriatingly, he kept his eyes on the road.

"It's not a bad plan. It just needs to be . . . refined."

"By *refined*, James meant to imply that Bartleby should not be the one who submitted the falsified accommodation letter."

"Yes, Anne. I got that from context, thank you."

"We don't know how the trigger for the cloaking was set up—a fake letter might set it off just like the real ones did," James explained, turning onto my street.

"So *you* should be the one to disappear. Is that what you're saying?" It was ridiculous. A misguided, entirely unnecessary bit of chivalry. My feelings sharpened the pitch of my words. "It was my idea, and it should be my risk to take."

James parked the car, killed the engine and turned to face me, infuriatingly calm. "The Oracle said whoever's behind this is close to *you*, Bartleby. Your working is glitching when students disappear. If anyone is going to solve this, you will. So, yeah, I'd rather be the one to disappear, because I have no doubt that you'll find me if I do."

I didn't know what to say to that, so I didn't bother responding at all. Instead, I undid my seat belt and climbed out of the car.

"Bartleby knew James's logic was solid," Anne said as I collected it from the backseat. "More than that, she knew Darya would agree with him. Nevertheless, she had resolved to do this herself."

CHAPTER TWENTY-EIGHT

Anne was with Bartleby all that weekend, endeavoring
to support her spirits and while away the many tedious
hours before the delivery of the letter; a needful exertion,
for as the time of reasonable expectation drew near,
Bartleby . . . had worked herself into a state of real
distress.

—NARRATORIAL COMMENTARY ADAPTED FROM
JANE AUSTEN'S *NORTHANGER ABBEY* BY ANNE

I SHOWED UP EARLY TO CLASS ON MONDAY, PAINFULLY AWARE OF THE
fake accommodation letter in my bag and the absence of Anne's
familiar weight. After agonizing over it that morning, I'd left
Anne on my dresser. I didn't want it to pipe up and give me away.

The classroom was mostly empty of students, although James
had already taken his usual seat. The sight of him caused a jabbing
sensation behind my temples. But he shot me a thumbs-up. He
was respecting my decision.

I breathed, willing away the small, scared part of me that
wished James could be the one to set the trap for Professor Delight. But this was my idea and my responsibility. If the professor
was behind this and decided to make me disappear along with the
other students, James would be able to keep investigating.

I took a step closer, clearing my throat. "Hi, Professor, can I
have a word?"

"Hmm?" He looked up from his notes, reading glasses poised halfway down his nose. "Oh, Ms. Bartleby. Just the person I wanted to see."

His tone was pleasant. Friendly, even. Uncertainty unsteadied me. What if he wasn't involved? What if I was wrong?

"I had a word with Amelia and Ursula about your work last week," the professor said. He set his notebook down and took off his glasses, tapping them into his suit-coat pocket. A high-pitched ringing filled my ears. "It's all sorted now," he elaborated. "Ursula's stepped aside and I'll be joining your committee . . ."

"You will?" I braced myself against the table. Uncertainty oozed away, replaced by an icy tension that made it difficult to breathe. My vision grayed and sparked around the edges as anxiety took hold. It wasn't supposed to work this way. Students chose their own committees, in consultation with their advisors. It was all in the graduate handbook.

And I wanted Professor Leighton on my committee. *Needed* her there. She'd been part of my entire Magic school journey, and facing the exam without her reassuring presence was unfathomable.

"Granted, it is a bit late for changes, but the necessary palms have been greased." He chortled, making it clear with a dramatic wink that no bribes had actually been perpetrated. "We all agreed that, given your recent shift in methodology, a committee member proficient in digimancy ought to be present during the exam. And, if you'll have me, the entire dissertation."

His smile turned sharp as we stared at each other.

"Uh, thank you?" I was supposed to be reaching into my bag right now, removing that fake accommodation letter and handing it over. But it was as if his announcement had short-circuited the connection between my brain and body. I wondered if Anne felt like this when it was glitching.

"Amelia mentioned that you'd considered pursuing accommodations for the exam, and that Ursula has been holding practice sessions with you as an alternative support given the trickiness of the timing. I'm happy to do the same if you stop by during office hours."

"Thank you," I repeated, numb. My ears rang, head already fuzzy with the beginning of panic.

The professor's nod was a dismissal. I shuffled to my seat, trying not to sway as the full extent of his words sank in. Instead of trapping him, I had the distinct feeling I'd stumbled into a trap myself.

"Shall we begin?" Professor Delight intoned from his lectern, and I realized with a start that the room had filled up. The professor smiled over us. He hauled the classroom's ancient projector screen down over the chalkboard and queued up a slideshow, diving in on his weekly project showcase.

I was too unsettled to follow. The Oracle's sticky notes had been clear that the people behind the disappearances were closing in. And now Professor Delight was on my committee, where he could smooth the way forward or hold my degree hostage. Determine whether or not I got to remain in the program. But why would he go to the trouble, unless he *was* involved with the disappearances? No professor voluntarily sought out *more* service work. From what I could tell, being a professor meant frantically scrabbling for pockets of time to devote to research amid ever-growing teaching, mentoring, and administrative demands.

Somehow, he knew I was investigating. Knew I was a threat that needed to be managed. But what had tipped him off? He couldn't know about my visit to the dean. Unless, maybe, Amelia had told him. I shivered, trying and failing to ignore this fresh evidence of her possible involvement. My degree was hanging in the balance, half of my committee was potentially plotting against me, and I had no proof. How in Hecate's name had I thought I could go up against a tenured mage to set things right?

Between one wobbly breath and the next, time caught up with me. I'd completely tuned out the professor's digimancy project showcase: he was already going over takeaways.

"As mages, we are free to make mistakes," he said, "just as

the team behind *Mapping Alchemy* did. The mark of greatness is to correct them." I risked a glance up and found that he was staring right at me. My belly rumbled and I swallowed hard to keep my breakfast down, some clinical part of me wondering if he'd roped me into his working somehow. If I was going green and transparent, just like Alse had. If I was about to disappear.

Shaking, I slid my things back into my bag and pushed to my feet, gagging and gulping to keep from vomiting. There was no time to excuse myself, no time for anything except to flee down the hall and fall to my knees, miserable, in a bathroom stall.

After my stomach turned itself inside and back a few times, I made my way over to the sinks, relieved to see my own wan face peering at me from the dirty mirror. I washed my hands and splashed water on my face, fear shifting into fury.

In the hall, James waited, arms crossed and expression at sharp angles.

"Are you okay? What happened?"

Fury bubbled over. I clenched my hands into fists, looking James in the eye. "I didn't have a chance to submit the letter." My voice was barely more than a whisper. "Because the professor had something to tell me. He's on my exam committee now."

James's face went pale. "What? How is that possible?"

I shook my head. "I don't know. But Amelia told him she'd steered me away from accommodations, so the trap isn't going to work." Not unless we redid the letter and James submitted it. But I wasn't sure we needed to trap him anymore. He'd caught me, but he'd given himself away in the process.

And—my heart sank with the realization—possibly Professor Husik, too, since she'd apparently been more than happy to agree to his unusual plan.

James rubbed his face. "It doesn't make any sense. Why? And why now?"

"When the Oracle's notes caught fire, someone was trying to prevent us from learning more. Do you think they could tell who was asking?"

James went pale. "Your questions were part of the divination, so they'd have been able to identify you—if they knew what they were doing."

"They knew what they were doing."

A surge of impossible, unreasonable triumph joined the rage coursing through my veins. If Professor Delight was worried enough to try to hold my degree hostage, that didn't just mean he was involved. It meant we had a chance of fixing things.

I didn't share that thought with James. Honestly, I was afraid of hexing it. Instead, I straightened my shoulders and held my chin high, buoyed by the possibility. I didn't need to trap the professor anymore. I just needed to take him and his conspirators down.

It was time to call Mags in on her promise.

I was going to need her sword . . . if she wasn't waiting to stab me in the back with it.

"STARSDAMNED SPAWN OF INBRED NEWTS." FROM THE FAR END OF THE hallway swear words reverberated like detonation charms. "You Crowley-stanning reality-fuckers really whipped up a festering-septic-spill of a reality for yourselves, didn't you? Hecate's mother-fucking dogs."

Magdalen was using all of her quite extensive vocabulary at once, an event that felt like it could potentially rip the fabric of consensus reality and leave us cast away on a sea of excruciatingly descriptive phrases that didn't bear thinking about.

James paused. "Should I wait outside?"

"Good idea." I grimaced. "I'll just make sure everything's okay and then let you in." Taking a breath, I slipped through my office door. It creaked and Mags turned, face flushed and furious.

Under her glare, I faltered to a stop. I hadn't wanted to believe she could be involved. I'd used her lack of magic as an excuse to put her at the bottom of my list of suspects. But she looked capable of anything right now. Murder. An institutional coup. International villainy. I'd underestimated her. Explained away her red-flag behavior this term. And maybe I'd been wrong to do it.

I couldn't quite breathe. Couldn't quite think. But Mags blinked, and recognition sapped some of the wrath out of her expression. She offered me a grim smile.

"Bartleby! I was hoping you'd come in today."

"Why? What's wrong?" The caution in my voice must have been obvious. Mags squinted at me and crossed her arms.

"What's up is *you were fucking right*. And I feel like the louse wiggling through Merlin's crusty pubic hair for telling you that you were just procrastinating."

I mirrored her, crossing my own arms, unsure whether to feel relieved or vindicated or just grossed out. I was tipping rapidly toward grossed out, the more those words pinballed through my consciousness.

"I know. Remember how you promised I'd have your sword? I came here to tell you I need it. Metaphorically, anyway. But what changed *your* mind?"

Mags's laugh was distraught as she ran a hand through her hair. The sound seemed to deflate her.

"Lots of people were worried about student absences and the Dean of Students's lack of response at the Federation potluck. Which, don't think I didn't notice you skipped." She paused to glower theatrically at me. "Then one of my students stopped showing up, right after submitting an accommodation letter. I remembered what you'd said and did some digging, and . . ." She gestured toward the external monitor on her desk. Its large display was filled with a spreadsheet. "It's easier to show you."

I joined her in front of the screen, trying to make sense of what I was seeing.

"Hecate's dogs."

"*Hecate's dogs* is putting it mildly. These are missing student reports from mage students and candidates who are currently teaching," Mags said. She scrolled through the document, which contained multiple dozens of reports, organized by instructor and including data like amount of time missing and class year and . . . My eyes started to glaze over, not with boredom but with a sense of complete overwhelm.

"This is . . . a lot."

Mags shook her head. "It's a starsdamned mess, is what it is. The Dean of Students's office and Public Safety are sticking to their magic flu story. But it turns out people are more than happy to share their concerns with a Federation representative when admin aren't getting results. Everyone I've spoken with has been able to confirm that their students submitted accommodation letters before vanishing. And my data doesn't include any courses with faculty instructors, so there could be even more students than the spreadsheet indicates."

I looked at Mags.

She looked at me. "What do we do?"

Instead of answering directly, I reached over and nudged the door open.

"James, you can come in now."

Mags eyed me.

The door creaked wider as James stepped inside.

"Did you catch all of that?" I was willing to bet he had, given how thin the walls were in this building.

"Yeah." James said. "How many students are we talking?"

"Twenty-five, that I know of." Mags frowned. "But there are a bunch of duplicate reports, and I've just started reaching out to nonMagic grad instructors who teach the gen-eds Magic students usually take." She turned to me. "Why are you calling in my sword now? Did you make another discovery?"

"We've figured out who one of the faculty behind the working is. Or I think we have."

"There have to be at least one or two more mages involved, based on what we've learned about the working," James added.

I quickly caught Mags up, outlining the broad strokes of Darya and Cy's Sherlock spell, the situation with the residence ghosts, the message I'd received from the Oracle and Professor Delight's maneuvering.

Mags pinched the bridge of her nose. "It just had to be faculty, huh?"

"This is too big for three mage students—or even three mage students and a PhD student—to take on alone. I think we need to bring in the Federation. Figure this out as a collective." Even just imagining it made me want to cry with relief. It wasn't what our graduate employee union existed to do. But since our students were disappearing, this was technically a labor issue for us. And the Federation had rallied for social justice causes before. It wasn't unprecedented.

"If you're already gathering data as a Federation rep, that makes the call even easier," James said. "We can't rely on faculty or the admin—this is our responsibility to set right."

Mags didn't have to be told twice. She snatched the office phone and stabbed a few buttons in rapid succession.

"On it."

CHAPTER TWENTY-NINE

Magic isn't always the answer. Sometimes you need to unionize.

—POSTER IN THE FEDERATION OF GRADUATE
TEACHING FELLOWS AND PRACTITIONERS OFFICES

THE FEDERATION HAD MOVED RECENTLY TO A BUILDING THAT used to be spillover office space, all bland paint and beat-up furniture. While the current Federation reps, two from every Magic branch and academic department, had done their best to make the space homey, stashing candles and pillows and snacks everywhere, it hadn't helped much.

Every flat surface was covered with clutter: brochures, pins, and signs from the last time we'd had to go on strike; flyers for various events; stacks of T-shirts.

At my request, James had bought a couple of pizzas for the group. We weren't the only ones who'd come prepared. There were already a handful of open boxes scattered around the room, and people were standing in clusters, slices balanced on napkins, chatting.

There had to be forty, maybe forty-five, people here. And, sure, that wasn't a big number if you knew that there were about three hundred students enrolled in Magic at the graduate level, and another two thousand or so enrolled in the university's more quotidian grad programs, but it was still a shock. If every one of them had lost a student, our spreadsheet had already almost doubled in size since this afternoon. And that still didn't account for students who'd gone missing in classes taught by faculty, or other missing grad students like Imani, whom we weren't able to flag.

As soon as Magdalen saw us, she climbed onto the nearest piece of furniture—sending clutter sliding—and let loose a high-pitched whistle.

"This meeting is called to order," she shouted. As a Federation representative for English, current Federation secretary, and the person who had called the meeting in the first place, this was her rodeo. I was more than happy to wait for my cue.

"As you all know," Mags said, "we called you together today to discuss a growing issue. Our students are disappearing. Or someone is fucking disappearing them."

A murmur of concerned agreement rippled around the room.

"My friend and officemate, Dorothe Bartleby, was one of the first people to notice something was wrong." Mags waved in my direction, and people craned to look. Instead of diving behind James, which was extremely tempting, I met their gazes.

This wasn't the sort of attention I wanted. As a first-gen student, my MO was very much *keep your head down and wow them with your work.* And if I'd had my preference, I would be doing just that. But sometimes, keeping your head down is the same as looking the other way. And this was not something I could look the other way from.

I needed the people in this room to come to the same conclusion.

"A while ago, Bartleby came to me with suspicions that I honestly thought were just the workings of a mind desperate for procrastination," Mags continued. That got her a few laughs. We *all* knew that mindset. We'd all lived it. "But she was right. Forty-one undergraduate practitioners and at least one mage candidate have gone missing—and those are just the ones that we know of."

That set the group whispering again, checking with their friends to make sure their group was accounted for.

"Who's the mage candidate?" someone called.

"Imani Joshi," James said.

There was more whispering. In the back of the room, someone stood.

"I haven't seen Hiroko for at least a week."

"I think my roommate, Shaun, might be missing," Hadrian added. "I assumed he was on leave and hadn't told me, but . . ." We could all finish the thought, so Hadrian didn't. The room fell slowly silent.

"So, that's possibly three missing graduate practitioners," Mags summarized. "All of the undergrads have been flagged in the early-warning system. Individually, we've tried to check in with them, checked in with various admin about them, reported them missing to the Office of Public Safety, cast spells to find them—to no avail. University administration clearly doesn't have the capacity to deal with this. Some might say they aren't trying hard enough, considering the scope of the problem. We thought it was time the Federation took matters into our own hands."

WE'D BEEN ABLE TO USE THE DATA MAGS HAD COLLECTED TO GENERATE an estimated timeline of disappearances. Alse was one of the first. There'd been two others who vanished before them, but the timeline was more chaotic after that. Between the end of week two and the start of week four, not only did the disappearances happen in quick succession, but also in increasing numbers.

As Mags walked the group through our data, James caught my eye. We were both thinking about Anne's spike in glitches. I was willing to bet it wasn't just narrating the missing students at random. It was narrating them at *the exact moment* at which they'd gone missing.

Reports and glitches had trickled down to almost nothing by last Thursday—the full moon—but not because the working had broken. All of the students were still, obviously, gone. There was another explanation, though.

Mags looked to me to share it.

"This is not a coincidence. All of the students we're aware of who went missing had just submitted accommodation letters."

"That explains the timeline," someone called from the back of the room. "Most accommodation letters are submitted in weeks two and three, after SAS has time to process students' requests and documentation." As the crowd shifted, I caught sight of the speaker. Rose, from Digimancy. She blinked rapidly, turning bright red. "My aunt is an Accessibility Specialist at another school," she said as if to justify her comment.

In the middle of the room, someone raised a hand. "Okay, so someone is disappearing Magic students who submit accommodation letters." As he brushed pizza crumbs from his polo, I placed him. Blake, a PhD from Environmental Studies Cy had brought over a time or two last year. "Why *now*? It's not like accommodations are a new thing. And why only target *Magic* students?"

I grimaced. This was the piece of the puzzle I hadn't been able to figure out. Shrugs and frowns passed from student to student, until a bike bell interrupted our failure of knowledge. I glanced up in time to see Darya's friend Evelyn push forward in the crowd. She was using her knee scooter to support her right leg, which was wrapped in a neon-green cast, and she rang the bike bell again as she rolled her way to the front of the room.

"I think I know why this is happening now. *And* why they're just targeting Magic students." She adjusted her T-shirt, which sported an infamous manga version of Merlin making an obscene gesture with the caption *Fuck you, I'm magic.* "The *Chronicle of Magic Education* has been reporting on this all term. Longer, actually. The board of the Association of American Magic Universities and Programs is deliberating about whether the ADA should apply to Magic education, because, and I can't believe I have to say this newt-shit out loud," she read from her phone, "'the possession of magic supersedes any mundane accommodations that might be requested.'"

The blood rushing to my head sounded like an ocean, hurling

itself against a rocky shore. Hadn't that subject librarian mentioned something along those lines, back at the start of term? If I'd been paying better attention, maybe I could have put the pieces together weeks ago.

"They're sending representatives to conduct focus groups on the issue. Not just with faculty, but students and staff at institutions around the country. Including ours," Evelyn added.

Puzzle pieces clicked into place, and the picture they were starting to reveal left me feeling sick. Someone wanted students out of the way, so they couldn't speak up about their own needs and experiences. Someone—Professor Delight, and maybe Amelia, too—was trying to rig the AAMUP's deliberations.

Several long, soundless seconds passed before the room exploded.

Mags began to whistle, trying to regain control of the crowd. When that didn't work, she marched into one of the tiny offices down the hall and came back with a megaphone.

"Hey!"

The anxious, urgent chatter quieted but didn't cease.

"I said fucking *hey*. Hecate's dogs, you're loud."

The chatter stopped.

"Thank you," Mags said. "So, we have the basic facts. Students are disappearing. They all submitted accommodation letters, which makes their continued absence very convenient considering Evelyn's revelation."

"It's not my revelation," Evelyn muttered. "Am I the only one who reads the *Chronicle*?"

"It still doesn't make sense," Blake said. "If they wanted to get all disabled students out of the way, their working wasn't very effective."

"Forty-one missing students isn't *enough* for you?" Rose asked.

"I mean," Blake sent his fingers through his curly black hair, "statistically, it's not a lot. But that's not what I meant. It's—The working left *Darya* behind, for Hecate's sake. No offense, but if I was an evil conspirator, I'd want Darya out of the way right off the bat."

Darya grinned. "I take that as a compliment."

"Maybe they figured that would look too suspicious," Hadrian said. "There have to be *some* disabled students around for the AAMUP rep to talk to."

"That," Evelyn said, "and disability isn't a static, constant thing. Everyone experiences it differently. Mine is temporary. For others it's an identity, and for others it's a medical condition."

"We contain multitudes," Darya agreed. "It's not an easy thing to select for in a working."

"But accommodations are," James said. "There are letters. Records. A database."

"Right." Darya looked thoughtful. "But however they're using the records, they must not be going back far. I renewed my accommodations at the start of fall term."

"And mine were approved in November," Evelyn added. "It's only a temporary accommodation, but they extended it through winter."

James nodded, as if all of this made perfect sense. "If whoever's behind this didn't want to have to manually alter the working for every student, setting it to loop in *new* entries would be an easy enough way to reduce the number of disabled students on campus before the representative arrives."

"So, they cleared out a bunch of students who can testify *and* made it look like demand for accommodations had dropped off." I didn't realize I'd said the words aloud until James caught my eye.

"Exactly. And because they're new accommodations, there's less chance of anyone putting two and two together. It might not be an ideal solution—if you're an asshole on an ableist crusade—but it's not *nothing*."

"Except *we* put two and two together. And from our perspective, even one missing student is too many," Mags said. "What we need now is a starsdamned plan."

"We need more than a *plan*," Lora cut in, appearing out of nowhere like an actual apparition. "We need a plan of *attack*." They joined Mags and me at the front of the room and looked out over the crowd, assessing. "We don't know what this working is, but we know some things about it. Like the fact that multiple branches are involved. Someone's using digimancy to mess with records, which tells us there's either an alchemist or diviner on board."

"Definitely a diviner," James cut in.

Lora kept going. "And there's also a necromancer blocking our attempts to find out what happened. People are reporting unusual ghost activity, but it's not the ghosts acting out and they're keeping me from talking to whoever or whatever *is*."

I already knew all of this, and my heart still plummeted into my stomach. I watched my colleagues as they processed what all of it meant. The working involved mages from multiple branches. It had outlasted the lunar cycle, which meant it was grounded. And the people behind it had access to student records—including accommodations.

I saw it the moment the room came to the same conclusion I had: the people we were dealing with weren't amateurs, and they weren't outsiders, either. They were in charge. Between one blink and the next, the group transformed from a calm collection of graduate students to a riot in the making. Outrage, fear, and disbelief manifested as a wall-to-wall roar. Everyone trying to shout at once.

"This is above our pay grade." Some dude I vaguely remembered from last year's all-branch meeting broke through the noise. "People are going to get hurt."

"Since when do you care about pay grades, William?" James asked. "Did you lose access to your trust fund?"

"Are you magic-addled? If faculty and admin are behind this and we move against them, we're done. Out of our program. Finished," William insisted.

"Burn it down!" someone shrieked.

"And ruin our own futures?" someone else bellowed.

"Someone is happy to ruin them *for* us. And at least we're equipped to fight back—our students weren't so lucky."

By that point, there were so many people shouting I couldn't process what anyone was saying. I found James's gaze, held it as the room whirled around me. Between anxiety, fight-or-flight, and the sensory overload of being in a semicrowded space with so many loud people, I was keeping myself from passing out by sheer force of will.

I'd pay for it later.

James's gaze helped ground me. I breathed, slowly, waiting for the noise to stop.

Mags raised her megaphone. "Fucking *stop!*" she shouted. "Behave yourselves. You aren't *stage* magicians, for *Hecate's sake.*"

The chaos ebbed.

"We should take this to the dean," someone insisted at the far edge of the room.

Beside me, Darya held out her hand. Mags passed the megaphone down.

"We already *did*," Darya said. The chaos threatened to break out again, but she eyed the room with her steely brown gaze. "It didn't go well."

Mags inhaled deeply and took back the megaphone.

"Our normal routes for dealing with this kind of thing have been, as Darya just confirmed, tried and found fucking lacking." She looked around the room. "As a member in full, I move to make this a Federation matter."

"Seconded!" Lora called.

"All in favor?" Mags asked. Hands rose, slowly then in a wave that spread across the room. It was obvious what the majority wanted, but rather than leaving Federation decisions to something as malleable as the obvious, there was a working in the building that triggered in just such cases. At the back of the room, a neon sign slowly flickered to life as it tallied our hands.

Motion passed.

There were a few discontented sighs, but for the most part this group decision created a sense of relief. We had a big and daunting task ahead, but none of us could say, individually, that we'd made the call.

"We're in this together now," Mags told the room. "We may have to take public action. But for now, we'll . . ." She fumbled, unclear on what our next steps were. When she turned to me, her expression went pleading.

I accepted the megaphone, standing on tiptoe as I addressed the gathered practitioners. "We're going to figure out exactly what the working is. We're going to figure out who cast it. And . . ." Anger and worry were still splashed across people's faces, all creased eyebrows and mottled skin. "We're going to make a ruckus like this campus has never seen so that everyone knows who was involved. Because if we don't, they'll just do the working again as soon as we've dismantled it. And when they do, we'll be included."

"Right," Mags broke the uneasy not-quite-silence that followed my speech. "This might work best if we break into teams. People can pitch in wherever they're willing and able. The first team will be investigating the working—how it functions and how we can stop or reverse it. Do I have any volunteers?"

Lora's hand went up as quickly as Darya's did. They eyed each other and kept their hands up.

Mags, catching sight of them as she surveyed the room, laughed.

"All right, then. Anyone interested in volunteering should speak to Darya and Lora after the meeting." She paused, bounced on her heels. "The second team will work to find out who is responsible for this working. We all know whoever volunteers for this team will be risking a lot. So, be sure."

In the silence that followed, nobody moved.

Sighing, I raised my hand. James raised his, too. I scowled. He smiled.

Mags met my eye with an apologetic smile before repeating her spiel. "If you're interested in volunteering for the second team, speak with Bartleby and James before you go." She took a breath. "The third team will work with me to start preparing our protest. Once we have some answers from our other teams, we'll need to be ready to move, so we should line up volunteers, plan dates and locations, that kind of thing." A large cluster of people moved Mags's way. She lifted her megaphone again.

"We'll meet about this nightly, or at least check in as our teams deem necessary, until the problem is resolved. Meeting adjourned."

With that, people went back to pizza and mingling, chattering in agitated clusters. Several people approached Darya and Lora, extending hands and grim smiles.

James joined me at the front of the room, opening a pizza box and thrusting it toward me.

"Eat," he said. "You look dead on your feet."

"Thanks?" I was almost too tired to be embarrassed. Almost. I took a piece of pizza mostly so I could hide behind it.

"Not that you don't look . . ." His eyes found mine, the pink of his cheeks deepening. But before he could finish that thought, a familiar mechanical whine cut through the illusion of privacy. Darya pulled up next to us.

"I hate to break this up," she said, "but it's getting late. Can we head out?"

Her words dissolved whatever energy had kept me going for so long. Exhaustion blanketed me, and I yawned so hard my jaw cracked.

"Good call." I looked from her to James. "I have to teach first thing."

CHAPTER THIRTY

To doubt his truth or good intentions was impossible; and yet, during the whole of their conversation, his manner had been odd.

—NARRATORIAL COMMENTARY ADAPTED FROM
JANE AUSTEN'S *NORTHANGER ABBEY* BY ANNE

I HEADED DOWN THE HALL TO THE THAUMATURGY BRANCH OFFICE after class, trying not to dwell on the way Alse, Pam, and Manesh's empty desks turned my classroom gap-toothed, skeletal. My twenty-eight remaining students had somehow looked like a ragtag group of survivors in spite of their numbers. Week five and midterms normally sucked the life out of everyone, but this was week five on steroids. On top of assignment deadlines, tests, and their missing friends, the possibility that someone might make *them* vanish next was ever present. Already, two of my students had withdrawn from their classes and gone home.

I couldn't help but feel a little bit relieved about that, though the entire situation enraged me. Despite making progress with the Federation's support, actually *protecting* more students from disappearing felt completely beyond my control. Maybe they'd be better off at home.

"Bartleby was as exhausted as her students. Worry and overwork were beginning to chip away at her ability to think and act decisively," Anne said from the depths of my bag.

"Thanks for the vote of confidence."

My phone vibrated as I passed our branch directory and hauled open the glass-paneled door. It'd been about a month since I stopped by to check my campus mailbox. Which meant I had a paystub to collect, in addition to any event flyers or memos that had accumulated.

I ignored the notification, waving to Faye. She sat behind the high front desk, reading glasses low on her nose as she peered at her computer screen.

"Morning."

"Good morning, Dorothe." She looked up with a smile, pulling her glasses off and letting them drop. The beaded chain that held them in place around her neck glimmered with hunks of polished moonstone. "Lucky timing, you stopping by. I was just about to send out an *email*." Her voice went singsong.

I stepped over to the desk.

"Your Branch and Field exam is officially scheduled. March first at nine a.m. in conference room 103b." Faye beamed.

I longed to share her undiluted enthusiasm. But I couldn't help tensing against the news. The seesawing possibility of the mascarons' parting shot echoed inside my head: *would've made a mage* and *would've failed*. I was uncomfortably aware of Anne's bulk in my bag, and I half expected it to glitch, repeating the mascarons' words for Faye and the entire branch office.

It remained silent, and I told myself that meant things would go differently this time. I'd already come up with a better spellwork demonstration. My argument about the magic function of early novels had evolved in a promising direction. I should plan for success, make a celebratory tattoo appointment, manifest a reality in which I wowed in my exam and advanced to mage candidacy and went on to have a noteworthy, illustrious career.

Chest tight, I mustered a smile.

"Thank you, Faye."

As I turned to leave, my phone vibrated again. And again. And *again*. I paused in the hallway outside the branch office to fish it out of my pocket.

DARYA

They accepted my article!!!!!!!

CY

Mage Watkins is almost in print. Watch out world!

DARYA

First publication, then a professorship! Brace yourselves!

CY

Mages' night out to celebrate when I get back?

DARYA

Perfect.

We can celebrate B's ABD then, too!

A Major Mage Milestones party!

I texted back my own bajillion exclamation points, despite the twinge in my chest. Darya's progress made me feel like I was falling behind. I was studying in small snatches of time I couldn't dedicate to other things. During office hours, or in the moments before my students trickled into the classroom, or late at night instead of sleeping. But it was barely scratching the surface of everything I needed to do.

My stomach burbled an acid premonition. I tried to ignore the feeling, walking down the hall toward the elevators.

"Bartleby did not trust in her ability to carry on with her own work," Anne noted. "Deep down, she was beginning to believe there would be no celebration to share with her roommates. She'd run out of luck."

"The end, Anne . . ." I tried to interrupt its narration, but it barreled on.

"Logically, Bartleby knew she still had a chance, but—but—

but—" The whirring sound that always preceded its glitches filled the hall, and I went still, breath caught on a mixture of dismay that yet another student had just vanished and hope that maybe *this* glitch would provide a clue we could really use. "—withdrawn, inaccessible, ghostlike in an endless and disorienting fog. The void encroaches—encroaches—encroaches—*encroaches-s-s-s-s-s-s*."

The crack of a cleared throat interrupted the echo of Anne's last word. I spun around, heartbeat lurching out of time.

Professor Leighton stood a few paces away, hand on a set of keys dangling from the lock on her office door.

"Dorothe?" She regarded me for a moment, eyebrows arched in concern. How much had she heard before Anne glitched about the missing students? Would she think less of me, of my work, after this glimpse into my insecurities? Or would she fixate on the glitching itself?

"Hi, Professor."

She left her keys hanging in the door and closed the space between us. "Was that your spellwork demonstration chattering away?"

I forced myself to nod. "It was. I'm . . . working on the glitching." It wasn't exactly untrue. If the Federation undid the nefarious working, stopped the disappearances, and restored the records, Anne wouldn't glitch anymore. Probably.

"Good girl." Professor Leighton grabbed my hands, pressing them together between hers in an almost grandmotherly way. "I may not be on your committee anymore, but I'm invested in your progress. You're prioritizing your work? Avoiding distractions?" Her grip tightened, almost imperceptibly, gaze sharpening from concern to something almost calculating. But that was anxiety talking.

I pasted on a bright smile. "Avoiding distractions."

Anne, blessedly, didn't contradict me. And Professor Leighton didn't press me on my answer, which meant she couldn't have heard much of Anne's narration before the glitch. She smiled, letting go of my hands to pat me on the shoulder.

"I won't keep you, then. Let me know if you'd like another practice session. My door is always open."

I wasn't sure if it was my lie, the embarrassment of Anne nearly exposing some of my deepest worries, or something else entirely that left me oddly unsettled. My heart limped quick like a frightened rabbit, determined to flee. I didn't deny it.

Back in my office, I shook off the weirdness and pulled up my favorite tattoo artist's booking form. I'd been too nervous to make an appointment last time I'd been facing down exams. Maybe that was where it'd all gone wrong.

"Bartleby chose a time on the day of her exam, determination coursing through her despite a tremor of anxiety," Anne said. "A *what-if* she distracted herself from by rolling up her sleeves and reminding herself of recent successes."

I'd only gotten halfway through the booking form, but I stopped to take Anne's suggestion. Tracing my fingertips over my tattoos, I walked myself through the milestones they marked. The antique grimoire with a platypus crest on my left forearm, which I'd gotten to celebrate my admission to the Magic program at Sublimity. The blackberry vine that twined from my right shoulder down to my wrist, to commemorate finishing my coursework. A constellation of fireflies peeking through the vine, one for every time I'd been nominated for the George Blackwater Award for Outstanding Mage Student Spell Composition.

Things didn't always go wrong. I wasn't always a failure. And one way or another, I was determined to have something to celebrate at the end of this term. I finished the form and hit *submit*.

A SMALL GROUP OF US MET THAT NIGHT TO TRY TO IDENTIFY THE WORKing behind the students' disappearances. We knew it had a cloaking effect and involved digimancy, but we needed more to go on if we were going to take it down.

"It almost certainly wasn't subtle," Darya said. "A working

involving this many mages with this large of an effect . . . It would have been massive."

"The data tells us the working was most likely done in week one," Lora added. "Or maybe the week before."

Mags nodded. "Focus your searches on things that happened around that time. Check social media, the school paper, the city paper, *everything*. Once we pinpoint likely workings, we can get someone to crosscheck with the permit office."

I reached for my laptop. Finally, something that felt doable. We were all researchers. Together, we could figure this out.

"And if you'd rather research in hard copy," Mags added, standing to gesture at the pile of campus papers, "we've got back issues of the *Prattler*."

Hands went up and Mags moved through the room like a TA passing out handouts. As she went by, I glimpsed a front-page image and headline that made me gasp.

Flowers in January: Campus's Magic Houses Bring Color to a Bleak Start of Term.

The photo was of the Bentham Cote woods on the day I'd seen James there, dancing amid snapdragons and foxgloves that writhed like flames. I leaned forward and grabbed Mags's arm just as she was handing the paper to another mage student.

"Let me see that?"

Mags pulled it away from the person she'd been passing it to and handed it to me. "What is it?"

"Just . . . the flower displays from week one." On that terrible mages' night out at the start of term, I had a fuzzy sense that Darya, Cy, and I had speculated about what the workings were for. They were massive, ostentatious even for the Magic houses, and *coordinated* in a way that intra-house magical showdowns usually weren't.

I scanned the article, confirming what I already knew. All

four Magic houses *and* the admin building had put on grandiose floral displays that day. They were all still active, too, though the wonder of them had worn off enough that they'd faded into the background of campus life.

That seemed telling all on its own. The Magic houses would have usually scrapped them by now. No point in ostentation if people stopped noticing. More unsettling, I'd seen most of them up close over the course of the term, and, aside from that first day, I hadn't seriously questioned their purpose.

"There's no way the flowers are just a stunt." I looked around. All eyes were riveted to me. "They aren't just *created* by a working—they *are* a working. Or part of one."

"But the flower displays happened on the fifth, and students didn't start disappearing until the sixth," Rose pointed out.

"Digimancy makes workings laggy sometimes." I'd learned that particular lesson all too well this term.

The more I thought about it, the more I knew. This *had* to be the working that had caused our students to start disappearing. Around the room, people were coming to the same conclusion. If it had been just one or two floral workings, it might have been dismissible. But five displays, tied to the Magic houses and admin building, grounded and still going? The power that would generate was enough to take out *all* of the students on campus, and half the city besides.

That wasn't what set my head spinning, though. While the rest of the room explored the implications of my realization, I dropped the paper and looked at James. Thoughts I didn't want to think blared in my skull.

He'd told me he wasn't involved. That he'd been dancing through the flowers because he'd seen the working and fallen into a trance. And I trusted him. I did. But the Oracle's notes had told me that someone close to me was involved. *So close*, the second message had said. And James was a diviner. We were *looking* for a diviner. It would be reckless not to at least think this through.

I glanced at him, guilty even to be considering it. From his expression, he knew what I was thinking. He'd gone pale, mouth a resolute line. But he nodded, once, as if to give me permission. *Go ahead. I understand.*

I closed my eyes, tried to block the awareness of his gaze as I imagined myself outside Bentham Cote in January. Hands clamped around cold wrought iron, watching flowers writhe like flames. James danced through my memory. But was he choreographing the flowers' motions, pulling them into manifestation and movement, or was the working choreographing him—the gravitational pull of shifting reality towing him through the inferno of foxgloves and snapdragons?

In my mind's eye, he spun between foxgloves, their heavy bells swaying against his exposed skin. I remembered thinking he must have some kind of protection against the deadly flowers. But Imani had mentioned a rash the next day in Digimancy. And magical intervention.

My eyes snapped open. I fished my phone out of my pocket, rapidly tapping in a search about foxglove exposure.

Contact with the sap of foxglove plants is likely to cause skin irritation.

I shot another look James's way. He tipped his head toward the row of offices at the back of the building. An invitation. I followed him back, anxiety settling.

He'd been telling the truth, I was certain of it. If he was some evil mastermind making students—including his own friend—disappear, he'd have taken precautions against plant-induced rashes.

James stepped into one of the closet-size offices, and I crowded in after him.

There was no door, so I kept my voice to a whisper. "Look, James, I had to consider—"

"I think you're right about the flowers. And I was there, right after the working. But I wasn't involved, Bartleby, I swear," he interrupted. "It's like I said at the start of term. I dropped off my VCR for Mims. Bentham Cote was having a '90s night and they wanted it to be 'authentic.' And then on the way out I saw the flowers and it triggered a vision." He wouldn't meet my eyes, and what had started as a whisper grew louder with emotion. "The one I told you about. With Anne's voice, and Imani. I got a horrible rash."

I grabbed his forearms. "I know, James. I believe you."

He stilled, surprise splashed pink across his face. "You believe me?"

"I had to think it through after the Oracle. But I remember Imani mentioning your rash in Digimancy." I let out a long breath, stepping closer to look deep into his eyes. As usual, they were the calm gray of a winter coastline, creased with worry but nothing else—nothing like guilt—that I could see. "I believe you. I trust you."

"We don't," Darya broke in. "The Oracle's prophecy said it was someone close to you, right, Bartleby? It looks like you and James have gotten very close."

The whole group had clustered outside the office. Twelve practitioners peered in at us, faces ranging from curious to outraged and hostile.

"Excuse us if we don't find your soulful eyes quite as compelling as Bartleby does," Lora added.

James winced, and I tensed, anticipating their next words.

"We'd like you to submit to a truth working."

"He didn't protect himself against the foxgloves." I looked from Darya to Lora, begging them to understand. "If he'd been responsible for the working, he would've done that. You know I'm right. We should stay focused on flowers. Figure out what else we can learn from them."

"I trusted him once, too, Bartleby." Lora's tone was sorrowful, not vengeful. I steeled myself against it, glowering at her and Darya and Mags and the entire group peeking around their shoulders. "He almost tanked my career."

"That was an accident." I sounded frantic, and I didn't care.

Truth workings weren't prohibited by student code, mainly because the administration wanted to be able to use them during investigations of academic misconduct. But they'd fallen out of fashion, more a tool of oppression than enlightenment and liberation. People had been outed during truth workings. Lives had been ruined. There was no way this wasn't going to be incredibly invasive, because there was no such thing as a *partial* truth. They couldn't use a truth working like a scalpel, just to ask a single question. What they'd be calling forth with this working was not some discrete objective fact, but something interconnected, rooted in James's lived experience as a thinking, feeling person.

The bees in my head reached a crescendo of insectoid rage. I balled my fists. "There has to be some other way."

All the blood had rushed out of James's face, leaving him waxen. Vacant, almost. After a tense moment, he shook his head. I squeezed my fists tighter until my knuckles strained and cracked. This was my fault. Lora and Darya had noticed my suspicion, followed my gaze to James. And he was paying the consequences.

"You don't have to do this."

He looked at me, eyes tired and sad, and brought his lips into the shape of a smile. "After what we learned from the Oracle, a small part of you will always wonder. So, yeah, I do. If I want to be part of this, alongside you, I do."

CHAPTER THIRTY-ONE

The way of paradoxes is the way of truth. To test reality we must see it on the tight rope. When the verities become acrobats, we can judge them.
—OSCAR WILDE, *THE PICTURE OF DORIAN GRAY* (1890)

THERE WERE MORE WAYS TO CAST A TRUTH WORKING THAN I wanted to think about. Scrying, potations, rituals. It was like that saying about trying to build a better mousetrap. Pretty much every major institution spent the '80s and '90s developing their own pet method.

The group didn't take long to debate, though. They decided on a working that used tarot as a tether.

We didn't even have to track down a deck. Chuck, a third-year in Divination, pulled one out of the pocket of his crimson-red, star-speckled broomstick skirt. Others rushed to clean off a coffee table, before which Chuck sank to his knees, slowly shuffling cards.

Lora and Mags guided James to sit on the couch opposite Chuck. I moved to sit next to James, but Darya caught my eye and shook her head.

"You'll muddy the working."

James grimaced affirmation. I sat in his line of sight instead; there if he needed me. His gaze stayed on mine, expression a silent plea: *I don't want to face this alone.*

Willing myself to be strong enough, I clamped my hands to-gether and waited.

Someone dimmed the lights, and Chuck passed the deck to James, instructing him to choose nine cards and arrange them in a circle. James obeyed with trembling fingers.

"This spread," Chuck explained, as James positioned the final card, "will call truth into the room. Nine points will guide us, taking us along James's life path. It will illuminate the shadows in his mind, let us glimpse James's inner sight, subconscious influ-ences, and, perhaps, his near future. Once read, it will bind him to answer our questions. It has been known to trigger visions in the subject being questioned." Chuck paused to look around the room, eyes landing finally on James. "Are you ready?"

James nodded, hesitating only slightly.

"To end this working, the cards must be returned to the deck by my hands," Chuck said. After a breath, he began. Cupping his hands over his ears, he rotated them until his fingers cradled the base of his skull. Then he tapped his rings there, rapid-fire, cross-ing and uncrossing his eyes.

The air in the room snapped tight, and Chuck huffed a ragged breath as he touched a fingertip to the first card.

"The seven of wands."

His voice took on a monotone, as if the words poured through him rather than from him, and static jumped from person to per-son. Scattered gasps and sighs rang out in the silence. I rubbed the backs of my arms, which prickled with raised hairs, eyes still on James.

"This life has been one marked by conflict. You were required to take a stand for something—maybe your identity, maybe a choice, but I think *both*—that others, close to you, did not believe in or agree with." Chuck locked eyes with James. And James was transfixed by that gaze, stilling and nodding as the words washed over him.

Slowly, and without looking away from James, Chuck reached over and tapped the second card.

"The lovers."

Every muscle in my body tensed. I shouldn't be here, listening to this.

"Your current state," Chuck told James, "is one of deep connection and fulfillment. Perhaps you've met someone, though this speaks to something deeper. A sense of seeing and being seen. Understanding. A choice you are making and have still to make."

Chuck moved in slow motion, fingers sliding toward the next card.

"The eight of swords." He paused for a breath after announcing the card, brows colliding as if he was having trouble interpreting its significance. "Your past situations and influences allude to confusion, lack of support, pressure to take a path that wasn't yours to take. Controlled by your parents. No, not *just* your parents. Your ancestors, one after another in a long, long line."

James flinched under the words, muscles bunching as if he was holding himself still. His eyes fluttered, trying to roll back in his head, and he groaned. My whole body trembled in sympathy. I closed my eyes and saw the carefulness that had come over him weeks ago, when he'd only *thought* I might know who his family was and measure him by them.

Chuck kept going, his speed increasing my dread.

"The knight of cups. Romance shapes your future, propelling you through trials, present and impending."

The next card resonated as Chuck tapped, a boom that rattled the room. Or maybe it just felt that way to me.

"The moon."

It slipped sideways under his fingertips, not quite reversed, but not quite upright.

"A constant presence follows, haunting you. It is everywhere, past, present, and future, in your waking and dreams. It illuminates a long, winding path. You have walked far already, and stumble onward, not knowing where it leads or if there's safety along the route. There is an internal crisis you're constantly reliving. Isolation. Trauma . . ."

He flipped another card and kept speaking, but I didn't hear anything else. James had risen to his feet with a graceful motion. He was dancing, eyes so far back in his head all I could see were the whites.

My skin prickled as I watched. I'd already believed him, but this was proof. This was what he'd been doing in the Bentham Cote flower display—magic, yes, but not a working he'd initiated.

"You have to stop this." I looked from Darya to Mags to Lora. "He was dancing, just like this, at the flower display. He was having a vision, just like he said."

Darya's face crumpled. Mags winced. Even Lora looked away, a pained expression there and gone on her face.

"I'm sorry, Bartleby," Darya said, "but you know it doesn't work like that . . ."

"Six of cups, reversed."

I flinched away from their pitying gazes as Chuck began to dig deeper into the ways in which James's childhood haunted him. To call this a truth working was to understate its brutality. This was a flaying.

James danced through the room, oblivious to our gazes and all the more vulnerable because of it. Trapped in some cryptic revelation as the rest of us poked and prodded into his psyche. And when this was done, when Chuck finished reading the cards, the real interrogation would begin. I couldn't be here for that.

I ran from the room before Chuck could tap another stars-damned card.

UNDER THE BUILDING'S AWNING, I WELCOMED THE GUSTS OF MISTING wind as a sharp penance. James had agreed to do the working, and as a fifth-year in Divination, he knew better than most what he was agreeing to. But it was my fault he was going through it, because he'd seen the suspicion in my eyes and felt the need to explain himself again. My fault they were peeling back the layers of his being, revealing the sorts of things that should be shared, voluntarily, over time, with someone he loved and trusted. If he ever shared them at all.

I doubted he'd ever want to share them with me now.

I sank to the damp concrete sidewalk and wrapped my arms around my knees, waiting for them to finish their dirty work.

Anger bubbled up with a terrible laugh. At Lora and Darya for insisting on the same thing I would have, if it had been anyone else but James. At James for agreeing to the working. But mostly? At myself. Passersby scurried a little faster at the sound, pattering footsteps moving rapidly past. I dropped my head and howled into my knees, a hedgehog hiding from my own mess, marking time by the progress of the cold as it crept from the sidewalk and deep into my bones.

Eventually, the door of the Federation headquarters jangled open, bell half-frozen and clunking rather than dinging. Footsteps approached me. I didn't look up. A warm hand squeezed my shoulder.

"Bartleby?" James's voice was cracked. Weary.

"It's done?" I peeled cautiously out of the ball of myself.

His expression was carefully neutral. "Let's go?"

I didn't care that the meeting was still going on inside. Wiping my face with my sleeve, I nodded. James extended a hand, and I took it, staggering to my feet after too long on the cold cement.

We rode in silence the whole way home.

At my front door, he pulled me into a hug and held me, tight, for a long time. Then he pressed a kiss to my forehead and got in his car and left.

WHEN SHE GOT HOME LATER THAT NIGHT, DARYA FILLED ME IN. AFTER the group decided they believed James—Darya couldn't meet my eyes as she recounted that part—they set plans in motion. Volunteers had been sent off to investigate at each house, to harvest samples of the flowers so we could verify that we'd pinpointed the right working and determine the best way to bring it down.

"They're going to bring them here, so I can run some tests. And Lora thinks we need to keep trying to contact the students." Darya wrapped her hands around her tea mug. "To be sure we understand the full extent of the working."

I wanted to growl. "We've already tried that. It hasn't worked." Lora had been there for those tries. Residence ghosts had *attacked* her, for Hecate's sake.

"They think," Darya continued, an edge creeping into her words, "they've figured out a way to keep the ghosts from attacking. At least for long enough to have a short conversation. But the students are moving around, like James theorized. We're not going to be able to find them in the dorms, not with all of the little workings students do in their rooms muddying reality. And we can't summon them to a location of our choosing, since they aren't ghosts. So, we'll have to risk talking to them somewhere else we know they'll be."

"Like classrooms?" I didn't bother looking at her as I asked the question. I wasn't shouting, but it was a close thing. She'd made the logical call, backing Lora, but the part of me that knew that didn't have much of a hold on my current reality. I pressed my tea mug against my cheek, willing its warmth to soothe away the roil of emotion.

Darya nodded, her voice taking on a softer tone. We'd lived together for three years, so she could tell when I was pissed and trying not to be. "If we can just *talk* to some of them, maybe they'll be able to give us the details we need to reverse-engineer the working. Even if they can't help us, it might help *them* just to talk to someone." She heaved a weary breath. "Anyway, Lora will be handing out Ouija boards, instructions, and supplies to anyone who wants to give it a try. They're bringing a kit by tomorrow before my class. You can use it later in the week."

"She found a way to do it without . . . ?" I didn't finish my question, but I didn't need to. Ghosts were so important to the workings of the university that warding against them was probably the easiest way to get expelled.

Darya nodded. "We think so. There's still a risk, but it's such a minor working Lora doubts it will be noticeable."

"That's . . . huge actually."

"It is." There were lines under the lines under her eyes as she sat back.

The tight knot of anger in my chest loosened just a bit. This had to have been an exhausting day for her, too, even if it had started with a big win.

As if reading my thoughts, she yawned, long and loud.

I'd been a terrible friend on multiple levels today. "I didn't even congratulate you in person."

Darya froze.

I let guilt untangle my anger even more. "So, congrats. You are a fucking *published* mage."

Her careful expression melted into a tired grin.

"All but dissertation," she corrected as though it was any normal day and we weren't tottering around the edges of a fight. "And only almost published. But thank you. I'm still not convinced it actually happened. It's way more likely that I hallucinated the acceptance email."

I snorted. "We both know that's not even a little bit likely."

Her smile grew, and my smile echoed hers. I leaned forward and grabbed her hand.

"I am not surprised at all. You're brilliant, and I'm proud of you."

Tears stung, pride and anxiety battling.

I wasn't jealous. I would not mar this moment, her moment, with jealousy. But I couldn't help but wonder whether I'd ever make it past exams to even *start* working toward this particular milestone. The choking tightness behind my ribs seemed to know the answer. Publication felt like it might as well be a mythical thing, it was completely illusory and out of reach. I blinked the tears away and grinned with Darya until the ache of my jaw made me forget the tightness in my chest.

DARYA LUGGED A OUIJA BOARD TO CLASS THE NEXT MORNING, FULL OF optimism. I wasn't quite so sanguine, but I'd still try it for myself tomorrow. In the meantime, I had other work to do. I refilled my coffee mug and slumped back into my chair at the kitchen table, tapping at the keyboard with one finger while I took a long drink.

"Bartleby had decided to catch up on some overdue reading," Anne said. I'd positioned it on a cast-iron potholder in the middle of the table, where it looked like a macabre centerpiece alongside the candles and salt-and-pepper shakers. "Both the subject librarian, Amanda Perez, and Darya's friend, Evelyn Itō, had mentioned *The Chronicle's* ADA coverage. Bartleby hoped that reviewing those articles would tell her something important."

"Mm-hmm." I clicked onto the website, setting my coffee down to type in a few search terms. *AAMUP* and *ADA* did the trick, revealing a series of articles by Selene Scoutt Price, the mage director of a teaching and learning center somewhere in the Midwest. A recent article hinted at what Evelyn had already explained.

Representatives were being sent to designated campuses to hear from faculty, students, and staff before the board delivered its own conclusions on the matter. I gulped my coffee, skimming quickly. Sure enough, our university was listed. What's more, there was a timeline for the visit: the representative would arrive on our campus during week eight, and stay through the start of week nine.

He'd leave the day after my exam.

Static frizzed up the back of my neck, as the memory of the mascarons' portent tried to turn itself into an earworm. *Failure. Could've been a mage. Run.*

Three weeks might be plenty of time to dismantle the working on our end. But that was assuming nothing got worse than it already was. If James had been right about what we experienced during our aleuromancy working, the missing students might not have that long. And without the dead setting things right, who

knew what effects the working might have on the rest of campus
over time.

My phone alarm went off, jarring me out of my anxiety spiral.
It was a reminder to go to Digimancy class. But I had no intention
of spending my day squirming under Professor D.'s watchful gaze.
I stabbed at the screen until the alarm stopped, then tapped into
my messaging app and pulled up my thread with James.

I'm skipping class.

With a thumb hovering over the send button, I hesitated.

After yesterday, was it fair for me to reach out? At the very
least he'd need some time to recover. And at worst . . .

I deleted my message and set my phone down, reaching for
my coffee.

The phone pinged. I snatched it up. A message from James,
and three little dots promising more.

Yesterday was intense.

I held my breath against the impulse to reply immediately, and
two more messages chimed into view.

Thanks for giving me some space.
Skipping class today.

I tapped a reply and deleted it, catching my upper lip between
my teeth. If I responded how I wanted to, I'd be doing the opposite of giving him space. I thumbs-upped his last message and put
my phone away.

For now, team two consisted of me. And only me. But that
was how it had felt most days in this program. Like I had to shoulder the burden of reality—of every possible reality—on my own.
And even if I knew now that it wasn't sustainable, I could power
through one more time. Hope against hope that if I pushed myself

to my limits, I'd find a way to do all the things that needed doing. Save my students. Finish my exam prep. Become a fucking mage.

"Bartleby's narration skull felt it too much, indeed, for many words," Anne said, paraphrasing *Mansfield Park*, "and meant to try to lose the disagreeable impression, and forget how much it had been forgotten itself as soon as it could."

I struggled to parse its ironically very wordy commentary, staring at it for a moment before I realized what it meant.

"I'm sorry, Anne. You're also part of team two. An important part. I shouldn't have forgotten."

Apparently mollified, Anne forewent additional quotable quotes. "Anne thanked Bartleby for her apology."

"Maybe you can help me make a list?"

Grabbing a sheet of paper, I wrote Professor Delight's name at the top. Below it, I added Dean Underhill. Between the way she'd dismissed Darya all these years and her lack of concern about our claims, she seemed like an obvious suspect. But my spark of motivation threatened to fizzle as I touched my pen to the blank spot beneath her name.

"Bartleby wondered whether she was in possession of enough data to add Professor Husik to her list," Anne said. "Yet, a larger part of her insisted that she didn't have the luxury to avoid doing so."

After an agonizing moment, I scrawled Amelia's name and punctuated it with a question mark. Their names were just the start. Opening my laptop, I pulled Mags's spreadsheet up. It had grown in size since Monday, and my smile was instinctive as I created a new sheet. I might not be good at proper investigation, but data wrangling I could do.

Some of the entries had notes about students' class schedules. Porting over every professor referenced in those was easy enough.

I alphabetized the names and started searching the internet, adding notes based on postings on ScoreUrProf, faculty websites, and whatever random syllabi I found floating around. One of the professors taught a class on Disabled Mages and Magical Activism, which made her unlikely as a suspect. Another led Thaumaturgy's pedagogical training workshop and championed the use of universal design to create courses that were accessible to more students from the start. He was also dating someone in Student Accessibility Services. A few more wrote explicitly about disabilities of their own. One even had a Spoon Policy in her syllabus that was obviously informed by the chronic illness community.

I crossed their names out and kept moving down the list, narrowing our pool of potential suspects so that when it came time to tear down this Heccing working, we'd be ready.

CHAPTER THIRTY-TWO

Follow these instructions CAREFULLY. If you attract the attention of a university ghost instead of a student and you aren't asking questions correctly, it is very VERY likely the ghost will get annoyed and break through the protections to possess you. And, honestly, you'll deserve it. I don't have time to go around doing exorcisms.

—HASTY PHOTOCOPY OF LORA MAMANI FLORES'S HANDWRITTEN SÉANCE INSTRUCTIONS

I SHOOED MY STUDENTS OUT OF THE CLASSROOM FIFTEEN MINUTES early. Most of them, anyway. Hopefully, a few hard-to-see ones had stuck around. I was pretty sure they'd been attending class for most of the term, and trying to get my attention by messing with my markers. Heaving a breath that set my bangs floating, I considered the empty room.

Only one way to find out, as soon as I warded against ghostly interference.

I retrieved Lora's supplies from my bag: custom air freshener she'd bullied a chemistry grad into making using rosemary, sage, and juniper compounds; a printout of a warding rune I was supposed to sketch in chalk on the door and windows; a small wind chime made of bird bones to hang in the doorway—it would make noise as the ghosts departed, which was how I would know it was safe to speak to my students. And finally, a custom Ouija board and planchette with a stapled packet of instructions.

I hung the wind chime and made quick work of the rune, tracing its cluster of concentric circles and texturing them with slashes and dots that were meant to subtly nudge ghosts away from the area.

Six minutes ticked by, each second agonizingly marked by the *tok tok tok* of the classroom clock, before the wind chime rattled. Referencing the instruction manual, I spritzed the air freshener in the four corners of the room and above the spot where I was planning to set up—warding the space from the ghosts, for at least a few minutes. It was such a minor working it shouldn't set off any university alarms. But because it was so minor, it wouldn't last. I needed to hurry.

I shoved desks into a large circle around the middle of the room, blocking the door. Just to be safe, I cast a cloaking, using Jane Austen's words to pull reality into shape around me.

"A mind lively and at ease, can do with seeing nothing, and can see nothing that does not answer."

The buzz of static electricity ran along my skin and out into the room as I spoke, setting the fluorescent lights crackling overhead. My head swam and floated at the same time. I closed my eyes and breathed deep until the feeling passed.

"Alse? Pam? Manesh?" My words didn't echo, which meant my working had stuck.

Collecting the Ouija board and instructions, I lowered myself to the grimy vinyl floor with a groan. Darya hadn't been attacked when she tried it. In fact, she'd been able to chat with Pam for a couple of minutes. But the sense memory of the Bone House ward ghosts' assault stole my breath for a long moment.

I forced myself to grab the intricately 3D-printed planchette, placing it precisely on the Ouija board. A steadying breath, and I posed a question to the room.

"Is anyone here?"

I closed my eyes, waiting. Nothing.

"Alse? Are you here?"

The planchette began to move almost immediately, zig-zagging across the board to stop, finally, over the art nouveau lettering of the word *yes*.

Hands shaking, I fumbled for another question from Lora's list. I couldn't get the pages of the Heccing packet to separate.

"I'm sorry our meeting was interrupted," I improvised, fingers still working at the pages. "I'm sorry this is happening to you. My friends and I are going to fix it."

The planchette wobbled, as if uncertain. I placed my fingers back on it, abandoning Lora's script. "What does the working feel like to you?" After another long moment, the planchette began to glide, first to the letter "F," then "U," then "Z," "Z" again, and "Y."

It's only a matter of time before they come fully untethered, James had said. But they were still here, for now. Getting tense wasn't going to help. I took a second to unclench my jaw and lower my shoulders.

"Fuzzy?" It wasn't really a question. The planchette moved anyway. "I," then "M," then, in such rapid succession that my fingers began to ache, Alse spelled the words *here*, *not* and *here* again.

It was almost the exact phrasing of one of Anne's glitches. My stomach knotted. "You can't see yourself? Is that what you mean?"

Instead of answering directly, Alse posed a question of their own. "A," and "M," and "I" and *real*, spelled out in that same rapid-fire way.

The other night's awful, rib-cracking tightness wrapped itself back around me as they spelled. If Alse was still clinging to consensus reality, odds were good for the rest of the missing students, but their question was proof that their hold was slipping. Unseen and unseeable even to themself, they currently *had* no boundaries. Or to use their word, they had *fuzzy* boundaries. The working was eating away at their sense of themself.

I struggled to swallow, forced myself to breathe as I dragged the planchette over the word *yes* forcefully, echoing with my own voice.

"Yes. You are real. You are here. You just need to hold on a little while longer, okay? We're going to figure this out."

I wasn't sure where they were in relation to me. This strange cloaking they were wrapped in was so thorough I couldn't perceive their breath, their body heat, or even the brush of fingers on the planchette. They were right here, sitting close enough to touch the Ouija board, and I couldn't reach out.

I repeated myself, whether for Alse or for me I wasn't sure.

"You are real. You are here. And we're going to fix this."

BY THE TIME I GOT HOME THAT NIGHT, DARYA HAD FILLED THE ENTIRE kitchen with plants. A row of canning jars in the windowsills contained cuttings of tulips and daffodils, sunflowers that shrank down into dandelions with audible *spurts* as I watched, lilies, and foxgloves. On the table, several of our mixing bowls held lotuses. A few coffee mugs supported tumbling cones of hyacinths and small sprigs of snapdragons.

"If you're staying," Darya said, "you'll need one of these." She was wearing a respirator, and she gestured at it before pointing me toward the counter next to the stove. "I'm working with some volatile plants."

I pulled my own respirator over my head and joined her at the kitchen table.

"I see your volunteers brought their ill-gotten goods over."

"Yes, they did." As she said it, Darya used a pair of forceps to pick up a cross-section of some sort of tuber and drop it into a canning jar full of glowing blue liquid. She spun the lid on quick as the liquid flashed fuchsia then shifted to a muddy brown before settling to the murky blue-black of a scummy pond.

"Have you learned anything from them?"

Darya raised her eyebrows theatrically to compensate for the respirator. "The working grounded in these flowers is definitely the one we're after."

I pulled out a chair and sat, hard. "Do you think they're like a living timer? The AAMUP rep is supposed to get here in week eight, so maybe they're just keeping the working going until then."

"Maybe. But I don't think the working is going to end when the blooms fade."

"What do you mean?"

"Most of these flowers aren't ephemerals or even annuals. They're tubers, rhizomes, and bulbs. The plants can live *years*."

Shock coursed through me, a splash of icy cold that slowly seeped into simmering outrage.

I could almost understand the twisted logic that led them to trigger the working at the start of term—they wanted to silence those most likely to speak out in favor of ADA accommodations, and piggybacking on the creation of new accommodation letters was an efficient way to accomplish that. But did they really not care that the working might catch a strangling hold, dig its thorns in deep and refuse to let the students go?

I already knew the answer.

I'd seen it every time Darya had to go to campus, playing bus roulette in the hopes that one of the handful the university had outfitted with a functional wheelchair bay would pull up. I'd seen it in the way my students quailed as they handed me accommodation letters. I'd seen it in the slapdash ramps and inaccessible buildings, the tiered lecture classrooms with steps between each row of seats, the back-to-back-to-back-to-back classes with heavy workloads and brutal attendance policies. I'd seen it in my own growing anxiety. My panic attacks. My spiraling sleepless work sessions.

The thing we were all trying to accomplish, the status we were trying to achieve, depended on the idea that all "good" mages should be able to push through, mind over body, burning the summoning candle at both ends regardless of the physical cost. The pursuit of Magic degrees inevitably left students broken on the other side. Mage was a disabling identity, but it made no real space for the disabled. Schools actively weeded disabled applicants out, or pushed them out over time.

"The good news is I think the working will fail if we destroy them. But we have to do it at all five sites at once." Darya squinted at the murky liquid sloshing in the canning jar on our table. "I need to do a few more tests to be sure, though."

I nodded. "Need any help?"

"Nope." Darya's voice was almost perky. "This is my jam. And besides, you look like you're about to keel over."

I shook my head. "I'm fine." I just had a throbbing ache at the back of my skull from the plastic smell of the respirator and whatever floral odors I'd breathed in before I put it on. "I think I'll go for a walk, though."

On the street, the half sphere of the waning gibbous moon winked out between fast-moving clouds. The sidewalks were wet, but the rain had stopped its incessant drizzle, at least for the moment.

I basked in the moonlight for a few seconds before heading toward the park down the road. It had been a while since I'd walked over, with everything that had been going on, but there was a swing there with my name on it.

Swinging in the dark was oddly comforting. Suspended between the twilit earth, streetlights flaring and porch lights beckoning, and the sparkling skies, stars and planets swirling in an endless dance, I felt centered.

As above, so below.

As I approached the park, the sight of a familiar green Subaru brought me up short. James leaned against it, underneath a buzzing streetlight, facing the trees that surrounded the park block. My whole body buzzed along with the light, worry and something else—something like excitement—rushing through me. I should call out. But he was lost in thought, and I didn't know what to say.

I settled on "Hey" when I was close enough to speak in my normal voice. James started and turned.

"Hey," he said.

"Waiting for someone?"

James smiled, slow and mischievous. "As a matter of fact, I

was." He stood, then, forcing me to look up as my eyes met his. "How's it going?"

I considered the question. "Good, actually. I think we're finally getting somewhere." I frowned. "How'd you know I'd be here?"

"Divination."

"Really?"

He laughed. "I stopped by your place. Darya told me."

"Oh." I wrapped my arms around myself, against the cold. "So, what's up?" It wasn't what I wanted to ask. But a barrage of questions that amounted to *how are you?* and *are you mad at me?* and *can you ever forgive me?* wasn't what either of us needed.

"I'm wondering if you want to grab some food?"

CHAPTER THIRTY-THREE

Unwearied perseverance and unceasing care were the qualifications on which James had secretly prided himself; and by which he had hoped in time to overcome all difficulties and obtain success at last.

—NARRATORIAL COMMENTARY ADAPTED FROM
ANNE BRONTË'S *AGNES GREY* BY ANNE

I PRETENDED NOT TO NOTICE HOW HAGGARD JAMES LOOKED AS WE pulled up to the burger joint. In the ghost-blue wash of the streetlights, the bags under his eyes were intense. His hair was a mess in a way that wasn't at all intentional, like he'd gotten one hour of sleep since I saw him last and it hadn't even been in a comfortable position.

James threw the car into park as I watched him. He slid the keys out of the ignition and pocketed them before noticing my gaze.

"Everything okay?"

I wasn't expecting the question, and I froze. He'd said he needed space, but he was here now. Did that mean he was ready to talk about it? I wasn't sure. I wasn't going to bring it up until he did.

"Fine." I fumbled with my seat belt. "I love this place."

James's confused smile was all lopsided dimples. "Me, too."

"They've got the best fries." I climbed out of the car and smiled at James over the roof. "Even if they do skimp on serving sizes."

James's face went serious. "I'll be sure to order extra."

We placed our orders and found a seat in a cozy corner booth. For a Friday, the place was dead. A few clusters of students and a family or two were perched around tables, but there were more empty seats than full ones, which was fine by me.

The hum of the restaurant settled around us like a comforter, the sounds of frying meat and percolating coffee combining into some sort of paranatural soporific.

James rubbed his knuckles into his bloodshot eyes, and I stifled a sigh. I couldn't *not* ask.

"Is everything okay with *you*?"

James blinked like he was trying to regain focus. "Sorry. I'm not feeling completely like myself."

I didn't want an apology. He wasn't doing anything wrong. I'd gotten him into this. I'd abandoned him during the truth working when he was scared and vulnerable—even though he'd wanted me to stay. And after, I'd just pretended everything was more or less normal.

I reached a hand toward him and then changed my mind and let it fall to the tabletop.

The waiter saved me from the awkwardness of that gesture. I snatched my hand out of the way as he set dishes down. Burgers and fries, with an extra side of fries. And coffee, of course.

"Do you folks need anything else?" he asked. He was about the same age my little brother was now, all gangly like an adolescent deer.

I shook my head and smiled. "We're good. Thank you."

James spattered ketchup over his fries with the enthusiasm of a forensics student re-creating a crime scene. He lifted a couple and held them out toward me.

"Abracadabra?" His toast was tentative.

I snagged a couple of my own and touched them to his. "Abracadabra."

For a few minutes, we savored the food, letting it be enough.

Letting ourselves be at peace. Neither the peace nor the potatoes lasted. When we'd reduced the food to crumbs, I pulled my hands into my lap.

"James, about the other night . . ." I looked down, picking at a hangnail instead of facing his gray eyes. "You wanted me to stay, and I couldn't handle it." I took a ragged breath, too afraid to look up. "It's just that, what they were doing?" Choking on the words would have been easier. I swallowed, tried again. "It's one thing for strangers to hear. They'll forget and move on with their lives. But those things . . . your truths . . ." There weren't any words that didn't seem ridiculous. I tried for alternatives. "If we're friends." If we were more than friends. "I shouldn't . . ."

Hecate's dogs. Just say it, Bartleby.

If he wanted to yell or blame me or go out of his way to avoid meeting in the future, well, I'd just have to deal. I pulled my hands out of my lap and ran them over my face, frustrated and awkward and not sure anything I was saying would make a difference. After a minute, I forced myself to stare into James's eyes.

"I only want to hear them if and when you want to tell them to me."

James watched with concern crinkling the corners of his eyes. As I finished, the ghost of a smile flickered and disappeared from his face.

"You think I'm upset with *you*?" he asked after a few torturous seconds.

I shrugged. "It would make sense if you were."

With one fluid motion, he slid out of his side of the booth and into mine, slinging an arm over my shoulders as he found my gaze. "We *are* friends, for your information." His voice dipped low as he stared down at me.

More than friends. My ill-starred goblin brain tried, but failed, to make me say the words aloud.

"And I didn't *ask* you to stay," he went on, shifting so that he wasn't staring directly at me anymore. His voice regained its usual timbre. I wanted to thank Hecate and curse her at the same time. "I hoped you might. But I understood why you didn't."

"Really?"

"Really."

His laugh was a fragile thing. "It wasn't all bad. It's nice to get confirmation, sometimes, about what's important. I don't know about you, but I'm great at lying to myself."

I risked a glance back up at him, very deliberately *not* thinking about two of the cards Chuck had drawn.

The lovers and the knight of cups.

Prophecy was notoriously flippant when it came to the interpretation of symbols. Lovers and romance could mean any number of things, really. That didn't stop me from hoping the cards had referred in some way to me. And loathing myself for it.

"I've done my best to shut the bad stuff away," he said, gaze tracking to the dark window, "to build a strong barrier between what I was supposed to be and who I want to be. But that barrier was breached, and it's going to take me a minute to move past that."

He'd told me about changing branches. His family's expectations. His own personal revolution. The scars, literal and metaphysical, he'd earned along the way. And I couldn't entirely understand, but I could empathize.

My family had never known *what* to expect for me, beyond the same life they'd lived, and their parents before them. Blue-collar job, marriage, and kids—maybe in that order. If I was very lucky, the life they imagined for me might include a fleeting chance, every now and then, to do something I loved. A novel read in stops and starts. A vacation somewhere middling, where at least it was possible to take a nap in the sun. The kinds of magic they could understand.

But I'd been born on a new moon, an emergency C-section that shattered my parents' world. My life was always going to be different than theirs, though the one time they'd acknowledged that and taken me to the local diviner, they'd been so shaken by the results it was worse than if they'd never acknowledged my difference at all.

Their surfeit of expectations still shaped me. It snuck up on me at the most unexpected times. Someone in class would talk about their study-abroad experience in undergrad or that one internship or that time at camp or some life-changing volunteer trip—all planned milestones on their path to *something* bigger—and I'd realize I hadn't known how to dream about my future, let alone plan for it, until I'd gotten here. Nobody had ever taught me how. I hadn't had milestones so much as a grasping, rambling journey that had somehow led me to this place.

My place.

I hadn't known exactly what I was choosing when I came. Not in the same way James knew when he switched branches. But my choice, like James's, had consequences.

I'd catapulted myself off the edge of my family's map of the known and possible and right into the big blank spot on the map. When they talked to me now, it was like I was some alien thing from another realm, fearful and unfathomable. And I *had* changed, fair enough. But that didn't mean the distance between us hurt less.

I couldn't imagine what family meant *exactly* for James. Couldn't fathom the weight of those expectations and that legacy. His experience was so different from mine. But I could understand the vining pain. I knew the precise way in which it sprawled and clung and choked at the most unexpected moments.

I wrapped my hand around his and squeezed. James squeezed back.

ONCE WE GOT PAST MY GUILTY CONSCIENCE, OUR SNACK TRIP STARTED to feel almost like a date. If dates involved trading notes on an ongoing investigation.

I caught James up on the Federation's efforts. We'd made contact with some students—Lora was going to get him a Ouija board tomorrow so he could try to contact Imani—and, according to Darya, we might know how to take down the working. Most of the pieces had fallen into place. We needed to identify who the rest of the mages behind the working were, and we needed to get ready for a major protest. Mags was handling the latter, but I'd made a bit of progress on the former. From my work with Mags's spreadsheet, I had a list of faculty who might be involved, but we needed to shorten it drastically, and fast.

"I'm going to owe Darya a huge favor." I groaned, entirely sincere.

"Why's that?" James asked around a mouthful of burger.

"I think it's time to have a chat with Pruitt Hockley."

James choked. "The Associate Director of Student Accessibility Services?" I nodded. "You think he'll share details about the faculty on your list?"

My smile was more bravado than anything. "If Darya paves the way."

Wiping grease off his hands with a crumpled napkin, James shot me an approving smile. "I have a thought, too."

I tilted my head. "Oh yeah?"

"Once we have a shorter list and we're mostly sure everyone on it is involved, we're going to need a way to gather information. Make sure we've pinpointed all the players."

"Players, huh? Since when are we in a heist movie?"

James shrugged. "What else am I supposed to call them? Conspirators? Monsters?"

"Monsters, definitely." I made a face. "What did you have in mind?"

"Since we *are* both dabbling in digimancy these days, I thought we might take a crack at a magically enhanced email." He leaned back and regarded me, smug despite the ketchup crust at the corner of his mouth.

I was too distracted by that ketchup, just at the curve of his lower lip, to process what he said immediately. As I tried not to stare, the words sank in.

"You want to make a phishing working?"

James leaned in, laughing. "Let's just shout that a little louder."

I made a face, dropping my voice to an intense whisper. "I'm sorry. I got a little surprised when you went from zero to infect-faculty-computers-with-a-magic-virus."

"It's not explicitly against student code," he whispered back. "We don't care about exam answers or anything like that."

His enthusiasm was contagious. "It's not our fault if the university's administrative documents haven't fully caught up with the twenty-first century."

"Not even a little bit our fault," James agreed.

CHAPTER THIRTY-FOUR

It was, of course, an indispensable part of Bartleby's business to verify the accuracy of her work, word by word. James assisted Bartleby in this examination. It was a very dull, wearisome, and lethargic affair.

—NARRATORIAL COMMENTARY ADAPTED FROM HERMAN
MELVILLE'S "BARTLEBY THE SCRIVENER" BY ANNE

IT TOOK US THE ENTIRE WEEKEND, BUT WE CRAFTED A FUNCTIONAL phishing working just in time for the meeting Darya got us with Pruitt Hockley. Which was why I was on campus, on a Monday, before 9 a.m.

Pruitt Hockley was a busy man. This was the only half hour he could spare.

He stood at the far end of the lobby, hands housed elegantly in his pockets. His dark brown skin and hot pink suit coat were a stark contrast to the grubby, industrial white of the walls. As we walked in, he drew his left hand out of his pocket and flicked his wrist so that the face of his rose-gold watch shifted into view.

"Mr. Hockley?" I hurried over and James lengthened his stride to keep up. "Thank you for making the time."

Hockley gestured toward the hall. "My office is right through here."

We followed, shoes squeaking on freshly waxed floors, down the hall and around the corner, to a glass-walled suite of offices on which *Student Accessibility Services* had been lettered in the official university hue of platypus purple.

Hockley unlocked the outer suite doors and led us through the sitting area toward a large office in the back. This space had opaque walls and a solid door, which Hockley closed behind us.

"Have a seat." He smoothed his tie as he took his own seat behind a slab of a desk with absolutely nothing on its surface.

I slid into the chair directly across from him. James grabbed a chair closer to the door.

"I understand you've got some questions." Hockley folded his hands artfully on the desktop. The man moved like a dancer, or one of those street performers who poses for hours at a time, every gesture a spectacle.

Dragging my gaze from his hands, I smiled. "Yes. Darya says hello, by the way."

Hockley twitched a smile but stayed silent.

Awkward. I cleared my throat.

"I'm not sure how much she told you . . ."

"Not very much," Hockley said. "She seemed to be mid-battle with a flower bulb."

Was that a joke? I relaxed, placing my own hands on the desk in mirror of Hockley's.

"That sounds about right. We're . . . I don't know how to say this diplomatically." I glanced at James, who grimaced as he shrugged. "So, I'm just going to say what I have to say. Darya trusts you, and I trust Darya." I took a breath. "As I'm sure you're aware, dozens of Magic students have gone missing over the course of the term. What's less obvious is that they're vanishing after submitting accommodation requests to their instructors." I laid out our evidence as clinically as I could, James chiming in when I missed anything important. Hockley's face remained impassive throughout, a semipleasant neutral expression he'd probably honed during faculty meetings.

I pulled my hands into my lap, leaning forward as I got to the point.

"I'm working on a plan. A group of us are. We need to know who's responsible because we think they'll just do this all again if we reverse the working without exposing them."

Hockley took his time to respond, soaking in the silence that followed my story. He inhaled, long and slow, and exhaled just as slowly.

He, too, moved his hands to his lap.

"A clarifying question, if I may?" he asked.

"Of course."

"You believe I can help because my office issued the accommodation letters? Do you have reason to believe my staff is involved?" The questions carried their weight in subtext: *Is this an accusation? Do you think I'm involved? What are you really here for?*

If we were right and administrators and faculty were behind this, they wouldn't necessarily have needed an inside person in this office. That didn't mean there wasn't one. Odds were that *someone* on his team had played a part in all this. It could even be Hockley himself, though I doubted it. Darya said he'd gone to bat for her more than once over ableist program policies. And anyway, we weren't here to start a witch hunt. We were here on the hope that SAS had collected information about faculty compliance over the years.

My glance at James was a question. He shook his head, so subtly I only caught it because I was looking for it.

Turning back toward Hockley, I lifted a shoulder and let it fall.

"We don't know. We have a list of faculty who may be involved, and we hope you might have data that can help us shift *mays* to *definitelys*."

Hockley's neutral expression went sour. "I don't know what data you're referring to." He stood, paced to the back wall where rows of filing cabinets towered, and raised his voice theatrically as he explained. "We only maintain records for *students* who use our services, and only for as long as we're legally required to maintain them." He dragged a column of drawers open, top to bottom, and turned to face us, hands once again elegantly in his pockets.

"I'm sorry to say I don't believe I can be of any assistance." He was going to kick us out. But then, why had he opened the filing cabinet drawers? "Now, I'm going to step out for coffee," he said, speaking at a normal volume again, "When I return, I expect you to be gone."

Did he suspect someone in the building was eavesdropping?

Before I could say anything at all, Pruitt Hockley stalked out of the room. The sidestep he had to do around James was the only inelegant motion he made as he left, clicking the door firmly shut behind him.

He was helping us, within limits.

In the rushing quiet of his wake, James stood and made his way toward the filing cabinets. I followed, resisting the intense urge to tiptoe.

Three drawers' worth of data, and we were supposed to find what we needed before he got back with coffee?

But the drawers were full of empty folders. James pushed them back in one by one, swearing.

"I really thought he was helping us out," he said with an irritated shove to the bottom drawer. It didn't rattle as much as the others as it closed. Suspicion, or hope, snagged my breath.

"Wait. Pull that back out?"

James pulled.

"Shut it again?"

James shoved.

"Does that sound weird to you? Compared to the other ones?" I crossed my arms as James experimentally opened and shut a different drawer, then slid the bottom one open and shut again.

"It does. A little less rattley?"

He pulled it back open and I sank to my knees, flattening myself against the plush office carpet to look *under* the drawer.

Sure enough, taped to the bottom was a thick manila folder.

I pried it loose. "Why do I feel like we are in a heist movie, after all?" My words came out a whisper.

James knelt beside me, his own voice hushed. "The way he

said they only keep records on students makes me think this file is not supposed to exist." He took a breath, eyeing the thing. "He obviously doesn't want *someone* to know about it."

"Yes, but who? And why all the theatrics?" It wasn't like the faculty in the file were lurking in the corridors to overhear him.

"Hard to say. But the idea that one of his staff is leaking information—or worse—didn't seem to surprise him." He shrugged, reaching to flip the folder open. It was densely packed with an assortment of printouts and handwritten notes.

"How long do you think he's been tracking this stuff?"

"Only one way to find out," James said. "How do you want to do this?"

I slid my phone out of my bag.

"He didn't say we couldn't take pictures."

WE RECONVENED IN MY OFFICE TO CROSS-REFERENCE SAS'S DEPRESS-ingly long file of problem faculty with my list of potential suspects. Hockley's folder contained at least five years' worth of data, as far as I could tell. And it wasn't sorted by branch or department. In-stead, it was jostled together by year and term. We went through everything, photo by photo, making note of incident reports that included faculty with appointments in the School of Magic.

It took us hours, but in the end, we had a list of five faculty who we were reasonably sure had been involved: Professor Cecil Osborne in Necromancy, Professors Arcadia Hobbs and Kenneth Alcott in Divination, Professor Mark Delight in Alchemy, and—dismay sent my stomach plummeting—Professor Ursula Leighton in Thaumaturgy.

I didn't want to believe it. I wanted to tear up the list and start over. But the evidence was there. Mr. Hockley's manila folder documented five separate cases, over the past three years, in which Professor Leighton had not only resisted implementing accommo-dations but also driven students who requested them out of class. The longer I stared at her name, the more pieces fell into place.

Her insistence that I focus on my own work, which only increased after my visit to the dean. Her emphasis on the possibility of failure, after that visit. The Oracle's prophecy that it was someone close to me. The easy way she'd stepped aside to allow Mark Delight onto my committee.

I'd been braced for my advisor to end up on this list. For Mr. Hockley's evidence to implicate her. It hadn't, though. And part of me wondered if this was why. If she'd been so dismissive when I brought up the possibility of accommodations because she knew how Leighton would react.

"Touch piece for your thoughts?" James asked.

I grimaced. Part of me wished that Anne were here, to explain for me. There was something cathartic about the way it blurted my innermost thoughts. Embarrassing, but also a relief. I'd suspected we were dealing with faculty and admin, but suspecting and knowing were very different things. And seeing Professor Leighton's name emerge had shaken me. But admitting that I was fantasizing about running away, hiding, heeding the mascarons' warnings before everything came crashing down around me, felt impossible. The words would douse the respect and belief I saw whenever I looked into James's eyes.

I shrugged. "I'm spiraling a little."

"Anyone would be." James grimaced. "I am, too, to be honest."

"I didn't expect there to be so many of them."

That wasn't quite true. It was more that I'd wanted to believe we might be wrong, that our professors wouldn't be involved in anything this hateful. That the people in power in our program wouldn't act so disgracefully.

"I don't think this is everyone." James looked at me, eyes even more tired than they had been the other day. "None of these people account for the flower display at the admin building. Someone higher up is involved. Maybe multiple someones."

His point was solid, and it hit me squarely in the gut. Whether it was Dean Underhill or someone else entirely, this wasn't going to resolve quickly when we started pointing fingers. It would get messy. And we might take ourselves out in the process.

James's mouth twitched. "This doesn't change anything. We're going to stop them."

"Yes, we are." I straightened my shoulders, imitating confidence in the hope of tricking myself into feeling it. Then I called up our phishing working. "Are you ready to send some emails?"

THE WEEK SPED BY AFTER THAT. WE BRAVED OUR WAY THROUGH DIGImancy. I taught and worked on my exam flashcards and met with my advisor for a practice session, somehow still finding the time to check our inbox every hour or so, waiting for our working to succeed.

Not everyone on our list would fall for our phishing email, so we cast a wide net, composing the working so that when a recipient clicked on our link, the magical equivalent of an automatic forwarding rule was created in their account. Every email they received afterward came to us.

That function was courtesy of the container full of lacewing larvae we'd used to buffer the working. Rose, who'd obtained them for us from one of her friends in Entomology, called the things junk bugs. Apparently, they collected detritus by impaling it on their spikes. That behavior imbued the fragile combination of magic and malware we'd concocted with the grabbiness of Velcro and the fierceness of the goathead stickers I'd stepped on so often as a barefoot kid in Texas.

Over the course of the week, we reeled in a lot of insignificant emails from the two faculty who did click: Kenneth Alcott and Cecil Osborne. Exchanges about articles in progress with the editors of academic journals. Administrative messages. Students asking for extensions on assignments. Junk mail. Nothing helpful to our investigation, though. Every time I started to spiral about that, I forced myself to breathe.

We still had time. Not much, but some.

After class on Wednesday, James and I huddled over my laptop. It was a New Moon, and I couldn't help hoping that meant a shift in luck for us. Still, I was so nervous we wouldn't find anything, I mistyped the password to the fake account we'd set up. Swearing, I tried again.

"What are we going to do if it doesn't work?" Instead of looking at James, I watched the screen, waiting for the inbox to load.

James cleared his throat. "About that . . . I might have—"

An email notification cut him off midsentence. We knocked our heads together, peering at the inbox.

"Sorry," James said.

I didn't care, didn't really feel the throb of pain. In our inbox, we had a new email thread. A series of reply-all messages to an email from Dean Underhill with the subject line **AAMUP representative dinner plans.**

Cecil Osborne–Re: Re: Re: AAMUP representative dinner plans

I still say we should run him through the Bone House wards as soon as he arrives instead of waiting to lay our preferred version of reality on him at dinner. Why allow him to speak to any of our students—and take the risk he'll pass his findings along before our dinner—when we can control the narrative from the get-go?

Kenneth Alcott–Re: Re: AAMUP representative dinner plans

Are there any additional preparations we ought to make?

~KA

Ursula Leighton–Re: AAMUP representative dinner plans

I shall look forward to it.

URSULA

Ivette Underhill–AAMUP representative dinner plans

My assistant has confirmed a reservation for five at
Kalemaris. March 2, 6 p.m. Please arrange your schedules
accordingly.

Best,

IVETTE

Another ping. I clicked out of the thread to see a new reply-all
response:

**Mark Delight–Re: Re: Re: Re: AAMUP
representative dinner plans**

There's something odd about this email. Delete
everything in this chain immediately. And contact IT.
Someone's downloaded a virus.

I took a shaky breath. "Hecate's dogs."

"We did it." James's grin was vicious. "Now we know who to
take down."

"Honestly, I'm surprised that our list of suspects was so spot-
on." I bit my lip. "I wasn't sure this was going to work." Despite
my expectations, our ridiculous phishing working had done its
job. I saved the emails to PDF, letting myself smile.

"What, because of the digimancy?" When I nodded, James's
expression went serious. "I'll have you know we had two of our
very best people on the job."

I snorted. "You've got that half-right."

"Are you implying that you don't think I'm one of the best people?" James's pout was melodramatic, surprising a snort out of me.

"You know that's not what I meant." He raised an eyebrow,
but didn't contradict me. "Anyway . . . how do we know we've
identified *everyone* who's involved?" I didn't want to bring down
the mood, but we didn't have time to rest on our laurels. Their
dinner plans with the AAMUP representative were for the night

of my exam, in nineteen days. Everyone else was waiting on us. Trusting us to make sure we'd identified all of the conspirators. "It seems like we've got the core group. But there could be more."

"About that . . ." James tilted his head, as if daring himself to go on.

That couldn't be a good sign. I folded my arms.

"I have an idea." James ran a hand through his hair with a scowl, sending that treacherous lock tumbling into his eyes.

I had ideas, too. About edging that hair out of the way and . . . James was watching me, face screwed up like he was about to say the worst thing I'd ever heard in my life.

My other ideas vaporized. "Oh, yeah?"

"You aren't going to like it," he said finally. "*I* don't like it." He huffed. "But I think it might work, if we're lucky. And I know I already suggested something like this. I swear I'm not trying to be a dog with a bone about it, but I think it might be our only option at this point."

I let my arms drop, exasperated.

"Are you going to tell me what this terrible idea is?"

"We use Anne." He cupped his hand to the back of his neck and grimaced.

He was Heccing right. I didn't like it.

"It's still narrating you," he explained as we walked to his car, "and we know it's capable of narrating people who are interacting with you because it mentions us from time to time. But the glitches mean it can probably narrate people who aren't interacting with you. That it can switch primary subjects, somehow. So, we use that."

I tensed and James corrected himself.

"I mean, we don't use the glitches. We know that won't get us anywhere. We use its regular narration. We can plant it in Professor D.'s office when we meet with him for one-on-ones in week eight." James unlocked his car and climbed inside, leaning over to unlock my door. "He's the only one we've got reliable access to."

I slid into the passenger seat, chewing on my bottom lip. It could work. If we could figure out how to keep it quiet, anyway. And how was I supposed to say no to that? I couldn't, not even if it meant risking my exam working.

"I know it's not ideal," James said. "But we can cloak it heavily and let it do its thing. It's the least dangerous option we have."

That was easy for him to say. If we decided to plant Anne in Professor D.'s office and it was discovered, the trail of breadcrumbs would lead right back to me. And only me. But I was already on Professor D.'s radar. My students needed help—dozens of students needed help—and I didn't have a better idea.

The university was warded against all the usual workings that could be used to spy. A plagiarism preventative. We'd found a loophole with our phishing working, but thanks to Professor D. they were onto that now. The odds that we'd get lucky and find another solution were vanishing. If Anne could *consistently* narrate anyone other than me, and if we could keep it quiet while it did, we had to use it.

"You're right." I narrowed my eyes, finding his. "But we're going to have to test it. For all we know, it might keep narrating me even if it's planted in Professor Delight's office. It's worked from a distance before."

James slung his arm over my shoulder. "Of course."

I sighed. "And in the meantime, we'll have to do something about the sound."

CHAPTER THIRTY-FIVE

It is a truth universally acknowledged, that a mage student in possession of a deadline must be in want of a distraction.

—NOTE ON THE BLACKBOARD IN THE MAGE STUDENT COPY ROOM

I SENT ANNE WITH JAMES, BUNDLED UP IN A BACKPACK AND WEARING Cy's cat ear trucker hat.

With plans in motion and nothing much to do until Monday, I spent the weekend trying to help Darya, getting shooed away, and retreating guiltily to prepare for my exam.

I knew, deep down in the marrow of my bones, that Anne's narration was divination. But I still couldn't quite demonstrate how it worked, let alone document the function for my committee's review. Because of my initial coding errors, Cy's Christmas Village had proven useless. But I didn't think Anne's narration would've worked on the village even if I had gotten the code right. Prophecies grabbed hold of reality in a subtler way than most other workings. Sure, they could be *connected* to objects—Excalibur being a prime example—but they were almost always *about* people.

Did that mean there had to be some consciousness involved for prophecy to change reality? Some awareness of the words and their meaning, on the receiving end, that allowed the magic to work? And how would I track that sort of thing?

I followed my questions into grimoires and journal articles, lost myself in my studies in a way I had so often before this term, when things were normal. Slipping into the flow was like a homecoming. Words and ideas clustered and shifted in my head, grouping and regrouping to my own personal choreography.

It was over almost as soon as it started. Monday morning came, and with it texts from James.

It worked.
Will fill you in after class.
Want to get a late lunch?

We made plans to meet at Glass Half Full after Digimancy.

Professor Delight started the day by handing out a signup sheet for our week eight one-on-ones. The paper contained a series of fifteen-minute time slots, scheduled during what would usually be class time on Monday and Wednesday.

James and I had planned for this. Still, I held my breath as I scribbled my name on the still-empty line next to the first slot on Monday. The thought of spending fifteen minutes, alone, with a professor who suspected I knew about his horrible activities—and had bullied his way onto my committee to keep me from acting on that knowledge—made me want to gag. I passed the sheet to Hadrian and wrapped my arms around my stomach.

At the front of the room, Rose spoke up. "Professor? How should we prepare for the conferences?"

"An excellent question," he said. "This time is for you. A chance to make sure your final projects are on track and that you aren't following a blind path."

His gaze flicked over Rose's head, slicing into me. "We'll ferret out any mistakes," he said, breaking his stare to smile back down at Rose, "and make sure you're set up to succeed."

I GOT TO THE PUB FIRST AND ORDERED A TALL GLASS OF A HABANERO
pumpkin ale, choosing a table as close to the fire as I could get.
The day was wet and cold and unrelentingly gray. My clothes were
sopping, despite the mud guards on my bike, and I did my best to
forget my misery with a long swallow. It burned in the back of my
throat, warming me.

I closed my eyes and sank back into my chair.

"That good, huh?" James asked. I sat up as he slid into the seat
across from me, drink already on the table. "Hey."

"Hi." I managed a smile.

James handed over the bag containing Anne. I hung it on the
back of my chair with my satchel.

"It worked?"

James's smile came slowly, but not because it was reluctant. It
took its time, spreading across his face. He was enjoying the moment. "It did. But not right away."

He wasn't just looking at me, he was gauging something I
didn't understand. I wanted to squirm. My cheeks and ears warmed
under his stare.

"At first, it kept narrating you." He said it suggestively, as
though Anne had been disclosing intimate details about me. Or
my thoughts.

My hands tensed around my glass. Had I thought indecent, or
even mildly embarrassing, things about him over the weekend?
Why did Anne have to be so uncannily good at narrating things
I didn't want it to notice? I took refuge in a long drink of beer.
When I set my glass down, James still wasn't telling. But he was
smiling at me, maddeningly.

"Are you planning on elaborating, or . . . ?" I slapped my
palms on the table, exasperated.

James smiled again, leaning back as if to contemplate my question. Then he sat tall and shook his head. "No. I'll let you find out
yourself." He shoved away from the table. "I'm hungry. Should
we order?"

Hunger was the last thing on my mind, but my stomach rumbled as he walked toward the counter. Traitor. I followed, but only because fries were on the line. When I caught up to him, he leaned in with a whisper.

"Check the logs later, if you really want to know."

LATER THAT NIGHT, JAMES TEXTED AGAIN.

Did you check the logs?

I'd been putting it off, afraid to learn just how badly I'd embarrassed myself.

Working on it.

Heart pounding, I scrambled off the couch to clear the clutter off the printer in my room. Ignoring the warmth flooding my face, I hooked the printer up to my laptop and pulled up Anne's logs.

The printer's quirk of printing all documents from last page to first had never actually worked in my favor before. I snagged the first several pages it spat out and scrambled onto my bed to read them.

Most were boring. Narrations of how late I stayed up, what I was reading, how many times I'd let my tea go cold.

And then I hit the series of entries that started three days ago, when I'd sent Anne with James.

Friday, February 12, 5:03 p.m. A narration of me telling James to be careful with Anne.

Friday, February 12, 5:04 p.m. to **6:00 p.m.** A series of bland commentaries about the car ride and the state of James's apartment (tidy, welcoming) and his cat (orange and apparently snack-oriented).

I turned the page.

More commentary about the cat.

And—
My hands started to tremble, breath unsteady.

Saturday, February 13, 3:32 p.m., Bartleby trusted
James with Anne because she trusted James with
herself, knowing that he could be relied upon to
take good care of both.

Saturday, February 13, 4:01 p.m., Bartleby longed
to know where James lived. She'd been almost
jealous when she learned that Lora had been there
and was actually jealous, no qualifiers at all,
that Anne got to know.

Saturday, February 13, 7:32 p.m., Bartleby wondered
what James was doing. She told herself it was
because she was worried about their experiment,
about the looming deadline, about the missing
students. And she *was* worried about those things.
But a bigger part of her wondered because she
wanted to know what James was like in the soft
light of the evening, relaxed and in his element.
What he ate, and what he read and what he
wore . . .

It went on, but I couldn't. My eyes skimmed ahead, heart
pounding, to discover what else Anne had shared. How embarrassed would I have to be, next time I encountered James?
Two entries down, a phrase stopped me short: **James wondered . . .**
I went back, reread the entry from the start.

Saturday, February 13, 7:59 p.m., James was
delighted by Anne's narration because its presence
in his home made it feel like a part of Bartleby
was there, as well. When Anne finally began to

narrate him, he put in earbuds and listened to
instrumental music, letting his mind wander. He
wondered what Bartleby was doing, imagined her
poring over research materials, chin propped
in her hand, hair falling to frame her face. He
traced the outlines of her tattoos in his mind,
thrilling at the beautiful images that let bits
of her soul peek out at the world, at once a
challenge and a plea.

Saturday, February 13, 8:00 p.m., That was what
James loved most about Bartleby: her brash
vulnerability. The way she admitted her failures
and shortcomings as if they were badges of pride.
The way being herself was a foregone conclusion,
and you could tell, if you took the time to
notice, that she wasn't going to apologize for it
even if the effort not to apologize threatened
to do her in. From the moment she'd fried those
computers in the lab, James had been fascinated.

My cheeks were burning now, but it wasn't with embarrassment. My stomach did that thing that happened when I took a
dip in the road too fast, or descended so rapidly from the crest of
a roller coaster that I almost wasn't breathing with the adrenaline.
I moved to keep reading, but the doorbell rang.

Shit. Shit, shit, shit.

Taking a deep breath, I did my best to center myself before
answering the door.

James might have been able to ignore Anne's narrations, but
I wanted to tear through the rest. I wanted to read every single
word Anne had narrated about James. And then read them again
and again, until the words tattooed themselves into me.

Maybe James would want to trace *those* tattoos, too.

I dragged the door open, unsteady at the thought and scowling to hide it. If it was a missionary, Hecate's dogs would be the least of their troubles. I wasn't in the right state of mind to politely send someone away.

But it was James, standing in the drizzling rain under our blinking porch light.

"Did you check the logs?" he asked, oddly formal. Or maybe nervous. I blinked up at him. The corners of his eyes were crinkled, hope and fear creased into his skin.

"Yes."

The word came out trembly, and he must have heard it. Or seen the way the logs affected me, the heat still flooding through me. His eyes widened, fear vanishing. He reached for me, lips finding mine. I pressed against him, hands searching, clutching at his jacket and shirt to pull him closer. The door slammed behind us and we startled apart, finding each other's eyes and laughing.

Taking James's hand, I led him inside. He gave me enough time to shut the door and throw the dead bolt before pulling me back toward him, sliding his hands around my waist. We made our way, entangled, into my bedroom. The logs were still there, pages scattered on my bed. I swept them aside with one hand, not willing to let go of James. I wouldn't let this stop before it was properly started.

James pulled away, his face as flushed as mine felt. Had I done something wrong? Misread this somehow? I tilted my head, opened my mouth.

He panted a question before I could get a word out. "Was it right?"

"What?"

"Anne's narration," he elaborated. "Was it right about—" he searched for the right words "—about you?"

I nodded, dared to ask my own question in return. "Was it right about *you*?"

His face smoothed into a lazy smile. He brushed my bangs out of my eyes. "What did it say about me?"

As he asked he stepped closer, pulling me back toward him,

leaving just enough distance between us that he could still see my face. He was waiting for an answer. My cheeks ached with blushing, but I found words and whispered them.

"That you're fascinated by me."

"What else?" His words were breathless.

"That you love my brash vulnerability." His smile deepened the crinkles at the corners of his eyes. "That you think my tattoos are beautiful."

His fingers found my upper arms, skimming over the thin cotton material of my shirt and setting my skin tingling beneath it. I took a step back, peeling off my shirt to reveal more of my collection: the shapes swirling up my arms and over my shoulders, down my ribs and abdomen. They continued even below that. Reminders that I was more than my mistakes. His hands found my bare skin, fingers tracing the patterns of plant leaves, fruit, insects, flowers and objects that called out parts of me I wanted to bring into the light.

"*You* are beautiful," he breathed.

Whatever remaining questions he might have had about logs and their accuracy were going to have to wait until the morning. The curve of his mouth was full of perfect promises.

Promises I was going to help him keep.

With a kiss, I began to unbutton his shirt, and together we made quick work of the rest of our clothes, tumbling into my half-made bed in one another's arms.

If Anne narrated what came next, it had the decency to keep its narration to itself.

CHAPTER THIRTY-SIX

Bartleby arrived at the Federation headquarters with a line from *Dracula* running through her head: "When we meet in the study we shall all be informed as to facts, and can arrange our plan of battle with this terrible and mysterious enemy . . ."

—ANNE'S LOGS, 19 FEBRUARY

MAGS WAVED AT THE ASSEMBLED GROUP. "THANK YOU ALL FOR being here," she said. "We've gathered information. We've made contact with some of the missing students. Now we need to decide if we're ready to take this working down. Team one, care to report?"

"Of course," Darya said. "Our working reversal is pretty well mapped out. We need to destroy the plants that are grounding the working all at once."

"And monitor Penant to ensure that student records are reinstated," Nathaniel said.

"Or magically re-create them, if they aren't," Hadrian chimed in.

"What about the ghosts?" Evelyn asked, voice tentative. "Will this undo whatever's made them so withholding and aggressive?" Hands rocketed up around the room, voices clambering to piggyback on her question.

"Taking down the working should set everything right." Lora

had to shout to be heard. Their use of *should* was unsettling, if not outright alarming, and a rumble of whispers underscored the group's dissatisfaction.

"Great!" Mags poured chipper energy into the exclamation, firmly closing the door on that particular topic. "I'm happy to report group three is also ready. We've appointed leads for each working site. I'll be coordinating the group at the admin building. Rose has volunteered to lead the group at Randolph House. Then we have Darya at Newton Hall, Lora at Bentham Cote, and Chuck at Sibyl House. Hadrian and Nathaniel have volunteered to lead a digimancy team to monitor and manage student records. We've been putting schedules together with shifts, because we need to keep the protests going even after the working falls."

Mags waited a beat before turning to me.

"That just leaves team two. Bartleby and James, would you take the floor?"

"Actually . . ." As the assembled practitioners turned my way, I removed Anne from my bag, adjusting it so it was facing the room. "I need to show you something, before we explain. *Once upon a time*, Anne."

After a long moment in which my eyes started to water and my lungs burned, Anne began to narrate. I inhaled, relief flooding through me almost as quickly as the oxygen did.

"Like all Bartleby's reasoning the thing seemed simplicity itself when it was once explained," it said, quoting Sherlock Holmes. I took a breath, ready to dive into my explanation, but Anne barreled on. "Bartleby and James had determined that, in order to be certain they'd identified all involved parties and accrued sufficient evidence of their guilt, it would be necessary to plant a surveillance device in one of the suspect's offices."

Hushed chatter swept through the room. Small exclamations of surprise and disbelief. Anne was not daunted.

"Bartleby's spellwork demonstration, although not designed for the purpose, meets the need better than most constructs

would," it explained to the room. "As an organic-digital narration construct, Anne produces logs that can be monitored from a
distance and creates a record which can be used to support claims
against the perpetrators."

"Your plan is to use your spellwork demonstration to *spy* on
faculty, on the off chance they . . . what? Say something incriminating?" William glowered at Anne, then at me. "That's a violation of student code."

"So is putting up runes to keep the university ghosts at bay,"
Lora said. "An even bigger one, technically."

"And these faculty are making students disappear, in case you
forgot." James's shoulder brushed against mine.

I took over. "Right. This is low risk. With any luck, we'll
have the evidence we need well before our deadline. I'll drop it
off on Monday—"

"Bartleby's knowledge of the plan was slightly out of date,"
Anne interrupted. Somehow, it managed its own dramatic pause,
despite speaking in its usual text-to-speech monotone. "James
would be the one to do the planting."

I glared and he smiled, sheepish.

"We bonded, I guess."

"Bartleby would need to keep Anne visible in order to discuss
her Digimancy project with the professor. There would be no
opportunity to hide the narration skull during the consultation,"
Anne explained.

It had a point, but its logic also had a major flaw. "Okay, but
who's going to pick it up, if James plants it?"

Rose raised a timid hand. "I had to schedule an alternate one-
on-one with Professor Delight because of a doctor's appointment."

My throat tightened around an irrational sense of betrayal.
It was *my* exam working; I was responsible for it. But this was a
group effort, and the group agreed with Anne and James. We took
a vote, and the *motion passed* sign at the back of the room lit up,
leaving me no grounds on which to argue.

James would use *his* week-eight conference to hide a cloaked

Anne in Professor Delight's office. Rose would retrieve it on Friday. If all went well, we'd get what we needed within that time frame. But we only had about a week to prepare.

"We're cutting it awfully close," Nathaniel said. "Are you sure this will work?"

"It will work."

James backed me up. "We've tested it. And we're doing our best, time-wise."

"We need to make sure Professor Delight can't hear your narration construct," Hadrian said. She frowned. "Most of the cloakings that might do that have been flagged as malicious by IT, since they're used for cheating."

She wasn't wrong. And the majority of the *sanctioned* cloakings I'd turned up only worked on visuals—smells and sounds still came through. We needed something that operated on all the senses but wasn't widely known. Something obscure, or old, or mostly forgotten.

Or all of the above.

Luckily, my exam prep meant I was familiar with a bunch of spells that fit that description.

"I think I have something." I handed Anne off to James so I could rummage in my bag for my photocopied facsimile of Ariadne Frecke's *Domestick Spelles*. Flipping through the pages of my grimoire, I scanned for the spell I'd marked.

To Soothe Megrims. No.

To transformme glass into china. Obviously not.

I skipped a few pages, thumb riffling the thick paper.

To beckome unobstrusive.

I paused over the page, scanned down the lines, tripping over the book's anachronistic use of the long S a couple of times in my haste. There was a note a few lines down.

Thisse working is particularly useful for housewives caring for aged relatives suffring nervous ailments, as it allowes one to minister to the invalid without inflicting pain and aches with too loud word or too buoyant step. Even smelles may discomfit the dear invalid and must be prevented. She who castes this spelle shall move according to her own whimme and remain unseen, unheard, and unscented until such time as the spelle is broken.

I'd scoffed at the spell the first time I encountered it, full of white feminist outrage: I should not have to make myself smaller or less for anyone else. Eighteenth-century housewives shouldn't have had to, either. I'd even ranted to Darya about it during a mages' night out, years later.

At least Ariadne Frecke took those poor folks' nervous ailments seriously, she'd said. *To Jane Austen they were a joke. Hypochondriacs.*

I smiled now, looking at the page. Using it was fitting.

"It's an old spell, so its use of incantation and object is . . . eccentric. But I think it will work." I looked around at the gathered practitioners. "Does anyone here embroider? Or play pianoforte?"

By the end of the night, we'd finalized our plans. We were going to ground our cloaking in an embroidered amulet, and the dormant magic in the object would be activated by a musical incantation. Chuck offered to complete the embroidery—a small, skull-size amulet with a circle of lavender around a lavish letter *U* (for unobtrusiveness). Hadrian turned out to be a pianist, and she volunteered to write a short etude to trigger the working.

On Saturday, we'd meet to test it.

MAGS HAD LET ME BORROW HER KEY TO THE FEDERATION HEADQUARTERS— with a chilling expletive-free warning not to lose it. I jammed it into the gummy lock and wiggled until the bolt slid back, pushing my way inside. James followed, carrying Anne.

"Spooky."

It was. And dusky and echoey and unfamiliar without a bunch of grad students crammed inside. I flicked the lights on.

Hadrian showed up a few minutes later, lugging a keyboard and trailed by Chuck. We set up in the middle of the room, standing around Anne, whom James had perched on a coffee table.

"So, what do we do?" Chuck asked.

Hadrian paused setting up her keyboard long enough to chime in. "What he said. I'm dying to know how this is going to work."

I flipped through *Domestick Spelles* to make sure I was remembering right.

The spell said we needed to play the song backward, measure by measure, while the person wearing the amulet either played or stood near the pianoforte. The working would end when the wearer either played or heard the song played "in its rightfull way."

"Fun," Hadrian said.

"Weird," Chuck added.

Hadrian cracked her knuckles. "We ready?"

I glanced at James.

"Before we try it on Anne, I'd like to test it." I didn't want a random working to accidentally vanish Anne forever, especially not before my exam. Plus, there was something about the way the light fell across Anne's orbital cavities made it look put-upon. It was becoming a pawn in our plans, and maybe it didn't want to be. Maybe it would prefer to narrate from the relative safety of the top of my dresser. When all of this was over, I was going to make it a more comfortable perch.

Hadrian shrugged. "Who's the lucky guinea pig?"

"Me."

James tried to beat me to the punch, almost bellowing, "I am." But I stepped between him and Chuck, reaching for the amulet. Chuck let me have it, and I slid it over my head.

"My exam working, my choice." I whirled to look at James. "Okay?"

He frowned but stayed put.

Hadrian clapped her hands together sharply. "I don't have all day. Can we start?"

As soon as I nodded, she started to play. The melody was pained and halting.

"I didn't practice it backward," she said. "Hopefully it doesn't have to be *good* to work. Those regency ladies weren't *all* exceptional musicians."

We stood there in silence for a solid thirty seconds after it ended. Nothing had happened.

"Second time's the charm?" She tried again.

This time, the melody rang out more easily.

When it was almost over, the notes warbled and warped, stretching before snapping into place. The room resonated with their absence, the working taking hold.

James was looking through me instead of at me, the notch between his eyebrows the only sign of his confusion.

I proceeded to walk around the room, chattering nonsense about the weather and compliments about Hadrian's hair (it was purple this week) and Chuck's clothes (which were always perfect).

After two minutes, Hadrian played the etude as she'd written it and, after the same odd warp and weft of the room's vibrations, I was visible again.

Hadrian clapped. "Hec yeah. That was badass!"

Chuck leaned back on the sofa, face a stunned grimace. "That was impressive. Were you making noise?"

"I talked to all of you and moved around the room."

"Should we test it on Anne now?" James asked.

I slid the amulet back over my head and handed it to James. He'd be the one to trigger the working when we planted it in Professor D.'s office, so he should do the honors now. He looped the cord around the skull, leaning the amulet gently against Anne's cheekbone.

"We'll need some way to attach this," he said. "So it doesn't jostle off and break the working."

I held up a finger. "Let's just see if it works on nonliving subjects first."

Hadrian started to play. After about thirty seconds, Anne snapped out of view, there and gone so cleanly I had to blink to clear my double vision.

"Good. Can you play it back?" My heart thrummed as Hadrian played the song.

As the etude ended, Anne snapped into view. I clapped and Hadrian did a mock bow.

"Thank you, I'm here all week," she joked.

This was going to work.

Except, we couldn't cart Hadrian around like some corporeal MP3 player.

"So far, so good. Let's see if it still works when the music is digital instead of a live performance." I gestured to James. He'd downloaded a music-composing app for the working, and he pulled it up now, handing his phone to Hadrian.

She tapped her etude into the composing app, using the digital keyboard to create a track that played backward and one that played forward. But Anne didn't disappear.

"Well, that was a bust." Hadrian sat back with a huff.

James frowned. "Maybe it's because the timing was off. You composed it faster than it actually plays."

Hadrian shrugged. "I guess that makes sense."

We tried it again.

James pressed *play*. The tinny midi sounds of the backward song poured out to the time of a metronome. Anne remained stubbornly visible.

"Nope. It's definitely not working," Chuck said.

It wasn't, and I could feel my heart pounding in my palms. There had to be a way to make this work.

"What do we do, then?" Hadrian asked. "We can't meet up before you make the drop. I'll be in Portland. It's my grandma's birthday."

"Do we know any other mage student pianists?" Chuck asked. We all shook our heads.

James crossed his arms. "We could use astral projection, maybe? If you can spare a few minutes on Wednesday?"

I groaned, realizing what had gone wrong. "I think there might be an easier answer."

All eyes turned toward me.

"I don't believe I'm about to say this, but technology isn't the problem—we're just using it wrong. We need a recording app. The music is an incantation in the spell, which means it needs to be performed by the casting mage. A recording is more in the spirit of performance than a composing app is."

James blinked at me, smile spreading.

"I can't believe it," Hadrian sniffed. "Our little copy-room girl is all grown up."

I made a face.

"Copy-room girl?" Chuck asked, leaning forward to squint at me. "*You're* copy-room girl? I imagined her taller. And more heroic."

I shoved my bangs out of my face.

"Very funny. Ha, ha, ha. Now, can we see if I'm right?"

James propped his phone up on Hadrian's music stand, hitting *record*. She played through the etude backward again, pausing so that we could start a separate track for the "rightfull" version. Anne wavered and vanished, then jolted back into view as Hadrian completed the tune.

I ignored my companion's hopeful expressions, breath half-held. "Let's try it again, just to be sure it works when it's only the phone."

Retrieving his phone, James moved closer to Anne and pressed *play*. The music began to march out of the cell speakers, backward, measure by measure.

James looked at me, and I stared back. Maybe if I didn't watch Anne, it would work this time. Maybe—

"Ooooh!" Hadrian squealed and clapped. "I think we have a winner!"

Chuck broke into beatnik's applause, fingers snapping as I whirled toward where Anne had sat a few seconds ago.

It wasn't there. I grabbed James's arm.

"Play it back?"

He played the normal version of the song and I stared at the empty spot until Anne popped back into view.

"That's disconcerting," James said.

"But functional," Hadrian added. "Which means I've done my duty." She packed up her keyboard and hefted it. "Best of luck with the drop."

"Good luck," Chuck echoed. "Let me know if you need more embroidery."

It felt anticlimactic. All that work, and now all we could do was wait for Wednesday.

DAILY DIGEST OF MAGICALLY PROMISING NARRATIONS, AUTOMATICALLY GENERATED FROM ANNE'S LOGS

DATE AND TIME	CONTENT
Monday, February 22 10:45 a.m.	For the whole of her meeting with Professor Delight, Bartleby was braced for a confrontation. If anything, though, the professor seemed distracted. He'd made perfunctory notes on her project, posing questions about her methods with all the mildness of a Professor Emeritus, thinking about his sun-dappled retirement. It left Bartleby feeling, for the rest of the week, that the other shoe must be about to drop.
Wednesday, February 24 11:15 a.m.	When it came time for James's meeting with the professor, Bartleby handed Anne to James with the instruction to *be careful*. It was not clear whether Bartleby meant *be careful with Anne* or *be careful of the professor*, but given the circumstances, it was likely a bit of both.
Wednesday, February 24 11:16 a.m.	James tucked Anne into his bag with care, slipping Chuck's embroidery in alongside the narration skull.
Wednesday, February 24 11:17 a.m.	Reaching for Bartleby like a man about to go to war, James pulled her into his arms. He kissed her like it might be the last time and guided their entangled bodies toward the bed.
Wednesday, February 24 11:50 a.m.	James drove carefully to campus and parked outside Pelley Hall, sitting in the running car for 3.5 minutes while he contemplated driving back to Bartleby's place and forgetting entirely about this blighted plan.
Wednesday, February 24 11:54 a.m.	James tied the embroidery to Anne, tight, with thread that looped down into Anne's nasal passages and back up around its upper jaw. He pulled his phone out of his shirt pocket and, after a bit of tapping, played the lurching backward song.
Wednesday, February 24 12:00 p.m.	James knocked on Professor Delight's office door, entering when the professor called, "Come in."

DATE AND TIME	CONTENT
Wednesday, February 24 12:02 p.m.	James had never particularly *liked* Professor D., but he was surprised now by how difficult it felt to hide his disgust and resentment as they chatted about James's project. How *dare* this man keep Imani and the other students from their lives and work? How dare he sit here, in his pristine office, playing at scholarly benevolence while he plotted and schemed?
Wednesday, February 24 12:05 p.m.	At Professor Delight's instruction to lay out his project "straight from the horse's mouth, as it were," James swallowed a spike of fury and did his best to muster enthusiasm for the topic.
Wednesday, February 24 12:13 p.m.	James didn't need to write down the professor's bland, reductive feedback to remember it. But taking notes supplied him an excuse to rummage in his bag. He quickly slid Anne out and nestled it under the desk, snatching a notebook and pencil before straightening in his seat.
Wednesday, February 24 2:28 p.m.	Professor Delight saw three more students that afternoon, each with a more disgraceful project than the last. The quality of graduate student endeavor had taken a definite swan dive since his day. He was doing his best to remedy that.
Wednesday, February 24 2:30 p.m.	At half-past two, Mark stretched and contemplated lunch. His foot nudged something under his desk. Something which his mind insisted he should take no notice of. His eyes narrowed, but he stood, collected his bag, and headed out in search of sustenance.
Wednesday, February 24 5:45 p.m.	Mark returned to his office to send a few emails before heading home for the night.
Wednesday, February 24 5:46 p.m.	As he slid into his leather desk chair, his foot once again nudged that unobtrusive *something* under his desk. Jaw tightening, he considered calling—no, he wouldn't allow himself to think of names. He'd handle this himself.

DATE AND TIME	CONTENT
Wednesday, February 24 5:47 p.m.	Vowing vengeance on whomever had done the deed that forced him to climb to his knees on the office floor and peer under his desk like some sort of overgrown toddler, Mark patted around, searching.
Wednesday, February 24 5:47 p.m.	His hands met nothing but empty space. With one final searching grasp, his fingers brushed something solid. He swore.
Wednesday, February 24 5:48 p.m.	After a few unsuccessful attempts at reversing the object's cloaking, Mark gave up trying to make it visible. Instead, he felt at it, hoping to intuit its nature from angles and textures.
Wednesday, February 24 5:52 p.m.	It felt like bone. And were those . . . teeth?
Wednesday, February 24 5:53 p.m.	Brow furrowing, Mark considered the week. There'd been nothing under the desk on Monday when he left. He was certain of that. The object had been placed there today. But he knew who it traced back to, even if the student in question hadn't darkened his door today.
Wednesday, February 24 5:54 p.m.	Carefully clearing space on his desk around the invisible object, Mark cast about for something hefty. The only thing that might do was his thermos. Double-walled steel that had withstood a decade of abuse, already. He emptied its contents into his waiting mug, screwed the lid back on, and took a few practice swings. It would do quite nicely.
Wednesday, February 24 5:56 p.m.	Adjusting the thermos in his hands, Mark oriented himself to the center of the empty space on his desk, and swung.

CHAPTER THIRTY-SEVEN

This spellwork demonstration demonstrates a key contention I will make in my dissertation. Namely, that [NARRATION IN EARLY NOVELS IS HECCING MAGIC FIND BETTER WORDS FOR THIS LATER]. Using a digimancy frame, I will [DO SOMETHING SMART HOPEFULLY. RASPUTIN'S BALLS I'M HOPELESS].

—DISCARDED DRAFT OF BARTLEBY'S EXAM PROPOSAL

I HEADED STRAIGHT FOR MY OFFICE THURSDAY MORNING, OPTIMISM bubbling despite my nerves. The Federation was ready and waiting for our go-ahead to take down the working. Anne was gathering evidence in Professor Delight's office, and Rose would retrieve it. Until then, all I had to do was wait. Which meant I had the whole weekend to focus on exam prep.

Was I less prepared than I'd hoped? Yes.

Did I still have some major things to finalize for my spellwork demonstration? Also yes. The way I saw it, there were a couple of ways I could prove that *Anne's* narrations were divination. The easiest—and riskiest—would be to get it to narrate my committee members during my exam. Faced with a skull spouting their own innermost thoughts, information that should be as unknowable to it as the past or future, they'd have no choice but to admit

I was right. My real problem was that I hadn't figured out how to establish that the narration in early novels was doing the same thing. But I had some ideas, and for the first time all term things were going right. Finding the students and finalizing my spell-work demonstration might actually be *possible*.

Outside my office door, I tripped. There was an empty box just where I'd be sure to stumble into it. Except, it was too heavy to be empty. My foot bumping into it would've sent it skidding if it didn't have *something* weighing it down.

I peered into it. There was nothing inside.

I shoved it with one foot, experimentally. It barely budged.

There was *something* in it. Something invisible. Something . . . *Unobtrusive.*

I went cold. Dropping to my knees, I reached into the box with both hands. My fingers traced along some sort of bone. Its edges were jagged.

So jagged. Fractured.

Hands shaking, I stood to unlock my office door and carried the box inside. There was only one thing that could be in the box. I forced myself to check Anne's logs, anyway, reading and rereading them until they seared into me. Until I couldn't pretend to be uncertain. I picked up my phone.

My trembling was so bad that I had to retype my message to James three times. Finally, I managed to send it.

He knows. He hurt Anne.

There had been no narrations after that final one, when Professor Delight attacked. Anne was more than hurt. It was broken. And I wouldn't know until James arrived whether or not it was beyond repair. I couldn't bring myself to reach back into that box to assess the damage.

Professor Delight would have been thorough in his destruction. I shuffled my shoulders up against the thought. James's texted reply was the only thing that kept me from bursting into tears.

OMW.

I could hold myself together until I knew the extent of the problem. Until then, I wouldn't let myself think about what this meant for our plans. Or my exam.

A knot formed deep in my throat, strangling me slowly from the inside out. I closed my eyes and breathed on a count of eight. In and out, over and over, until James arrived.

His knock on the door startled me; I rattled to my feet and let him in.

"Where is it?" James asked, skipping over *are you okay?* because of course I wasn't. Anyone could tell without even looking at me. I was radiating not-okayness.

I pointed to the box. He knelt next to it and tapped the things that made the app play our trigger song.

Anne seeped back into view, a fragment at a time. Or no, it wasn't an illusion of the working unraveling. The skull *was* in fragments, the whole crown of it caved in. Several of its upper teeth had been knocked out by the force of Professor D.'s blows.

Without meaning to, I made a sound between a gasp and a sob. The knot in my throat grew, making it hard to breathe or swallow.

"It's ruined." I reached for an accurate description. "Murdered." That felt right. Well, nothing about this felt right. But the word captured more of what I was feeling. The loss not only of an object, but also of a personality.

Anne was so much more than digimancy.

It didn't have any spirit matter lingering in its osseous tissue, but its skull had still shaped what it was capable of. I'd used the ultimate symbol of humanity, human mortality, to buffer my working. And its capacity for affect, for judginess and jokes, annoyance and sympathy, came from that buffer.

I was dissociating. I knew it, and I let myself withdraw into theory instead of dealing with the contents of the box.

I'd realized, weeks ago, that Anne was a very particular sort of prophecy machine and that prophecy required consciousness to work. But in my rush of excitement about that, I hadn't followed through to the inevitable conclusion: that all divination was channeled through not *one* consciousness but *two*. Diviner and divined.

Anne's full function, the complexity of its magic, clicked into place as I registered its loss. It wasn't words—or, it wasn't *only* words—that allowed narration to work magic. It was the biased, emotional point of view that shaped them and redefined everything within its frame.

Because Anne had personality, it could recognize ours. The realities we carried, on our surfaces and deep inside ourselves. It could create resonances between them. Its narrations—its words and its unique perspective—had illuminated truths that brought me and James together, like I was living in some off-kilter regency drama. It'd helped us understand what was happening to the missing students. It had shaped a story in which it was possible for someone like me—a struggling first-gen student who spent so much time trying not to be noticed that she'd failed to notice important things and people around her—to *help* in a major crisis.

And now Anne was shattered in a box on my dirty office floor.

James turned away from Anne to check on me. He frowned.

"You're shivering." He reached for my hand. "And you're freezing." My teeth began to chatter, but I barely registered his words, or the fact that he maneuvered me into my desk chair and wrapped his coat around me.

"Stay here. I'm going to get you some tea." He wrangled the keys out of the door, where I'd left them, and disappeared into the hallway.

Time stretched and compressed and he was back, shoving a warm mug into my hands, urging me to drink.

Behind him, Mags stormed into the room, unleashing a volley of her favorite swears at me. They increased in both volume and intensity until irritation overcame shock and I gathered enough energy to blink, then swallow, then raise both slightly trembling hands to flip my friend off.

Mags grinned.

"You're back. Now drink the tea your boyfriend's shoving at you. I'm going to make some calls," she said. She stabbed a finger in James's direction. "And you. Get Lora over here."

I took James's tea, too tired to address the label Mags had put on . . . whatever we were. James didn't seem to have noticed it. He was still kneeling in front of my chair, one hand resting on my knee, but he sent a quick text with his free hand.

I took one ragged breath, then another. When I was reasonably sure I wasn't going to eject my breakfast all over the office floor, I attempted a sip of tea.

At her own desk, Mags swore into a phone and slammed it down. "I called an emergency Federation meeting. Please tell me you got *something* useful before . . ." She trailed off, seeing the bleak look returning to my face.

"Nothing. You're welcome to look at the logs." The room threatened to spin. I closed my eyes.

"Maybe later," she evaded. "I trust you. But Hecate's dogs, Bartleby. He just *left this* outside the office?" Mags joined me and James at my desk, peering into the box. "It looks like he took a hammer to it." She winced.

"Thermos, actually." I heard myself slipping into a monotone, felt the shock creeping back in like ice up my fingers and arms. I didn't fight it. Honestly, it was welcome. Facing this was too much.

I slid out of my chair and knelt beside Anne's box. It was a shitty coffin, but it was Anne's final resting place.

Wishing I had a flower to lay over the skull's broken pieces, I traced a trembling finger along the bottom edge of Anne's orbital socket, where its cheek would have been in life.

From this angle, I could see a neon-green shape, peeking through the shattered cranial cavity—where the cloaking would have hidden it. I gently reached through fractured bone, removing a crumpled sticky note. Professor D.'s cramped handwriting filled the paper.

It's a pity; you would've made a wonderful mage.

So this was what the mascarons had been cryptically warning me about. Not just my exam, not just my investigation. Both, all at once. I swallowed an acid surge of rage and turned the note over, hands no longer trembling.

Tell anyone else you've misled to drop this investigation or suffer similar ruin.

Reading over my shoulders, it was James and not Mags who swore. Instead, Mags hoisted me to standing, told James to grab the box and my things, and guided me toward the door.

"Let's get you home." She hated when people made her go into a mom-mode at work, and I tried to apologize. That only made her scowl. "None of this is your fault. You saw a problem and did your best to fix it, even when it would have been better for you to walk away. That's all. You don't get to apologize for that, Bartleby."

She saw me safely to the passenger seat of James's car and pulled James into a whispered conference on the sidewalk. She didn't need to bother. I lay back against the seat and let my mind go blissfully blank.

"I'M AN ADVOCATE FOR THE DEAD, NOT SOME FUCKING BONE JOCKEY," Lora said. They stared at me, hands on hips. "I know you're in shock, but I need you to *listen*."

Lora'd come all the way to my apartment, by bus, at James's request. If this was why, she shouldn't have bothered.

"Can you bring it back or not?" I crossed my arms.

Lora pinched the bridge of their nose.

"Bartleby, you know as well as I do that the working would have broken with the skull."

I shook my head. "We don't know that for sure. It could

be . . ." What *could* it be? Hibernating? In stasis? This wasn't sci-fi; this was reality. Workings were easy to snuff out. They were only as strong as their tethering or grounding. Anne's skull hadn't just *grounded* my working, it had also been the buffer that made the technology work with the magic in the first place. Anne was gone.

But Lora was a starsdamned *necromancer*, for Hecate's sake.

James reached out and squeezed my knee. I shook his hand off.

"So it's not that you *can't* bring it back, it's that you won't."

Lora frowned. "Bartleby, Anne's gone. The skull has done its service. Let it be at peace. Let me inter it."

They might be right. But I couldn't bear it. Couldn't bear the thought of Anne in pieces in the ground.

"Get out." My words were deceptively soft.

"Bartleby," Lora tried. They stepped toward the box holding Anne, which James had set down next to my bags in the entryway.

I pushed to my feet, putting myself between Lora and the box.

"I said get out, Lora. Get *out*. Get *Out*. GET OUT."

With each repetition, I drove her toward the door. When they were through, I slammed it in their face and bolted it.

Fuck this fucking day.

I barricaded myself in my room.

CHAPTER THIRTY-EIGHT

As AAMUP board representatives visit campuses around the country, critique of the board's deliberations continues to roll in. An onslaught of think pieces by faculty and staff make two things perfectly clear: not only is the argument upon which this inquiry centers "ableist and completely off base," it is also a bald-faced attempt to return higher magic to the exclusionary chosen-one boy's club of days gone by.

—ARTICLE WRITTEN BY SELENE SCOUTT PRICE FOR THE CHRONICLE OF HIGHER MAGIC WEBSITE, 26 FEBRUARY

THAT NIGHT, THE ENTIRE ROOM FULL OF TEACHING PRACTITIO-ners could have held magic duels all around me instead of debating, more or less calmly, about how we should proceed.

I wouldn't have known the difference.

I'd shown up because some part of me recognized that I owed these people the courtesy of telling them the bad news face-to-face. That done, I'd sunk to the nearest couch and let the debate rage around me.

"We can figure out another way to pinpoint those involved. Go back to the Oracle, maybe," Chuck said. "Or get one of the missing students to spy for us, now that we're in contact with them."

"And put them even more at risk?" Rose demanded. "The people who worked the spell may be able to track them somehow. And the students we've spoken to have been confused. Their grip on consensus reality is fragile enough as it is—disrupting the routines they're clinging to might fracture it beyond repair."

Murmurs of agreement broke out.

"Besides," Hadrian interjected, forcefully, "we *have* a perfectly good working. We just need to re-create it."

I stopped breathing. I'd been dreading the moment someone would come to that conclusion. It wouldn't work. Even if the whole Federation pitched in funds for another skull and someone else bought it to get around the one skull per academic year policy and we invoked the university's emergency working clause to cut through permitting red tape, the results might not be the same. The skull that had been Anne *mattered* just as much as it mattered that Jane Austen was Jane Austen and not her sister or mother. And even if another skull *could* deliver the same results, Anne's working had taken time to develop.

We didn't have time. But I couldn't find the words or the energy to explain. I just shook my head, throat tightening around a sob I wouldn't let out.

James took one look at me and stepped in. "That's just it. It *was* a perfectly good working, but they're *onto* it now. They'll be expecting us to try spying. It's not going to work."

I could've kissed him on the spot. Or cried on his shoulder.

"James is right," Mags said. "We've got to find another way."

"A way that doesn't involve spying and still gets us all the proof we need in—" Nathaniel paused to think "—four days?" The skepticism in his voice was almost lethal. The conversation flatlined for what felt like an eternity.

"So," Evelyn said eventually, "we take down the working and we get the students to safety. We'll rent a bus if we have to."

There were enough murmurs of agreement that I forced myself to sit up and intervene.

"That might work to save these students in the short-term. But we don't know if taking down the working is going to restore their records. Digital files are more fragile than people are. The cloaking may have destroyed them." I glanced at Hadrian and Nathaniel, half hoping they might contradict me. That their work preparing the digimancy piece of our plan had positioned them to say, one way or another, how things were going to go. They only grimaced. "Without those records, the students have very limited options. They may not be able to transfer to other schools. If they're international, their visas might be at risk. Not to mention the tiny fact that if we can't produce records or sufficient testimony, the AAMUP might decide the anti-accommodations people are right. Professor Delight and the others will have won, either way."

My own fate was a foregone conclusion, and I wasn't going to appeal to them about it. But I was furious that anyone could be murmuring agreement so easily when over forty students were affected by this.

"They deserve better than that." I nearly choked on the force of my words. A surge of tears threatened to spill over and I bit my tongue to prevent them.

The room went quiet again.

Chuck cleared his throat. "We all know it's not ideal. But maybe other campuses made strong cases. Maybe saving these students is the best we can do." He didn't sound convinced. He sounded like he was pleading with himself and hating the process.

"Or—" Rose chirped the word like she was startled it had slipped out "—we pivot. Take down the working *and* get to the AAMUP rep before they can. We can tell the rep everything. And maybe get the *Prattler* to run it. And put it online. And—"

"Make people listen," Hadrian said. "I like it." She frowned. "Sucks for the students, though. Without proof, the professors who fucked them over will get to stay and keep working. It would drive *me* off campus."

"Still," Evelyn insisted, "we have to do *something*."

"Give us the weekend," Darya said, "to try to come up with a plan that saves the students *and* lets them stay if they want."

James leaned forward. "If we don't have a plan by then, we'll go ahead with Rose's idea."

"We'll need to start planning for our pivot," Evelyn said, obviously dubious.

"Then plan," Mags said. "I'll help coordinate. But it will take us a couple of days to get ready for the new pieces. We can give them until Sunday night, at least."

They took a vote. The *motion passed* sign lit up. Then my peers trickled past like a funeral line, offering pitying smiles, tentative pats, benedictions I didn't hear. As the door jangled shut behind the last of them, I bit the inside of my cheek to hold back tears.

JAMES PAUSED IN THE DOORWAY TO MY APARTMENT, WAITING FOR A RE-sponse to some caring, intolerable question. I'd stopped listening on the car ride home, but I forced myself to look up at him and attempted a smile. After a few stoic blinks, I gave up.

"Try to get some sleep," he said gently. "Or have some tea. Should I make you some tea before I go?"

I shook my head. "I'll be fine."

I was so parched my throat was burning, but I wasn't going to do anything about it. Doing that small thing, taking care of myself in that small way, would open the floodgates. I'd have to take care of other responsibilities, then, like notifying my advisor that I wasn't going to be able to take my exam. And deciding what to do with the broken pieces that had been Anne.

I shook my head again, harder. James pushed the front door open.

"I'll be back as soon as I can," he said. And then he was gone.

I collapsed onto the couch and turned on the TV, flipping channels until I found a cooking show. TV blaring and throat parched, I made a list of all the needful things I knew I'd have to face soon but wasn't going to do until I had no other choice:

I wasn't going to get a drink.

I wasn't going to change into comfortable clothes.

I wasn't going to email my advisor.

I wasn't going to pack my things.

I wasn't going to tell Darya and Cy to find another housemate.

I wasn't going to hack my CV into a bulleted list of marketable skills that *might* get me an entry-level office job twisting reality in small, banal ways that wouldn't even pay enough for me to rent my own place.

I wasn't going to call my parents and ask if I could live with them for a while. Just until I got on my feet again.

I wasn't going to cry. I wasn't going to cry. I wasn't going to— Starsdammit.

I WAS STILL CRYING, TWENTY MINUTES LATER, WHEN THE SCREEN DOOR creaked open and keys jangled in the lock.

"Darya?"

Someone walked in. Not Darya, then. But I hadn't sent James with my keys, which meant . . .

I pried my hot, gummy eyelids open and stared toward the door. "Cy?"

"In the incredibly teleportation-lagged flesh." He huffed as he dragged his suitcase in after him.

I sat up, wiping my eyes frantically.

"I'm gone for a month and a grubby TV-marathoner who can't even be bothered with a hug is all I get by way of welcoming committee," he said before his eyes adjusted and his expression shifted from playful to concerned. "Bartleby? What's wrong?"

I managed to avoid a fresh outpouring of tears as I explained. Even though he'd been here for the start of it, the story was a long one. So around the time I was getting to Mags's first Federation wrangling attempts, we wandered into the kitchen for some tea.

When I finished, Cy slid his hand through his hair in frustration.

"You do know I had cell service in England, right?" he said. "You could have reached out."

"Would you have told me to do something differently?" I was almost numb again after the crying and the telling. I wrapped my hands around my mug and breathed in the steam, hoping it would clear up my stuffy nose.

Cy made an exasperated sound. "Maybe. It's hard to say *now*." Then his voice softened. "But honestly, I think you made the best choices you could, under the circumstances."

The words weren't exactly comforting, and he knew it. If the *best* choices had landed me here, this had been hopeless from the start.

Slumping farther over my mug, I decided I'd check another item off my terrible to-do list.

"I think I'm going to go home for a while."

Cy choked on his tea.

"Home?" He knew my parents' place wasn't home to me anymore. It was one of the first things we'd bonded over. His family home wasn't home anymore, either.

"I'm not going to be welcome here for much longer. Especially after Monday."

Cy winced. "Your exam?"

It wasn't a question, really, but I nodded anyway. "And I don't have a way to cover rent without my teaching practitioner stipend."

He blanched. "Surely you can—"

"I can *what*, Cy? I don't have the required spell demonstration for the exam. And they aren't going to give someone who failed out of the program an adjunct role. It's better if I leave. Unless you think I should stick around and wait for Public Safety to requisition my magic artifacts and revoke my campus access."

Cy sat back as though I'd spit in his face. "No. Of course not. You shouldn't have to leave, either."

I pushed my tea mug away. "Yeah, well, it's starting to sound good to me." It was a lie, because the strain was beginning to show on his face. Something like grief flickered there, too. As much pain as I felt, I didn't want to pass it on. "I'm fucking exhausted. A break sounds like a gift from Hecate herself."

Using the explanation as an excuse, I shoved away from the table and headed to my room to collapse into my bed. I hadn't been lying about the exhaustion. But it took me a long time to fall asleep without Anne watching over me from its perch on my dresser.

CHAPTER THIRTY-NINE

Call parents
Finish Digimancy project report
~~Grade~~
Pack
~~Return library books~~
Email advisor
Withdraw from program
~~Talk to Cy and Darya~~
~~Draft a resume~~

—BARTLEBY'S TO-DO LIST, TEAR-SPATTERED AND WRITTEN
ON A TORN-OUT NOTEBOOK PAGE

B ETWEEN CHIPPING AWAY AT MY TO-DO LIST FROM HELL, SLOG-ging, dutifully, through my massive pile of grading, and procrastinating both of those things by collecting reams of useless evidence that Anne and early novels operated in the same way, I made it halfway through the weekend without another total collapse.

Anne was still in pieces, though I'd moved its box to my room after Cy had, uncharacteristically, offered to take care of it for me. Nothing in the box needed to be "taken care of," and nobody was going to convince me otherwise. Not Lora, and definitely not Cy.

As long as Anne was still present, in some form, I could pretend for milliseconds at a time that everything was normal. This was all a terrible preexam stress dream. I'd wake up on Monday to a world where all was right, and I'd pass my exam and advance to candidacy and start working on my dissertation.

James had been popping in and out since Thursday, ostensibly to work on a plan with Darya and Cy. Despite the fact that they were running out of time to come up with a solution that saved everyone but me, the three of them found an awful lot of opportunities to come to my room with more tea, food, and offers to talk than I could manage.

Eventually, I had to lock them out just to get the space to think. I could still hear them, pointedly not talking about me, in the other room. But the walls at least muffled the sounds, creating a small buffer between their attention and my raw psyche.

I tuned them out, sitting on the bed and fidgeting with my phone.

It was time.

I swiped through my contact list until I found my dad's number. My thumb hovered over it, trembling. Best to get this over with. My eyes flooded. I blinked the tears away and cleared my throat, dialing before I could second-guess myself.

Dad picked up on the third ring, fumbling to turn on his speakerphone.

"Hey, kiddo."

"Hey."

"Dorothe, honey, is that you?" Mom's voice was fainter, and accompanied by the clatter of dishware.

"Mom's here, too," Dad added, as if I needed the explanation.

I made myself laugh. No reason to worry them more than absolutely necessary. "Hi, Mom." There was a beat of silence that had become familiar over the years since I'd left. I took a breath, willed myself to break through the quiet.

"How's school?" Mom asked. "Will you graduate soon?"

I huffed in surprise, physically pained at the familiar question. We'd had this conversation so many times I'd lost count. Grad school didn't come with exact graduation dates, but my explanation never stuck. It would if I said what I had to say today. I finally had a definitive answer: I wouldn't be graduating at all. But I didn't know how to start, because I didn't know how to talk to them about failure. Every slipup I'd made over the years had only confirmed the fate they'd tried to steer me away from since that day in the diner.

I closed my eyes, trying to find the words.

"Dorothe?" Dad asked. "Did we lose you?"

"No." I opened my eyes, stared at the clutter tumbling out of my closet. "No, just thinking. School's great."

I forced extra cheer into my voice. I couldn't tell them now. I'd let it wait until I showed up back home. It would be easier, then. Or at least, unavoidable.

"Good," Dad was saying. "That's what we like to hear." He was following our usual template, even though I'd broken it simply by calling out of the blue.

"Did you need something, hon?" Mom asked.

What I needed was to be able to say *I messed up* and talk it through with them. To know that if I admitted things were rough, they wouldn't lecture me about my life choices or catastrophize about the prophecy. Wouldn't *we told you so* my career in Magic.

I swallowed down that need, bit the inside of my cheek against the bitterness.

"Nope. I just wanted to call and check in. How are things?"

They told me about their day-to-day, Bryan and his high-school sweetheart's prom preparations, Grace's middle-school soccer triumphs, their plans to come see me soon. They'd been saying that every year. If I was lucky, they'd have saved up enough to make it by graduation.

Except that they wouldn't. I wouldn't be graduating.

I bit my lip, forced a smile into my voice and asked follow-up questions until they told me they needed to go.

"Breakfast's ready," Mom explained. "I need to wrangle your siblings."

"Okay." I didn't want to end this conversation. It would be the last time my parents, who didn't understand a single one of my life choices, could imagine me as a successful adult out in the world.

"Love you, kiddo," Dad said.

"And miss you," Mom added.

I said the words back, as though they wouldn't be seeing me in a matter of days. And then I hung up.

THAT PHONE CALL UNRAVELED WHATEVER HOPE I'D BEEN HOLDING ON to that this would all work out.

It was Sunday morning.

My exam was Monday.

Anne was still a shattered pile of cranial bone in a box.

I threw my agitation into packing, dumping a hamper of clean clothes into my suitcase without bothering to fold them. I attacked the bedding next, wrestling my comforter into a garbage bag with my pillows and sheets.

Cleared of its linens, my bed gawped like a startled naked thing. Clutter peeked out from beneath it. And papers. Crouching, I gathered the scattered stack of printed pages into my hands and stilled.

Anne's logs.

These were the words that had brought me and James together. They were also the words that enabled us to send Anne to its doom. Something between a scream and a sob tore through me. Falling to my knees, I crumpled the pages in my hands, threw them, snatched at others that had drifted farther under the bed and tore at them until they were nothing more than a pile of macabre confetti. Garbage. They were garbage and I was going to make them disappear. I scooped them up and dumped them into the little bin underneath my desk.

That wasn't enough.

I needed to get rid of them completely.

Not even bothering to stand, I hobbled to my desk on my knees and threw my laptop open.

The logs were still pulled up, page still fixed to the words narrating Anne's brutal end. I didn't mean to read them. It was instinctive. Put words in front of me and my brain would parse them before I could even decide to try.

He wouldn't allow himself to think of names. He'd handle this himself.

I've got you now.

Thermos.

He swung.

I swiped to a blank part of the spreadsheet so I didn't have to see the horrible phrases.

Anne could have done it. If it had more of an element of surprise. If Professor D. had been distracted just enough to slip, to think of the names.

With help, Anne would have done it.

Hot tears sprang to my eyes and I dashed them away, angry. I was sick of crying. Sick of *feeling*. Blinking rapidly to clear the rest of the tears, I steered my cursor toward the red X at the top of the document. After I deleted Anne's logs, I'd never have to think about its last moments again.

But I hesitated.

I glanced back down toward the empty columns and rows at the end of the document. One last look.

The cells weren't empty. They were full, white noise composed of binary code. But in every cell, at the very middle of a sea of 1s and 0s, a letter.

0110101010100101001010101**B**010010100100100010010010101 0011
0101001010010100100100101 0**A**100100101010101000101010010010
101001010100010101010011 01**R**0010101000101000101000101010101
01010100101010010001010101**T**101010100101001010001010001 0111
0010101010100100100101 0010**L**01001010010101010101010100100 1010
001010100101000100100100 01**E**101000100100010001001000101 0101
100101010010101001010001 00**B**0010101001001010101111010100100
10010000001000010111101010**Y**101001001001001011101010101 0101

"James!" I screamed. "Darya! Cy! Get in here right now!"

They came, James and Cy springing around Darya's power wheelchair like reckless drivers, racing into the room until they pulled themselves to a stop around me.

"Look." I waved them toward the screen. "I want to make sure I'm not seeing things."

"Given the fact you just took at least a year off my life and you aren't dying or under attack," Cy panted, "you'd better not be seeing things."

"What are we looking at?" Darya asked, peering at the screen between me and Cy. On my other side, James's hand tightened on my shoulder. He'd been staring at code all term, just like I had. A few ones and zeroes were nothing, by comparison. He'd seen it already.

It took Darya and Cy a few extra seconds. Eventually, Darya turned to face me, eyes wide and nostrils flaring in horror. "Oh, Bartleby."

James, still silent, squeezed my shoulder again.

Cy, who was still catching up on pieces of this story, cocked his head. "I don't get it. You spelled your name in an early '90s computer geek way?"

"They're Anne's logs," James explained, after I tried and failed to find the words. "And the entries weren't here on Thursday. They're new."

"Anne is still functional." I broke the silence that threatened to swallow us after James's explanation. "Somehow. It's still fighting. And I've let it gather dust in a box."

It had always hated being left alone.

I pushed to my feet, forcing everyone around me to move back. "I have to fix it. There's still time."

James, Darya, and Cy seemed almost frozen in shock or confusion or—no, something worse. Caution.

They didn't think I'd come to the right conclusion.

Darya and James fought a nonverbal battle over who would break the news. Darya lost, grimacing at James before turning to me.

"Bartleby," she said softly, "those entries are from Friday. Yesterday was a full moon. Whatever's left of Anne's spellwork would have fizzled out."

James nodded. "There's a high chance that it was just the code and spellwork fighting without the buffer of the skull. Digimancy workings don't die pretty." He winced as soon as he said the word *die*, clearly regretting it. But it hung between us, and I flinched away.

"Anne is still working." I clenched my teeth. "I know it is."

My words had no real effect on James or my housemates. James's expression had gone puzzled, but Cy and Darya still just looked worried. Their cautious silence was worse than a slap to the face.

"If you aren't going to help me save Anne, then just get out of my way."

I snatched my phone and keys from the desk, lifted Anne's box to my chest, and stormed out of the room, leaving my stunned friends behind. Stomping into shoes, I pulled on a jacket and wrangled my way through the front door.

Nobody tried to stop me, but nobody followed, either.

I caught the bus, heading to campus and the only person I knew who *could* fix Anne. If I could convince them to do it. If they'd even speak to me at all.

AS SOON AS THE BUS PULLED AWAY FROM THE CURB, I TEXTED LORA.

Hey.

Five minutes passed. I tried again.

I need your help. It's urgent.

At the next bus stop, I kept myself from shooting off a volley of anxious messages by watching people board. They climbed on in twos and threes, flashing passes or tossing handfuls of change into the ticket machine. The bus turned down the road that would take us to campus. I watched the driver palm a couple of antacids and checked my phone. Lora still hadn't responded.

I know you said you couldn't help Anne, but I have proof it's still in there.

The bus huffed to a stop, brakes screeching. No answer.

I swore and tried calling. The phone went to voicemail as I climbed off. I tried again. They didn't answer, so I called Mags.

"Bartleby?" She answered on the first ring, probably surprised enough by my call to answer even though she kept a strict boundary between work and family time on the weekends. "Is everything okay?"

"No." I stopped in the middle of the sidewalk, unsure which way to go. I'd come to campus on instinct. I had no idea where Lora lived or if she'd be home. "I mean, I'm fine. Just . . . I need to get ahold of Lora. Have you heard from them since—" I didn't trail off so much as stop, cold, in the middle of my sentence. Mags got the point, though.

"I haven't talked to her," she said. "What's up?"

"They won't answer my texts or calls. Anne is still functioning—barely. I need her help."

Mags sighed. "They may not be ready to talk to you after the way you treated them."

That wasn't fair. I'd been protecting Anne. Lora might not see it that way, but she didn't have to: there were at least forty other reasons for her to help.

"This isn't just about me. Saving Anne could mean our plan is back on track." If Anne was still capable of reaching out to me through its logs, maybe it was still taking in data, too. Maybe it had been all along. And Professor Delight could have done any number of incriminating things after smashing it.

Mags stayed quiet. Maybe she wasn't going to answer. Maybe she was upset with me on Lora's behalf. Maybe—

"The other week they mentioned they've been writing at work on the weekends because their roommate's dissertation project is 'loud and squelchy.'"

"Work?" Where . . .

No.

Rasputin's *balls*.

"The Materials Lab." I said the words at the same time Mags did, turning to face that corner of campus. I couldn't see the building from here, but it loomed over me somehow anyway.

Cold wind hurled itself at sodden leaves in the gutters, failing to send them cartwheeling across cement and asphalt. It found every thin spot in my clothes.

I'd promised not to go back inside on my own. At least, not until I'd built up enough confidence that the ward ghosts didn't flag me as an intruder. I hadn't. If anything, I was more convinced than ever that I didn't belong. Or at least, convinced I wouldn't get to stay. And after what the wards had done to me the first time, I'd been pretty sure it would take hell freezing over to get me back inside.

Hell had frozen over.

I needed to save Anne. And maybe . . .

I squashed the small budding thing tickling deep in my chest. I couldn't think about maybes. I needed to stay focused.

Mags broke in on my thoughts. "But Bartleby, you can't go back in there. Lora said—"

"I know." I kept my voice firm. "Thanks, Mags." I hung up before she could recover from my interruption, shoving my phone into my pocket and picking up my pace.

CHAPTER FORTY

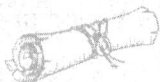

Free indirect discourse: a roving, third-
person point of view that allows the author
to create immersive worlds by hopscotching
through characters' consciousnesses. Some
mages contend that the technique is essentially
incantation, parallel to the reality-shaping that
happens during shared ritual workings.
—EXAM PREP FLASHCARD, HASTILY SCRAWLED
BY BARTLEBY IN A STOLEN MOMENT

MAGS

We've got a problem . . . Bartleby's heading into the Bone House.

DARYA

We know. James had a vision.

MAGS

Lora won't pick up when I call.

CY

We tried, too. We'll be there soon.

DARYA

If James's driving doesn't get us killed.

MAGS

Ok. OMW.

CY

Hurry. And bring that sword, if you still have it . . .

CHAPTER FORTY-ONE

In every known version of reality, order trends
inevitably toward entropy. Things fall apart. *As above,
so below*, as the saying goes. Magic is not exempt from the
laws of thermodynamics. Except when it is.

—PROFESSOR RUE HUANG, THEORIES OF MAGIC

I'M GOING TO HAVE TO STORM THE BUILDING." TALKING TO ANNE
felt natural, even now. "I know I promised Lora not to, but
if there's a chance you're still in there . . ." Lora had given me
her number to *stop* me from entering the building on my own
again. It wasn't my fault if they wouldn't pick up.

I needed to fix Anne.

Fixing Anne meant fixing the organic buffer that allowed
Anne's magic and code to play nice. As long as its skull was in
pieces, the working would keep imploding. Until, eventually,
Anne would be gone for real.

That could take minutes or hours. I might already be too late.
But I had to *try.*

Bone didn't quite have a mind of its own, but as a substance
that was closely linked with spirit—literally and figuratively,
through culture and folklore—it wouldn't cooperate with just *any*
magic that was thrown its way. In divination, some workings *used*
bone, but only necromancers could do workings *on* bone. At least,
I hoped they could. Lora was the only *actual* necromancer I knew

well enough to ask. They were also the only person I trusted to fix Anne.

I just had to convince them to do it first.

Around me, the breeze turned frigid, shifting direction and seeming to slow at the same time. A rustling, which I'd taken to be Anne's box brushing against my rain jacket, grew louder. Differentiated into voices.

Not this again.

You were warned.

Warned.

The heads above me peered down in judgment. I tried to ignore them, walking faster.

You could've been a mage.

Pity; you would've been a fine mage.

Pity, mage.

Mage, run.

You could've run.

Destruction.

Death.

Ruin.

Ruined the plan.

You ruined the plan.

Upheaval.

Inevitable.

It wasssss inevitable.

Failure.

Failing.

Failed.

I stopped, craning my neck. Who were these disembodied heads to judge me? To offer me these half-assed portents and expect me to, what, shiver apart under the pressure? Or become some sort of academic chosen one? They were glorified busts. Pale imitations of mages gone by. Mages they'd been meant to caricature as part of a starsdamned *prank*, for Hecate's sake.

"You've already said all that." I didn't even raise my voice.

"So, unless you have something new and useful to tell me, I've got more important things to do."

The wind paused, for a moment, in its blustering. Then it picked back up as the head nearest me glowered down. Its mouth writhed.

Good luck with your exam.

I glowered back. "What's that supposed to mean?"

But the breeze was already flitting away, setting budding tree branches rattling in its passage. The mascarons stilled into stony silence. I shot one last look at them and finished my walk to the Bone House.

"Good luck with my exam. Good luck with my Heccing exam." I looked into my box, frowning at Anne. "Who knew animate granite could be so Heccing sarcastic?"

Weren't those things only supposed to speak to students like once every few decades? Just my starsdamned luck; I couldn't get them to shut up.

I TRIED TO GO IN THE BACK WAY, EVEN THOUGH I KNEW IT WASN'T ANY safer than the front. But no matter what path I took, the Bone House guided me to the front stairwell. After looping back to it a fourth time, I fished my phone out of my pocket and dialed Lora. One last try couldn't hurt.

Straight to voicemail.

The only logical thing to do was leave. I started climbing steps.

The lights flickered, uncertainly, ahead of me. The wards seemed to be thinking. Considering my audacity. To waltz in here a *third* time and simply climb the stairs? Impossible. Unacceptable.

I wasn't quite holding my breath, but I was rationing air, each inhale a slow trickle, so that I could hear the building shift around me. Every creak of aged beams, every moan of pipes and drafty wind that shouldn't be audible. The lights flickered again, and long shadows stretched above me, outsized on the walls.

"Dorothe May Bartleby," a voice reverberated through the

stairwell, seeming to slip from one of the too-tall shadows even as it came from everywhere.

I tensed against it, recognizing it from half a lifetime ago. Lora had said something, that first time we met, about the wards liking to trot out dead grandmas.

"What do you want?" I looked from shadow to shadow. "I know you aren't my great-grandmother. She died thousands of miles away a long time ago. And if she's got any unfinished business left, it's got nothing to do with me or this building."

"You have a smart mouth," the shadow voice that *couldn't* be my great-grandmother's said. "But I like a little fire in a young lady. In my day, if you didn't have fire you didn't make it through. You'd be claimed by influenza or birthing or worse." The rattling cough that followed was as familiar to me as the voice.

"I know you aren't my great-grandmother." I repeated the words as I stared at the shadow who'd taken her voice.

"Well, certainly if you'd like I can disown you. But then my companions will feel no guilt or hesitation whatsoever about tearing you apart."

The shadow was becoming shorter and rounder as it spoke.

I huffed, edging up another step. I could just make out the second-floor landing, if I craned my head, and I was pretty sure I saw the outline of a door up there.

"Will this go any faster if I just *pretend* you're my great-grandmother?"

"Great-grandmother?" the voice asked with an offended sniff. "Since when did anyone call me *great-grandmother*? I was Granny, and you know it."

Maybe I *didn't* need to pretend. Maybe Granny was inexplicably haunting a building in Oregon instead of her home in West Texas. Or maybe something had drawn her here today. It seemed awfully convenient, but it didn't matter. I didn't have time to stick around to find out.

"Well, *Granny*, I know it's been a while and I'd love to catch up, but I have something urgent to take care of—"

"It can wait," shadow-Granny's voice boomed in the small space. "These nice ward ghosts tell me you've been trespassing." It cocked its head, considering me. "And I know my favorite grand-baby raised you better than that."

"Granny, it's an *emergency*." It was impossible to keep thinking of it, of her, as something *else*. She had the voice, the mannerisms, the turns of phrase.

"That's not an excuse, and you know it. All this fancy school-ing, and you're forgetting the simplest manners." Her shape con-densed further and further, light siphoned from windows and pooled in her features until she was the waxen-doll version of herself I'd glimpsed at her funeral.

She was standing close enough to touch me, and I almost flailed away, forgetting I was on the stairs. Steadying myself, I glared.

"You're going to have to try harder than that to get rid of me."

Shadow-Granny laughed, dentures ethereally bright. "You silly child," she rasped, "who said we're trying to get *rid* of you?"

My heart stuttered deep in my chest. I gripped Anne's box with damp hands, adjusting it as I tried to work up the courage to *do* something—anything—to get out of this mess.

The shadows that had surrounded me shifted then, and I could see them. Life-size wax dolls like Granny, bodies without anima-tion, most but not all in funeral garb. Some were in messier states of decomposition, their clothes disintegrating into putrid flesh. Others, hovering at the edges of the group, wisped in and out of tangibility like smoke.

The hair on the back of my arms stood on end, prickling up as I took them all in.

"I'm . . . I didn't mean any offense." My voice wobbled as I looked at the assembled group. "But I'm allowed to be here." I pushed more confidence into the words than I really had, recall-ing Lora's advice. That was what the wards needed, wasn't it? My confidence.

Granny was looming much nearer when I turned back toward

her. She shook her head, disappointed. "Who taught you how to apologize?"

I stiffened, shoulders straightening instinctively. I knew how to apologize. Knew that apologies could be shields just as easily as they could be olive branches. That they could become weapons even more easily, cutting both ways.

If I apologized here, I'd be culpable. I'd be conceding to this absurd claim that I'd trespassed and owed something to the dead because of it. And I would pay for my imagined crimes in something dearer than words or money.

Tightening my grip on Anne's box, I narrowed my eyes at my granny—or whatever she was—and cast about for the right combination of words. Not an apology: an incantation.

But Jane Austen finally failed me.

I couldn't think of any words to hold up between my dead great-grandmother and myself. Nothing fierce and full of purpose enough to keep literal ghosts at bay.

"Dammit, Bartleby, *think*," I chided myself, not caring anymore whether this shadow-version of Granny heard me swear.

Prose wasn't going to cut it, but maybe poetry would help. I took a breath, planted my feet and reached for some Robert Browning. That morbid Victorian weirdo might just get me out of here.

"'What's dead can't come to life, I think. So, friend, we're not the folks to shrink.'"

It was an odd rhyme, and I couldn't remember the name of the poem it came from or what the words meant in context. But I repeated them over and over as I took one tentative step, then another. The wave of exhaustion that flooded me as I recited the couplet one final time sent my arms trembling. I fumbled Anne's box, caught myself on the handrail. Anne wobbled and steadied inside.

Granny laughed. "You want to speak stories at us like they're weapons?"

I ignored her and kept climbing. The second-floor landing wasn't getting any closer.

"I have stories, too, dear. The kind you won't want me to tell."

Hecate's dogs.

Behind me, Granny's silent friends pressed closer. Numbness erased a swath of me, nerves shifting from high alert to nothing in a fraction of a second.

"There was once a little girl who liked to read," Granny began.

Dread flooded me, but I focused on my footing.

"She was too small for books. Too small to make sense of the words tangling on the pages. But she began reading a full two years before her peers. Her parents called her a prodigy. Others, less generous in their assessment, called her *witch*. She was born on the darkest of nights, you see, when the moon turns its face and all manner of evils may run riot."

I took another stubborn step as something crashed in the distance.

"Everyone in her little life knew she was special. Some knew she was doomed. Either way, the knowledge set her apart, a stranger in her own hometown, her own family," Granny said, considering her gray cuticles with a curl of her lip. "In the wide world, surrounded by people who *truly* shined, the girl found herself set apart in a different way. She was a dim bulb, living in constant fear she'd either burn out or be replaced. She didn't belong there any more than she'd belonged at home. Any more than she'd belong *anywhere*. Too bright for her beginnings, but not bright enough— never bright enough—for bigger things."

At some point during this speech, my eyes found Granny's and locked there. I wasn't surprised by her words. Hecate knew I'd thought them thousands of times myself. But it was my lack of surprise that gave them power, let them take an iron grip on consensus reality.

Her story transformed around me, a burning net of energy that had me tangled, knotted, bound. Worse: the ghosts weren't hovering at a respectful distance anymore. They'd closed in.

CHAPTER FORTY-TWO

Here's the thing about the honored dead, / If they don't
lift you up, they fuck with your head . . .

    —SONG WRITTEN FOR THE CAMPUS BATTLE OF THE BANDS
BY GRINNING AT THE DAISY ROOTS, WHO BROKE UP
IMMEDIATELY FOLLOWING THEIR FIRST PERFORMANCE,
REPORTEDLY DUE TO "INTENSE HAUNTING"

I WARNED YOU, GIRL," GRANNY HISSED, DRAGGING SIBILANTS FROM
thin air.

The wave of ghosts fell on me, pinching, scratching,
gnashing rotten teeth. It was a repeat of the assault in the void,
except this time I could see them in the harsh light.

White-green fingers dragged along my skin, blue-green nails
flicked out, dry and shriveled, to gouge. At every point of contact,
I went numb.

I was losing myself, one small piece at a time.

"All you had to do was apologize," Granny said, observing the
scene dispassionately from one step above. "All you had to do was show
a little bit of *contrition*." Granny's laugh was vicious. "Stubborn girl."

I ignored her, focusing instead on a line from *Sense and Sensibility*. "'I will be calm. I will be mistress of myself.'" I whimpered
as ghoulish groping hands balled into fists, delivering blows that
ached in the absence of pain. Numbness spiked deeper and deeper
into me. I clung to the incantation, refusing to break.

And then they turned toward my box, decrepit hands questing toward Anne.

"Do you know what happens to bone among the dead?" Granny asked conversationally. I didn't respond. Didn't have to. A fingertip brushed one of Anne's shards, and the place where it landed turned to powdery white dust.

"Stop. Please, stop. I'm allowed to be here."

Fighting against my bonds, I fell to my knees to shield the box with my own body.

If I were a better mage, if I really *belonged* here, I'd rip myself free of Granny's words, sling workings as the wards took me down. I would know the incantations to ensure mutual destruction, instead of this pitiful wordless defense I was barely managing now. I would call forth so many variations of reality that this place would buckle under the weight of them. The constants would put right whatever I made wrong, but not before I'd sent shadow-Granny back to the red clay of her own grave.

I huddled around Anne, waiting for the ghosts to finish their work, to destroy me as Lora had predicted. Because I *wasn't* a better mage. And I really, truly did not belong. Granny was right about that. Even if nobody else had noticed yet, the wards could see it clearly. I was out of shape with this place and this program, non-Euclidean, an imposter.

But no. That couldn't be entirely true.

An imposter wouldn't have noticed students needed help. Or if they did, they wouldn't *do* anything about it, especially with prophecy dogging their heels and one last chance at exams slipping between their fingers.

The academy's antiquated, elitist systems had made it perfectly clear in hundreds of subtle and not so subtle ways that I could never belong. This last, desperate effort to fix Anne wouldn't change that, whether or not I succeeded. But I'd built a place here for myself, anyway.

And if I couldn't stay? If I didn't get to become a mage, blazing with skill and scholarship? The least I could do was make sure my students got the chance they deserved. Make a place for them on my way out.

As soon as I got out of this starsdamned stairwell.

I fought against the strangling net, reaching for stories as I struggled to my feet. No memorized passages or stanzas of poetry sprang to mind with Granny's story about me still reverberating in my bones. It was as if she and the ward ghosts had burned an entire library out of me. A library I'd spent years building, all on my own. They had no right to take my words. Panic surged into the sharp clarity of realization.

They hadn't taken *my* words.

"That's an old story," I began, staring Granny right in the eye. "I've heard it—and told it—so many times, I'm starting to think I've outgrown it."

Another crash, closer now, and something that sounded suspiciously like the clang of elevator doors drew some of the ghosts' attention away.

But Granny held my gaze. She knew I wasn't done. I took a breath, already so harried and disoriented I didn't need to cross and uncross my eyes to grab hold of reality with my incantation. Shifting my shoulders against the pressure of the net, I said what I needed to say.

"In fact, I'm starting to think it's time for me to tell a new story."

My ears popped as the words caught hold, and a wash of power cascaded over me, untangling the knotted story-net in which Granny had snared me. My body tingled as blood circulated freely. I could move. I could run. But I held my ground, waiting for what I was pretty sure the crashing and clanging had been foreshadowing.

I didn't have to wait long.

Light blazed into the stairwell on a volley of swear words. Mags, sword held high, charged into the small space. Someone— probably Darya—had cast a working on her weapon; it glowed bright, slicing shadows away from the space as Mags waved it back and forth. James and Cy followed close behind her, huddling in the small strip of consensus reality the sword cleared for them.

"Hurry!" Darya yelled from the landing next to the elevator. "I can't keep this door open for long."

The ward ghosts swarmed James, Cy, and Mags before they could reach me. My friends gained ground, but the dead just kept coming—help wasn't going to reach me in time. That was okay. Their presence was enough to recharge me.

I picked up Anne's box and faced Granny.

I might not be the brightest mage in the room. I might not *belong* here in the same way my friends so clearly did. But it didn't matter. There would always be brighter mages, brighter scholars, no matter how many metaphorical rooms I walked into. And some of them? Some of the brightest I'd ever met? They were here, and they believed in me. They'd stood beside me all along. They'd listened to me and decided that I was *right* and this fight was ours. Hec, Mags didn't even have magic, and she was fighting ghosts, anyway. For me, and for our students.

But there were better things we could be doing with our time.

The thought was startling in its clarity. I couldn't feel anything anymore. My body was completely numb, wrapped around the box that held Anne more by instinct than anything else, so the idea of it was free to burn its way through me. In its passage, I began to itch, tingling as feeling came back.

"Enough." My voice thundered through the stairwell.

The ghosts paused. Granny arched a wiry brow.

"I won't apologize." The dead began to moan, angrily. Granny held up a hand, checking them, and turned back to me. Pride and grief and something a lot like rebellion sliced a grin across my face as I stared her down. "I *am allowed* to be here."

For the first time, I really meant it. Not caring whether any of the ward ghosts believed me, I brushed past the waxen-doll specter of my grandmother and joined my friends on the landing.

"We aren't done here, missy," Granny hissed after me. "Mark my words. We will finish this conversation."

I tensed, instinctively, ready for an attack. But before I could turn to insist that, no, we abso-Heccing-lutely would *not* be finishing this conversation, the stairwell door slammed firmly shut behind me. The lingering traces of the stairwell's abstract horror-scape dissolved, a dirty bubble of dish soap bursting, leaving me alone with my friends on the second floor.

LORA SWORE WHEN WE BURST INTO THEIR QUIET STUDY SPACE.

"Rasputin's fucking balls, Bartleby, you *promised* not to come back here," she said. "And . . . for Hecate's sake. You're smoking."

They jumped up from their table and rushed forward, patting out the smoldering patches on my clothes. She went still when she noticed the others. James held the door open as Mags swaggered in, sword in hand. Cy sauntered behind her, looking entirely unruffled despite having been harried by the dead. Darya brought up the rear, arms working the wheels of her backup—and more portable—wheelchair. She came to a stop next to Mags and waved at Lora, cheerfully.

When James shut the door, I cleared my throat.

"Look, I know you're mad at me and you're probably right to be, but Anne is *still functional* and I need your help."

I set Anne's box on the table.

Lora didn't look at Anne. Instead, their eyes tracked over to the altar where their ñatitas lounged amid ofrendas and accessories. A feather boa. Cigarettes. Flowers.

The gaze she turned on me was horrified. My stomach flipped itself inside out.

"Did you really just tell off your own grandmother?" Their tone was half-accusatory, half-impressed.

"I didn't have much of a choice." I crossed my arms. "You weren't answering your phone. And the wards . . ." I didn't want to think about them. How close I'd come to giving in.

As if he could hear my thoughts, James made a growling sound.

Ignoring it, I focused on Lora. "Fix it, please."

Lora's eyes flicked to the box, where a powdery haze still surrounded the fragmented remains of the skull.

"Mierda," she whispered. They met my eyes. "Look, Bartleby, I believe you," she said, "but this isn't something I can fix on my own. Bone work is complicated. It requires an entire coven."

"Which is why we're here," Cy drawled.

Lora ran their hands through their hair. "We'll need blood," she said. "Preferably from a lineage the dead recognize."

James stepped forward, already rolling up his sleeves. "We've got it."

Lora raised an eyebrow. "And . . ." Their eyes tracked over to the ñatitas. Were they walking her through this? "Containing material," they said after a second, "that bridges life and death."

Darya actually squealed. "I knew that powdered death cap would come in handy eventually."

Lora's expression shifted from dubious to neutral. She was starting to think this might be possible.

I reminded myself to keep breathing. "Anything else?"

Lora looked to the ñatitas. "We'll need someone to perform a ritual of rebirth. Whatever the Hec that means."

Cy strode forward. "I believe I can manage that."

Lora looked around the room, neutrality fading into tired optimism. "The only other thing I could use is some six-hour-energy."

Mags cleared her throat, shifting her sword to her nondominant hand to dig something out of her pocket. She tossed a vial to Lora and turned to wink at me. "I think that should take care of the *IOU*."

All I could do was gawp at her, literally speechless.

Lora laughed, a sharp sound that was more surprise than mirth. "I guess we're doing this." They turned to look me in the eye. "But I have to warn you, I can only fix the *skull*." The implication of her words was obvious, but she carried on, anyway. "Bartleby, even if you're right . . ."

I cut them off. "It might not work. The working might have

come unbalanced. It might have unraveled completely in the time it took me to get through the wards." I ran my hands down my face, unwilling to consider the possibility. "I know. Just, try. Please."

Darya and Mags made a quick run to the Science Library to retrieve a small stoppered vial of powdered death cap, which Darya brandished triumphantly when they returned.

Things moved quickly after that. Lora downed the six-hour-energy and coached everyone through their roles. Darya poured the death cap in the groove of the lab's containment circle. I laid Anne's pieces out inside.

"Take a seat," Lora said, when I tried to step back out.

"Why?" I crossed my arms.

"You're connected to Anne," James explained. "You are part of what ties it together."

Anne waited. *Object.*

I cradled it. *Gesture.*

James bled and Lora chanted. *Incantation.*

And Cy danced, while Darya and Mags watched, hopefully. *Ritual.*

Bit by bit, each fragment of bone hovered before melding into its rightful place, bright new cranial seams the only sign that Anne had ever been shattered. The working was transforming Anne into a patchwork thing.

Time—inscrutable, immeasurable—passed. As we snatched hold of it, reality pluralized. The working took on a fluttering, floating quality, like we were bobbing in a sea of possibility. Power swelled then broke as the working reached its peak. The euphoria that spread through me, all warm sun and salt breezes, didn't help the uneasy slosh of dismay in my guts.

Anne's skull, mostly whole again, stared empty-gazed from the cradle of my arms.

It didn't speak.

I sagged over it, unable to watch my friends in their continued working. I could feel their worry, their exhaustion, their pain.

Lora's voice went ragged. Cy's dedication to performance was the only thing keeping a grimace from his face. I chanced a look at James, who was so pale he looked almost translucent. My stomach lurched.

I needed to stop this. We'd tried, and we'd failed, and it was time for me to admit it. Sometimes, consensus reality *couldn't* be coaxed into a different shape. I closed my eyes, throat tightening around the words.

A monotone voice broke the silence before I could speak.

"Bartleby waited in the Materials Lab like it was limbo, dreading her inevitable descent into hell," Anne said. It was channeling Dante. This had to be a hallucination—my imagination fevered, as my favorite author would say. But Anne persisted. "Bartleby's efforts had worked. Anne was returned to functionality."

I opened my eyes. My friends had frozen, watching me. They'd heard it, too.

It'd worked. Our ritual had worked.

I clasped Anne to my chest, crying with relief and triumph. Darya cheered, and her voice was a pulled pin. The room exploded with celebration, all but drowning out Anne's next words.

"Bartleby's relief at Anne's revival was short-lived," it said, the text-to-speech tones of its voice undeniably sorrowful, "because her narration skull revealed that it had not generated any incriminating logs during its period of disrepair. Bartleby realized that there was only one way forward now; they'd run out of time and other options."

I took a shaky breath. As usual, it was right.

We had today and tomorrow to undo the working and bring our missing students back. We were going to have to use the rest of today to rally the Federation. Which left Monday to secure the evidence we needed to *keep* our students here once we brought them back.

Nausea hit, and it wasn't just the first sign of cosmic cost taking its toll on my body.

There was only one place I'd be able to collect that evidence, now that Professor Delight knew I knew about his involvement. Only one situation in which he *wouldn't* expect an attack.

Because what kind of mage student tanks her own Branch and Field exam? Especially when it's already been tanked for her.

CHAPTER FORTY-THREE

At first, Bartleby did an extraordinary quantity of studying. As if long famishing, she seemed to gorge herself on grimoires. There was no pause for digestion . . . but she went on silently, palely, mechanically.

—NARRATORIAL COMMENTARY ADAPTED FROM HERMAN MELVILLE'S "BARTLEBY THE SCRIVENER" BY ANNE

WE SLAMMED PAINKILLERS AND ANTACIDS WITH AN ASsortment of caffeinated and electrolyte-packed beverages to put off the cost of our magic for a few more hours. It didn't entirely work, but we were all used to pushing through the pain.

Darya and Cy double-checked supplies and prepped posterboard signs while Mags made calls. As soon as the malicious working went down and we had hard evidence, the Federation would launch a protest. Rituals didn't have to be magic to be powerful.

The chaos made it easier for me to keep the full truth from my friends. I told them that I was going to use Anne to confront the professor *after* my exam, when the committee called me back into the room after a short period of deliberation to let me know if I'd passed.

Distracted by everything that had to happen before 9 a.m., they accepted my story. Mostly. Every so often, I caught James watching me, eyes narrowed in concern. He was the only other person who knew both Anne and Professor Delight as well as I did. He hadn't confronted me about it yet, but it was clear that he knew my plan didn't add up.

For one thing, I had very little control over what Anne chose to narrate. I could nudge it to begin with my *once upon a time* command. And I could usually get it to stop. But the only way to *truly* prevent its interruptions was to cast our cloaking, and I'd have to uncloak Anne for the spellwork demonstration.

Professor Delight was not going to give me an opportunity to confront him after the exam. He'd show up to watch me fail, and then he'd get out of there. I *had* to confront him while I still had a chance at passing.

My stomach balled in on itself.

At the start of the term, the thought of losing my shot at becoming a mage had been enough to send me into spiraling panic. Now I was going to tank my chances, intentionally. I hated the plan. I wanted to hide and pretend it wasn't going to happen. But my confrontation with shadow-Granny had made everything clearer for me. What I was doing here, and how I could make my mark. I was going to ensure that my students were safe and free to return to their lives, even if it cost me the life I'd worked so hard to build.

My thoughts must've been all but written on my face, because the next time James shot a worried look my way, he frowned and came over to join me.

"You're not telling them everything," he whispered, glancing at Darya and Cy, who were conferring over the notes and printed pages filling the kitchen table.

Mags paced behind them, cell phone plastered to her ear.

"I've told them everything they need to know to get the job done." I didn't look at him.

"And, conveniently, not enough for them to stop you from sabotaging your own exam."

I turned to face him.

"James . . ."

"I just want you to know that I know." He reached for my hands. "I know what you're planning, and I know why. I'm not going to make this harder for you by trying to convince you not to do it. Even though it's killing me not to." He exhaled, hard. "If you've decided it's the only way, it's the only way. But I want you to know that I see you. And I wish that I could do something— anything—to pay the price on your behalf."

I squeezed his hands, glanced at my friends. "Just . . . don't let them find out. Or if they do, don't let them intervene." My career was over, either way. I didn't want them to try to save me if it meant this had all been for nothing.

"You know how I tell people about that working in the computer lab?" James asked. Head tipped, his eyes were wide and intense as if he wanted to take me in, memorize the moment.

I nodded. Why he insisted on painting me or my ridiculous mistake in that light, I didn't understand. Thanks to him, there were people who actually believed my digimancy fail was heroic. But he was the only person who thought *I* was heroic. The only one who looked at me like I could do anything I set my mind to.

"*This* is the story I'll be telling from now on."

My vision blurred. I squared my shoulders and closed my eyes, breathing deep. While I tried to hold back tears, James bent and kissed my forehead, a brush and he was gone. I blinked until my vision cleared.

By the time I'd composed myself, James had joined my housemates in the kitchen, paint pen in one hand and poster board in the other. He smiled at me and turned his attention to the poster.

I wrapped my arms back around myself and headed into my bedroom. I wasn't going to cry or agonize or brace myself for the inevitable. I was going to have a conversation with Anne about what needed to happen tomorrow. It probably already knew, considering how easily it seemed to parse my innermost thoughts and expose them to the world. But Darya had been right, after our aleuromancy working, to ask its opinion. I hadn't followed her example before planting it in Delight's office, and I regretted that.

I wasn't going to make the same mistake again. I'd ask it for help. Bribe it with a hundred outrageous hats, if I had to.

And after that . . . for the handful of hours I had left before my exam, all I wanted to do was pretend. I was going to finish my spellwork demonstration slides—even though I wouldn't get to use them. And then I'd review my notes while watching terrible TV and munching on a variety of snacks until the sun came up. Or until I fell asleep in a pile of chip crumbs and powdered cheese. Whichever came first.

I WAS STILL AWAKE WHEN THE SUN ROSE.

The house was eerily quiet. Nothingness thrummed in my head, louder than the usual chaos of thoughts that rattled around inside.

I'd expected anxiety brain. Panic. At the very least, nervous anticipation. I wasn't numb, really. Not like I had been in the wards. And I wasn't disassociating, either. But I was resigned. I knew what I had to do, and I was prepared to do it.

I got up and got dressed.

In the back of my closet, the outfit I'd planned to wear to my exam, a jumpsuit and jacket that made me feel wise and powerful and stunning all at once, hung ready. I pulled it out and stared at it for a full minute before returning it to the rack.

I wasn't going into that room today to pass my exam.

Instead of the jumpsuit, I chose slacks and a black button-up that was zigzagged with colorful lightning bolts. I did my makeup, bold brows and dark lips. Staring at myself in the mirror, I smiled. Feral. An imposter revealing herself, just before gutting the reigning monarch. I put on my rings and I shrugged into my leather jacket.

I was going to war.

Collecting Anne, its amulet, and my notes, I headed into the kitchen. The room was a wreck, covered in protest signs and papers, used coffee mugs stacked precariously on top of notebooks, empty pizza boxes, and balled-up napkins.

I started coffee and settled in amid the mess.

This was what I loved most about living here. Not the clutter, but the camaraderie it spoke to. The urgent work we pulled off at the last minute, again and again, because we had each other to lean on. The sense of belonging and becoming, intertwined.

When the coffee was ready, I snagged a used mug and scrubbed it quickly. Cy stumbled into the room as I worked.

"Did you make enough for two?" he asked, collapsing into a chair. Behind him, the hum of Darya's power wheelchair was followed by a plaintive, "Save some for me!"

I fished two more mugs out of the mess and washed them.

Cy leaned backward far enough to yank open the fridge and snag some creamer.

I poured the coffee, sliding mugs to my friends before filling my own to the brim. We drank in silence, words unnecessary. They'd known I'd be up early, that I'd head out without waking them. And they'd dragged themselves out of bed to prevent that because they'd also known I'd need the company.

When I pushed away from the table, Cy, blinking sleepily over his coffee, finally broke our silence. He raised his mostly empty mug and cleared his throat.

"To good luck," he said.

Darya, catching on more quickly than I did, raised her own mug. "To well-being."

I sat back down and lifted my own mug, rounding out the traditional toast: "To the beneficence of the universe."

We clinked our mugs together with a murmured "abracadabra," slamming back the dregs of our coffee.

As I climbed out of my chair, I turned to Darya. "If you see our students . . ." I trailed off. What would I even say? But Darya nodded. She'd think of something. "Thank you," I added, glancing from Darya to Cy, "both of you, for doing this with me. For believing me."

Darya smiled and Cy shrugged, setting his silk dressing gown fluttering.

I left before we got any more sentimental. I needed to hold it together.

"I will be calm," I muttered, reaching for Austen's words again. "I will be mistress of myself." Retrieving my bike from the garage, I slung my bag over my shoulder and headed to campus.

MY PRETERNATURAL CALM LASTED UNTIL I WAS IN THE ROOM. IT WASN'T a particularly special or awe-inspiring space. In fact, it emanated dullness. A windowless room a little bigger than a standard office, occupied by a large conference table and, at the far end, an aging flat-screen monitor on which I could display slides.

Aside from Faye, who unlocked the door for me and bustled around, straightening chairs, I was the first one there.

"I've got some cake at my desk just for you," Faye said. "When this is over and you're ready to celebrate."

I wanted to cry. "Thank you. That's so nice."

Faye shook her head. "It's nothing."

I took a seat at the head of the table so that I was facing the door with my back to the wall, cradling my hands in my lap until my advisor breezed into the room a few minutes later.

"Dorothe," she exclaimed, arms outstretched. I stood and hugged her. "How are you feeling? Excited? You're going to rock this."

I mustered a smile. "A little nervous." But not about the exam.

University policy, while often Byzantine, was brutally clear about one point: mage students only passed the Branch and Field exam and advanced to candidacy if their committee agreed *unanimously* that they should. With Professor Delight on my committee, there wasn't much possibility of that, no matter how well I did. Maybe if I backed off, let Delight and his conspirators get away with their plot . . . But I wasn't going to do that. And getting Delight to name names meant I needed to use my spellwork demonstration for something other than proving my theory about early novels and narration workings.

Professor Husik nodded, as if this was only to be expected. "Remember, everyone here wants you to succeed. You've done the work. Now you get to wow us."

I wished that were true. Longed for the version of this day that my advisor described. It wasn't going to happen. After this, even Amelia wouldn't want to work with me.

I closed my eyes and took a deep breath as the rest of my committee arrived. Professor Matthews took a seat across the table from Professor Husik. I couldn't help but notice how close it was to the door. As the only nonMagic member of the committee, she clearly felt a bit uncertain about the whole thing. Professor Huang followed her in, sitting next to Professor Husik. Moments later, Professor Delight swept in, taking the seat at the foot of the table, directly across from me, with a knowing smirk.

Faye had a brief whispered exchange with Amelia before heading out. She wiggled her fingers at me, smiling, and shut the door behind her with a thud.

My stomach lurched at the finality of the sound.

This was it.

What should have been the last hurdle between me and my dissertation was, instead, the last hurdle between me and my expulsion.

At least I'd get to enjoy the question period, before unleashing hell.

For the next forty-five minutes, I would pretend that this was just my Branch and Field exam. That I had half a chance of passing it. That I'd get to eat Faye's cake. That there would be a celebration tonight at Glass Half Full, with a table full of friends toasting me.

"We're here today to examine Dorothe Bartleby's preparedness for mage candidacy," Professor Husik said, voice brisk. "Shall we begin?"

CHAPTER FORTY-FOUR

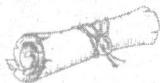

> When they came to converse, Bartleby was soon sensible
> of some mental change. The subjects of which her heart
> had been full had now become but of secondary interest.
> —NARRATORIAL COMMENTARY ADAPTED FROM
> JANE AUSTEN'S *PERSUASION* BY ANNE

THE FIRST PORTION OF THE EXAM FLEW BY. PROFESSOR HUSIK kicked off the question period before ceding the floor to Professor Delight. He was bafflingly civil, asking simple methodological questions before calmly handing the baton to Professor Matthews, who interrogated my literary interpretations with a series of questions about the theoretical underpinnings of my approach to Austen's work, and in particular my definitions of narration and free indirect discourse. Finally, Professor Huang leaned forward, notebook in hand.

Their questions were the trickiest, and I kept waiting for anxiety to freeze me up, to steal the words from my mouth. But ironically, knowing I was going to fail made answering easier. The only thing I had to care about was helping my friends get our students back.

When I finished, Professor Huang nodded. It was a small gesture, but I could tell by the look on their face that I'd done it. I'd convinced them—if not of my argument itself, at least that the subject was worth further exploration.

Grief hit, so intense I was dizzy with it. If things were different, I would have passed this time. I would have fucking passed
my exam.

Professor Husik closed her notebook with a smile. "That con-
cludes the question period. We will now take a ten-minute break,
and when we return Ms. Bartleby will provide a spellwork demonstration."

My stomach clenched, and I took a seat as my committee
members trickled out of the room for bio breaks. Professor Delight
lingered behind the others, considering me. His expression spoke
volumes, full of patronizing pity and anger and a wild glee that
was held barely in check. It was a gaze that seemed to say, *I hope
you enjoyed this, because we both know what comes next will break you. I
will relish watching your career go up in flames.*

A long, stuttering heartbeat, and he was gone. I held on to my
water bottle and repeated the words that had become my mantra.
"I will be calm. I will be mistress of myself."

It was that or fall apart.

I REVERSED ANNE'S CLOAKING WHILE THE COMMITTEE WAS TAKING
their break, positioning Anne so that its empty orbital sockets
would stare right at Professor Delight.

"Bartleby was nervous now," Anne intoned to the empty
room. "But she gathered strength from the knowledge that her
plan would work."

"Thanks, Anne." I rested a hand on it. Hopefully, it was right.

I forced myself to breathe. To keep moving. Rethinking Anne's
position, I propped it on top of my facsimile copy of *Domestick
Spelles* so it would be closer to eye level for the professor.

I wanted to unbalance him, as much as possible, before Anne
began narrating.

If I were in his position, I'd be expecting me to do one of two
things: share a sob story about the untimely demise of my working and attempt, unsuccessfully, to pass by describing it instead; or

reveal a brand-new skull upon which I'd recast my working over the weekend—in flagrant violation of university policy.

Some professors never expect collaboration to be an option. They never expect that cohorts might be doing their best to support each other, even when it's more convenient to go solo. The communal is a power they don't understand.

I was going to use that awareness gap to push Professor D. over the edge.

"Bartleby's friends were in position," Anne added as the committee began to trickle back into the room.

It was time to team up with a magic construct of my own creation to goad one of my committee members into self-incriminating in front of a room of his peers.

No big deal.

I took a deep breath as Professors Huang, Matthews, and Husik settled into their chairs. Mark Delight strode in slowly behind them, clearly looking forward to what was to come. Until his eyes fell on the skull in the center of the table, bone lace-like with sutures that weaved back and forth across its surface. His expression didn't change, except for a brief crinkling around the eyes and a general stiffness as he lowered himself into his chair.

Good. I'd made him less at ease. Now for the harder part. To truly unsettle.

"Are we ready to proceed to the spellwork demonstration?" Professor Husik asked the room. A round of nods and murmured yeses gave me the go-ahead I needed.

I eased my way in, gesturing at Anne to indicate the presence of my working.

"My demonstration working uses a digimancy framework to test one of the core contentions of my project—that narration was, in its early literary manifestations, quite literally magic. Since the magic involved has been part of our reality for so long it has become inert, testing that claim requires an oblique approach."

I paused for a breath, sneaking a look around the room at my committee. Three of them sat with politely interested expressions.

Professor Delight's professional demeanor had melted, just enough that I could see his impatient confusion. Was I going to bomb this thing, or not? I smiled, fiercely, in his direction.

I was going to bomb this exam like no mage student had bombed an exam before me: with intense panache. And I was going to take him down with me.

"The idea was that I would be able to use the construct not only to identify patterns indicative of potential magic at work in a large corpus of early novels, but also to create new narrations by recombining those patterns in new arrangements."

They all nodded like they were following along, but Professor D.'s expression grew increasingly wary. I was not the nervous wreck I should be.

"Due to some unanticipated functionality, I initially believed the working had failed. Three aberrances stood out. First, the construct, Anne, began to narrate *me* almost immediately, with a depth of insight that was uncanny. Second, the construct did not respond to the commands I created in the code packet. And third, with increasing frequency the construct began to glitch, seeming to narrate nothing from an omniscient point of view at irregular intervals."

Only a bit more framing, and I'd hand things over to Anne. I breathed and continued. "Review of the code and spellwork revealed a handful of small errors. I've addressed most of them."

I looked at Anne; its lace-like sutures lent it a terrible beauty. If nothing else, I'd managed to salvage *it*.

"Over the course of the past several weeks, I have come to the following conclusions—about which I am happy to speak at more length after my demonstration. First, that the glitches were not glitches, after all. Rather than narrating nothing, as I originally assumed, it became clear that the construct was drawing upon the institutional repository, narrating from the cloaked perspective of the students who went missing—and whose records were erased—over the course of this term."

Professor Delight's scoff was full of outrage, but Professor Husik held a hand in his direction and smiled at me.

"Go on, Dorothe."

I drew myself up, relaxed my shoulders, and continued.

"Second, while the construct was meant to create *fictional* narrations, its ability to narrate me was still indicative of magic. The magic of narration isn't worked outwardly, not at first. It begins with inward changes. Put plainly: narration is divination."

Even Professor Matthews was nodding now. I took a breath, allowing myself a smile as I wrapped up my presentation.

"Narration reshapes consensus reality by giving us access to the interiority of others, allowing us to know people in a way, and from a unique perspective, that's not supposed to be possible. That knowing carries beyond the page, into the way we are with each other. Person by person, reader by reader, reality shifts." I paused for effect, looking around the room with triumph singing through me.

"My construct—" I gestured again at Anne "—*could* narrate anyone here."

Professor Delight's gaze narrowed as I locked eyes with him. I opened my mouth, the next words on the tip of my tongue, but Anne's hard-coded sense of dramatic timing kicked in.

"Professor Husik leaned forward," Anne said, "excited to see the working in action."

Amelia broke character as a stern examiner, laughing and clapping. I kept my eyes on Delight.

"But it is a truth universally acknowledged that a construct in possession of the power to narrate must be in want of a *good* story." My words didn't waver. I could be proud of that, later. "Something dramatic." I waited a beat before concluding my remarks. "I cede my remaining minutes to Anne, my spellwork demonstration." I cleared my throat. "*Once upon a time.*"

Delight's hands, flat against the table, scraped along the vinyl and formed themselves into fists. It was the only movement he made.

"In ceding the floor to Anne," Anne began, "Bartleby relinquished all remaining hope of passing the exam. While she had demonstrated the divinatory qualities of her construct's narration, there would be no time for her to walk through the presentation she'd prepared about how the skull's narration illustrated the magic at work in early novels. There was something more important at play around this seminar table. Something nefarious."

Delight sat rigid, staring at Anne. A vein along his jaw pulsed. The rest of the committee looked on in confusion.

"Since January, dozens of Magic students had gone missing. After reporting to the clearly overwhelmed Office of Public Safety, Bartleby took matters into her own hands to find them. Her investigation revealed that one of the people around this table was involved in the disappearances."

"This is highly irregular," Professor Matthews chimed in, "even for *your* school."

Professor Husik frowned—though I wasn't sure if it was at the dig on the School of Magic, the interruption, or my spellwork demonstration. "Noted," she said. "Now, shush."

Professor Matthews slumped backward, sliding her hands underneath her thighs.

"The professor in question believed himself safe . . ." Anne continued. At its use of the pronoun, all eyes swiveled to Professor Delight, who pretended not to notice and held himself rigid, the polite smile on his face a rictus. ". . . after attempting to destroy Bartleby's spellwork demonstration, which had been about to narrate the names of his fellow conspirators."

Delight's face went a shade paler, but he was otherwise unmoved.

"I'm afraid that your working is creating fantastical fiction, at best, Ms. Bartleby," he said. "Libel, at worst." When he spoke, his voice was cold and unconcerned.

Professor Matthews murmured agreement. "What proof do we have that the construct is *actually* accessing a person's innermost thoughts? And what do these accusations have to do with Ms. Bartleby's proposed dissertation?"

Anne, unbothered, continued to speak in a monotone text-to-speech voice that somehow managed to sound wry. "Professor Matthews continually regretted her decision to work at a state school. She'd attended the best universities. She should be on the East Coast doing *real* research instead of toiling away here, spending most of her time on teaching and service."

Professor Matthews squeaked in surprise and let her protest lapse into embarrassed silence.

"I'd very much like the demonstration to proceed," Professor Huang said. "Don't you agree, Amelia?" Beside them, my advisor smiled.

Delight growled, so low I almost didn't catch the sound.

"We could cut the demonstration short." It was the only concession I was prepared to make. "If Professor Delight would rather narrate his own story." I swear I heard my advisor snicker, though her face was a neutral blank when I snuck a look her way.

Turning back to Professor Delight, I waited for an answer. A tiny twitch of one eyebrow was the only response he gave. But his face was a shade pinker than it had been before. I took that as a good sign.

Anne finished its tale.

"The professor focused quite intensely on *not* thinking the names of his treacherous colleagues," Anne said. "Though he knew well that the effort to *not* think the names would inevitably fail. One cannot intentionally *not* think of something, when one has identified what not to think about, for long. And, he reflected, he wasn't being compensated well enough to keep their secrets when his own were being dragged into the light."

Anne paused as the angry color that had begun to flood Delight's face washed away, leaving him an awful shade of bluish white.

"Nevertheless, dread seized him as he contemplated what would happen when he inevitably slipped up. What *they* would do to him. He decided to—"

He moved as Anne spoke, slipping a quick hand into the

pocket of his suit jacket and hurling a small object lengthwise over the table at Anne, a guttural snarl punctuating the motion.

As the object hurtled toward it, Anne finished its sentence "—attack."

My yelp of surprised dismay felt separate from me. I floated above myself, unable to empathize with my body's distress.

Professor Husik flicked a wrist, freezing the object in mid-air. She stood and snatched the bottle—an alchemical potation of some sort—sliding it safely into her pocket.

At almost the same time, Professor Huang reached into their briefcase and pulled out a pair of handcuffs, the gray metal studded with little pebbles of moon rock. They threw these at Delight with a series of rapid commands in . . . Cantonese, maybe? And the cuffs wrapped themselves around Delight's wrists one at a time, effectively binding him to his chair.

At my baffled look, Professor Huang explained. "I had these made when a student attacked me a few terms ago. I haven't left the house without them since."

"You will be made to account for your actions." Delight stopped flailing in his chair long enough to snarl. "If I were you, I'd reconsider my course and apologize."

Professor Huang shot him a look that clearly telegraphed their desire to thwack him across the back of the head. They had no intention of apologizing, and neither did I.

Enraged by the reaction, Delight bellowed and began stringing together a curse. Nothing happened, except that he moaned when his working didn't take. The moon rock in the cuffs prevented it. Professor Huang, closing the distance between them, thwacked him, anyway.

"We'll have none of that, thanks."

I removed Anne from the table, packing it away for lack of anything better to do. But Anne's voice boomed as I lowered it into my bag.

"Professor Delight cursed Dean Underhill and his sniveling colleagues as he struggled against his bonds. He would have thought six mages, one a dean for Merlin's sake, could outwit a poor excuse for a mage student."

Delight was shocked into silence by Anne's pronouncement. He sank into his chair as if all of his bones had evaporated. Across the long table from him, I mirrored his movement, sagging backward with a sigh. Anne went on to name Professor Delight's accomplices as he mentally cursed each and every one. He named everyone on our list, and a few more besides. A couple of assistant deans, some staff administrators, the cemetery caretaker.

I'd done my part. Now it was up to the committee.

The absurdity of the thought struck me, and I almost laughed out loud. In another reality, where I hadn't had to make this decision, I would've been thinking the exact same thing, waiting patiently in the hall to learn whether or not I'd passed my exam. In another reality, I'd be moments away from becoming mage, all but dissertation.

I shook the thoughts away and turned my attention to the rest of the room.

Professor Matthews had pushed her chair back and away from the table. "Highly unusual," she repeated to herself, eyes closed and breathing rapid.

Closer to me, two of my committee members were unfazed.

"Thank you, Rue," Professor Husik said, setting down a cell phone that, in the chaos, I hadn't seen her pick up.

"Of course," Professor Huang replied.

"Will you keep an eye on him while I check on poor Professor Matthews?" Her tone went wry as she said *poor*.

Professor Huang growled. "With pleasure. I take it you've called the provost?"

Professor Husik was already moving toward Professor Matthews. "Mm-hmm." She paused and turned to face me. "It would be very helpful if you'd stay to make a statement."

I managed to nod.

"And Bartleby?" I didn't want to, but I looked up. Her smile was gutting. "You were splendid, for what it's worth."

I nodded again.

I had been. But we both knew it wouldn't matter. As I waited for the provost to arrive, I pulled out my phone, sending the text that would spur my friends into action.

It's done.

CHAPTER FORTY-FIVE

A fresh round of protests rocked campus this week, as graduate students gathered to call attention to an ableist conspiracy in which a number of Magic faculty and administrators
have been implicated. "Magic has a long history of eugenicist
thought," commented graduate student Darya Watkins, leader
of the protest outside Newton Hall. "There are still those who
think it should be accessible only to an elite group—chosen
ones, you might say. They're wrong."

—ARTICLE IN *THE PLATYPUS PRATTLER*, 2 MARCH

I WANDERED MY BUILDING, A LOST SOUL WITH NO DESTINATION.
Eventually, I found myself in the hall that led to my office.
And there, leaning against the wall beside my office door, was
James. I barreled into his arms. Wordlessly, he wrapped them
around me, resting his chin on top of my head.

The simple gesture dissolved my last traces of numbness.

"It's going to be okay." He planted a kiss on top of my head.
"You're going to be okay."

I cried, right there in the hall, letting him whisper soothing
promises that comforted me, even though I knew they weren't true.
Eventually, tears spent, I sniffled a question into his damp shirt.

"How are you here? I thought you were supposed to be at
Sibyl House."

Gently unpeeling himself enough to meet my eyes, James

shared a sad smile. "The others knew what you were planning to do. I didn't tell them," he said. "And they reassigned me to Bartleby duty." He kissed me on the forehead. "Which suited me fine, since I would've been here either way. They've got enough people at the protest sites."

I nestled my head against his chest, nodding. "I'm glad you're here." And I was, even though some distant voice in my head—one that sounded a lot like shadow-Granny—threatened to overwhelm the warmth of his arms with chilling doubts. *If they knew, why didn't they stop you? Why did they let you sacrifice your career, girl? They would've fought you on it, if they'd thought you really belonged.*

"Let's get you home," James said. "You must be exhausted."

I was. But if I went home, shadow-Granny's voice might take over.

"No." The word came out strangled, and James pulled up short, eyebrows colliding.

"No?"

"I don't want to go home." My phone buzzed. I fished it out of my satchel and stared at the screen, unsure whether to laugh or cry. **30 minutes until this event: Tattoo.** I'd failed my exam, but I still had a success to celebrate. In fact, if Professor Delight and the others got what they deserved for casting their monstrous working, this would be both the biggest failure and success of my life.

"There's somewhere else I need to be."

I'd done it. I'd lived through the starsdamned fulfillment of my childhood prophecy. My career might be over, but I was *free.*

And by Hecate, I was going to mark the occasion.

TRAFFIC SLOWED AS WE MADE OUR WAY OFF CAMPUS. WE PASSED THE Bentham Cote protest, where there was no trace of the magically enhanced snapdragons and foxgloves I'd seen on the first day of term. Most of the people marching through the trees were grad students I recognized from the Federation, all of whom had taken precautions for the flowers. But it looked like they'd attracted some students from other programs, maybe even a few community members. Darya had planned for that, sending volunteers over to spread some concoction of hers on the grounds just in case the foxgloves had left behind a nasty surprise.

Signs reading NOTHING ABOUT US WITHOUT US! And MY DISABILITY MIGHT BE INVISIBLE BUT YOUR ABLEISM ISN'T, and NO JUSTICE, NO PEACE bobbed above the crowd. Their stamping feet and chanting voices transformed into a wave of sound—no, a crashing roar—even from here.

I pressed my hands against the car window, staring with surging pride and rage and exhaustion and grief. We'd done it. We'd taken down the working. I'd gotten the evidence we needed. And between that and these protests, the university *had* to take action. It wouldn't be able to sweep us under the rug.

"So, where are we going?" James asked. He kept his eyes on the traffic light, caution in his tones.

"Sublime Inkantations."

"That tattoo shop?" He glanced at me, brows raised, just as the light turned. Behind us, someone honked. James hauled his attention back to the road reluctantly, taking a right.

"Yep."

"Are you planning to explain why?"

"I like tattoos."

James snorted. "Really? I hadn't noticed."

From the backseat, Anne chimed in. "Bartleby wished to mark her success, as she had all of her successes before."

"Is that . . ." James glanced my way. "Is that what your tattoos are?"

My cheeks burned. "It's not, like, an ego thing. If that's what you're thinking."

He shot me another quick look, brow furrowed. "It's not."

He didn't ask what it *was*. And I'd avoided telling him about my childhood prophecy all term, reluctant to let him see how far back my mess truly went. Reluctant, if I was being truly honest with myself, to say anything that might make him stop thinking of me as a hero—ridiculous as it was that he did in the first place. Now . . . I needed him to understand.

I told him everything. Small details, like the way the cupcake, with its too-sweet chemical strawberry tang, had sat heavy in my stomach because I could tell my parents were nervous about something. Bigger things, like the prophecy itself. The ways it had shaped me and my parents, warping our relationship over time.

James drove with his head tipped toward me, listening.

I clamped my fingers into fists, squeezing and releasing over and over as I finished my story. "Anyway . . . by the time I graduated high school, failure had been hanging over me for so long it was all I saw when I looked in the mirror. It was all I could imagine for myself." I shucked my shirt up, showing him the *Sense and Sensibility* quote—*Know your own happiness*—and stack of books on my abs. "I got my first tattoo the night after graduation, to push back. It helped." I took a deep breath and let it out, keeping my own gaze on the road. "They all help. To be honest, they're a lifeline. Reminders that I am more than that horrible prophecy. More than my failures. I get one for every success, no matter how silly or small. I know that probably sounds ridiculous."

"No." James pulled into Sublime Inkantation's parking lot. "That doesn't sound ridiculous at all. I think about my scars in a similar way. They're reminders that I'm not my parents' version of me. Not that I want more of them." He parked under a bare-branched tree at the back of the building and shifted to look at me.

My cheeks began to burn again, for more pleasant reasons. At least, until Anne piped up.

"James wondered what sort of tattoo Bartleby would get to commemorate her latest success."

I grinned as I unbuckled and opened the passenger door. "I was kinda thinking a skull would be fitting."

Anne was clearly at a loss for words, because it resorted to quoting *Emma*. "Bartleby wanted neither taste nor spirit . . . The gesture took Anne agreeably by surprise."

JAMES WENT PALE WHEN KURIO—MY TATTOO ARTIST—PRESSED THE needle to my skin and got to work. I relaxed into the sunburn buzz, trying not to laugh as James averted his eyes.

"I didn't know you were squeamish, Southeil."

The muscle in James's jaw tensed. "I'm not. I just . . ." He cupped his palm around the back of his neck. "I can't stand the thought of other people in pain."

Kurio found a tender spot right as I started to say that I wasn't, and a hiss escaped me before I could stop it. James winced.

"Sorry." I grit my teeth as the needle dug in. "It mostly doesn't hurt. But you don't have to stay, if this is hard for you to be around."

James swallowed. "No. I want to be here. I'll just distract myself." I hissed again as Kurio hit another tender spot, and James's voice went faint. "Somehow." He pulled his phone out of his pocket and started tapping at it.

"To think I was convinced you were a necromancer."

James scoffed, eyes lifting to mine for the briefest second before dropping back to his phone screen. "Now you know better."

For a few minutes, the only sound was the tattoo gun's relentless *burrrrrrr*. It rattled down into my bones, shaking me up as it transformed me. I closed my eyes, welcoming the change.

Kurio wasn't a chatterer. They preferred to work with their headphones on—music quiet, so they could hear me if I needed anything—and slip into hyper-focus. It was one of the reasons I kept coming back. The other being the superb quality of their work. Usually, I'd have queued up an audiobook and settled in. But usually, I was alone.

"Got it," James said, almost under his breath.

I cracked an eye open.

"Got what?"

"A solution. You should get another try, considering everything. And I found this buried deep on the School of Magic's website." He raised his phone screen, reading aloud. "'Should you wish to apply for an exception to a program policy, you may do so by submitting the *Petition to Waive a Magic School Policy* form.'"

"It can't be that simple." I'd have crossed my arms, if Kurio didn't have one of them pinned. "You're telling me all I have to do, after all of this, is fill out a form?"

James chewed his lower lip. "Well, it says they only grant petitions 'in extreme circumstances.'" His eyes found mine. "But I'd say these circumstances are fairly Heccing extreme."

"Okay." I let out a breath. The bees that usually cluttered up my head had made their way to my stomach. "What does the form say?"

James tapped a couple of times, muttering at his phone until it showed him what he wanted.

"It says you need to write two short statements, no more than five hundred characters each. One to explain your request, the other to provide supporting evidence and your rationale."

So far, it seemed doable. Although I wasn't sure how I was going to cram everything into five hundred characters. I wanted so many things. Not to have failed my first exam. Not to have had to torpedo my own career. Not to have to wonder, every time I ran into a mage or professor on this campus from now on, if they secretly resented students who needed accommodations or even just a little help now and then. If they looked at those students—at me—and saw a tarnish on the reputation of Magic scholarship. If they'd one day do their best to force us out. And, more than anything, I wanted the administrators who ran the program to know how fucked up all of this was without me having to try to explain it. Without even this small amount of added labor, on top of everything else.

"And . . ." James's gazed flitted up, but he didn't quite meet my eyes.

My stomach pinched, as if the bees inside had grown agitated and begun trying to escape. "And?"

"You need a statement from your advisor and the Director of Graduate Studies."

"Professor Leighton?" My laugh—pure, outraged disbelief— was violent enough that Kurio quirked a shaved eyebrow at me. I mouthed a silent sorry and they got back to work.

"Considering the circumstances, they'd have to accept a statement from someone else."

"Maybe. But who else would I ask?"

"Professor Huang? They did a stint as Divination branch chair a few years back. They have clout. Or you could ask your branch head."

The last time I'd run into Professor Paris—at the Thaumaturgy wine and cheese last term—she hadn't even recognized me. There was no way she'd write a compelling statement on my behalf.

But Professor Huang might.

For the first time all day, I felt a sliver of something light and warm slip through the gloom wrapped around me. Hope, I realized.

Over the buzzing of the tattoo gun, Anne announced my intentions. "As soon as she had use of both of her arms again, Bartleby would send the necessary emails."

I WROTE TO AMELIA AND PROFESSOR HUANG ON THE CAR RIDE HOME, trembling with anxiety. And hope. And exhaustion. It had been a long, long day.

If this didn't work, my time at Sublimity would be over in a couple of weeks. I'd be expelled from the program, which would mean I'd lose my teaching contract. And without that, I'd be unable to pay my rent. I'd have to go home, confess to my parents that I'd finally failed, just like they'd always known I would. Live on their terms, under their roof.

Hecate's dogs, I needed to stop telling myself this version of the story.

It was going to work. I was going to petition the School of Magic for an exception, and they were going to give it to me.

I slashed the back of my hand across my eyes and forced myself to look at James.

"Have we heard from any of them yet? Imani? Alse?"

James started to shake his head. But, as if my words were an invocation, his phone began to ring.

He fished it out of his pocket and glanced at the screen.

"It's her." His tone was gentle, words spoken not in surprise but in relief. He pulled over to answer. I shifted in my seat, meaning to look away—to offer him some modicum of privacy—but James arched an eyebrow at me and stabbed the speakerphone icon on the screen.

"Imani?" His voice wavered.

"James! You actually pulled it off!" Imani's shouting voice peaked the phone's speakers.

"Are you okay?" James asked, ignoring the unpleasant sound and backhanded compliment in favor of getting practical information.

Imani laughed, a short, sharp sound. "I am weeks behind on all of my work and my parents are going to be insufferably clingy," she said. "So, no, I am not okay. But I will be fine."

"Do you need anything? Food?"

I was beginning to realize James's go-to move in any vaguely stressful situation was to feed people. It was an admirable trait. I focused on that instead of the uncomfortable twisting feeling in my gut. He was going to go to her. Comfort her. And she'd been through more than I had. She'd been in some terrible liminal space that ate away at her sense of reality for weeks. He'd be justified.

I slid down in my seat.

"Did your genius girlfriend get the proof to pin those bastards?" Imani asked instead of answering James's question.

I was confused enough that I had to sit back up. *What?*

James looked at me, a smile outmaneuvering the concern in his gaze. "She did." He wasn't denying it. Wasn't trying to push back against the label.

"Then, I'm good. That's all I need. My housemates have the food covered, believe me."

In the background, Zach shouted, "Ghosts can come *back*!"

"Celebratory pizza on Zach?" James asked.

Imani laughed. "How'd you know?" She paused for long enough that I started to wonder if the call had dropped. "Thanks," her voice wavered, "to both of you."

"What else are cohort BFFs for?" James asked.

Imani huffed a small laugh. In the background, the doorbell rang.

"I'll talk to you later, okay?" she said after another, not-quite-audible, shout from Zach. "I'm being summoned."

She hung up. James stared at the phone for a second before sliding it back into his pocket.

I reached out and touched his shoulder. "I'm glad she's okay."

"Me, too." He cleared his throat and started the car, steering us back into the flow of traffic. He was silent for long enough that I started to feel desperate.

"Genius girlfriend, huh? She sounds cool."

"She is." One hand snuck its way up to the back of his neck, sheepish. "And, uh, I hope she's my girlfriend."

"If she's as smart as you say," I said, carefully, "then she would very much like to be."

James risked a glance my way, detecting the impending *but* in my tone.

I dispensed with our weird third person fiction, all the doubts I'd tried to shove away flooding back in at once.

"James, I still don't know how this is going to play out . . ." The words hurt coming up. I wrapped my arms around my stomach, letting myself trail off. Speculating wouldn't do any good; either the petition would work or it wouldn't.

"They're going to grant you that exception." James didn't look at me, though the tension of his neck and shoulders told me how much he wanted to. "It's not fair, otherwise. Your committee's decision was never going to be unanimous. The school's admin will have to see that."

"I hope so," I whispered, but the words didn't hurt any less. Because he was right. It wasn't fair. I'd wasted so much time thinking I didn't belong here, and now—when I'd finally found my place and my people, finally allowed myself to trust that I might be enough—it might all be torn away. But Magic school wasn't fair. It never had been. "I want to stay."

"And you *will*. We'll find a way to make it happen."

He smiled at me, expression so fierce and determined and full of longing that I wanted to catch the moment between my hands, hold it there like the fireflies I'd cupped in sticky palms when I was a kid, and sit with the wondrous glow.

I wanted to say *yes, I'll be your girlfriend*. I wanted to demand that he pull over on the spot so I could kiss him breathless. But if I did, and the petition didn't work . . . that would break me. It would break *everything*.

I belonged here, working higher magic with my housemates and friends. With him. And now that I'd realized that, I couldn't settle for some half-measure version of this life. There wasn't a reality out there in which I could be content watching the people I cared about do the thing I loved most while I stood on the outside looking in. I'd resent them for it eventually. And that resentment would poison us.

"It wasn't that Bartleby didn't want—" Anne began.

"*The End*, Anne." My words were tear choked, but firm enough that it stopped immediately. Easy as it would be to let Anne speak for me, this was something I had to say for myself. I kept my eyes on James, watched his knuckles go white around the steering wheel.

"James."

He met my eyes for only a moment, looking twice as haggard as he had after that starsdamned truth working. And I hated myself for that. He knew what I was about to say, or he'd guessed the outlines of it. But I kept going, anyway. I belonged here, but Dean Underhill and Leighton and Delight and the others weren't the only ones in higher ed, or even at Sublimity, who wanted students like me gone. Until I knew one way or another how this was going to go . . .

I took a breath, my throat doing its best to close around the words. "You have no idea how much I *want* to be your girlfriend, James. It's just, everything is so up in the air. I can't make any commitments right now."

James adjusted his grip on the steering wheel, knuckles going whiter. "You've had a hard day. Let's get you home," he said, after a long pause.

I spent the rest of the day trying not to think about the way James's expression had closed off. I hadn't said no, but it'd felt a lot like a no coming out. Like an ending, reverberating through our story too soon. He must've felt it, too.

I curled up on my bed, exhausted but unable to sleep. Eventually, Anne began to narrate—bursts of names and information as the missing students returned and their records were restored. We'd done it. We'd really, truly done it. I dozed off to the sound of their stories being set right.

CHAPTER FORTY-SIX

A representative of the AAMUP is on campus this week, amid ongoing protests about ableist conduct in the School of Magic. Six faculty have been placed on administrative leave as the Office of the Provost looks into protestors' allegations.

—ARTICLE IN *THE PLATYPUS PRATTLER*, 4 MARCH

MY NIGHTMARES CLUNG LIKE SPIDERWEBS, MAKING MY SKIN crawl as I followed Darya onto the bus and tumbled into a seat near the wheelchair bay.

I'd tossed and turned all night, and I could still see Granny's dead, waxen face when I closed my eyes, leering as I informed her that it was time for me to tell a new story. My subconscious had rendered the memory of that moment perfectly, from the streaky light to the powdered bone floating in the air like pollen. It'd played and replayed in my sleep. But where its rendering was perfect, its riffing was diabolical.

In the nightmare version of our confrontation, my words didn't break me free from Granny's net. If anything, they tightened it around me until I was almost choking.

"Do tell, dear." Granny laughed, leaning toward me so that the mothball taint of her breath burned in my nasal passages. "Whatever gave you the idea *that* was possible? Everywhere you go, there you'll be, as they say."

"Bartleby!" Darya poked me, startling me out of the night-mare haze. "Were you even listening?"

I rubbed my face. "Sorry."

I needed to shake this off. I *was* still me. But I'd broken free of my prophecy, finally. And, given how many adaptations of *Pride and Prejudice* I'd consumed in my lifetime, I knew it was possible to tell new stories with the same old characters. I just had to figure out how. Straightening my shoulders, I focused on Darya.

"We're headed to Randolph House today." She waved her phone as if citing a text message. "According to Cy, James is at Bentham Cote, marching with Mims."

"Thank you for finding that out."

Darya frowned. "Did he do something to upset you yesterday?"

"I don't want to talk about it."

"Okay, but just say the word and Cy and I will hex him six ways from Sunday."

I mustered a smile. "I know."

The bus pulled away from the curb, rattling into traffic and toward campus.

"Are you sure you're up for this?" Darya asked.

"Yep."

I wasn't. Exhaustion had a chokehold on me. My shoulder felt raw because of my new tattoo—more like a battle wound than a reminder of success. And I was more than a little haunted by my nightmare. But I'd already canceled class, and marching alongside my peers would be therapeutic—as long as I didn't have to face James.

It would also, hopefully, distract me from the lack of messages in my inbox.

At Randolph House, I fell into step behind Darya, who'd kit-ted out her power wheelchair with paperboard signs and disability pride flags. She had a clipboard with her, and every once in a while she veered out of the picket line to show it to somebody, fire in her eyes. I stayed in line, marching and chanting until my voice was raw and my legs were rubber and there was no room in my head for any worries, any plans, anything at all except the call and response of protest. *Hey, ho, Sublimity, you cannot get rid of me.*

Perversely, that was when the emails began to trickle in.

I saw the first, a boilerplate message from Faye on behalf of the graduate committee, while taking a water break.

Dear Dorothe Bartleby,

This email serves as notification that the status of your academic standing has changed to Academic Disqualification. Your exam committee was unable to reach a unanimous decision in favor of your candidacy. Written assessments of your performance and recommendations will be shared with you in 1–2 weeks. Per program policy, you are permitted to complete any winter term courses in which you may be enrolled or teaching before withdrawing from the program.

Crouched in the shade of the Randolph House portico, I waited for the tears to come. Instead, my hand clamped hard around my phone, trying to turn itself into a fist.

If Anne were here and not at home on my dresser, it would quote some furious, devastating book. George Eliot's *The Mill on the Floss*, maybe. *Bartleby's first flush came from anger,* I could imagine it saying, *which gave her a transient power of defiance.*

The imaginary narration helped. I stood, sliding my phone back into my bag.

The email didn't change anything. I'd known it was coming, and I was going to submit my petition to waive the policy as soon as I pulled together the materials. Running on sheer stubbornness, I brushed my cheeks dry and rejoined the picket line.

Cy joined us on the bus ride home that evening, comparing his own mysterious clipboard with Darya's before settling in for the ride. They began trading news as I repeatedly refreshed my inbox.

"—and we think all of the students are back now," Cy was saying when my attention finally drifted back to their conversation. After ascertaining James's whereabouts this morning, he'd joined Mags at the protest outside the admin building. "Mags said most of them are heading home to regroup. I suspect some of them will be transferring. But pretty much everyone was willing to stay for the rest of the term when Mags told them about the AAMUP representative."

"Speaking of which, I'm meeting with him on Friday." Darya's laugh wasn't triumphant, it was bloodthirsty. "He's going to hear a lot about what we think of their proposal."

"Good." A little of Darya's bloodthirstiness made its way into my voice. At least *something* was going right. Something like justice might come out of all this mess in the end.

"Word is they've already put several of the conspirators on administrative leave," Darya added. "Leighton. Delight. The dean, too. Please tell me that's more than just a rumor."

"It was announced about an hour ago," Cy confirmed. "Well, not announced, so much as communicated delicately to a select group of people, including the Federation officers, since the Federation took responsibility for the demonstrations."

"I guess we'll see if the administration actually follows through. But—" Darya's tones leaped from bloodthirsty to gleefully slaughterous "—whatever the university does, I know for a fact that several of the students and their families are pursuing lawsuits."

My phone buzzed in my hands and I startled, jerking it up to find new messages from Amelia and Professor Huang, their statements of support attached.

As I followed Darya and Cy from the bus stop to our apartment, I read and reread Amelia's note.

Dorothe,
You were splendid, as I predicted. I am, of course, more than happy to support you in any way I can.

Please find my statement attached.

Good luck,

AMELIA

They were kind words. Supportive ones. And Professor Huang's email contained more of the same. But Amelia's sign-off left me uneasy.

I belonged here, with Darya and Cy and James and Mags and Lora. But that didn't mean the administration would make room for me, that I'd be allowed to stay. And I couldn't help feeling a creeping sense of *denouement*.

The last days of the term were slipping away. I had two class sessions left to teach, one Thursday and one next week. After that, there'd be a small mountain of grading to finish.

And then . . .

I tried to cling to that angry defiance from earlier, barricading myself in my room to submit my petition. But Anne gave the lie to my pretense, narrating my fears the entire time.

"OH, GOOD, YOU'RE ALIVE," CY DRAWLED, THE MORNING OF MY CLASS'S final session. "Darya was about to make me get up and check." He was sprawling across the couch, a coffee mug propped on his chest. Darya, lounging on the battered love seat and using her power wheelchair as a footstool, craned her head to look my way.

"I was." Her voice took on a more hesitant tone. "How are you?"

"Fine."

The past eight days had toppled like dominoes, in quick succession. There'd been no word about my petition, and the uncertainty had made it impossible to sleep for more than a few fitful minutes at a time. I'd probably sleep like the dead tonight, though. Because my wait was over. I had my answer.

Petition denied, the subject line had read.

Apparently, Professor Delight wasn't the only mage on my

committee who'd voted to fail me. Professor Matthews had found the whole ordeal shocking and unprofessional. With a fifty-fifty split, the School of Magic felt that there was insufficient evidence that I would have passed in different circumstances.

I wasn't ready to tell my housemates, though.

I shuffled a little farther into the room, trying to blink away my bleariness. "Is there any coffee left?"

"Bartleby had suffered from dreadful nightmares," Anne announced from my dresser down the hall. "And had woken to find reality more devastating than her dreams."

Darya narrowed her eyes. "Fine, huh?"

I groaned, sinking onto the arm of the couch in defeat. "I heard back about my petition."

"And?" Darya asked gently.

"They denied it."

"Why?" Cy bolted upright, sending his coffee cascading. It puddled on the carpet. "What grounds could they possibly have?

"Professor Delight wasn't the only one who voted against me." The words left a bitter aftertaste. I tried to swallow it away.

"Oh, Bartleby." Darya's expression went anguished. "We'll figure this out, okay? It's not over yet. We—"

I waved her words away. "What is there to figure out? I failed. Twice. And my petition was denied. Maybe Granny was right."

My housemates traded baffled looks.

"Granny?" Cy managed.

I wanted to laugh. I wanted to scream. All that emotion, colliding together, came out as a sound—half hiccup, half sob. It sent my bangs tumbling into my eyes. I swiped them out of the way, scowling.

"In the Bone House, Granny joined the ward ghosts and tried to trap me with a story about my childhood prophecy. I told her I was going to tell a new story. She's been showing up in my dreams ever since, insisting it won't do any good. And it looks like she's right, after all."

Cy smirked. "Well, obviously. You're going about it all wrong."

"Pearson!" Darya threw a pillow at his head.

Cy caught it, midair. His smirk was gone, but there was a smug set to his lips. He hoisted the pillow, pretending to toss it at Darya, before spinning to hurl it at me. "Even Jane Austen had an editor."

I was so stunned by the comment I caught the pillow with my face. My ears popped as it flopped to the carpet. I stared at Cy, rubbing static electricity from my arms.

"What was that for? And what do you mean, *even Jane Austen had an editor?*"

Darya looked from Cy to me, something awfully like a smile crinkling at the corners of her lips. "I think he means you don't have to do it alone."

Cy's shrug was languid. "More or less."

"We know things are hard right now," Darya added, "but we're here for you. We'll figure something out. Together. Just tell us what you need."

I pinched the bridge of my nose, squeezing my eyes shut against a rush of tears. I loved her for her optimism, I did. But trying to catch hold of it myself seemed more impossible, more dangerous, than attempting a major working with no containment circle or ghosts to prevent catastrophe. The petition had been my plan.

"Coffee. I need coffee." I marched into the kitchen without another word. But they'd anticipated I would do that. An invitation, thick textured paper with gilt lettering, waited on the counter in front of the coffee machine.

> **You're cordially invited to Darya's Major**
> **Mage Milestones celebration. Thursday,**
> **Week 10, at Glass Half Full. 7 p.m.**

Underneath the letterpress type, Darya had scrawled a quick note.

You owe me a celebration. I promise we'll celebrate you soon.

An unseen hand clutched my heart, fingers leaving bruises where they squeezed. We were supposed to celebrate together. I wanted to crumple the note, throw it away, but that wouldn't stop the ache. Instead, I left it on the counter and headed to campus.

CHAPTER FORTY-SEVEN

Bartleby was sorry, but could not repent. On the contrary, her plans and proceedings were more and more justified and endeared to her by the general appearances of the next few days.

—NARRATORIAL COMMENTARY ADAPTED
FROM JANE AUSTEN'S *EMMA* BY ANNE

SHOULDERING MY WAY INTO MY CLASSROOM FOR THE LAST TIME this term—and possibly ever—I tried to forget my housemates' strange behavior, ignoring the lump in my throat.

Tired, familiar faces watched me cross the room. I dumped my bag and raincoat into a chair and turned to consider them. My heart kick-drummed as I scanned the back row, where Alse, Pam, and Manesh clustered together, trying and failing to be inconspicuous.

Some of the tension inside me evaporated. I hadn't expected to get to see them again. But they were back. They were here, and their presence buoyed me.

I smiled at them before turning my attention to the rest of the class.

"At the beginning of term, I told you that you'd all been hexed. Most of you believed, before taking this class, that you weren't good spell writers. I'd like to know whether your feelings on the subject have changed."

I snapped and surveys floated down to the desks, already keyed in to a working that would visualize the data they provided on our whiteboard.

As students completed their surveys, the whiteboard revealed their secrets—many of them still felt uncertain in their skill as spell writers, but none of them considered themselves "bad" at it anymore. I'd failed at many things this term, but I hadn't failed in this.

Taking a seat on my lectern-table, I swung my legs, considering them. "You've learned and accomplished more than this survey can capture, over the past nine weeks. And before we part ways, I'd love to hear what resonated with or inspired you the most this term. What will you be taking with you from this class?"

"I learned that my spells power the entire university," Grigori joked. "The administration should be paying me to be here."

Waite raised xir hand. "I learned that there's more to spell writing than typing out a list of spell ingredients and instructions."

More hands went up, and Reed practically shimmied until I called on her. "I learned that I'm a better spell writer when I have feedback. Like, I don't have to think of everything all on my own or all at once."

Her takeaway reminded me of what Cy had said this morning, setting off a pressure shift in my skull so intense that my teeth ached. I tried to shake it off as I sent the class on their way.

Over the general cacophony of departure, I heard a sneaker squeak against the vinyl flooring and a politely cleared throat.

Alse, Pam, and Manesh had hung back.

"Ms. B.," Pam said, "we, uh . . ." Her sneaker squeaked again, as she shifted her foot awkwardly. Alse cut in.

"They told us you were the one who realized what was happening at first," they said.

"They told us what you did," Manesh added.

"To make sure we'd be okay when the spell came down," Pam explained.

I readied myself for thanks I didn't want. I'd done it because I had to. Because I was angry, no *furious*, that someone—anyone—had the audacity to decide that some students didn't belong. And also because I needed my time here to mean something, even if it was going to be cut short. Magic, at its simplest, was the act of shaping and sharing realities. And that was exactly what I'd done this term. I'd worked with my friends and the Federation to craft a reality in which this wasn't okay. In which these students *did* belong, beyond a shadow of a Heccing doubt, because we said so. In which I belonged, too, because of them. For them. It wasn't heroism, like James kept insisting. It was the biggest *fuck you* to the academy I could muster.

But all magic came at a cost, and part of me had known I would be the one to pay ever since we'd done the working to save Anne. Or maybe before even that, when the mascarons started talking to me.

"We wanted to know if you're teaching this class next term?" Pam asked.

"We have to take it again," Manesh explained, "and we'd like to take it with you."

Alse folded their arms, eyes on my satchel instead of me. "Do you have like, a course reference number or something?"

I could feel my smile wobbling as I hesitated, uncertain how to respond. Whoever had told them about my exam hadn't explained that failing this time meant I was out of chances. I couldn't bring myself to explain now. Not with fear and need and something else, something vulnerable and hopeful, flickering across their faces.

Somewhere along the way, their belonging had gotten all tangled up in mine, and when I left, they'd be paying, too.

It wasn't fair. I *wanted* to be here next term. Wanted these three in my class again. Wanted, more than anything, to stay. But my petition had been denied. The School of Magic would not waive their policy on my behalf. And, much as I longed to see my way through the mess of my career to a solution, I wasn't sure it was possible. It was why I'd pushed James away. Why the thought of Darya's celebration hurt so much.

I needed to come to terms with reality, prepare myself for what life would look like after Magic school.

The absurdity of that thought hit me like a fist. Maybe Cy was right, and I *had* been going about this all wrong.

This was *Magic school.* I was a mage student, for a few more days at least. I was here to wield higher magic: to tear down dysfunctional realities and shape new ones from their raw matter. And what were policies if not workings that added up to an institutional reality? Dry, inexorable documents charting out the way things should be.

I straightened my shoulders, regarding my waiting students.

"Of course you can retake the class with me. I'll let you know as soon as I get my course assignment." It wasn't a lie, not really. It was a story. And I didn't know the ending yet, but that shouldn't—couldn't—stop me from telling it. Because reality reshaped itself around stories.

They thanked me and left, pausing to wave at the classroom door. "Goodbye, Ms. B!" Alse called. "Have a good spring break!"

"See you next term!" Another snippet of story, and the words ricocheted through me, transforming my reality as I spoke them.

The rules said *I* had to pass or fail, all on my own. *I* had to petition. And when that didn't work, *I* had to walk away. According to the rules, my belonging was determined solely and entirely by *me.* But that wasn't how belonging worked. It was a web, not a single strand. My belonging had always been entangled with my students' and my friends'. Cy was right, in his smug way. And so was Reed, spouting my own lessons back at me.

I didn't have to figure it out alone. *Nobody* had to figure it out alone. And that meant—

My startled laugh echoed in the empty classroom.

It was hard to focus, hard to breathe. Adrenaline spiked through me, and I clenched my fists against the wild feeling. I snatched my satchel and started running, down the hall and out of the building toward Bentham Cote.

I had to find James.

THIRTY MINUTES LATER, I WAS POUNDING ON JAMES'S FRONT DOOR, desperate for him to be home. His cousin, Mims, had disclosed his address with dramatically rolled eyes when I'd shown up, panting, on Bentham Cote's porch. She had apparently been apprised of who I was at some point over the past several weeks. Either that, or she was a lot more willing to give out addresses than phone numbers. I'd have to clarify that with James later.

If he was home.

And if he'd speak to me. Or even answer the door.

I pounded again, shouting. If he wasn't going to open the door I needed to at least have my say.

"James? If you're in there, I'm sorry. I was afraid and I pushed you away and played it safe, but I didn't want to do either. I *don't* want to do either. And I'm not going to. I want—"

The door swung open. Just inside, James finished pulling a shirt on and braced himself against the door frame, revealing unshaven cheeks and bleary eyes. The imprint of a crocheted blanket pressed into his forehead and cheek. He'd been asleep. It wasn't even 10 a.m. yet.

His expression shifted from half-asleep to confused to . . . something. He shoved through the screen door that still separated us and put his hands on my shoulders.

"Bartleby? Is everything okay?"

I nodded, then shook my head, confused by the intensity of his gray eyes.

Was he worried or angry?

"It's not." My voice came out a whisper. I got louder as I went. "But I think it's going to be. I want to fight. I want to stay. I want—"

I could see something in his eyes. Pain or regret or confusion.

It couldn't be an echoing want.

I shuffled back, forcing James to let go of my shoulders, fold his hands under his armpits.

"I owe you an apology," I carried on, not quite meeting his eyes. "I pushed you away. I gave up on myself and on us. It's not what I wanted to do, but it's what I thought I needed to do." I took a ragged breath. "I was wrong. It was shitty of me. And I know it might be too late to say it, but I'm sorry."

I might not be able to fight the assumptions and judgments and bullshit forever, even with help. My career might still die a slow, horrible death. But while I had the tiniest chance, I had to *try*. To keep trying. And I wanted him by my side while I did.

My eyes had wandered to my feet, so I didn't see James move. I heard a step. Then his fingers were soft on my chin, nudging my gaze upward until my eyes met his.

I could see the responses flashing through those eyes, fast and intense and discarded as quickly as they arose. After a second, he rejected them all with a growl, leaning in to kiss me.

My nature rejoiced in his, as the alchemists in our program might say if they were being saucy. I arched into him, tiptoeing to better return his kiss. He groaned, pulling me closer, before pulling away.

I blinked up at him, mind still focused on the feel of his lips on mine.

"It *was* shitty," he said. "I didn't know what to do, Bartleby. You were hurting and you pushed me away and . . . I had to respect your choice, give you your space." He ran a hand through his hair, let it rest for a second along the back of his neck. "But I wanted to drive back to your place and beg you to try. *Convince* you to try."

I traced my fingers along his cheek. "I'm sorry."

He found his smile again, leaned down close. "If you haven't noticed, I've been stuck on you since you fried the entire copy room. Nobody else has measured up."

I snorted, outraged but pleased. "What is it about that working? Did you start believing your own story? I'm not a hero. It was an *accident*."

"An accident you walked away from," he corrected. "You messed up in a big and embarrassing way and you just kept going. You didn't let it stop you. You got up, brushed off your ego, and moved on. You grew past it." His lips brushed along my cheek right beside my ear. "It is one of the single most remarkable things I've witnessed in my time here." His voice dropped to a whisper. "And I've seen a lot. They have a Magic program at this school, you know."

I didn't know what to say, so I kissed him.

CHAPTER FORTY-EIGHT

Bartleby—the anxious, agitated, happy, feverish
Bartleby—set her heart at ease for a time.
—NARRATORIAL COMMENTARY ADAPTED FROM
JANE AUSTEN'S *NORTHANGER ABBEY* BY ANNE

JAMES FUMBLED THE DOOR OPEN AND GUIDED US INSIDE WITH-
out disentangling from me. Our movements were a piece-
meal waltz as we made our way from the open living area
toward the single room of his bungalow.

Somewhere along the way, a cranky meow interrupted our
nonverbal conversation. James stopped kissing me long enough to
mutter a testy, "Mind your own business, Wynn," before guiding
us the rest of the way into the bedroom and closing the door.

With his arms twined around me and his breath hot and
ragged against my neck, James whispered a question.

"So, Ms. Bartleby, am I qualified for the position?"

The feel of his lips brushing against my sensitive skin sent
chills running up and down the length of me. I moaned my response without meaning to. "Yes."

His soft kiss distracted me further. But I found my way back to
the question. "Wait—what position?"

"I assume—" he paused for another kiss "—since you're here—"
a nibble "—that you may have an opening for a boyfriend." His

voice was softer, vulnerable, with the last words . . . afraid, even now, that I might reject him.

"I may need another demonstration of your qualifications."

His moan was so soft I almost didn't catch it, a sound of want and frustration and need. I pulled back just enough to look into his eyes.

"Yes. Of course, yes. If you still want me." My heart pounded, even though he'd spent the past fifteen minutes demonstrating how much he wanted me. Even though I'd heard the desire in his voice.

James's smile was slow and sure.

"Well then, girlfriend," he said, and the words sent more chills rumbling over my skin, "let me demonstrate further." He wrapped himself back around me, and our conversation switched to a mostly nonverbal exchange.

WE SPENT ALL OF THAT DAY AND MOST OF THE NEXT TOGETHER, SE-questered in our own reality. As I lounged on his couch Thursday afternoon, James tended to Wynn. The cat waited grumpily by his food bowl, yowling when James took too long, to his feline mind, to open a can of wet food.

He was larger and oranger in person than he looked in the photos on James's social media, and after he'd finished eating he stared at me, green eyes round with interest.

"He's a bit standoffish," James said after I tried to coax the cat to join me on the couch. "He doesn't meet a lot of new people."

Wynn slunk out of the room, presumably to find a place to nap.

"I'll win him over eventually."

James smiled. "I'm sure you will."

We sank into companionable silence, and as I sipped my tea I took in the contents of the studio-like space. A TV hung on one wall, bordered on either side by battered wooden bookcases that were overflowing with a mix of modern and antiquarian books.

A cat tree occupied the other corner, and a few plants had been propped in windowsills, giving the space a welcoming feel.

James watched me look around, waiting while I twisted on the couch to get a full view of the room. When I sank back into the cushions, he spoke.

"It's not much, but I like it."

"I think I imagined it would be fancier." I meant the words as a compliment, but he didn't hear them that way. A flicker of disappointment came and went in his eyes, and he looked away.

"When I changed branches, my family cut ties. Financial and otherwise." His jaw tensed. I wanted, irrationally, to track down his parents and have a few words. They likely wouldn't speak to someone like me, let alone listen. But that wouldn't stop me from telling them exactly what I thought about their behavior, given half a chance.

I reached out to rest a hand on James's arm. "It's a relief. I wouldn't feel at home in a fancier place."

He was already smiling when he turned back toward me.

I made my face stern. "But now that I have this information, we need to have a conversation about why you let me bully you into feeding me. And half of the Federation."

He laughed, leaning forward and kissing me before I could launch into said conversation. When he'd thoroughly distracted me from the topic, he sank back into the couch, grinning.

"Speaking of food, I believe we've both been invited to a celebration. We might want to think about getting ready, if you plan to go."

The thought of Darya's mage milestones party brought consensus reality crashing down around me. I sat up so fast I sloshed my rapidly cooling tea all over my still-bare thighs. We hadn't even talked about the School of Magic's response to my petition, or what else I could do to stay.

"What's wrong?"

"I meant to tell you . . ." I twisted my fingers together, eyes on the carpet. "My petition was denied. I'm going to fight it, somehow. I just . . . don't know how yet. And I was hoping to have a plan before I asked Darya and Cy for help."

James curled a knuckle under my jaw, gently nudging my gaze to his.

"You don't need to have a plan to ask for help." His seriousness melted away, mischief sparking. "And I know for a fact you really, *really* don't want to miss this party."

My heart pounded.

What was so important about this party? Darya had invited me *right after* my petition got rejected, and she was normally more considerate than that. And now James was insisting I didn't want to miss it.

I could feel hope fluttering at the back of my mind—butterflies instead of bees attempting to fill my head for a change. But that was ridiculous. I hadn't even asked them for help yet. James just knew how much I cared about Darya, how important it was to show up for my friends.

I barely registered the tickle of dripping tea as I stood. I *did* owe Darya a celebration.

"Okay. Let's go."

GLASS HALF FULL WAS PACKED. DARYA HAD BOOKED THE PARTY ROOM in the back, so we ordered our drinks and made our way deeper into the building. About half of the people between the bar and the back room were familiar, mage students and adepts and undergraduate practitioners and even a few faculty. I caught a glimpse of Professor Huang and my advisor, chatting next to the fireplace.

The sea of faces was startling—no, uncanny—out of the context of the university's offices and seminar rooms.

I could feel my resolve cracking already.

There were too many people. Or too many people who probably knew about my exam. All of my instincts told me to hide, to run, to save whatever sense of dignity I had left as a scholar. I took a breath and let it out slowly. James fell into step next to me and caught my hand in his.

"Hey. You okay?"

I meant to nod, offer a quick "fine." Instead, I shrugged.

"This is harder than I thought it would be."

There were any number of ways he could have interpreted my words. Jealousy about Darya's success, her ability to hit program milestones and race past them to even bigger ones like publication. The difficulty of celebrating at all when I was facing the fight of my grad school career. But somehow, he saw right to the heart of it.

James tugged my hand with just enough force that I had to slow and turn toward him.

"Everyone who knows you also knows you would have passed that exam in your sleep, if you hadn't needed to tank it to help our students. All of our students. And friends." He tucked a tumbling lock of hair behind my ear while he waited for me to meet his eyes. "You know that, right?"

I didn't mean to shake my head.

Doubt was a habit my body clung to, even if, intellectually, I *knew* I belonged.

"Well, they do. It matters—to Darya, and to all of us—that you showed up." He paused, gray eyes narrowing as he took in the way his words had ratcheted me up to full tension.

He understood that, too, without needing clarification. "And if anyone makes you feel otherwise, I promise to 'accidentally' spill my entire beer on them."

My laugh was shaky. "That might be taking things a step too far." I didn't hate the idea, though.

"Just give me the word, and . . ." He mimicked a clumsy spill. I laughed again.

We made our way to the back, where Darya was definitely not wondering where I was. She was surrounded by people, midtoast. I stumbled to a halt, swallowed.

Shit.

Maybe the celebration part was going to be more difficult than I thought, too.

I urged myself to start moving, but my body didn't listen. I'd frozen in place. James waited, patient, at my side while I breathed hard, willing myself to take the last few steps.

"Bartleby!" Darya called, catching sight of me. "You're just in time." She waved us over.

People were already eating. In fact, Cy, Mags, and Lora were splitting a table full of appetizers just a few feet away. So Darya couldn't mean we were just in time for *food*. But the invitation I'd received had given me no other clues about what the night might hold.

I was forced to skip over all of the other things I'd planned to say on the car ride over. Things like *you were right* and *I'm going to need your help*.

"In time for what?"

Instead of answering, Darya winked, and a million things happened at once. The lights dimmed. The music changed to something more in my taste than Darya's, all acoustic guitars and melancholy harmonies.

Chairs squeaked as they were pushed back from tables, and the chatter quieted even as the shuffling, stomping noise of people reorganizing themselves reverberated through the place. James guided me toward the table where Cy, Mags, and Lora sat, pulling out a chair for me before taking his own. The seat he put me in faced the room, like a reception desk or a throne. It gave me an unobstructed view of the people gathering. Beside me, Mags raised her glass and clinked it repeatedly with a spork.

"If this turns into a flash mob, I'm leaving immediately," I whispered, more to myself than to James. He laughed, anyway, finding my hand under the table and squeezing it. I held on to him, a secret lifeline.

"It's not a flash mob," he whispered back.

How did he know? What in the name of Aleister Crowley's sentient syphilis was going on?

Darya approached the table at a leisurely pace, power wheelchair motor humming softly. She turned in her chair and searched in the bag strapped to the back until she'd fished out a slightly smushed gift box, just large enough to hold a volleyball or . . .

When she passed it to me with a flourish, I sighed and opened it quickly, fingers not sparing the beautiful floral wrapping paper, already annoyed.

Some Merlin-level fuckery was going down, clearly, because it was Anne in the box, looking impossibly smug for a skull wearing a pink hat with cat ears.

"*Once upon a time*, if you wouldn't mind, Anne," Darya prompted when I'd pulled it from the box and positioned it on the table.

"Over the course of the last week, the Federation of Graduate Teaching Fellows and Practitioners had rallied in protest . . ." Anne intoned.

"We know," I interrupted. "The protests at the sites were important, but you already narrated this at length. Could we please not?"

Anne ignored me. ". . . of the committee's decision to issue Dorothe Bartleby notice of academic disqualification," it continued.

My breath left me in a rush.

"Citing the great need for Bartleby's actions," Anne kept narrating, "and noting that an intentionally botched exam should not count against a student who has acted in critical support of the student body at immense personal cost, the FGTFP submitted an open letter to School of Magic admin—and the provost—on Thursday. It had hundreds of signatures."

I looked around the room, at the gathered people, tears welling. "You . . . what?" Under the table, James's grip on my hand tightened, just enough to keep me steady.

"Lora Mamani Flores handed Bartleby a packet of papers," Anne carried on.

Lora shot an annoyed look at Anne, but promptly passed me a thin stack of papers. They were printed emails. The correspondence between FGTFP leadership, our program admin, and the provost.

"Skip to the last page," Mags stage-whispered. At some point, she'd sat back down and snuck a pile of chips and artichoke dip onto her plate.

I did as she suggested, eyes darting over the words so fast I didn't believe them at first. I read them again and again before they sank in.

"The School of Magic recanted their judgment, striking the status of academic disqualification from Bartleby's record," Anne said. "In light of her services, she was awarded a timeline extension and her second exam attempt had also been stricken from the record. In spring term, Bartleby would start fresh."

Anne's recap gave me time to catch my breath, but with the whole room waiting for me to respond, I still struggled to breathe.

"I—" The single syllable was all I managed. I swallowed, twice, and tried again. "This was supposed to be Darya's celebration."

An amused laugh trickled through the room. Darya gloated, "I told you we'd celebrate when we could celebrate *together*. I haven't changed my mind."

My throat tightened around unshed tears.

"Thank you," I sputtered. "Thank you all. I can't believe you did this for me." My words sounded half-accusatory. But I hadn't even had to *ask*. "I can't . . ." I shook my head. "I can't thank you all enough. It means so much."

Everyone near my table moved to hug me at once. As they did, applause rang out, a mix of clapping and cheers and, from somewhere in the back of the crowd, a single voice shouting one of the chants we'd used during last week's protests.

"Better together, united we stand."

Others took it up, banging on tables, until the whole pub rang with our makeshift drumming and raised voices. I joined in, shouting until I was hoarse.

WHEN THE NOISE DIED DOWN AND THE CROWD TRICKLED BACK TO THEIR own tables, I whirled on my friends.

"*This* is what your mysterious clipboards were for? You gave me that whole talk about being there, if I needed help, and you were *already helping*." I sounded irrational. Angry instead of grateful. Darya and Cy traded a look, bursting into conspiratorial giggles. My outrage grew. "And when exactly did it become acceptable to lure your housemate to a phony celebration on entirely false pretenses?"

"Excuse me?" Darya screeched. "There's nothing phony about this celebration. You fought for our students—for us—and we wanted to fight for you, too."

"I'll cheers to that," Mags said, holding her glass aloft. "To good luck."

"To well-being," James chimed in, catching my eye with a smile.

"To the beneficence of the universe," Darya said.

Lora held up their glass before anyone could lean in to complete the traditional toast, sneaking an extra blessing in. "To crafting kinder futures."

Cy tilted his head, considering, then followed Lora's example. "Hell with tradition. To telling new stories."

I took the group in. Not just their smiling faces and raised glasses, but their generosity. Their willingness to give their time and attention and effort, even when supposedly wiser heads advised us to keep our eyes on our own paper and problems. These people, my found cohort, were going to revolutionize the way we studied and thought about magic. They were already doing it. And I was proud to stand beside them, for however long I could.

"To us," I said, and we clinked our glasses together with an enthusiastic "abracadabra."

★ ★ ★ ★ ★

ACKNOWLEDGMENTS

A novel is, at its heart, a working. A complete reality, conjured from words and sentences, paragraphs and pages. Like so many workings, it's one that requires collaboration to pull off. I am lucky to have had some of the very best collaborators anyone could ask for. Thank you to my agent, Rebecca Matte, for seeing the reality I was trying to create and not only believing in what it could become but also championing it tirelessly—even when you were supposed to be on vacation. And to my editor, Dina Davis, who encouraged me to dig deeper and enriched Bartleby's story and the world of *Higher Magic* in profound and exciting ways: I'm so grateful to have had your feedback and support.

Many thanks to Tamara Shifman, Gina Macdonald, and Kathleen Mancini for the fantastic proofreading and copyediting (you are all clearly practiced thaumaturgists); to Erin Craig, Tara Scarcello, and Imogen Oh for the cover art of my dreams; and to Sophie Amoss (narrator) and Carly Katz (producer) for the wonderful audio edition.

I would also like to thank the many other skilled and talented publishing alchemists at MIRA, Harlequin, and HarperCollins who helped transform my words into an honest-to-Hecate book, including but not limited to: Margaret Marbury, Nicole Brebner, Evan Yeong, and Fiona Smallman; Ana Luxton, Lindsey Reeder, Randy Chan, Ashley MacDonald, Diane Lavoie, Rachel Haller, Pamela Osti, Puja Lad, Alex McCabe, Ambur Hostyn, Riffat Ali, Brianna Wodabek, Daphne Guima, and Jaimie Nackan; Denise Thomson; Reka Rubin, Christine Tsai, and Nora Rawn; Sophie

James and Heather Connor; Loriana Sacilotto and Amy Jones; Katie-Lynn Golakovich; Bailey Thomas, Melissa Brooks, and everyone in Sales (your magic is beyond my ken, but I am immensely grateful for it); and anyone else I might have missed—thank you all so much.

To the Future GOATs, my Viable Paradise 2022 cohort, and the Inklings: I am a far better and happier writer thanks to your friendship and support. I can't imagine doing any of this without you all. Thanks especially to Anna Marian, Erik Grove, Ishmael Grey, K.S. Walker, Liv Tarcov, Michelle Denham, Mona West, Reed Mingault, RJ Taylor, Samantha Paine, Tracy Hoagland, Valerie Kemp, VH Chen, and Zohar Jacobs for beta reading and underbrain percolating.

Speaking of Viable Paradise, my time there was the best kind of magic. It helped me see myself, my writing, and this book in new ways. I'm so grateful to the faculty and staff who made it possible, and especially to Max Gladstone and Sherwood Smith for their insightful feedback on an early draft.

Thanks to my PhD advisor, Dr. Heidi Kaufman, for always making me feel like I belonged in higher ed and *also* for pushing me to imagine my life beyond the tenure track. And to the incorrigible women who advised and mentored me throughout my college years: Dr. Betsy Wheeler, Dr. Carol Erwin, Dr. Nina Björnsson, Dr. Shirley Robinson, and Dr. Patrice Caldwell.

To my found cohort, which spans institutions and even continents, and especially to Eleanor Dumbill, Katie Jo LaRiviere, Angela Rovak, Anna Brecke, Anna Wagner, and Matt Poland. The real PhD is the friendships we made along the way.

To GTFF 3544 and the grad students alongside whom I went on strike at the end of my first term in PhD school: you taught me that we're stronger together and that some things are more important than degree progress, even if you're an anxious first-gen student who only just got here and secretly feels that she doesn't belong. None of that rubbed off on me at all, clearly.

To Wenyi Zhao, for all of the long, inspiring conversations

about global education and for your incredible friendship. And to my colleagues, whom I have the honor of working alongside to support student-centered learning, accessibility, and inclusion. I have learned so much from you about what I want the academy to be, and I hope that tired but clear-eyed determination spilled over into my characters.

To my partner, Cabb, who has never questioned that I could pull off this weird, long-form magic called novel writing, and who kept me well supplied with snacks, coffee, and shoulder rubs along the way. To my four-legged writing assistants, Charlie, Max, Jones, and Nellie, for making me take walks when I needed them and occasionally stealing my pens, just to keep things interesting.

And to you, for reading. In doing so, you've completed the final steps of this working. Thank you for making magic with me. *Abracadabra.*